MERICK CITY LIBRARY

Invisible Ar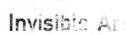

ules

Also by the same author

Trail of the Dead
Blood Price

JON EVANS

Invisible Armies

HODDER &
STOUGHTON

First published in Great Britain in 2006 by Hodder & Stoughton
A division of Hodder Headline

A Hodder and Stoughton Book

1

A CIP catalogue record for this title
is available from the British Library

Hardback ISBN 0 340 896051
Trade Paperback ISBN 0 340 89606 X

Typeset in Sabon by Hewer Text UK Ltd, Edinburgh
Printed and bound by Clays Ltd, St Ives plc

Hodder Headline's policy is to use papers that are natural, renewable
and recyclable products and made from wood grown in sustainable
forests. The logging and manufacturing processes are expected to
conform to the environmental regulations of the country of origin.

Hodder & Stoughton Ltd
A division of Hodder Headline
338 Euston Road
London NW1 3BH

To Rachael, Ben, and Rowan

Acknowledgements

I must begin by thanking The World's Greatest Agent, Vivienne Schuster at Curtis Brown UK; her compatriots Carol Jackson and Betsy Robbins; and her American counterpart Deborah Schneider.

Thanks to my endlessly helpful publishers: Carolyn Mays and particularly, as always, Alex Bonham at Hodder & Stoughton; Iris Tupholme, Kate Cassaday and Lisa Zaritzky at HarperCollins Canada; and Anika Ebrahim at Jonathan Ball.

Thanks to Martin DeMello for the tour of Bangalore. Thanks to Raven Alder, Robert Hansen and Jesse Kornblum, for showing me around (and a good time at) DefCon. Thanks to Ganious for providing the venue.

And thanks to everyone who put me up, and put up with me, for the year that I wandered around the world ostensibly researching and writing this book. California: Allegra Lundyworf, Jack and Linda Valentine, Maria Alexander, Steve Braun, Peter Rose, and everyone from Camp Crackistan. Iraq: Ryan Lackey and Adam Fritzler. England: William Hanage, Sophie Breese, Michael Carlin, Nicholas Greenfield, Chong and Andrea, Jorge and Jo, Max and Kelle, Paul and Sasha, Rachael and Ben and Rowan. Montreal: Rayna Anderson, Jo Walton and Emmet O'Brien, Winnie Tom and Jim Withers. New York: Sarah Langan, Neil Katz, Maggie Cino and Linda Tom. Paris: Doug Cushman, Nigel Dickinson, Michael and Xanthe Lancaster. Toronto: Nona Robinson, Donna Tom, Lisa Hayes, Linda Brennan and Ray Van Kleef. Vancouver: Chris Hemming and Nathan Basiliko. Sydney: Judith Cox.

And, especially, in Toronto and Waterloo and Muskoka and Florida, my family.

Acknowledgements

The following books were enormously helpful. *Another World is Possible If . . .* by Susan George; *Disposable People: New Slavery in the Global Economy* by Kevin Bales; *Global Uprising: Confronting the Tyrannies of the 21st Century* edited by Neva Welton and Linda Wolf; *Hacking: The Art Of Exploitation* by Jon Erickson; *The New New Thing* by Michael Lewis; and *The Rough Guide to India*. Thanks also to defcon.org, google.com, livejournal.com and wikipedia.org.

I India

Karnataka

1

The bridge is out. No: it has never been in. Danielle nudges the gear shift into neutral, splays her legs out on either side to support the motorcycle and stares disbelievingly. The road before her continues smoothly for some sixty feet, then unravels into a leprous mass of concrete, from which a tangle of rusted girders reaches across the Tungabadhra river towards a similar span on the other side. It fails to arrive by forty feet.

Whoever did not finish this bridge's mid-section neglected to inform the National Geographical Survey of India, whose map of the state of Karnataka, currently tucked into Danielle's day pack, claims that the bridge successfully traverses the dark river below. The next crossing is fifteen miles away, along gouged Indian roads that would eat up at least an hour, and it is already afternoon, and Danielle isn't sure that she can reach her destination at all from the other bridge. For a moment she feels defeated.

Which is fine. This is a chore, not a mission. A favour to a friend, and one she already wishes she had not accepted. A valid excuse to back out would be a relief, and how much more valid can you get than this impassable ruin of an incomplete bridge?

But wait. She sees motion. Something stirs in the water by the opposite shore, next to the pillars that hold up their third of the bridge, and then what looks like a large floating wicker basket shaped like an inverted dome, maybe ten feet in diameter, emerges from the shadowed water. It carries two men. One uses a leaf-shaped paddle to propel the basket-dome – *coracle*, a distant corner of her mind informs her – towards the south side of the

3

river. The other man waves and points somewhere behind her. His smile flashes white against his dark skin. Danielle looks over her shoulder and sees a little dirt trail, about a hundred feet back, that separates from the road and falls steeply to a muddy landing on the river bank.

They cannot seriously be thinking of ferrying her motorcycle across. It's a small bike, but still a heavy machine, and their overgrown basket looks as if it has all the structural integrity of a banana leaf. But here is *another* coracle, coming behind the first, and this one moves slowly, because it is loaded with half a dozen Indian villagers, several heavy sacks of grain and a man sitting on a motorcycle much like hers. This coracle bobs low in the water but amazingly does not sink.

Danielle reluctantly decides she cannot abandon her errand just because the river must be crossed by fragile-seeming ferry instead of bridge. She wheels the bike around and steers down the dirt path to the river bank, controlling brake and throttle gingerly; she has no helmet, it has been years since she spent much time on a bike, and low-speed motorcycle manoeuvres are always potentially treacherous. When she gets to the landing, a flat patch covered by shallow mud, she turns off the engine and looks towards the approaching coracle ferry. The paddling has stopped. Both men gape at her with wonder and bewilderment.

For a moment Danielle doesn't understand. Then she realizes. They thought she was a man, thanks to her close-cropped hair, and the truth has struck them dumb. She is probably the first woman riding a motorcycle by herself that these men have ever seen, and an exotic white woman at that. And this is the sticks. Yesterday's journey, Goa to Hospet to Hampi, was a route that sees plenty of white women travelling solo, but although Hampi with its many Western backpackers is only ten miles away, this broken bridge is definitely off the beaten track. This is real rural India. A whole different world. She doesn't feel threatened by their stares, not with the sun beaming down, and several women visible in the other coracle, and a handful more now watching her from the opposite shore, but she does feel distinctly uncomfortable.

For a moment she wonders whether this is what being a movie star is like; everybody wordlessly watching you, knowing that you belong to an infinitely glamorous and more exciting world than theirs. She wishes she had brought a male companion. Not that that wouldn't have created its own set of problems. But suddenly those problems seem better than feeling like a target. A target only of attention, right now, but such attention makes her nervous.

The empty coracle, a woven basket of thumb-thick branches lined on the outside with plastic wrap, reaches the shore. The non-paddling man steps out and motions her to get off the bike. She doesn't want to. She suddenly wants to turn around, ride straight back to Hampi, e-mail Keiran and tell him he can find someone else to run his international errands for him. But Danielle has spent the last few years of her life systematically forcing herself to do exactly those things that make her uncomfortable or frightened. She knows she is mostly the better for it. She wonders, though, as she stands back and allows the man to straddle her motorcycle and expertly roll it on to the coracle, whether one day this constant struggle for self-improvement will propel her into disaster.

The vessel's interior is wet, but the motorcycle's weight distorts the flexible hull enough that all the interior water pools beneath the bike's tyres, and Danielle stays mostly dry. She sits cross-legged on the surprisingly comfortable wood, avoiding the ferrymen's unflagging stares, and watches the unearthly landscape around her.

The wide, fast Tungabhadra river, lined by tall coconut trees, carves a path through jumbled ridges of colossal reddish boulders that somehow look both crystalline and water-warped. Roads and villages are built in the shadow of these boulders, which look like handfuls of fifty-foot pebbles dropped by the gods, balancing and leaning on one another in seemingly unnatural ways, as if child-giants had used them as playthings, piled stacks and mounds of them, then abandoned them here when they grew bored. It's hard for Danielle to shake the notion that this place was meant for creatures of far greater scale than mere human beings.

And then there are the ruins. Most human constructions here are ancient, the bones of the Vijayanagar kingdom that ten centuries ago ruled all of southern India. Half-collapsed stone-work; still-intact ziggurats densely carved with Hindu gods and idols, some of their features worn away by the centuries, but still enormously imposing; high ornate walls standing forlornly in tilled fields; kilometre-long pillared colonnades. Once these were royal residences, temples, elephant stables, public plazas. To the west, Danielle can make out the crumbling remains of a massive stone bridge that once spanned the palm-tree-lined river. This thousand-year relic doesn't seem much more ruined than the rusted iron and cratered concrete above her.

A few squat concrete boxes have grown around the northern end of the modern bridge, and clusters of thatched huts are visible in the distance, between the hills and ridges. Dots that are men and women can be seen cultivating small oblong properties, brown fields of grain and deep green banana plantations. A large whitewashed temple to some Hindu god is visible at the top of the highest hill. But the modern buildings, roads and plantations look wildly out of place.

As they approach the northern bank Danielle winces, realizing that she forgot to agree a price before embarking. She expects a demand for some outrageous amount of money, and she is not in a good position to argue; a woman on her own, on the wrong side of the river which only these men can help her cross. But the man asks her for only twenty rupees, less than fifty US cents. His accent is so thick, and the price so surprising, that he has to repeat it three times before she is certain she has understood. She wonders why, unlike just about everyone else in India, these men do not see the central goal of their interaction with a foreigner to be the acquisition of as much wealth as possible by any non-violent means available. Maybe so few tourists come here that these men have not learned how to be usurious.

Or maybe they are frightened of foreigners. If Keiran is right, they have good reason to be frightened.

She wonders what time the ferry stops. Surely she can get back before nightfall. Even if not, surely she can pay someone to paddle her back across. And even if that fails, surely some family will put her up for the night. She has money, after all, and a white woman's glamour. Even in the worst case, it will be an adventure. Danielle kicks her engine into life, shifts into gear and starts north.

2

The road is old sun-baked asphalt, grooved and pitted but not bad by Indian standards, and virtually deserted. At first she is relieved by this emptiness. Her motorcycle skills are rusty, the Bajaj Pulsar's gearing system is counter-intuitive to anyone who learned to ride a motorcycle in the West, and the Indian roads she has grown accustomed to – seething, anarchic, horn-honking maelstroms of buses, cars, cattle, auto-rickshaws, cyclists, pedestrians, children and dogs – are a constant threat to life and limb and sanity. But after about ten minutes Danielle begins to find the solitude eerie. This is the most alone she has been since the moment she landed in New Delhi six months ago. She is a little relieved when she passes a wheezing Tata bus going in the opposite direction. She has to steer to the edge of the road to avoid it, and the stones its wake kicks up rattle against her motorcycle and her right leg, but its presence alleviates the feeling that she has left all civilization behind.

The habitations she passes do not. Tiny clusters of eight or ten structures, most of them made of tree branches, with palm-thatch walls and roof lashed together by vines, straight out of the Stone Age. Only a few concrete boxes with slanted corrugated-aluminium roofs, the road itself and the occasional metal bucket or plastic roof tarpaulin hint at the existence of the twenty-first century. This is by far the poorest part of India she has seen. The land grows stonier as she passes, less bountiful. Everyone she sees is working the fields, men and women both. She supposes it is harvest season. They turn and stare as she passes. Many of them look gaunt and weak. Not malnourished, there is plenty of food even here, but sickly. The women wear dull, ragged robes. Everywhere else Danielle has been in this country, even the slums of Delhi, women wear vibrantly coloured shawls or saris.

The road begins to ascend, steeply enough that the Pulsar's engine growls loudly at the challenge. The bike trembles increasingly beneath her and Danielle asks fate not to let its engine give out, not here. It is nearly new, but it is Indian-made, and that means unreliable. Then, as the road winds upwards, the cracked asphalt suddenly ends, replaced by dirt and rocks.

For the next half-hour Danielle worries too much about steering around the larger rocks to have any time for other concerns. She is so focused on the strip of road immediately in front of her motorcycle that she doesn't see the train tracks until she is almost on top of them. She bumps across the rails and brakes to a halt.

It takes her mind a few moments to return from its tight focus to the larger world around her. To her left, the tracks follow a valley, paralleling a small creek, until they disappear beneath the sinking sun. To her right, they end next to a long, large concrete platform, on which two gleaming metallic cranes are mounted, each the height of a four-storey building. A smooth road, unmarked but easily four lanes wide, climbs eastwards from the platform, up towards a ridge-top radio antenna. A small modern building sits beneath the cranes, adorned by a satellite dish. All this new construction looks brain-wrenchingly dissonant amid the stony wilderness, especially after the thatched huts Danielle passed half an hour ago.

This land is too dry and steep to support any settlements, but two men stand outside the small building, staring at Danielle. She considers stopping and talking to them, asking for directions to the recipient of the package she carries, but decides against it; they work for the mine, surely, and will not be sympathetic towards her errand. The Pulsar bounces a little at the steep lip where the dirt track joins the asphalt road, and Danielle winces. The last half-hour of hard road, on her motorcycle's insufficiently padded seat, has been decidedly uncomfortable, and she is not looking forward to the return journey. She spurs the bike into its fourth and final gear and barrels up the perfect road, ignoring the slack-jawed stares of the two Indian men, wishing again that she had turned this errand down, or at least begun it earlier. Only a few hours of daylight remain.

Despite her hurry, when she passes the antenna at the crest of the hill and sees the mine, Danielle stops the bike and gapes for a good thirty seconds. The entire valley beyond the ridge has been dug out, replaced by a colossal rectangular pit, its dimensions measured in miles. The pit plunges so deeply into the earth that Danielle cannot see the bottom. Several ramps and an enormous elevator descend into the abyss from a walled complex of long, low buildings, dotted with satellite dishes, on the other side of the mine. The trucks and massive construction vehicles she can see inside the compound's walls look like Tonka toys next to the vast sandpit that is the strip mine.

The Kishkinda mine. Producing mostly titanium, but also copper, nickel and small amounts of gold. And, according to her ex-boyfriend Keiran Kell, incidentally poisoning thousands of desperately poor local residents with toxic chemical by-products called 'tailings', while Indian authorities are paid both officially and unofficially to look the other way. To say nothing of the environmental devastation, the scale of which Danielle could not previously have imagined. The mine has erased a good twenty square miles of the earth's surface.

She digs the e-mailed directions out of her pack, double-checks them, then continues. The road bends around the northern end of the mine, heading for the complex. Danielle looks for a small dirt track that veers off the road near the north-eastern corner of the mine, just before the road turns south, towards the compound. After about a mile she sees it. And the roadblock between it and her. A chain hangs chest-high across the road, strung between two granite boulders, and a half-dozen Indian men in khaki stand behind it, waiting for her. A jeep is parked by the road behind them.

Danielle slows down a hundred feet from the roadblock, more annoyed than concerned. After six months in India, she is confident that, regardless of whether the men are police or Kishkinda mine security, reverse racism and a little baksheesh will get her past them in a few minutes. She has come too far to be repelled by a mere roadblock. Danielle stops the motorcycle in front of the chain, smiles, and says, 'Hello.'

Five of the men carry lathis, bamboo clubs with leather handles. They look like toys rather than weapons, but Danielle knows that a single blow can knock out a grown man; she once saw a half-dozen policemen armed only with lathis drive off an angry crowd of hundreds, at a movie theatre in Delhi that had sold too many tickets. The sixth man carries both a lathi and a revolver on a belt. It is he who says, 'Please off the motorcycle.'

Danielle dismounts. At five foot nine she has at least three inches on all the men. 'Are you police?' she asks.

'Passport,' the man says.

She pauses, then, with just a hint of haughtiness, repeats, 'Are you the police?'

'Give me passport.'

She decides not to push the point. Whoever they are, she clearly isn't leaving without showing ID. She produces her travel pouch from beneath her jeans, withdraws her passport – concealing, as she does, the other, Republic of India, passport tucked into her pouch, with a thousand US dollars folded inside – and gives it to the man. He does not seem impressed by the coat of arms of the United States of America.

'Danielle Leaf,' he reads aloud, looking at her picture, then flipping the pages until he finds her India visa and entry stamp. After examining them he puts her passport into his back pocket.

'Wait a minute,' she says. 'I need that back.'

'Luggage,' the man says.

'You have to give me my passport back.'

'Give me luggage.'

Now Danielle begins to worry. There's something about this man's stony, expressionless face. The other guards watch her with fascination, but their leader seems entirely incurious. She is suddenly acutely aware of how powerless she is right now. But, she reminds herself, she has done nothing wrong, and surely nothing bad is going to happen to her within sight of this billion-dollar Western-owned mine. She gives him her day pack. He turns, walks over to a flat boulder and begins to array her possessions atop it. She instinctively starts to follow, but two of the other men raise lathis to block her path. They are all around her now. She hadn't noticed them surrounding her.

She swallows, tells herself to be patient, to take no notice of the irrational fear that is beginning to clutch at her gut, and waits. The leader withdraws a cell phone and makes a call. For a moment she is surprised it works out here; then she remembers the antenna on the ridge. The Kishkinda mine must have its own cell network. He has opened her passport and is reading aloud from it. Danielle looks back at her motorcycle and sees that the key has been removed. She opens her mouth to demand its return, definitely nervous now, but the leader speaks first, something in a sonorous Indian language. The lathis that block her way are removed and he beckons her to follow.

The few possessions in her day pack – Geographical Survey map, *Rough Guide to India*, the printed directions, two Snickers bars, a bottle of water, spare toilet paper, disposable camera, small flashlight, Leatherman multi-tool, cigarette lighter, her own Reliance-branded cell phone – are carefully spread over the boulder. Placed among them is a fist-sized package of transparent plastic wrapped around some sort of dried herb.

'What's that?' she asks, genuinely bewildered.

'Is in your luggage.'

'No, that's not mine.' She says it in a tone of simple clarification.

'Is in your luggage. Cannabis.'

For a moment she doesn't understand. Then her skin goes cold with the shock of comprehension. She stares at the small package of drugs that has been planted among her possessions. 'No,' she says. 'No. That's not mine. You put that there.'

'Cannabis,' the leader repeats. 'You criminal. You come now.'

'No,' she repeats. 'That's not right. That isn't mine.' She looks at the little man with a gun and begins to feel angry. She feels as if she is taking part in a miniature morality play illustrating what is most wrong with India. 'This is ridiculous. You think I'm going to pay you? No way. Absolutely not.'

'You criminal.'

She glares into his expressionless eyes for a moment before realizing that of course she is going to pay a bribe. Better that than be jailed. 'Let me guess,' she says. 'I can pay a fine to you right now, right? And then you'll let me go? How much? Ten dollars?' She immediately kicks herself for having been the first to name a price.

'Not money,' the man says. 'We not want money.'

This is so unexpected it takes her a moment to absorb, and causes her anger to flicker and dissipate. This is not simple bribery. Something else is happening here. Something very wrong, she can feel it, see it in their body language, the way they look at her. 'Then what do you want?'

'We want you. Danielle Leaf.' He speaks her name softly, like a lover.

Danielle stares at him. The other men are all around her again.

'You come now.' The leader takes her arm, firmly, and leads her to the jeep. Danielle lets him. She does not know what else to do. Her head whirls with confusion.

'You can't do this,' she says, her voice so feeble and breathless she is not even sure he hears her. 'I'm an American. You can't do this.'

He pays no attention. She wonders dazedly whether she should try to run, but she knows she cannot get away from them, and now it is too late anyhow, she is in the back of the jeep, between two of the men, and the leader has started the engine, they are driving towards the mine complex. No. Not the mine. The jeep turns and bounces off-road, up the same little track Danielle had intended to follow, the track that was meant to take her to Jayalitha, whose passport Danielle carries. They are not going to the mine, where at least she would find organization, Western management, some kind of accountability. They are taking her somewhere else. Somewhere private, isolated. When she realizes this, her gut clenches into an icy knot. She feels as if she is falling from a great height. The word *abducted* flashes into her mind. Danielle tries to think of something she can do, some means of escape, but it is too late for that. All she can do is sit and wait, heart thudding, her whole body damp with sweat, until they reach their destination and whatever awaits her there.

3

The concrete hut that serves as Danielle's cell is about ten feet square. The corrugated aluminium ceiling slants upwards, six feet high at one end and nine at the other, attached to rusted prongs of re-bar that protrude every eight inches or so from the rough concrete tops of the walls. The wall on the shorter side has a window about a foot square, barred by an iron cross. Opposite the window is a door, exterior-hinged, locked by an iron bolt that thunked loudly into place after Danielle allowed herself to be pushed inside. At first being locked in was almost a relief. When you are a woman captured by six armed men of unknown allegiance and motivations, solitary confinement is far from the worst available option.

Red sunlight spills into the hut from the window, the uneven gaps between the aluminium roof and the concrete walls, the cracks around the door. A wooden bench and two metal buckets, one empty and one full of water, are the only furnishings. She can tell by the smell that the empty one has been used as a latrine. Thankfully the hut is well ventilated. An iron ring is set into each side wall. Danielle doesn't like the look of them. And there is a thick lace of dark stains on the walls, floor and bench. Stains that might be blood.

The hut stands like a sentinel near the lip of a high westward-facing bluff, and through the barred window she can see the sun set over the jumbled boulders of the alien landscape. She sees no other buildings. To get up here, the jeep had had to turn off the dirt track into one that was virtually non-existent, then fight its way up five minutes of brain-rattling trail. After she was put in the hut, the jeep drove away. She knows they have left men on guard outside to watch her – she can hear their low voices, footsteps, the rasp of matches when they smoke.

They're just trying to scare you, she tells herself, trying to stay calm. *Nothing terrible is going to happen or it would have happened already.* She forces her hoarse breath under control, puts *pranayama* lessons from yoga classes to use. She sits down on the bench, but her fear produces too much nervous energy; after a moment she gets back up and paces, despite the hut's oven-like heat which soaks her in sweat. It is the not knowing that is worst. Who these men are, what they want, who or what they are waiting for, and why they took her to this godforsaken place rather than a real prison. Right now, prison would be a relief.

When she hears the growl of an approaching engine, she presses herself up against the door, trying to see through the cracks. Only a very narrow wedge of the world is visible, across which a jeep passes before rumbling to a halt. A car door opens and shuts. Men exchange a few words in an Indian language. Footsteps approach. Danielle takes a step back, breathing heavily, her body trembling with tension.

The bolt slides and the door swings open. The uniformed leader, the man who planted the drugs, stands next to another Indian man, this one taller and slightly pudgy, dressed in casual but expensive-for-India shirt and slacks. The other uniformed men cluster behind them. The tall man takes the uniformed leader's lathi and walks into the hut. Danielle has to step back to avoid a collision. The door closes behind him.

'Sit,' the man says.

Danielle, eyeing the bamboo club in his hand, obeys.

'You are in very great trouble, Danielle Leaf.' His English is accented but good.

'They put that bag in my pack. It isn't mine.'

'What are you doing here?'

She has already decided on her answer. 'I'm visiting a friend.'

'Who?'

'Her name is Jayalitha.'

The man frowns. 'How do you know her?'

'I don't really. She's a friend of a friend. Our mutual friend told me I should come see her if I was in the area.'

'And who is your mutual friend?'

'A man named Keiran. In London.'

'Why are you in India? Are you with an NGO?'

'NGO? No. I work here. In Bangalore. I'm a project manager for Infosys.' This is no longer true – she quit that job four months ago, after only six weeks – but she still has her Infosys ID card, and hopes to impress him with her invocation of her former employer, famous across India.

'Remove your clothes.'

He says it in the same distant tone in which he has carried on the rest of their conversation. She stares at him. 'What?'

'Remove your clothes. For the purposes of searching. You may retain your underclothing.'

She decides it is time to draw a line in the sand. 'No. Absolutely not. If you want to search me, have a woman do it, I won't let

15

you. You haven't even told me who you are. Are you the police? I want to see some identification.'

He looks at her for a moment, then shifts his grip on his lathi so he is holding the bamboo club like a paddle, his right hand folded over the leather handle and his left gripped around the middle, and then he stoops slightly and, moving from his hips, slams the free end into Danielle's mid-section.

Danielle doubles over, clutching reflexively at her stomach, falls off the bench and on to the ground, her mind numb with pain and shock. She can't breathe, the wind has been knocked out of her, her lungs and throat feel sealed shut. She thrashes and gags for air like a landed fish, unable to think of anything but her desperate need for oxygen. The world begins to go grey around the edges. Then her lungs open miraculously and she can breathe again. It hurts like fire but she sucks air in greedily, and for a moment she lies on the damp concrete floor and just breathes, curled into a fetal position, moaning slightly on each exhale, unable to believe what has just happened to her. She cannot remember the last time she was physically struck by anyone or anything.

'Get up,' the man says, prodding her forehead with his boot, his voice alive with excitement. Danielle cringes away from him, hisses with pain as she pulls herself up to her knees, looks up at the man who has just hit her. His lips are parted, slightly, and his eyes are intent on her. He looks excited. She can tell he is holding himself back; what he really wants is to hit her again, and again after that, until she is bloody and broken.

'I tell you one more time,' he says softly. 'Remove your clothes.'

Danielle wants to fight, but he has a club, and she is weak with shock and fear, and even if she somehow won this battle, there are more men outside, one of them with a gun. Slowly, painfully, she stands, takes her shoes off, begins to remove her clothes. She feels dizzy and has to lean against the wall behind her. A deep red mark is already forming on her stomach where the lathi struck her. She feels nauseous, feverish. She wonders whether she has internal injuries. She doesn't look at the man but knows he is watching her undress with fervent attention.

'Give me that,' the man says, pointing at the travel pouch made visible when she pulled down her jeans. Danielle obeys, standing as far away from him as possible, now wearing only underwear and socks, shivering despite the heat. He opens it, sees the credit cards, the three thousand cash rupees, and the Republic of India passport. Jayalitha's passport. He takes it, reads through it, finds the dollars within.

'You come to all this trouble for nothing,' the man says, pocketing the money and her travel pouch. 'Of what use is a dead woman's passport?'

Danielle stares at him dully, trembling, dreading what comes next. The man raises his lathi, and she crouches, terrified but ready to try to fight: but he uses it only to rap twice on the door, which opens.

'You stay here some time longer,' the man advises her. 'I come again. I think we have many more subjects to discuss.' He smiles. 'We shall talk and other things.'

He leaves. The door shuts behind him. Danielle stares into space from where she is, not moving except to breathe, for some time, long after the jeep roars away, until twilight has faded to darkness.

It is past midnight before she accepts that escape is impossible. The roof will not peel off. The iron bars in the window will not be forced loose. The door will not open. She tried removing the laces from her shoes, tying them together and dangling the resulting lasso through the crack between roof and wall, hoping to catch the end of the bolt that locks the door, but her laces aren't long enough, and even if they were, even if she had all week, she doubts she could ever loop them around the bolt and pull it open, not working by feel in near-total darkness. She still has her wallet, in her jeans pocket, but there is nothing potentially useful therein, only a few hundred rupees and her Citibank ATM card.

Danielle sits in the corner of the hut, knees to her chest, shivering despite India's tropical heat. She feels exhausted but not tired, physically but not mentally drained. It is terror which keeps her alert. They can do anything to her, and probably will. If they are willing to hit her like that, then there is little, maybe nothing, they will not be willing to do. Including murder. She may die here in this hut. That is not dramatic hyperbole. That is a cold, hard, very real possibility. And if it comes true, it will be bloody and painful – by the time death comes she will likely be grateful for it.

It is almost impossible to believe that her life could actually end tomorrow, in this concrete box, at the hands of that man, that all the complex intertwined strands of herself could be suddenly guillotined, hopes and fears and memories extinguished like a snuffed candle. Surely it can't really happen. Surely her story can't end like this; none of the stories she has ever seen or heard end like this, abruptly and brutally in a concrete box – even the horror stories make more sense. But then most of those stories were fiction. This is real life. Real life doesn't follow the rules of stories. Real life dives into dead ends and finishes without warning.

She tries not to think about what they might do to her. She wants to think that she will fight them, defiant to the end, but remembering what happened to her when the man hit her with the lathi, how quickly she was reduced to cringing obedience, she doesn't think such vows of courage mean much when they are set against real violence and pain. Almost everyone tells themselves they would be brave. Danielle suspects only a very few actually are.

'It isn't fair,' she whispers. She was doing a favour for a friend. She was doing the right thing.

In a story she would be rescued. But there seems no hope of that. She will not be missed at the ashram for another two days, and the people there know only that she was going to Hampi. Keiran will be expecting some kind of e-mail confirmation that his errand has been performed, but how long a silence will prompt him into some kind of action? Her best hope is the man in Hampi who rented her a motorcycle. But what will he do, and when? Nothing that will find her. Probably nothing at all, for a few days. Eventually he and the ashram and Keiran may gather their knowledge, eventually her route may be traced, but that will take weeks.

She thinks of Keiran with fury. If he hadn't sent her . . . He should have known. He obviously didn't, he would never have deliberately sent her into danger, but now, because of his mistake, and her willingness to do a favour for a friend, Danielle might die, might actually *die*, tomorrow. Or whenever they grow sick of her. She tries not to think about how long they might keep her here, and what they might do to her while she lives. She has always felt contempt for women who live in fear, who refuse to walk city streets alone at night, who stay as far away from roadsides as possible for fear of men in cars who might swoop in and abduct them. *Better half a life than a life half lived*, she used to say. Now it seems she is going to pay for that boast, now she is in the midst of the worst nightmare of those women: abducted by a gang of violent men, imprisoned, helpless, knowing that no one will come to her aid.

She buries her face in her knees and tries to meditate, to breathe deeply and think of nothing, but every breath hurts, and her mind returns again and again to terrifying images of what the day may bring, and each time she gasps involuntarily and tenses up so powerfully that her abdominal muscles ache and the bruise hurts like fire. Eventually she starts to cry. She tries to prevent the tears, she knows they are useless, but they flow unstoppably.

The heat wakes her. She is sprawled on the concrete floor, her shirt pillowed beneath her head, with no memory of falling asleep. It is only a little past dawn, but the sun-baked hut is already sweltering. She pulls herself stiffly to her feet. Most of her muscles ache, and every motion provokes agony from the dark, swollen bruise on her stomach which has grown to the size of a man's fist, a halo of red around a dark core where the lathi hit. She uses the latrine bucket, and drinks water from the other. She doesn't want to do either, but she is desperately thirsty and has more pressing concerns than dignity and illness anyhow. At least there doesn't seem to be any internal bleeding. The faintest of silver linings.

She wonders how she looks, smeared all over with dust and sweat. Like a refugee, no doubt. Like a victim. It will be hard to play the haughty untouchable white woman, but that is almost the only card she has, to try to intimidate them into sparing her. She doubts it will work. Whatever glamorous otherworldly aura she may have had was erased when the man struck her with the lathi and she fell gasping to the ground.

There are men outside, at least two of them left here to watch her, she hears their low murmurs, the hiss of some kind of gas stove, a few metal clinks. They must be cooking food, or heating water for *chai*. She tries not to think of food. It has been a gruelling eighteen hours since she has eaten, and she is savagely hungry.

Then she hears the jeep's approaching engine, and her heart begins to jackhammer in her chest, all thoughts of food forgotten.

4

She decides she will wait until the door opens, then charge out right away, try to break through them, disappear into the brush. They will be expecting it. It won't work. But she has to try.

The jeep pulls to a stop. A door opens. And Danielle hears an unexpected voice: male, with an accent she can't place but definitely Western, growling, 'Get your fucking hands off me.'

Then the voice of the man who hit Danielle: 'You require education.'

A thunking sound, followed by two lighter thuds, and then cries in an Indian language. Someone sprints around the hut.

Danielle turns and looks out of the barred window. A white man, heavily muscled and military-fit, tattooed, barefoot, wearing khaki slacks and no shirt, with a black eye and bruises on his chest, his wrists handcuffed behind his back, runs to the lip of the bluff. When he realizes there is no way down, he turns to face the five Indian men who pursue him wielding lathis. The man who hit her, and four others in uniform.

At first it seems too unfair and one-sided to be called a confrontation. But then the handcuffed man pirouettes on one foot, moving with a dancer's grace, and his other leg whips out, the heel catches one of the uniformed men on the jaw and knocks him sprawling with an audible *clunk*, bone on bone with only a little skin between, and the handcuffed man continues the movement, spins towards his pursuers, kicks with his other leg into the crotch of another uniformed man, and then he ducks under one lathi and sidesteps another, moving with extraordinary speed and fluidity, every motion flowing seamlessly into the next, and his next step takes him halfway past his three remaining attackers, and Danielle is beginning to dare to dream that he might escape or even defeat them, so cinematic are his motions, when a lathi cracks into the side of his head and all the fight drains out of him. He sags to one knee, like a boxer hit by a knockout punch, and then they are all on him, beating and kicking him, and by the time they drag him to the hut and force him inside with Danielle, his face and body are torn and bloody.

The man lies groaning in the corner, wrists still cuffed behind him, as the jeep pulls away, leaving three guards to watch them. Danielle stares at her unexpected visitor.

'Are you OK?' The question sounds idiotic even as it leaves her lips.

'Water,' he rasps. 'Is there any water?'

She brings him the water bucket, helps him sit up, which he does wincingly. She cups water in her hands and lets him drink from them.

'Thank you,' he says.

'How are you? Do you think you'll be OK?'

He tries to shrug. 'Define OK. I don't think there's anything permanent. No broken bones. Who are you?'

'My name's Danielle. I'm American.'

'Who are you with?'

'With? I'm not with anyone.'

He looks at her and, amazingly, manages a half-smile. 'No shit,' he says. 'Then you really are in trouble.' His accent is strange but his English is fluent.

'Who are you with?'

He wriggles a little, adjusting his position to the least uncomfortable option, before answering. 'Justice International. We're a small NGO. We organize oppressed peoples to prevent human rights violations. And, you can see, if we're very lucky, we get to *become* human rights violations.'

He pauses to spit blood into the corner. She cannot believe he is being flip after the beating she just saw him receive. His lips are swollen and distended, she thinks at least one of his eyes will swell shut, the tattoos on his muscled arms and torso are half obscured by ragged cuts and bruises, his dark crew-cut hair stained with blood. She takes her shirt off, dips it in the water bucket, and stoops next to him, intending to clean him up a little.

'Let it clot first,' he says. 'You'll waste your time. And shirt.'

She asks, 'This sort of thing happen to you a lot?' His sardonic tone is infectious, and makes the situation a little easier to bear. As does his presence. He is both a distraction and a welcome indication that the situation is more complex than she had previously realized.

'More than I'd like.'

'What's you name?'

'Laurent.'

She interprets it as a woman's name at first, then realizes. 'Are you French?'

'French Canadian. Originally.'

'Was that some martial art out there?'

'Several of them.'

'Did they teach you that at Justice International?'

'No. The French Foreign Legion.'

She looks at him. 'Seriously?'

'Seriously.'

'So is Laurent your old name or your new name?'

'New.'

'What's your old name?'

He half smiles. 'Ask when you know me better.'

'You think we'll have time for that?'

'They haven't killed us yet.'

She sits back. 'Who are they?'

'You don't know?'

She shakes her head.

He says, 'Local thugs. Literally. Thug is an Indian word. They're Kishkinda's unofficial muscle. Dirty deeds done dirt cheap, and fully deniable. Disappearances, torture, murder. This district's been at war for years. Small, cold, but vicious. The mine and the money made it worse, but it's much older. Caste, politics, last century's blood feuds. Why don't you know this already? Are you really a lost tourist?'

Danielle explains.

'Christ on a tabernacle,' Laurent says. 'Bad case of wrong place, wrong time, eh?'

'I guess.'

'Who's this Keiran? What's his interest?'

'I don't know. I used to date him. He's a computer expert. He's doing some work for these anti-globalization protesters who want to shut down the mine. They wanted to bring Jayalitha over to England. I guess to help them.'

'Jayalitha is dead.'

Danielle sucks in breath sharply at this confirmation. 'Did they kill her?'

'Yes. I knew her. She was collecting evidence about the damage the tailings are doing. Slow poison. Cancer. Birth defects. It's like

Chernobyl squared. Ten thousand people live where they dump the tailings. Most not even connected by road. Jayalitha went to every village, documented everything, taped interviews, photographs, evidence. She could go where we couldn't. So they killed her.'

'Jesus,' Danielle says inadequately. 'What do you think they'll do with us?'

Laurent shrugs. 'One hand, you'd think if they want to kill us, we'd be too busy being dead to be chatting. So, jail or deportation. Bothering to plant drugs on you, that's a good sign. Other hand, maybe it's just delay, for our execution the decision must come from higher up, they're waiting on that.'

'They don't have any reason to kill us.'

'They have lots of reasons. One, it's easier. Two, we won't bother them again. Three, deterrent for other do-gooders. Unless we become martyrs. Ever wanted your face on a protest poster?'

'No,' Danielle says. 'I'll fucking kill him.'

He looks at her. 'Who?'

'Keiran. If I get out of this I'll . . .' She stops, unable to think of a revenge suitable for the immensity of his mistake.

'Don't be hard on him,' Laurent says. 'He just fucked up. Easy to do from far away.'

'I don't want to die here.'

'It's amazing. We have so much in common.'

'How can you joke?' she asks.

'How can you not?'

She nods, slowly.

5

Laurent and Danielle sit companionably next to one another, beneath the window, their backs to the wall, out of the sun. Occasionally she mops sweat off both of them with her shirt. At least all his cuts, mostly small and ragged, have now clotted shut.

She feels weak from hunger and the brain-sapping heat, and they are almost out of water, but these things do not worry her. She has too many worries already, there is no room for any more.

'What brought you to India?' he asks.

'I got a job. In Bangalore.'

'Why take it? I'd think Americans wouldn't come.'

'I don't know. I was in law school, NYU, and I couldn't stand it any more. I don't know why. I guess I needed to do something drastic. So I came here. Then I quit the job and went to a yoga ashram in Goa. It's not as flaky as it sounds. I'm not like one of those New Age Ayurvedic women.'

'Right this moment it doesn't much matter to me if you are,' Laurent says drily.

'I guess not. Anyways, I was doing yoga teacher training at this ashram. I just graduated last week. I was just about to leave, go back to Boston, as soon as I got the certificate.'

'And Keiran knew you were in India, so he asked you to deliver Jayalitha's passport,' Laurent says. Danielle nods. 'No indication there might be trouble?'

'No. All he said was that the roads were bad and I might want to go with a friend from the ashram or bring a driver. But after four months in an ashram what I really wanted was to get away from everyone else for a little while, and I was feeling all Little Miss Invincible Biker Chick. Yeah. That worked out well, huh?'

Laurent smiles. 'So you were to give Jayalitha her passport and then leave? Only that?'

'No. I was supposed to help her get back to Goa and put her on a plane to England. We were supposed to be in the airport right now. And here I am. Locked up, and beat up, and fucking starving. I'm glad you're here. If you weren't I'd be going nuts right now.'

'I'm glad you are here too,' Laurent says solemnly.

'What happened to you?'

'I was collecting groundwater samples in a village not far from here. One of the villagers must have informed on me. I woke up surrounded.'

'How did you go from the French Foreign Legion to that village?'

'It's a long story.'

Danielle looks at him. 'You got something better to do with your time?'

'Perhaps not.'

'Actually,' she says, 'begin at the beginning. Why join the Foreign Legion in the first place?'

Laurent shrugs. 'I had an unhappy childhood.'

'Unhappy how?'

'In the usual ways. Followed by a troubled youth. Again in the usual ways. My story is simple. I wanted to be someone else. And the Legion offered a way. And a certain glamour. And extremity. I've always been drawn to extremes. I despise the ordinary. So here I am, extraordinarily uncomfortable. I don't suppose you know how to pick locks?'

'Sorry. They don't teach you that in the Legion?'

'They do, but these Indian cuffs are unusual. I don't think I can open them while in them. Do you have anything that might work as a pick?'

She shakes her head. 'They took my day pack. And my travel pouch. I've still got my wallet. Nothing much useful in there. Some coins. Shoelaces. That's about it.'

'No underwire in your bra?'

'Sorry. Sports bra. I was dressed for comfort not style.'

'Pity.' He looks at her appraisingly. 'You know, even under the circumstances, you are remarkably pretty.'

Danielle half laughs. 'Are you actually hitting on me?'

'I'm stating unarguable facts. Another is, we must escape.'

'Feel free.'

'Thank you.' He gets to his feet and surveys their cell. After a moment he turns on one foot and kicks sideways at the door, lightly, not so much a blow as the application of pressure. Then he moves to the window, and carefully examines the corrugated ceiling, there only an inch higher than his head.

'Aluminium,' he mutters. 'Steel is much stronger than aluminium.'

'Great. Got any steel?'

'Yes. On my wrists.'

'Taking us back to the no-lock-pick problem.'

'Your earring.'

Danielle blinks. It has been years since she has removed the crescent-moon earring from her right ear. She has lost awareness of its existence as a thing separate from herself.

'Take it out,' Laurent says. 'Time for a crash course in lock-picking.'

It takes two frustrating hours, in which Danielle repeats the same tiny motions again and again, and impales her thumb a dozen times on the hook of her earring, before his left cuff finally pops loose.

'Got it,' she says, too tired to be triumphant. The concentration required by the process, added to her weakened state, has made her dizzy. She sags back against the wall as Laurent takes the earring and applies it to the other cuff. It takes him less than a minute. He flexes his newly freed wrists in front of him experimentally, still holding the handcuffs, a heavy Indian design that looks like a pair of chained-together horseshoes, locked by cylinders shaped like huge bullets.

'Now what?' she asks.

Laurent picks up her bloodstained shirt, wraps it around his right hand, pulls the loops of the handcuffs over that cushion, and walks to a corner next to the window, where the ceiling is lowest. His strong jaw, deep-set eyes, solid build and long, muscle-knotted arms combine with his ragged cuts and purpling bruises to make him look almost simian, half man, half beast. If she had not seen it herself Danielle would not believe him capable of the kind of martial grace he showed outside.

'Now,' he says, 'brute force and ignorance.'

He makes a handcuff-strengthened fist, takes a few deep

breaths. Then he crouches slightly and, exhaling sharply, un-
leashes a textbook uppercut into the ceiling, near one of the iron
prongs that connect roof and wall. The *clang!* is so loud that
Danielle instinctively covers her ears.

The impact strength of steel is three times that of aluminium, the
roof is old and thin, and Laurent is strong, highly motivated and
skilled. Most of the force of the punch comes from his powerful
legs. It has to go somewhere. It goes into a visible dent that flattens
part of one of the corrugations. The next punch causes that whole
area of the roof to crawl slightly upwards on the rusted iron prong
that anchors it. Laurent keeps punching, getting into a rhythm,
breathing deeply, crouching, then, on the exhale, uncoiling upwards with all his strength. Danielle hears the men left to guard
them outside, chattering worriedly between the metronomic
clangs. So much for sneaking out.

The rebar prongs that support the roof have been flattened
slightly, so that their tops are a few millimetres wider than the rest
of their length. This prevents the aluminium from just sliding off,
but does not long prevent it from tearing free of the first prong,
under the pressure of Laurent's onslaught. He moves to the next
length of rusted rebar and continues to punch. He is breathing
hard now, but his motions are as elegant as before. Soon the roof
breaks free of this anchor as well. He continues, machine-like,
despite the beating he took only a few hours earlier, the cuts and
swollen bruises all over his face and body. Danielle finally realizes
that Laurent actually means to peel a corner of the roof off the hut
and go over the wall.

He does not stop until the roof has been torn from four anchor
prongs, two on either side of a corner. Then, breathing hard, he
reaches up towards the ceiling, only an inch taller than his head, and
simply pushes. For a moment all his muscles stand out in sharp
relief. Then, with a roaring, tearing sound, the whole corner of the
roof folds upwards to an almost perpendicular angle, opening up a
triangle of space some two feet on each side, allowing in a blinding
ray of noontime light that silhouettes him dramatically.

Laurent stops to catch his breath. Danielle stares at him in awe.

'Thank low Indian standards,' he says hoarsely. 'Wouldn't have worked on a Western roof.'

Outside, their guards hold a nervous-sounding conversation. She expects them to charge in, but they do nothing. Maybe they have been ordered not to open the door under any circumstances. She knows from her six weeks at Infosys that Indians do not delegate authority well, and their low-level workers tend to be almost physically incapable of showing initiative or dealing with unexpected situations. She is suddenly deeply grateful for this trait.

'Any water left?' he asks.

'A little.'

He drains the last puddle from the water bucket.

'What do we do now?' she asks.

'Now it's like the First World War. Wait for the right moment, then go over the wall.'

She looks at the wall.

'Can you climb that?' he asks.

'If I need to.'

He smiles. 'Good girl.'

Considering what he's just done, she decides to ignore his patronizing tone. 'How long do we wait?' she asks, her voice low.

'Long enough to be unexpected,' he says in a normal voice.

Ten seconds pass. Fifteen. Twenty. Then, without warning, Laurent vaults on to the wall like a gymnast.

From his crouch atop the wall, first he jumps straight up, and Danielle sees the end of a lathi describe an arc through the space beneath his airborne legs. Then he leaps down and Danielle hears the collision of bodies. Without allowing herself to think, she grabs the rebar prongs herself, engages *moolabundha* and *uttayanabundha*, the yogic names for muscular locks in the pelvic floor and abdomen that provide the body with the internal leverage she needs right now, draws herself most of the way up the wall, brings her right leg up above her head to brace against a third prong, and uses that lever to pull herself over the top.

On the other side, Laurent and one of the guards stand opposite one another, both holding lathis. The other two guards already lie senseless on the ground. Both Laurent and his opponent turn and stare at Danielle for a moment, amazed by her appearance. Then Laurent strikes out, quick as a cobra, there is a dull rapping noise, and the third guard falls.

'I didn't think you'd climb it so fast,' Laurent says as Danielle lowers herself to the ground.

'I thought you might need help. I guess not.'

'No. But thanks for the good intentions. We need to go before they come round.'

Danielle says, 'I couldn't agree more. Which way?'

'A village, over that hill. They're friends. I hope. Don't be happy yet. We're not safe. We won't be safe for some time. They'll be after us within the hour.'

6

The village is a collection of a dozen single-room structures made of branches, vines and thatch, located in a flat patch between two ridges, on either side of a thin stream. As Danielle and Laurent approach, holding commandeered lathis, they join half a dozen women, wrapped in dull shapeless cloths, returning to the village with spine-warping loads of firewood on their heads. The men who wait for them wear dhotis, like pale kilts, stained with years of wear and filth. Most are shirtless, but a few wear tattered T-shirts.

Both men and women seem less curious about their battered white visitors than Danielle would have expected. Maybe they are too exhausted; the women must walk for hours to find firewood – there are few trees in these stony highlands. Maybe, after growing up in a place like this, they are incapable of being curious, they have never developed enough imagination.

Chickens, pigs and dogs pick their way among and inside the buildings. Small, ragged fields line either side of the stream, to the end of the valley. Danielle doesn't know much about farming, but even she can tell that the crops here are sparse and stunted. A few bullocks graze farther afield. Every thatched hut has a few plastic buckets and watering cans, metal pots and implements, candles, cigarette lighters, empty whisky bottles that Danielle is appalled to see – how can anyone in a place as poor as this spend money on whisky? A few of the huts are adorned with Bollywood movie posters, and colourful pictures of deities, Ganesh and Krishna and Lakshmi, decorated with marigolds, are found in nearly every one. A simple wooden cart, four wheels on a frame, the most elaborate machine in the village, stands next to the single dirt track that leads away from the village, over a ridge and to the north.

It would be bad enough without the sicknesses. But those are everywhere. Of the sixty people in this village, fully a third have a visible illness or deformity. Children missing legs. Adults with rubbery, cancerous growths on their throats, abdomens, faces. Limbs so devoid of muscle they are only bone wrapped in skin. Men and women whose every breath is a loud, rasping struggle, overcoming deformations in their throats. Babies born missing an eye, or with faces warped like melted plastic. It is like visiting a leper colony. Danielle's exhilaration at being alive, at having escaped, slowly dissipates into appalled horror. She has never even imagined misery like this.

A group of men, relatively hale and hearty, sit around a small open fire, smoking *bidis*, cheap Indian cigarettes made from individual dried tobacco leaves, and drinking from clay cups what Danielle angrily realizes is whisky. One of them sees Laurent, recognizes him, stands to greet him. The others glance over at them and then away, uninterested.

'*Namaste*,' Laurent says to the standing man, pressing his hands together in front of his heart and bowing.

The man returns the greeting. He seems neither pleased nor displeased by Laurent's presence.

'Dr Lal?' Laurent asks. 'Is possible?'

The man gives Laurent the sideways Indian nod, bringing his ear almost to his shoulder; not quite as much a 'yes' as the Western nod, but a definite acknowledgement. Without another word, he stoops to put his cup on the ground, then turns and walks away.

'One of our doctors should be near here somewhere, doing vaccinations,' Laurent explains.

'Should we go with him?'

'No. He'll find him faster alone. We need to rest.'

Danielle can't argue with that. Now that they are safe, however briefly and tentatively, bone-deep weariness has fallen on her like an anvil. She finds a relatively inviting patch of grass, some distance from the whisky drinkers' fire, and sits. Laurent does the same.

'Is this the village where they captured you?' she asks.

'No. No one here would report on us. This is a village of friends. But they will search for us here. We need to leave very soon. If we are found here we endanger the entire village.'

'Endanger how?'

'They might burn every building. With the families inside.'

'That's crazy,' Danielle says, shocked. 'There has to be . . . Can't the government do something?'

'There is no government here. Delhi and Bangalore are too far away. Government officials don't go where there are no roads. Think of this as a different planet. The state authorities are bribed by Kishkinda, the local authorities *are* Kishkinda, and even if someone was willing to believe illiterate farmers, they don't dare testify in court, they know their families would not survive. As Jayalitha showed. And even if the government did get involved, this isn't as simple as "evil Western company exploiting the poor". The Indian government owns a one-third share in the mine. And there are rifts among the local people, mostly caste but also money – the landowners support the mine. You understand, these people around us, these are the lucky ones. This is a village of free men. Most people in this district are slaves.'

'*Slaves?*'

'They call it debt bondage, but it's slavery. Most lower-caste men and women here, nine in ten, spend all their lives farming their masters' fields, in exchange for a single kilogram of wheat per family per day, and a single acre to grow enough vegetables to feed their family with, if they have any strength left over after twelve hours in the fields. If they flee they are killed, but the sad truth is, the idea never even occurs to most of them. Their debts constantly increase, and then the debt, meaning the slavery, is inherited from parent to child. Some of the families here have been slaves for a hundred generations. The federal government tries to buy their freedom and give them money to live on, but of course the programme is thoroughly corrupt, especially here – all that money goes straight into the landowners' pockets. Don't misunderstand. It's not unique to Kishkinda. There are millions upon millions of slaves in India. The men and women you saw working the fields on the way here? Slaves, all of them.'

'Slaves.' Danielle shakes her head. It seems insane, that thousands of people could live in feudal slavery amid these barren, windswept ridges, only a short train journey from Bangalore, city of tomorrow. But then this is India, a nation torn between medieval and ultra-modern, where physics researchers in Mumbai study string theory a few miles from the largest and most awful slums in Asia, a country where hundreds of thousands of computer programmers graduate every year, but hundreds of millions of subsistence farmers live on less than a dollar a day.

Danielle closes her eyes. Then tiny fingers tug at her shoulder. When her eyes fly open, she is lying on the grass, having fallen asleep without knowing it. A dozen children have clustered around her and Laurent, their eyes bright with wonder, chattering incomprehensibly. Most poor Indian children have learned to ask white strangers for 'one pen' or 'one rupee', or at least to say 'hello', but these know no English, they only want Danielle's attention. Three of them, two boys and a girl, have faces so deformed Danielle has to fight instinctive repulsion. One girl is missing a leg; another has a grotesque tennis-ball-sized growth on her throat. A boy with some kind of elephantiasis has to use his hands to drag his bloated legs and body along the ground. She is almost glad she cannot understand anything they are saying. That would be too heartbreaking.

'God,' Danielle says. 'Is this all from the mine?'

'This?'

'Their . . . their faces.'

'Yes. Tailings, dumped upstream. Toxic waste. Of course, Kishkinda denies it. They produce sheafs of faked studies saying the water is safe and the land has not been poisoned. And people believe them. No, not really. People simply don't care. One billion people in India. Too many already.' Laurent ruffles a boy's hair. 'These children are expendable. Let them suffer. Let them die.'

Danielle can't think of anything to say.

'There's Dr Lal,' Laurent says. 'I hope he can help us.'

Dr Lal rides into the village on a creaking, wobbling bullock cart, driven by the man Laurent sent. A large water bottle and a black shoulder bag sit on the cart next to him. The doctor, skinny, twenty-something and ponytailed, wearing very dirty khaki cargo pants and a T-shirt that may once have been tie-dyed, disembarks gingerly and shakes hands with Laurent.

'What happened to you?' Dr Lal asks.

'Thuggery,' Laurent says. 'We need to get to Hospet.'

Dr Lal purses his lips. 'I see. Will they be looking for you?' His Indian accent is barely noticeable. Danielle guesses he has studied in America.

'Yes.'

'There is only one road.'

Laurent says, 'I know.'

'Perhaps we can try to hide you?'

'That's what I was thinking.'

The doctor nods, American-style, and has a brief conversation with the driver, who turns the cart around and leads it to the edge of the village, towards a small mountain of hay that has been piled and left to dry.

'If my parents and professors could see me now,' Dr Lal says, smiling slightly. 'There were no courses on cloak-and-dagger work in Iowa. Such an oversight. I can dress those cuts while we wait.'

'I'm fine,' Laurent says. 'They're shallow.'

'As you wish. Be sure you clean them when you can. Are you all right?' he asks Danielle.

She nods.

Dr Lal looks around. 'I don't think I've been to this village before. It seems healthier than most.'

'You can't be serious,' Danielle says.

'I'm afraid so. The free villages are terribly sickened. The debt slaves are much healthier. I suppose sick workers are discarded. There are villages like this with a cancer rate of six in ten. And always much higher among children.'

'God. Is there anything you can do to help them?'

'I have my bag of tricks,' Dr Lal says. He indicates his black case. 'Justice International keeps us well supplied, no mean feat in India. I'll vaccinate them, I'll medicate them, I'll treat them as best I can, I'll keep careful records. Some of them will respond. But most won't.' He sighs. 'We don't have enough volunteers. And most stay less than a year. I may not stay much longer myself. It isn't the money. It's . . . in Mumbai, or Bangalore, I would mostly treat patients who wouldn't sicken and die no matter what I do.'

Danielle looks at the children who surround them, some of them smiling and excited, others shy and downcast, all of them fascinated by today's exotic visitors.

'Come,' Laurent says, taking her arm. 'Our limousine is almost ready.'

*   *   *

Four hours later, Laurent and Danielle enter the city of Hospet on the back of the bullock cart, hidden beneath bales of hay piled upon layers of jute cloth. The jute feels like sandpaper, the cart is made of hard many-splintered wood, and the road is as warty as a toad's back; her bruised stomach aches as if aflame; but as she lies on the cart, squeezing Laurent's hand in hers, Danielle's mind is occupied not by pain and discomfort and exhaustion, but by two other, sharply contrasting things – the sheer exhilaration of still being alive, and the bright hopeful eyes of the wretched village's misshapen children.

Hospet is a busy, modern Indian city, and when they emerge from cover, in an alley near the open market, the profusion of noises, smells, colours and people is almost overwhelming, hallucinatory in its intensity, after the isolation of the last two days. Stalls heaped with mangos, coconuts, papayas, bananas; goat carcasses hanging in the air as small boys use rags to wave flies off them; machine-gun haggling from all around the dense crowd of women in bright saris, moustached men in dark slacks and pale shirts, and the odd Westerner in stained cargo pants. At the edge of the market, auto-rickshaw drivers shout at one another for some perceived slight, revealing teeth stained red by betel nut, as chauffeurs relax behind them in bulbous Ambassador cars.

'You said you had your wallet,' Laurent says. 'Is there any money in it?'

'Yes.' Danielle checks. 'Almost five hundred rupees.'

'Please give fifty to our driver.'

Danielle passes fifty rupees, about one US dollar, to the man. He takes it with the same lack of emotion with which he agreed to help them escape. He and Laurent exchange *namastes*, and Laurent leads Danielle into the market. The mingling smells of food make her mouth water and her stomach cramp with hunger.

'They will be looking for us,' he says. 'We must take the first train to Bangalore. We will be safer there.'

'Do I have enough money?'

'For third class. It won't be comfortable.'

They eat street food in the market, chapatis and *aloo parathi* and *chai*, ten rupees per person, the finest meal Danielle has ever eaten. They then buy T-shirts to wear, fifteen more rupees apiece. A nervous twenty minutes pass at Hospet Junction railway station. There are a few white backpackers, but Laurent and Danielle stand out, especially he, barefoot and bruised, his left eye swollen shut, easy for his captors to find. But nobody approaches them.

Daytime third class is worse than Danielle imagined. All the seats are taken, and the overflowing throng of fellow-passengers presses against her on all sides, forcing her to stand in various aching, uncomfortable poses. Vendors selling coconuts, *chai* and deep-fried *pakoras* somehow pass through what seems like a solid mass of humanity, holding vats of boiling water above their heads as they jostle and elbow their way through, but somehow, miraculously, disaster is perpetually averted. Even after Danielle manages to garner enough personal space to sit cross-legged, a privilege she knows she is only accorded because she is white, the eight-hour journey seems to stretch into forever.

But eventually, late at night, they reach Bangalore, once India's garden city, now its modern high-tech hub, the most Westernized city in the country. Danielle has never been so grateful to arrive anywhere. She is also so tired she feels almost drugged. So is Laurent, she can see it in his glazed eyes. It feels very strange, and very draining, to have escaped desperate peril, then travelled from a fourteenth-century village to a twenty-first-century metropolis, all in one day.

They leave the train and pass through the main hall, where, in typical Indian style, workers are prising up what seem like perfectly serviceable stone tiles in the train station's main entrance hall and replacing them with new ones, rather than working on any of the ten million sites in Bangalore that actually need repair. It isn't until they are outside that she realizes she has no idea where to go. She hasn't been in Bangalore since quitting Infosys four months ago. There were a few people at work she might be able to stay with, in an emergency, but she doesn't have their phone numbers, only e-mail addresses.

'My ATM card,' she says, thinking aloud. She checks her wallet and nearly drops it, exhaustion making her move clumsily, as if carrying an enormous burden. Relief floods into her at the sight of the silver card with the Citibank logo. How strange that this little piece of plastic, and its four-digit code, can be the sole difference between comfort and desperation.

'We should go to the police,' she suggests.

'The police?' Laurent shakes his head. 'No. Here that is never a good idea. Everyone who is anyone is for sale. And Kishkinda have much more money than you. It will only be a beacon for them.'

'You think they'll still be after us here?' Until now she has assumed that once they reached Bangalore they would be safe.

'They have a long arm and a long memory. We won't be safe anywhere in India.'

'Then what do we do? We can get money, but we can't leave the country. They've got our passports.'

'A hotel,' Laurent says.

'They'll want our passports too.'

He manages a tired smile. 'I think we'll find a five-hundred-rupee note works just as well, at the kind of hotel I have in mind. Worry about tomorrow tomorrow. First we must rest. Rest is a weapon.'

Berry's Hotel, on Church Street, obviously dates back to the days of the Raj. Its foyer's mahogany panelling, ancient leather couches and iron-lace elevator doors have a certain decaying stateliness. Unfortunately the same charm does not extend to its rooms, where the most noticeable features are low ceilings, exposed wiring, rusted plumbing, cracked furniture, stained linoleum and torn bedding, but Danielle is too tired to care. She is just glad that they found an ATM quickly and that the hotel's obsequious proprietor was happy to take money in place of identification.

She and Laurent fall on to the room's two twin beds and pass out so quickly she does not even remember to undress, much less pull the cover over her. Not that they need covers. Bangalore, a thousand metres above sea level, is cooler than most of India, but it still feels like a hot summer night in Boston.

She spends the night trapped in nightmares of a labyrinthine prison, pursued by men with warped faces in business suits, carrying lathis, down endless grey corridors that echo with the howls of dogs. She wakes to Laurent's gentle but persistent shaking, and half sits, supporting herself on her elbows, still dazed. Her dreams slip from her mind like sand through fingers. She welcomes the amnesia.

'I'm sorry,' he says. His voice is grim. 'You need to get up.'

'What for? What's wrong?'

'Have some coffee.' Two paper cups with bright red COFFEE DAY logos sit on the table between the beds. 'I made some phone calls. I have news. None of it good.'

7

'I called my group's office here,' Laurent says, as Danielle struggles for full consciousness. 'No answer. I called the national office in Bombay. Again no answer. Those phones should always be answered, twenty-four hours. I called headquarters in Vancouver. They don't know exactly what's happening either. Almost all of our people in India have been arrested. The government are calling Justice International a drug-smuggling ring. Our people in Kishkinda as well, they say they grew and supplied the drugs. Most of all they want to arrest us.'

'Us? You and me?'

'They seem to believe that you are one of us.'

'But . . . the police. You're saying the Indian police want to arrest me for being a drug smuggler.' The words sound ridiculous leaving her mouth.

'Exactly.'

'That's crazy.'

'Yes. It is crazy. It is also very real.'

Danielle stares at him, trying to absorb the blow. She has not escaped yesterday's danger. She is not safe. She is, incredibly, a wanted criminal. Maybe, she tells herself, this is just another dream. Maybe she will wake into a more pleasant reality any second now. This is too awful. It can't really be happening.

She shakes her head to clear it. 'I need to understand exactly what is going on.'

'The what is very simple. Kishkinda poisons the ground around the mine, doing terrible things, as you saw, to those who live there. My group tries to stop them. They think you are one of us. And they have declared war. They cannot attack us directly now we have escaped, so they have the police come after us.'

'Just like that? They just tell the police what to do?'

'Bribes, false evidence, political influence,' he says. 'They have millions upon millions of dollars. More than enough to put us in jail.'

'We should go to the consulate.'

'No,' he says sharply. 'No. The consulate will help if you are arrested. They will not help you escape arrest. They will inform the Indian police if you go to them.'

'But if we turn ourselves in, publicly, they won't dare to—'

'Of course they will. Do you know how many Westerners are in Indian jails on drug charges? You know the bureaucracy and corruption here. Do you really think the police were one hundred per cent correct with every such conviction? Believe me, some of them are innocent men with powerful enemies. Do you really believe it can't happen to you? My group will fight this, but you know what Indian courts are like. Slow, corrupt, incompetent. No. What we must do is leave the country. We won't be safe until we escape India.'

'How? We don't have passports, we can't get new ones, and the police are after us.'

Laurent nods. 'That's the essence of the problem.'

'Jesus.' Danielle sits up, reaches for a cappuccino, sips it. She feels as if she has stepped into quicksand, that she will soon be sucked down and suffocated whether she struggles or not. This is something too big and pervasive to tackle on her own. She feels like she has already used up all her luck and resourcefulness. She can't handle being on the run from false drug charges in a foreign country.

'I just want to go home,' she says faintly.

'I'm sorry. That isn't possible.'

She has to call someone for help. But who? Her parents? She can just imagine how they would react. Oh, they would try to help, certainly, with all the money she might ever need, with outraged calls to their congressman and senator and the Indian ambassador, careful to work only through the proper channels – and she knows none of it will serve to conceal the fact that they will believe the allegations that their fucked-up black-sheep daughter is smuggling drugs from India. She can almost hear her father: *How could you get yourself into this?* She can imagine her mother telling her to turn herself in for her own good, her own safety. No. She will go to her parents if she is arrested. Their kind of proper-channels influence might help her then. Not before.

'What I don't understand is why,' Laurent says. 'We've been fighting Kishkinda for years. They think nothing of disappearing an Indian, but a Westerner – until now we might be intimidated, roughed up, but having us arrested, let alone *all* of us arrested, never before, that is very visible, very risky. For them as well as us. Something extraordinary has stirred them. I'm sorry. You seem to have come just as someone hit the Kishkinda beehive with a very big stick.'

'Just my luck.'

'I don't think it was luck. I believe the people holding this stick are your friend Keiran and his group.'

Keiran. Danielle has almost forgotten it was he who got her

into this mess. Maybe he can help her. If anyone can, in a situation like this, it's Keiran Kell.

'What do you know about them?' Laurent asks.

'Nothing. Except it's totally out of character for him to be working with any group at all. Much less anti-capitalist protester types.'

'What is he like? What does he do?'

'Well.' Danielle knows that talking about Keiran is a betrayal of their friendship. But she trusts Laurent, their situation is desperate, and she angrily feels that at this point she pretty much owes Keiran a betrayal to even the score. 'He's a hacker. Or was.'

Laurent raises his eyebrows. 'Hacker?'

'Breaks into computer systems. At least he used to, when we dated. But now he's all legal, does computer security for some investment bank in London.'

'He must have gone back to his old pursuits.'

'For a bunch of anti-globalization protesters? That's so not his politics. He's basically the British version of a redneck libertarian.'

Laurent shrugs. 'Maybe they bribed him. Maybe blackmailed. Regardless, whatever he hacked from Kishkinda has them running scared. And chasing us.'

'Sorry,' Danielle says, feeling irrationally responsible for her ex-boyfriend.

'Don't be. For one, it's not your fault. For two, I'm glad of it. Remember, his group and mine are on the same side. If they scare Kishkinda, it means they have found a weakness. I wish them luck. Maybe I can even help them.'

'You won't be helping anyone if you wind up in jail here.'

'True,' he admits.

'Are we safe here? Do you think the police will check the hotels?'

'It's certainly possible.'

'Then we should go,' she says, alarmed.

'Maybe we should. But where?'

She thinks for a moment. 'Goa.'

'Goa?'

'We can stay at the ashram as long as we need. They don't really keep records. And there're white tourists everywhere. We'll be anonymous. And Kishkinda might own Karnataka' – the Indian state that includes both Bangalore and the Kishkinda mine – 'but Goa's a whole different state. They won't have as much influence there.'

Danielle gets off the bed, wincing from her bruised stomach.

'Are you all right?' he asks.

'I'll live. Just don't tell me any jokes for a few days. How are you?' She looks at his swollen eye and the red, scabbed-over cuts visible on his face and arms.

'It's nothing,' he says dismissively.

Danielle instinctively looks around for something to change into and realizes she literally owns nothing but the filthy, sweat-starched clothes on her back. She takes a deep breath and tells herself not to worry about the big, life-swallowing problem, to focus on the little things, that is the only way she will be able to cope with this. One hour at a time.

'All right,' she says. 'Before we go to Goa, let's go shopping.'

She takes him to Westside, a five-storey department store that would not look out of place in London or Boston. It was this store, its designer clothes, organic groceries and English books, and especially its soothing air-conditioned environment, which kept Danielle sane during her first culture-shocked weeks in India. It still feels like an oasis. Maybe she should claim sanctuary here, like in a church in the Middle Ages. Surely no policeman would dare arrest her among these racks of clothes and pyramids of soap.

She buys a small backpack's worth of sensible travel clothes and toiletries. When she changes, she discovers that the bruise on her stomach where the lathi struck her is darkly purple, and if she reaches either arm too far in any direction, it responds with a bolt of gasping pain. She wishes for a shower. She showered earlier, in the hotel's lukewarm water, but then had to drip dry and don her worn, dirty clothes. She is glad she has kept her hair very short since coming to India.

Laurent is waiting for her by the main entrance, in new slacks, sandals and a dark T-shirt. Like her, he now carries a small black backpack. They step outside into the seething heat of Bangalore proper, upon sidewalks that seem to have been victimized by a recent massive earthquake, through teeming crowds of well-dressed pedestrians, past men in tailored suits and women in bright saris, street vendors selling coconuts, crumbling century-old brick buildings, brand-new glass-and-steel architecture, leg-less beggars, hyper-modern Internet cafés. They eat at KFC, otherwise populated by Indian yuppies on lunch break from their high-tech jobs. It is hard to believe, in this modern, globalized, alternately choking and glittering city of eight million souls, that just a few hundred miles away, poisoned children are dying as their parents look on, helplessly ignorant of what they can do to help, whole villages full of people who have never made a telephone call.

After they eat, Danielle flags down an auto-rickshaw; three wheels on a cheap motorcycle chassis, with a thin open-sided roof, painted brown and yellow, shaped like a beetle's carapace, covering the driver and the two passenger seats. There isn't much room in an auto-rickshaw. They have to sit right up against one another, packs on their laps.

'Bangalore Junction,' Danielle orders.

The driver responds with a sideways Indian nod, yanks the long handle on the floor that starts the engine, and charges into seemingly impermeable traffic as if auditioning for a place in the Light Brigade.

Bangalore sprawls across a huge area; their journey takes them the better part of twenty minutes. It is not so much a distance traversed as a sequence of terrifying collisions barely avoided. Indian roads are horrendously overcrowded, 'lanes' are as rare as unicorns, and all drivers act as if imminent reincarnation is a fate devoutly to be wished. Danielle and Laurent, accustomed to this, barely notice the apparently lethal surges of traffic around them. They hardly talk. The squalling horns and unmuffled auto-rickshaw engine drown out anything quieter than a shout, and the haze of engine fumes is caustic to the throat.

Danielle lets her mind drift. Laurent's shoulder muscles feel like warm iron against her. She wonders whether he has always been strong, or whether the Foreign Legion built those muscles. She wishes she could do yoga, a run-through of the *ashtanga* primary series would clear her head, but they don't have time, and she won't be capable of anything strenuous until her bruise heals. She looks down at Laurent's thick hands, folded atop the backpack on his lap. He seems somehow hyper-real, more present than the rest of the world around her. She finds herself wondering how his fingers would feel entwined in hers, touching her, caressing her face and lips; she feels a sudden strange urge to grab his hands and bite them lightly, taste the sweat-salt on his rough fingers—

She catches herself and twitches with dismay. This is ridiculous. She is running for her life. She doesn't have time for this kind of idle daydream. Of course, she tells herself, making herself think in abstractions, that's exactly why it's happening, intense situations like this are bound to draw people together, danger as an aphrodisiac, her genes screaming at her to get busy reproducing *now* because it looks as if maybe she won't have another chance. She is attracted to him, yes, of course – Laurent isn't classically handsome but he is athletic, graceful, beautiful in a raw animal way, and he did enter her life like the archetypal knight in shining armour. But right now she has to focus on what's important, her own escape to safety, not on the man next to her, the physicality of their bodies pressed against one another. As distracting as that is.

'This may be difficult,' Laurent says, as they approach the station, and she starts out of her reverie. 'Foreigners are supposed to have a passport to buy a train ticket. And I don't think Indian Railways will be as easy to persuade otherwise as Berry's Hotel.'

45

'I know.' Indian Railways, unlike most of India, actually works with reasonable efficiency; its trustworthiness and reputation for integrity exceed those of the police, the courts, the government and the military combined. 'That's OK. I have a plan.'

'I hope it's a good one. There are police here. They will be watching for us.'

Her stomach tightens painfully. She had somehow not considered that probability. For a moment she wants to abort the plan, turn around, go back to the hotel and think of something else – but there is no something else. They won't be safe in Bangalore. They need to get to the ashram. And no other route to Goa will be any easier.

8

'I'm really sorry to trouble you,' Danielle says, doing her best to sound embarrassed instead of terrified. Every time she sees any kind of uniform, her heart writhes in her chest. Fortunately, the ticket office is overcrowded, and a hefty percentage of those waiting here are backpackers. With any luck all white people look alike to the Indian eye.

The towering blond Dutch couple look down at her sympathetically. 'I understand,' the man says. 'I lost my passport at a hotel in Thailand once. It was my first time travelling.'

'Of course we'll help you,' the woman says. 'Our train doesn't leave for another two hours, we won't mind standing in line again.'

'By now I think we won't even *notice*,' the Dutchman says, and both of them laugh. Danielle and Laurent smile back. 'Just remember, as long as you're on the train, your names are Johann and Suzanne. Do you know how much the tickets will cost?'

'Fifteen hundred rupees,' Danielle says, offering them four five-hundred-rupee notes. 'Please take the rest and have a nice meal somewhere, from us.'

'Oh, no, we couldn't,' Suzanne says, detaching three of the notes from Danielle's hand. 'It wouldn't be right. Just wait here, or in the cafeteria. But don't eat anything! I think the food there is very dangerous.' They laugh again. 'We'll bring you the tickets in half an hour.'

'Thank you,' Danielle says, feeling a little miserable about lying to these nice people, even if it is in the noble cause of her own self-preservation.

It is only twenty minutes before the Dutch couple return. Doubt is on their faces, and for a moment Danielle fears the worst, but they are holding two computer-printed Indian Railways tickets.

'I'm afraid the next train is full,' Johann says. 'We bought you tickets for the overnight train. I hope that's all right?'

'It's fine,' Laurent assures them. 'Tonight is fine.'

Danielle isn't sure of that, she was counting on being out of Bangalorc as soon as possible, but she supposes it's better than nothing.

Killing time before the train, they stop at one of Bangalore's many Internet cafés, which sell an hour of computer time for as little as ten rupees, less than twenty-five cents, surely the cheapest Internet access on the planet. Danielle logs into her Hotmail account and composes an e-mail to Keiran, explaining what is happening and why she needs his help. It is hard to make everything that has happened in the last few days form into a coherent order in her mind. She falls back to instincts learned in her year of law school, imagines she is writing a brief. The simple recitation of facts takes longer than she expected. It makes it seem more real, somehow, re-reading her own description of what happened, ordered in neat rows of words. After selecting the SEND button she is more frightened than ever.

'When does the train leave?' she asks Laurent.

'Four more hours.'

She nods. 'Let's get a drink.'

They order a pitcher of Castle beer at NASA, a bar on Church Street, just off the thronging neon-brand-name chaos of Brigade Street. Beyond NASA's chromed airlock, the tables are decorated with glittering rockets, the walls are curved and ribbed brushed metal in a vaguely *2001* style, and a *Star Trek* movie plays silently on the giant video screen. The music, Tricky and the Prodigy and Tupac, was hip five years ago in the West, and is loud but not too loud for conversation. The crowd is young and extremely up-wardly mobile. It even features Indian women dressed in smart jeans and T-shirts, and one very daring one in a halter top, drinking with boyfriends or even co-workers, an unimaginable sight almost anywhere else in India. Danielle is sure no police will come looking for them here.

'To survival,' she toasts sarcastically, offering up her glass.

'To you,' Laurent says, lifting his glass to clink against hers. 'You've been extraordinary. Strong as steel. Most women, it's sexist to say but it's true, most women would have collapsed, could never have coped.'

'I was pretty close to collapse before you showed up. Even if I'd gotten out of that hut, I'd never have made it here without you.'

'I'm a soldier. Dealing with situations like this is my job. With you it seems to be a natural talent.' He smiles. 'Perhaps you should join the Foreign Legion.'

'I didn't think they accepted women.'

'No,' he admits. 'But for you they should change their mind.'

'High praise, I'm sure. You're definitely the first person ever to call me "strong as steel". Usually it's more "strong as butter".'

'Why is that?'

She shrugs. 'I give up on things. You know how hard it was for me to quit smoking?'

'Very difficult?'

'Piece of cake. One week and I was fine. Quitting is for quitters. And me, I'm a natural quitter.'

He looks at her quizzically. 'It doesn't seem that way to me.'

'Yeah? I quit pre-med to do English lit. Then I quit college to be an artist. Well, drug-culture slacker really, but I called it being an artist. Then I quit art to go back to college and start law school. Then I quit law school for the job here. Then I quit the job for the ashram. And you know, if it wasn't going to be over in a few weeks anyways, I would have quit that too. Without even talking about relationships. Oh, but there I pick quitters too, so frequently they end it first. Saves me time and trouble.'

'Why do you quit?'

'Men or careers?' she asks.

'Both.'

She pauses to think before answering. 'I guess it's the same reason both ways. I feel cheated. I have this image of how I want them to be, and the way they present themselves, and then I try them out and they're just stupid bullshit. College is a bunch of snobbish twerps trying to get stoned and get laid. Art is a bunch of pretentious assholes with poor personal hygiene telling each other how great and famous they're going to be some day. Law school, the worst kind of abstract plastic inhuman crap. Jobs, pointless drivel, they eat your soul and time and give you nothing back. Ashrams and Ayurveda and all that so-called enlightenment bullshit are for damaged people to put tiny little bandages over their huge personal fissures so they can pretend they're not fucked up any more. And men, don't get me started. They tell you they love you. Then an hour later they see some teenager with big tits and they want to follow her down an alley and fuck her. And I never learn. See, they're all really great at first. You see trouble, sure, right from the start, but you see so much *potential*, you just know that *some day* it's really going to be *great*. Men and careers both. Being a starving artist and doing a lot of drugs is really cool because you know that one day the Guggenheim will call and you'll be famous and everyone you know will be so jealous. You just know you and your latest troubled boyfriend will be perfect one day, you'll look back on these days of him stealing money from you and laugh. You're sure of it. You're just paying your dues. It's just the prelude to perfection. And then one day you wake up and you realize, the Guggenheim isn't going to call, he isn't going to start helping you without being asked, this isn't going to turn into something wonderfully different, this is no prelude, this is *it*, this is your life, and it's going to stay your life unless you do something. So what do I do? I do something. I quit.'

Laurent looks at her.

'Jesus,' she says, embarrassed. 'I'm sorry. I don't know where that came from. I don't usually babble like that, I swear. Only when I'm in imminent danger. Sorry. Jesus. No more beer for me.'

'No apology needed,' Laurent says. '*Au contraire*. I understand completely. And it doesn't mean you're weak. Not at all. It means you're strong. It's the ones who accept the half-life, the damaged life, who are weak.'

'Well. Nice of you to say so.'

'I say it because it's true. You're no quitter. You're a seeker.'

She smirks. 'I asked Bobby Dylan, I asked the Beatles, I asked Timothy Leary, but he couldn't help me either . . .'

'*Exactement*. You've never found anywhere you felt you belonged?'

She hesitates. 'Maybe once. I spent a summer in Baja California once. One of the years I pretended I was an artist. My boyfriend was a scuba instructor. I did a lot of diving, became a divemaster, like an assistant instructor. He was a shit, but I liked it there. That was . . . Yeah. That was good. Do you dive?'

'A little. With the Legion.'

'Anyway. He was a shit. We broke up. Sometimes I think, maybe I could go back there, start up a dive shop.'

Laurent nods. 'But that would take money, and—'

'No. Money's not a problem.' She swallows. 'My parents are rich. Very rich. There. So, yeah, whatever that means. Maybe I'm just a spoiled rich girl who's never had to deal with real consequences. God knows I've heard that often enough. Sorry. One of the things about growing up rich is that you get so fucking awkward and guilty about it. I own an apartment in Manhattan, you understand? My parents were so excited about their prodigal daughter getting into law school at NYU they bought me an apartment. Outright, no mortgage. Broke their fucking hearts when I dropped out.'

'So why didn't you go back to Baja California?'

'I don't know. It would have felt like cheating. Like quitting. Ironically. Like, I would have lived in my own little safe corner of the world, teaching rich tourists how to dive, and one day I'd find some grateful sensitive Mexican hunk to cook me dinner every night, but I would never have really done anything, you know? It would have felt like a total retreat from the world. So I came here instead. Big mistake, huh?'

'That,' Laurent says, 'remains to be seen.'

'What about you? You woke up one day and decided you wanted to join the Foreign Legion? What's your real name?'

'On my passport it says Laurent Cinq-Mars.'

'But that's the name the Legion gave you?' she asks.

'The name I chose for myself when I joined.'

'Cinq-Mars?'

'French for March fifth,' he explains. 'The day I came to the Legion recruiting office. In Quebec, when unwanted babies were left on church steps, they were named after the day of discovery. Same idea. I had thirty francs in my pocket. I spent all the money I had on the flight to Paris. And I couldn't go back to Canada.'

'Why not?'

'I would have been killed.'

She blinks. 'Seriously?'

'I was deeply involved with very dangerous people.'

'So this whole running for your life thing is old hat to you, huh?'

'No matter how many times your life is threatened,' Laurent says, 'believe me, it never becomes routine.'

'So you were a gangster, then you were a soldier, now you're an activist?'

'Not so different from you. Quitting an old life, trying on a new.'

'Just like changing clothes, huh?' she asks.

'Not quite so easy. As I think you know.'

'Maybe I do. So what's your real name?'

'Laurent is my real name,' he says firmly.

'Fine. What was your first name?'

'I'm not yet drunk enough to answer.' He smiles thinly as he says it, but a burr in his voice hints that she should let the subject go.

'OK. How'd you get so political?'

Laurent purses his lips. 'I was stationed with the Legion in a number of poor countries. Mostly in Africa. I saw the injustice of the world. And I decided to do something about it.'

'Simple as that?'

He nods. 'It really is that simple. Deciding to do something. I'm surprised you've never made the decision yourself.'

'Yeah. Well. I guess I tell myself I'm trying to figure out how to get myself right first, then I'll worry about the rest of the world.' She takes a sip of beer. 'That's not the truth, of course. It's just what I tell myself.'

'And what's the truth?'

'The truth is I just don't give a shit. Or didn't, anyway. I always knew there were people starving and dying of malaria and getting tortured to death. Everyone knows that. Sometimes when I saw something horrible on TV I'd feel bad for a moment and call their number and give them five hundred bucks. And feel really good about myself for a week. But normally, it's not just me, most people, normal people, we just don't care. We'd rather go see a movie and forget about it than actually do something. I know that sounds awful, but that's the way it is.'

'Yes. It is awful. It is the way it is.'

'More beer?' she asks.

'Do we have time?'

She glances at her watch. 'Two hours.'

'Time enough.'

* * *

Danielle is a little tipsy, not drunk but warm and confident, when they emerge from the bar and flag down an auto-rickshaw. When they get in he puts his arm around her, and she instinctively leans into his strength, puts her head on his shoulder, closes her eyes, rests her palm flat on his muscled chest. The rickshaw pulls away, into the squalling cloud of horns and engines and screeching brakes that is Bangalore traffic. She lifts her head up, opens her eyes and looks at him for a long moment.

'What's your real name?' she asks, without really knowing why.

He kisses her. A lurch of the rickshaw parts them for a moment, long enough to smile at one another. Then he wraps her in his arms, and their next kiss lasts all the way to Bangalore Junction.

'This isn't a good time,' Laurent murmurs when the auto-rickshaw pulls to a halt and they separate.

'I guess not,' Danielle says, breathless. 'We have a train.'

'They might be waiting for us.'

'They better not be.'

Laurent finds this very funny. He is still chuckling about it when they approach their train, the *Mas Vasco Express*, Indian Railways number 7309, bound for the city of Margao, although the destination station is actually called Madgaon, presumably to confuse Western travellers. They check the computer print-outs on the side of the carriage to ensure that Johann and Suzanne van der Weld are indeed scheduled for second-class sleeper births 61 and 62.

Danielle at first thinks that the tap on her shoulder is Laurent. But when she turns she sees two small, moustached Indian men in brown uniforms, insignia on their shoulders and lathis in their belts. Laurent stands rigidly next to them.

'Tickets,' the older policeman says. 'Passports.'

9

'Are you the police?' Danielle asks.

She can barely hear her own voice, but she seems to have been understood. 'Railway police,' the younger man says. 'Tickets and passports.'

'Tickets. Of course.' She starts fumbling with her backpack, stalling. 'Honey, do you have the tickets, or do I?'

'I'm not sure,' Laurent says, unstrapping his own backpack, pretending to search within.

Danielle tries to think. They haven't been arrested, so they haven't been identified, and the tickets are in Johann and Suzanne's names. But they have no passports. That will look suspicious. The more suspicious they look, the less chance they have of ever leaving Bangalore. Stalling won't work, their train doesn't leave for another fifteen minutes. But there must be some way out of this.

Inspiration hits. 'You're very late,' she says loudly, making her tone that of angry complaint. 'We asked for you ten minutes ago. What's wrong with you people? What if we were in danger? How can it take you so long to get here?'

She glares at them, pulls out their tickets and waves them in their faces confrontationally. 'There you go. Now what are you going to do about it? We demand full compensation. I'm an American. I'm not going to let you people cheat me like this.'

Their stupefaction is exceeded only by Laurent's.

'Excuse me,' the older policeman says warily, 'I do not understand.'

'You don't understand? It's not complicated. Don't you speak English? Do. You. Speak. English?' she asks shrilly, her voice growing louder with every word. People within a twenty-foot radius turn to stare at them.

'Yes, madam, of course I speak English,' the older policeman says, with barely concealed annoyance. 'I do not understand the nature of your complaint.'

'I already told the boy I sent to get you. We paid for full-price first-class tickets, and they gave us these!' She waves the tickets again. 'Second-class! I demand the tickets we paid for and financial compensation for our trouble! Just because we're white doesn't mean you can cheat us like this! I want our first-class tickets right now!'

'Madam, I think there has been some misunderstanding—'

'You're goddam right there's been a misunderstanding! And it's your job to fix things up and make us happy! Now are you going to do that or are we going to have to go to your manager?'

'Madam—'

'What's your name? You and your assistant both, I want your names!'

'Madam, perhaps you should come to the ticket office with us,' the younger policeman says, his voice soothing. 'Perhaps we can sort this out there.'

'You certainly better,' Danielle huffs.

Laurent gives her a slightly stunned look as they fall into step behind the police. Danielle puts on her best flouncing Ugly American walk, and glares at every Indian they pass. Some of them shrink away. Danielle has to fight to conceal a smile. She feels giddy, as if she is on some kind of drug, dancing on the edge of a cliff.

In the ticket office they cut to the front of the line reserved for FOREIGN PASSPORT HOLDERS, RAILWAY OFFICERS, VIPS, AND FREEDOM FIGHTERS, earning themselves a glare from those next in line, a half-dozen Overseas Indians clutching British passports. The older policeman has a brief conversation in Hindi with the sour-faced woman behind the counter, whose wrinkled face is adorned with a bright red dot on her forehead. Then he turns to Danielle. 'Tickets, passports and receipt.'

Danielle blinks, then turns to Laurent. 'The receipt.'

Laurent looks at her.

'For Christ's sake, Larry, the train's leaving soon,' she says impatiently. 'Give me the goddam receipt.'

'I . . .' Laurent nods. 'Just a moment, yes, of course, I have it here somewhere.' He unslings his backpack again and begins to search through it. 'It's in the inner pocket here, I'm sure of it.' He rummages and his face falls convincingly. 'Maybe the outer pocket.' But the outer pocket is empty. 'Honey,' he says, 'I don't know where it went.'

'You don't know where it is? You *lost* the fucking *receipt?*' Danielle allows her voice to ascend into a screech; easy to do, with her gut churning with anxiety. 'What the fuck is *wrong* with you?'

'Now, honey, calm down,' Laurent says faintly, 'it'll be OK.'

'I don't care,' Danielle says, turning to the policeman. 'You must have hired one of your pickpockets to steal it. We know you're all corrupt. We know you people have your little tricks. But not this time. I want our first-class tickets, and I want them right now, do you understand?'

'Madam,' the older policeman says stiffly, no longer concealing the anger in his voice, 'if you have no receipt, then you have no case, and I will thank you not to abuse my colleagues and myself in this manner any further.'

'Who's your supervisor? I demand to speak to your supervisor!'

'Madam, you have no receipt. There is nothing we can do for you. I must ask you to leave immediately and stop causing a disturbance.'

'How dare you—'

'*Immediately,*' the policeman stresses, steel in his voice.

'Honey,' Laurent says, taking her shoulder, 'we have to go. The train is leaving. We can't be late. We'll miss the flight.'

Danielle looks at him, then at the stony, contemptuous expressions on the two officers, the woman behind the window and those whose queue they have hijacked. 'You haven't heard the last of this,' she warns. 'I will be writing a very strongly worded letter to the Minister of Railways!'

'Come on,' Laurent says, pulling her.

She shrugs him off. 'Get your hands off me!'

Head high, she storms out of the ticket office, followed by

Laurent. He falls into step beside her as they climb the stairs that lead up to the platform. They board the train without looking at each other. It starts moving before they even make it to their berths. They sit down on the bench-like bottom berth, opposite a white backpacker couple in their early twenties, exchange a look, and then both of them dissolve into slightly hysterical laughter. Their berth-mates look on with puzzled expressions.

Danielle lies in Laurent's arms, soothed by the hum and gentle rocking of the train. She slips her hand under his shirt, runs it gently along his scabbed movie-star muscles, and holds it to his heart, feels it beating slowly beneath her palm. She is grateful for his warmth. Indian Railways always turns the temperature in their air-conditioned compartments down to *arctic*, and this is especially evident on the top bunk, to which they have retreated for the sake of privacy. On the other side of their berth, on the lowest of the triple-tiered bunks, the young British couple sit and read their Lonely Planet guide. Indian Railways also tends to clump foreign travellers together.

'Back at the station, that was incredible,' Laurent says. 'I truly thought we were finished. How did you think of doing that?'

Danielle basks in his praise. 'Just reflex. Law school, years of getting hassled by cops, dealing with lowlife druggie assholes, I guess I picked up a few instincts.'

'You should join us.'

'Excuse me?'

'You're smart, capable, you know how to deal with India, you're perfect for us. You're exactly who Justice International needs.'

She says, 'I thought Justice International was all in jail except for you.'

'That won't stick. Even if it does, we're not surrendering the fight. You saw the children of Kishkinda. We can't give up on them. Maybe we can both join your friend Keiran's group. Make common cause.'

'It's . . .' She hesitates. 'It's really noble that you spend your life fighting for that kind of thing. I admire it. It's wonderful. But I just don't know if I could do it. I can't live like this.'

'It's not all running for your life,' he says, amused. 'It's just the decision to make the world a better place. Maybe you're not ready for it. But if you make it, you won't ever feel cheated by it. You won't want to quit. You'll get frustrated, you'll get furious, but you'll never wonder if you're wasting your life. I promise.'

'Must be nice. Having a mission.'

'It is.'

'I'll think it over,' she says.

'Do.'

She kisses him, long and hungrily, then lets go and whispers, 'I'm looking forward to having a room to ourselves.'

'So am I.'

'I can tell.' She smiles. 'Can I stay up here with you? At least for a little while?'

He says, 'If you're comfortable.'

'Don't let me fall.' The berth is very narrow.

He shakes his head solemnly. 'Never.'

Margao station at six in the morning is quiet, misty and deserted by Indian standards. The stalls on the platforms, little stands that sell *chai*, crackers, samosas, chocolate bars, pistachios, newspapers, even a few John Grisham novels, are not yet open, and the vast and oppressive station, all cracks and rust and peeling paint, feels like a tomb. Its main entrance hall contains only a few dozen people, sitting in small circles drinking tea, or sleeping in family groups on colourful woven mats. Only a handful of would-be taxi and auto-rickshaw drivers approach Laurent and Danielle as they exit. They eventually agree to four hundred rupees to go north to Anjuna; a fortune by Indian transportation standards, more than half the price of the thirteen-hour Bangalore–Mangalore–Margao rail journey, but then it is an hour's drive away.

Margao, like most Indian cities, is an ugly, overcrowded mess, but once they cross the bridge over the long, wide tidal river that divides Goa in two, the countryside turns rural and pretty. The dark ribbon of road winds its way through thick green foliage, red earth, golden grass, lagoons lined by palm trees, and villages of small but solid modern buildings, already busy at this hour. Nearly every village has a house with a wall facing the road on which is painted a huge blue-and-yellow ad for mobile phones, informing passers-by, 'An IDEA Can Change Your Life'. Men in drab shirts repair motorcycles; women in blinding saris shop in the little stores, or at the markets that sell vegetables, heaping bins of grains and spices, clothes. Some stalls sell religious goods, Hindu figures and garlands of yellow flowers, like everywhere in India, but also rosaries, candles and garlanded pictures of Jesus. Goa, half converted by the Portuguese in the sixteenth century, is still largely Christian – albeit with a very Hindu flavour, as pictures of a blue-skinned Jesus attest.

The Satori ashram is on a large, mostly untended patch of land a few miles east of Anjuna proper, walled by chain-link fence. Two women at the wooden gates, presumably waiting for their own ride, wave casual hellos to Danielle as she and Laurent emerge from the taxi. Danielle knows their faces but not their names. It feels odd to be recognized and greeted. She realizes she left the ashram only five days ago. It feels like five years.

'Come on,' she says. 'Let's get settled. We'll be safe here.'

Goa

10

Three days later, thirty thousand feet below Emirates Flight 502, the Arabian Sea glitters in the sunlight like burnished steel. Ripples form a complex pattern on its surface, interlocking ridges of water spread across a vast area. Much like what Keiran would see if he were to watch a small patch of ocean from a sailing boat. A fractal pattern, repeated at every scale. Like a coastline, whose peninsulas and outcrops inevitably include perfect miniatures of themselves, the tiniest element governed by the same laws as whole continents and oceans. Keiran takes a moment to appreciate the elegance of the universe, then returns his attention to the chess game on the seat-back screen before him.

'Don't you get bored of winning every time?' Estelle asks from beside him.

Keiran looks over to her, and to Angus in the seat beyond. The pixieish American woman and the small, fine-featured Scotsman stand out amid the plane's mostly Indian and Arabic passengers like mustard splashes in a coal mine; she has purple-streaked hair, his glittering front tooth sets off the strands of gold woven into his dreadlocks, and their bare arms are adorned by tattoos.

'No,' Keiran says. 'Their computer plays the Alekhine Defence every time. That's truly bizarre. I'd love to meet whoever programmed it.'

'But you still beat it every time.'

'Deep Blue it's not. But every game is different.'

'Is it too much to ask for you to focus on what we're here for?'

Angus asks. 'You haven't taken that laptop out since we left London. I thought you had work to do.'

Keiran pauses for a moment to consider possible replies. Then he says, 'I don't know about you, Angus, but I'm here because you fucked up colossally. Which puts you in a curious position vis-à-vis lecturing me on how exactly I spend my time.'

'Christ. I don't know how many times I can say it. I'm sorry. I didn't know.'

'As if sorrow and ignorance somehow make it better. I'd actually rather it was deliberate and you felt good about it.'

'My information was that it would be perfectly safe,' Angus says.

'Yes. Exactly the information I passed on to Danielle. Which very nearly got her raped and murdered. If I'm not very receptive to your complaints just now, it's because I try not to listen to idiots.'

Estelle puts her hand on Angus's. 'Keiran, please,' she says. 'People make mistakes. Then other people accept it, and we all move on.'

'I'll be happy to move on. Soon as I'm confident you won't make any more catastrophic errors.'

'And how exactly are we meant to convince you of that?' Angus asks.

Keiran shrugs and returns to the Alekhine Defence.

The town of Calangute comes as an unwelcome shock. The biggest tourist destination on the Goa coast, it is a Technicolor vision of tourist hell, screeching with shouts and car horns and unmuffled motors, smelling of dust and exhaust fumes and too much humanity, full of cheap hotels slapped together out of uneven concrete. Its streets are clogged with fat blustering English tourists who resent the country they have travelled to for being insufficiently like Britain, Indian hustlers with angry eyes who physically pull tourists into their shops, taxi drivers who tell outrageous lies to get fares, and middle-aged Europeans who will not speak to anyone with dark skin except with peremptory orders. Even Calangute's long, glorious beach cannot redeem it.

'Don't worry,' Estelle says in the taxi, noting Keiran's appalled expression. 'You get used to it. And anyway, we're staying near town, not in town.'

'Thank Christ for that.'

The crowds and buildings thin out as they drive north, until there is only a narrow strip of cafés, restaurants and lodges to their left, between the road and the beach. The right side of the road borders waterlogged grassland patrolled by a few cows. They cross a tidal river via a concrete tunnel bridge, and enter an area of spacious estates hidden behind high walls. The driver follows Angus's directions to a pair of spiky iron gates, the only aperture in a stone wall topped with mortared broken glass. Angus gets out of the car to punch a five-digit code into a numbered panel next to the gate. He shields his hand, but Keiran instinctively watches the relative motions of his arm as it jabs back and forth, and guesses the code is either 13854 or 46087.

The house is blue, three-storeyed, with two satellite dishes visible on top. Keiran identifies the dishes as Sky India TV and a VSAT Internet connection. He is pleased to see the latter. The driveway winds through lush, well-maintained gardens, to mahogany doors adorned by a brass knocker shaped like the Sanskrit symbol for Om. The veranda runs right around the house.

'I see we'll be roughing it,' Keiran says.

Angus smiles. 'Builds character.'

'You never did explain how exactly your crew of unemployed anarchists and social castaways came into all this money.'

'No,' Angus says, as he pays the taxi driver. 'I didn't.'

Keiran takes his laptop bag and small backpack, both of which he carried on his lap, and watches as Angus and Estelle unload their bewildering amount of luggage from the boot and the other half of the back seat. 'Nor did you explain why you've got enough gear for an Antarctic voyage.'

'That we can tell you,' Estelle says. 'We decided Goa might be a good secondary base of operations.'

Keiran raises his eyebrows. 'Setting up shop in the tiger's mouth, eh?'

'As long as we keep it quiet,' Angus says, 'the, shall we say, flexible regulatory environment might work to our advantage.'

'Could you give us a hand with some of this?' Estelle asks, overloaded with bags nearly as big as she.

Keiran considers. 'I could.' He makes no move to help.

'Jesus. Are you always such a prick?'

Keiran looks at her. He doesn't know Estelle at all well. Until receiving Danielle's e-mailed report of danger and disaster, all his contact with their group had been via Angus himself.

'No,' he says after a moment, walks over and picks up a heavy pack. He has every right to be angry with Angus, but none to take it out on Estelle as well. 'Sorry.'

She nods, partially mollified. Angus draws out a large, ornate, old-fashioned key from an inner pocket, and they follow him into the luxuriously appointed house.

'We should ring Danielle, let her know we're here,' Angus says.

Keiran says, 'I believe her guru frowns on telephones. We'll have to go to the ashram ourselves.'

Keiran is drained by thirteen hours of planes and airports, his clothes are thick with sweat from India's alien heat and humidity, but he connects his laptop to the house's satellite uplink and checks e-mail before he showers. This journey is the longest he has gone without Internet access for several years. He is relieved to be back online. He was beginning to feel exiled, stripped of one of his physical senses.

A sign in the washroom warns in bold type that toilet paper must be discarded in the small lidded wastebin, rather than the toilet, lest the finicky Indian sewer system choke on it. Another sign warns that the water is not drinkable. A few tiny gecko lizards dart about on the roof and walls, flicking their tongues.

Keiran doesn't mind their presence. Even a luxury holiday home like this cannot be made both gecko-proof and livably cool. And he likes geckos. Their extraordinary climbing abilities are a miracle of science; gecko paws are covered by filaments so fine that they form a powerful quantum bond with any surface, allowing them to climb on anything, like Spiderman. Plus they eat mosquitoes. Indian tourist authorities claim that malaria has been eradicated in Goa, but the World Health Organization's website treats that claim with considerable scepticism.

He dresses in grey slacks and grey T-shirt. Normally he wears all black, but that would be near-suicidal in the Indian heat. His day pack is black canvas decorated with a Linux penguin. When he descends to the foyer, Angus and Estelle are waiting for him, clean and newly dressed, he in cargo pants and a red shirt, she in a green sarong and a sky-blue blouse filigreed with black. It's an eye-catching ensemble; with the purple streaks in her hair she looks like the top half of a rainbow. Keiran admits to himself that he resents Angus a little for having so pretty a girlfriend.

'Shall we?' Angus asks. 'The taxi is waiting.'

'Shouldn't we just hire a driver for the week?' Keiran asks.

Angus and Estelle exchange a look before she says, 'We wouldn't be comfortable with that.'

'Why on earth not?'

'When you hire a taxi, you're dealing with an independent local entrepreneur. That's fine. But hiring a driver for an extended period is like having a servant. It would be too close to exploitation.'

Keiran stares at her. 'It's exactly the same thing either way. You pay a man to drive you around.'

Angus shakes his head. 'There's a difference.'

Keiran considers arguing, but just shakes his head at their Alice in Wonderland politics and follows them to the taxi.

The Satori ashram is essentially a disorganized summer camp for unhappy Western women. Its inhabitants sleep in individual

A-frame huts but bathe, cook, eat, take Ayurvedic lessons and do yoga together, in big tents or out in the open. Keiran sees Tibetan monks in saffron robes, Indian men in designer clothes and the occasional tanned Western man in locally purchased drawstring trousers, but most of the population consists of white women, early twenties to late fifties, with stringy hair and grimly reverent expressions. A few of them wear saris, generally with Western clothes on beneath. Teams of women wash pots, prepare food, chop herbs, clear weeds and clean huts. There is no obvious nerve centre; past the car park, in which half a dozen cars and twenty motorcycles rest, several different paths lead into the ashram's large property, past haphazardly strewn buildings. Keiran, Angus and Estelle wander for several minutes before the third woman they ask recognizes Danielle's name.

'Oh, she's not with us, she's doing the teacher training with Tara and Guru Virankasulam,' she says, speaking the last name reverentially. 'They'll be at the other end of the property.'

It is a five-minute walk to a tent-like structure with open walls, a hardwood floor and pillars, and a canvas canopy rather than a roof, where nearly fifty people, almost all of them women, all of them extremely fit, are in the midst of a strenuous yoga class. A red-headed woman and a bald, elderly Indian man conduct the class. Both are clad in saffron robes. The guru calls out what Keiran supposes to be the Sanskrit name for a stance, and then, as the men and women strain to attain and sustain the pose in question, the red-headed woman goes among them, adjusts their stances, sometimes forcefully, and scolds them for minute failures.

It is an impressive spectacle, this sea of athletic, sweat-glisten-ing bodies moving in unison, their loud Darth Vader breaths in perfect sync, as they lift themselves off the ground, balance precariously on hands or heads or one foot, and twist and fold their bodies, human origami, into poses that must near the limit of human capability. It takes Keiran a little while to pick out Danielle. He hasn't seen her in more than a year, and she has cut her hair very short. He sighs with relief, to finally see her in the flesh and know she is all right, that his dreadful mistake which so endangered her can after all be repaired.

They retreat to a crude wooden bench beneath a copse of trees, within sight of the canopied wooden floor, to wait for the class to end.

'That's pretty intense,' Estelle says. 'I mean, I do *ashtanga* yoga too, I can go through the whole primary series, but nothing like that.'

Keiran nods. He too is impressed. Danielle practised yoga when they dated, but never approaching this level.

A shirtless, heavily muscled man, almost hairless yet vaguely ape-like, approaches them. His long arms are tattooed with vaguely military sigils, and he has bare feet and a black eye. He pauses, squints for a moment, and says, 'Are you Keiran?'

Keiran looks at him. 'Who wants to know?'

'You're here for Danielle?'

Already out-informed, Keiran doesn't want to let anything more slip, but Estelle says, 'Yes.'

'You must be Estelle. And Angus. I'm Laurent. Justice International.'

Hands are shaken all around. Laurent all but crushes Keiran's hand.

'Thanks for coming,' Laurent says.

'Thanks for helping her out,' Keiran says stiffly, already deciding that Danielle is too good for this lout.

Angus says, 'You knew Jayalitha.'

'I did,' Laurent agrees.

'Are you sure about what happened to her? Is there any chance . . .'

'I didn't myself see it, and they left no evidence,' Laurent says, 'but don't let that stir false hope. There is no doubt. I'm sorry.'

Angus looks at Estelle, who takes his hand and clasps it between hers.

'Those *bastards*,' Angus says. 'They will pay. I promise you, I will see them pay for that. Jaya was, she was . . . extraordinary.'

Laurent nods.

'What happened to her?'

'They burned her in her own house. With her family and all the evidence she gathered. By the time I arrived there was nothing but ashes and bones.'

Angus grimaces. Estelle closes her eyes for a moment. A silence follows.

'How did you know her?' Laurent asks.

'We met her when we came here a few years ago,' Estelle says.

Angus picks up the story. 'Jaya was working in a hostel in Cochin, saving up money to marry her husband. It was what they quaintly call a "love match" around here. Meaning both families were appalled and there were death threats all around. Her husband was from Kishkinda, as you may know. I don't remember his name.'

'Tamhankar,' Laurent says.

Angus nods, satisfied. Keiran suspects he knew Jaya's husband's name perfectly well; that was a test. 'Yes. He's Kannada, and Jaya is Tamil.' He pauses and his face tightens again. 'Was. Was Tamil. They will regret what they did to her. I know that sounds hollow, but it's the truth.'

'It's only a rumour,' Laurent says, 'but I heard it was a man called Vijay, from the Bombay office, who killed her. It might have been him that captured me and interrogated Danielle. If so I think he has military training. He was new, I'd never seen him before.'

'Vijay,' Angus says, tasting the name. 'From the Bombay office. Keiran, I want you to look into that. Vijay.'

Keiran nods.

'When did it happen?' Angus asks.

'Two days before Danielle arrived.'

'Just ten days ago,' Estelle muses. 'Jesus. What an evil thing to do.'

Another silence.

Laurent says, 'Danielle will be very happy to see you all.'

'She won't be long now,' Estelle says. 'They're in *shivasana*.'

Keiran glances at the yoga class, whose members are now lying back on their mats, arms and legs splayed out to the sides, eyes closed, silent. It reminds him of the famous picture of the Jonestown victims in the 1970s, hundreds lying dead in neat rows.

'I've been doing my due diligence,' Angus says to Laurent. 'Reading up on your group. You have an impressive track record. I think we could do good work together.'

Laurent nods. 'I was thinking that too. Common cause.'

'You've got the organization there in the field. We've got money, and contacts, and certain other advantages. Like him,' he says, indicating Keiran. 'Your ground war, my air war, together we might beat these bastards.'

The yoga class disperses, its members glowing with sweat and endorphin bliss. When Danielle sees Keiran, her face stretches into a wide grin and she pelts across the field like a delighted child. She rushes to him and he hugs her, tightly at first, until she grunts with pain and pulls away.

'Easy,' she gasps, 'I'm still a bit bruised.'

'Shit. Sorry.' He backs off. 'Is that from . . .'

Danielle nods awkwardly as Laurent casually drapes his arm around her.

'Oh, Jesus,' Keiran says. 'Those *fuckers*. Dani, I don't know what to say. I am so sorry.'

'What did they do to you?' Estelle asks, her voice soft.

'They just hit me the one time. That's all. This little tinpot dictator with a lathi. But then Laurent showed up and saved the day.'

'After she released my handcuffs,' Laurent says. 'It was a joint effort.'

'It was entirely my fault,' Angus says. 'I sent the passport. I told Keiran it would be perfectly safe. You have every right to be absolutely livid with me. I had no right to ask you to go. I never imagined they might do that to you, but obviously I should have. I'm fucking . . . I don't even know the right word – abashed and mortified and grovelling don't even come close to my level of guilt.'

'Mine too,' Keiran mutters. 'For believing you weren't full of shit.'

Angus gives him a weary look.

'Well,' Danielle says. 'Just don't let it happen again, OK? Once in a lifetime is more than enough. Trust me. But, you know, as long as you can get us out of the country, all's well that ends well.' She smiles faintly. 'There were even certain fringe advantages.' She looks up at Laurent, who leans down and kisses her.

'Speaking of getting out of the country,' Keiran says, trying to hide his annoyance at the way Laurent is pawing Danielle, making it clear she is his property. He digs in his penguin pack and produces a digital camera. 'I need pictures of the both of you. Laurent, over there, with the sky behind you, that will be easy to edit out.'

'What's this for?' Danielle asks.

'Your new passports.'

Laurent blinks as the camera flashes. 'You can give us passports?'

'Fake ones. But good enough to fool Indian customs on the way out.'

'What about when we land?' Danielle asks, taking Laurent's place.

Keiran snaps a picture of her. 'You just can't *imagine* how it happened, but somehow you lost your passport in the airport in India. It's not hard to prove you're American. They might put you in a holding cell overnight, that's all, until they confirm your identity.'

'And they might call the Indian embassy to see if we're wanted by the authorities here,' Laurent says sceptically.

'Indeed they might. But the Indian embassy will say they've never heard of you.'

Laurent looks at him. 'How can you be sure?'

'Trust me.'

'Keiran, I don't mean any offence, but trusting you is how Danielle got into trouble in the first place.'

Keiran looks at him expressionlessly.

'Don't worry,' Danielle says. 'If he says they won't know, they won't know.'

Keiran explains, 'It's what I do.'

Keiran, Angus and Estelle decide to visit Anjuna's beach before returning to the house. Anjuna's meandering main road, lined by restaurants, hostels, shops, Internet cafés, travel agencies and money-changers, extends for two miles from the highway junction to the sea. At the waterfront, beach cafés overlook the surf, and a nightclub hidden behind tall fences stands on a high bluff. The town is far more easygoing than Calangute with its seething chaos. White people are everywhere, most of them young and very fit, on foot, on motorcycles, eating in cafés, throwing frisbees on the beach. As they descend the sandy path that leads to the beach, Angus is twice offered ganja and ecstasy by local men ostensibly selling souvenirs and psychedelic paintings. Keiran supposes Angus's dreadlocks make him a magnet for drug dealers.

'So what do you think?' Estelle asks Keiran, as they walk over rocks and on to the long strip of soft, golden sand.

'Of what?' Keiran says.

Angus says, 'Our new friend.'

'I think he's a dangerous idiot.'

Angus looks at him. 'His shagging your ex-girlfriend wouldn't make you a wee bit biased here, would it? And besides, you think *everyone* is a dangerous idiot.'

'So do you. It's one of the wonderful common threads that make our friendship so rich and vibrant.'

'I'm touched. But it's not true. I only hate most people. The useless, selfish cunts who grow up rich and turn a deliberate blind eye to the dying poor all around them. Ordinary people. Laurent, however, happens to be a member of the tiny minority that actually works to help them.'

Keiran says, 'Danielle was born very rich indeed, and I don't see her slaving away to save Aids patients in Zimbabwe. How do you feel about her?'

'Sod off, straw man. By "rich" I mean everyone ever born in a First World country, as you well know. Don't waste my fucking time with all these petty class distinctions among the haves. We're all haves. And I think she has potential. I even, and this really makes me a starry-eyed dreamer, think you have potential.'

'Better check into the hospital, mate. I think you're having an aneurysm.'

'Ever the comedian. What do you think of Laurent?' Angus asks Estelle.

She says, 'I like him. But what matters is that he can help us.'

'Help you or help the poor?' Keiran asks.

Both of them look at him, bewildered.

'Oh, I'm sorry, I forgot. They're one and the same. How convenient.'

'What exactly are you saying?' Angus asks, an edge in his voice. 'You think we're in this for our own good? You've seen how we've lived for the last ten years. You've seen the bruises. You've visited me in prison. You sell out to work in an investment bank and then you have the fucking nerve to suggest that *I'm* the hypocrite?'

'I couldn't have sold out. I never bought in.'

'Always quick with the smooth, contemptuous one-liner. Dodge the question. Maybe I'm wrong about you after all.'

Keiran says, 'It's not your noble goals I question. Yes, you want to make the world a better place. The problem is, you're totally fucking wrong about how to do it. You want to save the world? Be my guest. But you're going about it in exactly the wrong way.'

'Meaning what?' Estelle asks.

Keiran thinks for a moment, then shakes his head. 'Never mind. What do I care? What do you care what I care? Nothing to both. I owe you my life, and I'll pay my debt, and then I'll go back home. No sense fighting over politics while we're at it.'

They walk in silence for a little while. Then Estelle says, 'Keiran, it's fine if you don't want to talk politics. But if you ever do, I'm always interested in hearing the views of someone as smart as you are.'

Keiran nods. 'All—'

'Even if you are needlessly abrasive.'

'All right. Maybe we can talk politics when I'm in a better mood.' He pauses. 'And I'm sorry.'

'Answer me this,' Angus says to him as they walk. 'What is it you want out of life, mate? What lives in your dream world?'

Keiran doesn't miss a beat. 'Rolls-Royces stuffed full of twenty-pound notes. Non-unionized people with dark skin scurrying to obey my every whim because they know they'll starve to death if I sack them. Huge dams flooding vast tracts of old-growth rainforest. Perpetuating the Chinese iron fist in Tibet. A world full of people who eat nothing but genetically modified McDonald's French fries, and Chiquita bananas they bought at Wal-Mart. Helping plan the American invasion of Iran. *Fifty-year patents.*'

'Very funny,' Angus says sourly.

Keiran grins. 'I try.'

11

Estelle comes to join Danielle for yoga the next morning. Still basically strangers, they are a little skittish around each other, and Danielle is glad when small talk ends and the class begins. She clears her mind, focuses on her breath and body, as they move through the *namaskaar* series, the warm-ups before the primary series begins.

The class is gruelling and fast paced, and though Estelle is fit and experienced, she has to stop and rest a few times in *balasana*, child's pose. Danielle pushes herself through the strain, past the sweat and hoarse breaths and aching limbs, until the rhythmic powerful *ujjayi* breathing at the core of the practice manages to extinguish past and future, until she is entirely in the now, all body and no mind.

At the end of the class, they lie back in *shivasana*, which Danielle privately calls *naptime*. She feels sore and wrung out, but deliciously loose and relaxed, at peace with the world. Whatever happens will work out, somehow, she is sure of it. She tries to ignore the nagging voice telling her that that's just endorphins talking, that real problems aren't fixed just by going to a yoga class for an attitude adjustment.

After the class Danielle and Estelle sip tea in the ashram's open-air café.

'Thanks for having me here,' Estelle says. The remains of her Southern accent are more palpable now; she seems to have let down her social guard. Danielle feels more at ease too, now that they have sweated together.

'No problem.'

'Did you like living here?'

Danielle looks around and chooses her words carefully. 'It was a valuable experience. I think it's best that it didn't continue much longer.'

'What are you going to do next?'

'I haven't really thought past getting out of the country in one piece.'

Estelle nods. 'Understandable. Here's one option you might want to think about. Angus and I, we don't know you well, obviously, but we do like you. Keiran speaks very highly of you. And you're obviously tough as old nails. We'd like you to think about working with our movement in some capacity.'

Danielle's instinct is to immediately decline. This is what she always does, when she is asked to join or support a political group, a gallery, a movement. She assumes, whenever asked, that she is being approached for her and her family's wealth. But Estelle probably doesn't even know she is rich, Keiran isn't likely to have mentioned it. And besides, Estelle is right. Danielle *has*

73

been tough and resourceful. Their desperate escape from Kish-kinda feels far enough behind her now that she can feel proud of it. It feels good to be approached because of what she is, what she can do, rather than her ability to write fat cheques. Danielle isn't sure it's ever happened before.

'I'd have to think about it,' she says.

'Of course.'

'What capacity do you have in mind?'

Estelle says, 'Depends on what you're comfortable with. But we might, for instance, have you help organize protests. We're considering a possible major protest in Paris in two months' time.'

'That's what you do? Organize protests?' Danielle says dis-believingly. 'That's why you hired my ex-boyfriend the über-hacker?'

'No.' Estelle hesitates, then says, 'Our inner circle does more challenging work. But we can't ask you to join that yet. That's not a decision either side can make lightly. We have to completely trust the people we work with. You understand, we don't necessarily play within the rules set down by governments.'

Danielle looks at her. 'What does that mean exactly?'

'Well, I can give you a lot of soothing euphemisms, but what it really means is, we break the law. No violence against people, unless absolutely necessary, and it hasn't been yet. But we can't afford to play nice. Not in a world where ten per cent of the population holds the other ninety in chains. Oh, it's not official slavery any more, not on paper, but poverty, ignorance, disease, corruption, they add up to the same thing.' Estelle's voice turns grim as she speaks, her eyes harden, she seems to change before Danielle's eyes from a friendly, playful woman into a vengeful angel. 'Strong preying on weak, rich feeding on poor, like fucking vampires, everywhere you look. And it's the strong and rich who make the laws. We can't be bound by the law if we want to break the chains. Legalized slavery and mass murder, that's what it boils down to. You were there. You saw them dying in Kishkinda.'

Danielle doesn't say anything. Estelle's sudden transformation is unnerving, as if the pixieish purple-haired woman has been possessed. Danielle isn't ready for a heavy political conversation, or this kind of righteous passion.

'Sorry,' Estelle says, reading Danielle's reaction. She smiles sheepishly, lets her fury dissipate. 'Didn't mean to go into lecture mode. But if you think you want to do something about what you saw, let us know. We can help you set up in Paris, we've got friends and places there, or wherever else our next action is. We take care of each other.'

'Everyone's trying to recruit me,' Danielle says. 'Laurent too.'

'We're hoping to work with him too. He seems like a good man.'

Danielle nods. 'So does Angus. How long have you known each other?'

'Since my divorce. Three years, I guess. Not like it sounds, I was already separated when we met. I married a Brit when I was twenty-one and stupid. I was all packed up, ten days away from flying back to Alabama for ever, when I met Angus. At a protest, appropriately. And ten days later I decided, at Heathrow, at the gate, I didn't want to get on the plane.'

'Wow. Like a movie. Romantic.'

'Maybe a bit like you and Laurent, if you don't mind me saying so.' Estelle pauses. 'You want to know something I haven't told anyone else yet?'

Danielle looks at her warily. 'OK.'

'Maybe I shouldn't, but, honey, you give good trust vibes.'

'If it's something legal, maybe you shouldn't—'

Estelle laughs. 'No,' she says, 'don't worry. It's not like that. Angus asked me to marry him, before we came here.'

'Wow.'

'Yeah. Wow.'

Danielle wishes Estelle hadn't said anything. She hardly knows this woman. She isn't ready to discuss her marriage proposal. But she can hardly ignore the topic now. 'What are you going to say?' she asks.

'I told him I couldn't answer him yet.' Estelle sighs. 'Not that I don't want to spend the rest of my life with him. I do. I love him desperately. But marriage, having seen how it goes wrong . . . I'm divorced, my parents are divorced, my brother is divorced, it's not a great family track record, is it? And let's face it, with what we've devoted our lives to, what are we going to do, settle down in a house in the country and raise a brood? There's a famous poem in the UK. It starts, "They fuck you up, your mum and dad. They may not mean to, but they do". I mean, the whole *concept* of marriage is . . . suspect, I think. For people like us, anyway. I'm sorry. I've been brooding like crazy. Picking at it like a scab. As if we haven't got enough else going on, he had to spring this on me too.'

'He seems like a good man,' Danielle affirms again, inadequately.

'Yes. Yes, he is. I'm sorry. I don't mean to drop this on you. But I haven't had anybody to talk to. It's not like I can have a heart-to-heart with Keiran.'

Danielle smiles at the notion.

'How long did you date him?' Estelle asks.

Danielle thinks. 'Four months? Five? Not that long. But he's about the only ex I ever stayed friends with.'

'How did you meet?'

'In California. He was working for some dot-com cyber-punk start-up that went nowhere. I was living in Oakland, in this warehouse squat we called a collective loft, doing a lot of drugs and pretending to be an artist.' Danielle half smiles. 'A match made in counter-culture heaven.'

Estelle says, after a moment, 'He has a very strong personality.'

'At first he often seems like the world's biggest asshole,' Danielle agrees.

'And then?'

Danielle sighs. 'With him it's a matter of respect. It's almost childish. His problem is he's too smart. I mean, I've met a lot of smart people, I'm sure you have too, but take it from me, Keiran's on a whole different level. He's so smart he feels total contempt for just about the whole rest of the human race. He assumes people aren't worth talking to and it's up to them to prove otherwise. So at first he treats you like dirt. But then if he sees you do something smart or interesting or valuable, whatever, he turns into a pretty decent human being. I mean, he's still sharp tongued, you have to grow a thick skin, but he's not as bad as he seems at first. He's totally trustworthy, if that's what you're worried about. He'd walk through fire for his friends. Complaining loudly the whole way.'

Estelle nods. 'That's more or less what Angus says.'

'Maybe he's different now. I've seen him maybe five times in the last four years. People do grow up. But he doesn't seem to have changed much.'

'I think his emotional age got stuck at twelve,' Estelle says, and then looks dismayed by her own words. 'Sorry. That just came out. Maybe he'll grow on me.'

'He usually does,' Danielle agrees. 'Like a cancer.'

That afternoon, Danielle sits in their hut and stares at her Certificate of Completion, verifying that she has successfully finished the Satori ashram's prestigious yoga teacher-training programme, and tries to feel some sense of accomplishment beyond that of a Girl Scout who has received a merit badge. She can turn this piece of paper into a career, if she wants, go back to America and teach nine or nineteen classes a week. The idea does not appeal. She adores yoga for itself, but the notion of teaching it to stressed-out yuppies who will never devote themselves to it as she has is repellent.

The door opens and Laurent enters their hut. He is mildly surprised to see her. 'Shouldn't you be away bending yourself into a pretzel?'

'I'm done,' she says, showing him the certificate.

'Congratulations. Does that mean we're supposed to leave?'

'No. The next group hasn't arrived yet. And anyways, I'm sure I could stay as an assistant teacher if I want.'

'Do you want to?'

'No.'

Laurent nods. 'You know, I think I will miss this place.'

Danielle looks around. Their home for the last week is exceedingly spartan; two-by-fours hammered into an A-frame shape with visible cracks between the planks, a misshapen table, folding chairs and a crude bed with a lumpy mattress and flower-print sheets, canopied by a tattered mosquito net. But she will miss it too. Despite the uncertainty, the constant spectre of danger, this has been one of the best weeks of her life.

'Let's celebrate your graduation,' he suggests. 'Go for a ride.'

'We're supposed to meet Keiran and the rest tonight.'

He smiles. 'That leaves all day.'

They rent a motorcycle from a teenager in Anjuna with a Limp Bizkit T-shirt. Laurent rejects the first machine they are offered and settles on a battered but smooth-running Yamaha. Danielle thinks for the first time of the man in Hampi who never regained the Bajaj Pulsar that the Kishkinda men stole, and makes a mental note to find some way to repay him.

First they go to the beach, which extends for almost a mile between rocky headlands. Westerners, Indians, dogs and a handful of cows roam and play on its sand, which is fissured by a winding tidal river. Several fishing boats are stationed above the high-tide line, dark wooden hulls about thirty feet long and six wide, each with a single outrigger pontoon the size of a person, attached by ten-foot-long wooden struts. The boats are full of folded nets that smell of fish. The water is warm and glorious. Laurent and Danielle frolic, body-surf, play-fight, lean back and float and let the waves wash them where they will. When they walk back on to the beach, the hot sun dries them within minutes.

They remount the Yamaha and zoom through Anjuna, past its cafés and tattooed young Israeli backpackers, fill up at the local Bharat Petroleum station, and ride northwards on the coastal highway, the glittering blue of the Arabian Sea to their left, vivid green jungle to the right. Danielle rides with her arms wrapped tightly around Laurent, her head on his shoulder, wind in her face, the Yamaha engine rumbling contentedly beneath them, and thinks: *This is happiness. I am happy.* She knows they are still in danger. She does not know where she and Laurent will go next, or whether he even wants them to stay together. But she manages to expel all that from her mind. It is only the future. This is the present, and in it she is happy.

They stop for fresh coconuts and pineapple and cool-drinks, the Indian term for sodas, in a small, dusty village an hour's drive away. They stop again when they spot an empty beach on the way back. There they find a secluded nook, in the shadow of a huge rock, where they have long, slow, tender sex that brings tears to Danielle's eyes. They return to Anjuna and wander its vast, kaleidoscopic, twice-weekly market, which attracts thousands of tourists and hundreds of locals. Finally they ride south to Calangute as the sun sets, casting a rosy glow on the entire world before it dips into the ocean's warm darkness. Danielle is blissfully exhausted by the time they finally reach Calangute's Le Restaurant, where Keiran, Angus and Estelle wait for them.

'What I'd like to know is why they're after us in the first place,' Danielle says.

'Yes,' Laurent agrees. 'My whole organization, arrested and jailed. Danielle and I captured, and who knows what they might have done to us. Just as your group sends Danielle to Jayalitha. I can't believe this is just coincidence.'

Angus shrugs apologetically. 'And I can't believe it's not. Jayalitha was collecting evidence for us, we wanted her to come back to the UK with it, but no bombshells.'

'No point in speculating,' Keiran says decisively. 'We simply don't have sufficient data for any conclusion. Let's get everyone out of here safely, then try to find out what happened.'

'How long do we have to wait here?' Danielle asks.

'Your new passports should arrive in forty-eight hours. Mulligan's finished with them, visas, stamps, everything. He's

DHLing them tonight. Two-day delivery or your money back. You should be safe enough until then. Just avoid anyone who might ask for ID. And try to blend in, stay in places with lots of other tourists. Kishkinda might have sent their own people to look for you. Don't go anywhere that you stand out.'

Laurent eyes Keiran. 'I thought you were a *computer* security expert.'

'Good hackers understand all security systems,' Keiran says. 'Hardware, software, wetware, meatware.'

'Wetware? Meatware?'

'Brains. Human beings.'

Laurent nods. 'These brand-new passports of ours – what happens when we pass through outgoing customs, and the Indian officer types the fake visa number into his computer?'

'Define fake,' Keiran says shortly.

Laurent has to think about the answer for a moment. Then he says, 'Not issued by a legitimate authority.'

'Define legitimate authority.'

'For a visa, the national government in question.'

Keiran gives Laurent a patronizing look. 'Can you be more specific?'

Danielle suppresses a sigh. It's apparent that Keiran has decided to dislike Laurent. Apparently he hasn't grown up any in the last four years. He doesn't look any different, either; still a tall, slender man with pale skin, spiky dark hair and almost disturbingly luminous green eyes. And he still wears impatience as his default expression.

'The foreign ministry?' Laurent suggests, vexed by Keiran's questions. 'What are you getting at?'

'No. When embassies issue visas, when customs officers check them, they don't call the foreign ministry. They punch the number into their computer. The legitimate authority is not the foreign ministry but their database. Your visas are as real as anyone's.'

'You're saying you broke into the government of India's computer databases?'

'Please,' Keiran says scornfully. 'It wasn't even hard. Their security is shockingly inept. Patches *years* out of date. Their network was reasonably hardened, but once I got on to it, a script kiddie could own that database.'

Laurent nods slowly. 'I'm impressed.'

'We still have to buy your plane tickets. Where are you going from here?'

Danielle and Laurent look at each other. They haven't discussed this at all. Danielle quails at the thought of talking about it in front of the others.

'We'll get back to you tomorrow,' she assures Keiran.

'Do you want to come stay with us until you go?' Estelle asks. 'We've got a lovely huge house, five bedrooms, more than enough space. And Angus cooks. Good thing, too, 'cause all I can make are grits and boiled peanuts.'

'That's nice of you,' Danielle says, smiling at her. She decides she likes Estelle, who seems much more relaxed, more comfortable in her skin, with Angus beside her. The same seems true for Angus; they are one of those couples who seem to take the jittery edge off each other's personalities. 'But it's too much hassle to move our things tonight, and then tomorrow there's no point in moving for just one night.' And, she doesn't say, the ashram is safer.

'Also,' Angus says, 'there's some kind of party tonight, if you'd like to join us.'

She blinks. 'A party?'

'A beach rave up by Arumbol,' Keiran explains.

Danielle chuckles. 'You're here twenty-four hours and you've already found a party. Keiran, you'll never change.'

She means it fondly, but she can see, by a wince that quickly vanishes from his face, that he is genuinely stung. She guiltily wishes she could take her comment back.

'Everyone needs a little playtime now and then,' Estelle says. 'Come by the house at eleven if you're interested.'

*   *   *

Danielle is quiet on the ride back to the ashram. This last week, living in the ashram, waiting for Keiran to arrive, spending every moment living with potentially imminent danger, has been awful, yes, but also thrillingly intense. She and Laurent have clung to one another like children in a storm, each has barely let the other out of their sight. Being separated was inconceivable. Now their time here is almost over. They have never even talked about what they will do if they make it out of the country. Danielle supposes it was a silent mutual agreement not to jinx their escape. But now they have to talk.

She still knows little about the man she has spent almost every waking moment with for the last ten days. They have traded plenty of colourful anecdotes, from his life in the Foreign Legion and hers as an American counter-culture nomad, but no actual history, and he tells his stories as if they are of no more importance than amusing tales from a dusty old book, as if they happened to someone else. She has told him about some of her exes, but he has never once mentioned any other women, though she is sure there must have been many. Nor has he spoken of any friends. She knows he is gracious, considerate, strong, brave, smart, funny and devastatingly good in bed, but she has never seen any real emotion in him – the closest he has ever come is his annoyance at Keiran tonight. It is almost as if he is a robot, built to be the perfect boyfriend, with enough of a dangerous past to make him romantic, but no actual baggage.

She doesn't know why Laurent has made such an impact on her, why the thought of leaving him makes her feel sick. It isn't just the intense, romantic nature of their first encounter, the way he saved her from some awful fate, their escape from peril like a knight and a princess in a fairy tale. It isn't just that, unlike in most of her relationships, he rather than she is the prize, it's Laurent who is more beautiful, glamorous, untameable, exciting. It's that when he's away from her, she feels old, dull, forgettable, but when he's with her – she has never felt so intensely alive.

'You're quiet,' he says, as they walk back to their hut after passing the ashram, nodding to people they recognize as they pass. All the women smile extra brightly at Laurent. Everyone likes him.

They re-enter the hut and he relaxes back on the bed. Instead of joining him and letting him wrap his strong warm arms around her, as she normally would, and as she wants to, she sits on one of the folding metal chairs and says, 'We should talk.'

He cocks his head. 'Something wrong?'

'Yeah. The future.'

'What's wrong with it?'

She says, 'Does it even exist?'

'Is this a metaphysical question?'

'No. What happens the day after tomorrow?'

He looks puzzled. 'We get our passports and leave the country.'

'Yes. But where are you going? And where am I going? Are we going to the same place? Are we going together? What happens to us now? We haven't talked about this at all.' Danielle is breathing hard as she speaks. She realizes she is clutching her thighs tightly with her hands and forces them to let go.

It takes Laurent an agonizingly long moment to answer. 'No. No, we haven't talked about it. I confess I thought, I suppose I just assumed, that we would both go to the same place, and we would be together there like we are here. If . . .' He takes a deep breath. 'I know this has been strange and sudden between us. Are you saying . . .' He stops again. Then he says, simply, 'Do you want it to end when we leave? Is that what you think is best?'

'No! No. I want . . . I don't know *what* I want. But I know I want you to be there.'

Laurent looks at her and says, 'I want to go to whatever place you go.'

She blushes with relief and begins to smile.

'But I don't know if that will be possible.'

Her smile vanishes. She feels as if someone has just poured a bucket of ice into her stomach. 'Why not?'

'I have duties. You know that. My friends and colleagues have been arrested. Jayalitha has been murdered. Kishkinda continues to poison thousands. I can't give up the fight and go back to America with you.'

Danielle can't argue with that. Laurent is a knight. He cannot abandon his cause in the midst of battle.

'If I wasn't here, where would you go?' she asks.

'It doesn't matter. The important thing is, I would work to come back here.'

'I don't think I can live here. I don't think I can live like you do.'

'I know.'

They look at each other.

'Come with me,' he says. 'Come to Paris. I think I will go there with Angus and Estelle, find common cause, perhaps bring our groups together. Come with me.'

'But you just said—'

'Please. Worry about the distant future when the distant future comes. Come with me. We'll go together. Please.'

She aches to say yes. But as much as it would hurt to end things, maybe it would be better now than later. Even if the very thought is like imagining tearing her own arm off. 'I have to think it over.'

He nods. 'I understand.'

They look at each other.

'Come here,' he says.

It isn't a request. She walks to the bed and stands over him for a moment, smiling slightly, before he pulls her down, draws her beneath him, almost rips her clothes as he tears them off, then entwines her hands in his and pins them above her head, kisses her passionately as he slowly lowers himself to her, careful as ever of her fading bruise.

'Stay with me,' he whispers.

Danielle arches her back, presses herself against him hungrily. Sex with Laurent is amazing. He is almost too good in bed. She knows she is only the latest in a long string of women. It is ridiculous to think of a future with him. Maybe here in India they make sense together, but back in the real world it will be like trying to tame a wild animal. He isn't the kind of man she should fall for. But it is much too late for that. All she wants is to be with him. She decides not to think about it, not now. Instead she closes her eyes and allows raw animal pleasure to extinguish all rational thought.

They hear the party before they see it, in an isolated bar between the beach and the spiny headland that protrudes into the water at its end. The space is little more than a large open wooden floor with an L-shaped bar in one corner and an impressive sound system in another, at which a shaven-headed DJ plies his trade, his face as intent as that of a surgeon doing tricky work. Lines of tables outside the bar proper, on the beach, are laden with stubby bottles of Castle beer, plastic water bottles, Marlboro Light packets, purses, day packs, discarded clothes. Most of the chairs are empty. The crowd is here to dance. About two hundred people, mostly in their early twenties and in exceptionally good shape, maybe a dozen of them Indian, writhe to the fast-paced thumpa-thumpa-thumpa beat. Tattoos, dreadlocks, bare-chested musclemen, women in sarongs and bikini tops, the harsh smell of cigarettes and the sweet smell of pot.

Danielle didn't think Laurent would be interested in the party, but it was he who roused her at 10.30 and suggested, all but insisted, that they go. Further unwelcome evidence that she doesn't actually know him. She dressed in a short skirt and a tight shirt that leaves her midriff bare. She wouldn't have dared do this in Bangalore, but in hedonistic touristic Goa, it is tame. Laurent wears white yoga pants and no shirt, as when she first saw him, without the handcuffs. Estelle is in a bright sarong and a blue bikini top, Angus in cargo shorts, his slender torso bare. Keiran, dressed in black jeans and black T-shirt, leads them on to the floor. He is obviously looking for someone.

They have to push through the crowd; very few people make way for them. The noise is sufficiently loud to preclude most conversation, but Danielle hears harsh glottal noises that she recognizes as either Arabic or Hebrew. Of course. Travelling through India for a few months is a rite of passage for young Israelis after they complete their military service, which explains this crowd's youth, fitness level and fuck-you attitude. Danielle supposes that if this was her first chance to cut loose after two years spent looking for suicide bombers on the West Bank, she wouldn't be much inclined to worry about the well-being of strangers either.

The people Keiran knows – friends of friends, apparently – number half a dozen, all male, all with shaved heads and tattoos. The rest of the crowd gives their group more space than most. After a quick shouted conversation in incomprehensible English, Keiran takes something from one of his friends and leads Angus, Estelle, Danielle and Laurent back on to the sand, far enough away to hear one another.

'How do you feel about chemical enhancement?' he asks.

Danielle frowns. Laurent raises his eyebrows. 'What sort?'

'I believe the American slang is "rolling". My friends just dropped ten minutes ago. If you want to get in sync . . .' He holds out an upturned palm, on which are five gel capsules. 'Work hard, play hard, that's my mantra.'

Danielle shakes her head instinctively. She hasn't touched drugs for years. She has walked out of parties solely because people started passing joints around. Not that she isn't tempted. Ecstasy was always her favourite drug. But she doesn't do that any more.

Laurent takes two of the pills and offers one to her.

'Come on,' he says, smiling. 'Moderate excess might do you good.'

'I gave it up.'

'One night won't kill you. No need to be a puritan. You can enjoy life and still live it the way you want.'

Danielle looks at the drug in her lover's hand. She knows that the experience of doing ecstasy together is, or can be, a powerful emotional bond. But she knows this from damaged, drug-dependent relationships.

'Come on, Dani,' Keiran says. 'All the cool kids are doing it.'

She wants to slap him. But instead her hand reaches out, as if self-propelled and takes a pill from Keiran. It doesn't occur to her to wonder about safety or purity until a moment after she swallows it. Laurent follows her example. Keiran offers the last two to Angus and Estelle, who look at each other, obviously tempted, but politely decline.

'Israeli-made, top quality,' Keiran assures them. He takes his own pill and passes a bottle of water around to wash down the drugs.

They return to the dance floor. It seems uncomfortably remote now, its denizens menacing, the music harsh and too rapid. Danielle wishes they hadn't come, that she and Laurent had stayed in bed. She dances, but her heart isn't in it. She wants a beer, but no. One drug at a time. She even wants a cigarette, which she quit years ago. It's as if this night all her old vices have returned to haunt her.

Time passes. Laurent seems to be enjoying dancing, and anyway it is too loud to talk. Keiran has a long conversation with his Israeli skinheads, and then they are back on the dance floor, throwing themselves around with graceful rhythmic abandon, their faces glowing with bliss. Not Keiran. It hasn't hit him yet.

Then Danielle starts to feel the drumbeats grow more powerful, vibrating through her, through everything, seemingly shaking the air, the floor, the earth itself. Time seems to slow down. Or maybe she has sped up. The drums keep pounding out their staccato demands, but space has somehow grown between the beats, she can easily pick out every element of their complex rhythm. She feels very warm, but comfortably so, and her surroundings have become somehow deeper, more present, as if thickened in some barely perceptible fourth dimension. Both time and space feel warped, distended, but at the same time ordered with crystalline perfection. Colours seem more vivid, sounds are clearer, the warm wind is delicious on her skin, and every human face and form around her seems impossibly beautiful. Danielle feels a wave of energy surge within her, filling her whole body with throbbing strength and power.

She looks up at Laurent. He is so beautiful. He is beautiful even sober. On ecstasy he looks like a god. He smiles at her. She can tell it hasn't hit him yet. But Keiran's eyes shine with understanding. They exchange a beaming smile. She is glad Keiran is happy, he deserves it, it isn't easy being him, deep inside he is shy and misunderstood, his brain works in ways the rest of the world doesn't comprehend, so he has become distant and short tempered. Danielle understands that now better than ever. She would like to sit down with him on the beach, hold him tightly, listen to him, understand him, while running her hands over the rough denim of his jeans, the cotton of his shirt, his smooth skin and spiky hair, not sexually, she doesn't feel the least bit sexual right now, but just to feel the sensations, now that the pleasure response of all five of her senses has been amplified tenfold. But she doesn't want to leave Laurent. And she wants to dance.

The music calls to her. She throws herself into it, moving with perfect clarity of thought and motion, every step an epiphany, and she is surrounded by impossibly beautiful, wonderful people, heroes and princesses, all of them unique and gorgeous and precious, and, oh God, here is Laurent, a smile stretched across his face, he puts his arms around her, dancing with her, they move in perfect harmony with each other and the music, he is so warm, she presses herself against his bare chest and gasps with delight, she feels she might explode from the perfection of this moment, but she doesn't, and it doesn't end, it goes on, and on, and on.

'I forgot how good it could be,' Danielle murmurs to him, she doesn't know how much longer later. They are on the beach, she can feel every particle of sand against her skin, that feels wonderful, but nothing compared to Laurent's body pressed against hers.

'If it's been a few years, then it's like your first time all over again,' he says.

'I want to know all about you,' she says. 'If you like. I don't mean to press you. But if you want to tell me, I want to listen.

Growing up. Coming here. The Legion. Anything you want to say to me,' she laughs, 'and not just when I'm on drugs. I want to listen.'

He traces the outline of her face with a finger. 'You're so beautiful,' he murmurs. 'I wish we could stay here, like this, for ever.'

'Me too. Me too a whole lot. Do you have any water?'

He produces a bottle. She drinks deeply, ecstasy makes you thirsty, but not too deeply, cuts herself off because she knows most deaths due to this drug are actually caused by hyponatremia, drinking too much water. She passes back the bottle, glad she is able to maintain at least some judgement in the midst of this overwhelming storm of pleasure.

'Let's dance,' he says, and leads her back to the dance floor. She wants them to hold each other and talk instead, but she follows, and when they are again immersed in the storm of sound and motion, she lets the music carry her away. Every motion, every sway or shake of the hips, feels flawless, she moves with the instinctive grace of a ballerina, in perfect sync with the beat.

Eventually she realizes she is coming down. She still feels wonderfully energized, but only physically, the psychoactive effects have worn off. According to her watch it is 1 a.m. Two hours have passed since the drug hit. She wishes it didn't dissipate so quickly, or at least that she could remember its effects better, recall more than a few glittering fragments of grace and perfection.

Keiran approaches them. 'Want to go for a walk? Cool down a bit, then catch a taxi back home?'

'Sure,' Laurent says. 'Let me get some water first.'

He soon returns from the bar with fresh water, deliciously cold. Angus and Estelle, undrugged and thus exhausted, join them, and the five of them walk back up the beach. Angus and Estelle walk hand in hand, talking in low voices, chuckling at private jokes. The ocean to their left sighs rhythmically. The stars and moon above are bright enough to read a newspaper.

'Where did your friends go?' Laurent asks Keiran.

'Back to their house, to smoke spliffs and chill out. Not really my scene.'

'How do you know them?'

'Online, mostly. Lots of good Israeli hackers. But they don't know what I'm up to. They think I'm here on holiday.'

Danielle is glad to see that Keiran is treating Laurent at least civilly now. Then again he is on ecstasy.

'How long will you be here?' Laurent asks.

'I'm going back to London as soon as you're home safe. I do have a job to go back to. I mean a day job. In addition to the work.'

'And what's the work?'

Keiran shrugs. 'Same as ever. To own fill-in-the-blank's whole computer network. Here the blank is Kishkinda.'

'You can do that?'

'If anyone can.'

'You don't lack confidence,' Laurent observes.

'No. I don't.'

They walk on. Danielle lets her mind drift to a crazy notion of Laurent living with her in Manhattan, bringing her bagels every morning. Before she knows it they are in Arumbol proper. It seems smaller and more relaxed than Anjuna.

A cab, conveniently, is there waiting for passengers. It's an Ambassador, not a large vehicle, and Estelle winds up riding on Angus's lap in the front, with Keiran and Danielle and Laurent in the back. They instruct the driver to go to the ashram and then the rented holiday house in Calangute. Once they are in motion Danielle takes Laurent's hand in hers, leans against him and closes her eyes. She isn't tired, there's still enough E in her system that she feels vibrantly alert; she just wants to focus on the feel of him, the smell, the way his rough fingers curl gently around hers.

Her reverie is broken by Keiran's sharp voice. 'This isn't the right way.'

She opens her eyes. She can't tell where they are exactly, somewhere on an empty road, forest to either side.

'Short cut,' the driver explains.

Keiran shakes his head. 'This isn't right. We want to go south. This takes us east. I saw the map. Turn around, this route will take ages.'

'Short cut,' the driver repeats, showing no inclination to follow Keiran's advice.

'No, this is the longest cut available. We should be going exactly the opposite way.'

'Let it go,' Angus says tiredly. 'He's the driver. Maybe the map's wrong.'

'It happens,' Danielle agrees, thinking of the incomplete bridge that was supposed to cross the Tungabadhra, what feels like years ago. She nestles her head in the crook of Laurent's neck. Maybe Keiran is right. In fact, he's almost certainly right, she knows very well that this isn't the kind of thing his searchlight mind gets wrong. But what does it matter? They have already agreed on the price.

It is odd, though, that a local driver would go in so exactly the wrong direction.

A tiny, ice-cold kernel of worry appears at the base of Danielle's spine. Then it begins to thicken and grow, like ice spreading across a winter lake. Either Keiran is disastrously wrong, or the driver is disastrously wrong – or he is deliberately taking them away from the coast, into Goa's quasi-rural wilderness. He would only do that if he had been paid to do so. If, for instance, he had been given pictures of certain white people, and told there was a great reward for taking them to a certain place in Goa's remote hinterland.

'Guys,' Danielle says, sitting up straight. 'Guys. I think Keiran's right. We should go the other way.'

'It's OK,' Laurent says soothingly, 'we'll be fine.'

'No it isn't. Why is he taking us out here? Tell him to turn around. Make him turn around.'

'Stop the car,' Keiran orders. 'Stop the car right now.'

'Short cut,' the driver says blandly, stepping on the accelerator.

Estelle looks back at Keiran and Danielle, then at Angus. Then she says, loudly, 'Stop this car right now or I'll stop it for you.'

'Here,' the driver says, rounding a bend at such speed that his passengers are thrown together by the centrifugal force, and then, appearing out of the wilderness forest before them, they see a Bharat Petroleum station, alone on a thickly forested road, like the famous Hopper Mobilgas painting. The station is lit by a pair of white fluorescent tubes that project from fifteen-foot-high poles in the shape of hockey sticks. Their light illuminates the station surreally in the otherwise perfect darkness; it looks too vivid to be real life.

A gas station. He was just taking them to a gas station to fill up. Danielle and the others relax, and Danielle giggles with embarrassed relief, as the driver parks in the gravel in front of the pump, switches off the engine, opens the door and gets out.

'Sorry,' Danielle says. 'Sorry. I guess I've gotten paranoid.'

'Perfectly understandable,' Estelle says. 'I was getting pretty worried too.'

Then Keiran says, his voice taut, 'This is no petrol station.'

After a silence Angus says, 'Looks like it to me.'

'That pump. It's not connected to anything. There's nobody in the building. And our driver's done a runner.'

Danielle realizes Keiran is right. Their driver is gone, and the station is deserted. It isn't just closed for the night, in fact its construction isn't even complete – bundles of rebar still sprout from its unfinished roof, and the pump stands at an angle on its concrete base, not yet connected to the gas tank beneath. Relief is replaced by cold terror as she looks around. They have been driven to this deserted site and deliberately abandoned.

'Everyone out of the car,' Angus orders, opening the door.

Danielle follows Laurent out. Her limbs feel beyond her own control, as if she is a passenger in her own body; she watches herself clamber out of the door with some amazement at the way all her limbs manage to gracefully coordinate. The situation feels unreal, far more hallucinogenic than the chemicals she ingested earlier.

The five of them cluster beside the car, standing rigidly, senses straining, trying to see or hear something in the perfect blackness all around them. But nothing moves and the only sound is a faint buzz from one of the fluorescent lights.

'Where did he go?' Danielle asks, meaning the driver.

'Around the building,' Keiran says.

'Maybe we should look for him.'

'Right,' Estelle says. 'Charge into the darkness. I've seen too many horror movies to sign up for that one, thank you very much.' A faint quaver in her voice undermines her bravado.

'They must have found us at the party,' Keiran says, his voice devoid of emotion, just solving another puzzle. 'They saw us leaving, sent someone to run ahead and set up the fake taxi.'

Laurent says, 'I'm going to try to start the car.'

They watch as he gets into the driver's seat and proceeds to wrestle with the steering column. Hot-wiring it, Danielle supposes. She wonders where he learned that. In the Legion, or his shadowy life before.

Keiran draws out a mobile phone. 'No signal,' he reports.

A flash of light from the west draws all their attention. Headlights, approaching, swinging back and forth as the vehicle follows the curves of the road.

'We were followed,' Angus says quietly. He steps closer to Estelle, moving automatically, ready to protect her.

Danielle holds her breath as the lights approach, fiercely tells them to keep moving, as if with the force of her mind she can propel them farther along the road and away from the gas station. But the vehicle slows as it approaches.

'Laurent,' Danielle says, '*hurry*.'

The vehicle is an open-sided jeep carrying half a dozen Indian men in dark clothes. It reminds Danielle very much of the one that carried her up to the hut where she was held captive. It turns into the gas station at speed and pulls to a gravel-spraying halt in front of the Ambassador just as Laurent coaxes the taxi engine into growling life. Danielle tenses, about to try to leap into the taxi and escape, take their chances in a high-speed chase.

Then there are half a dozen loud barking noises in quick succession, curiously hollow, like a sledgehammer hitting concrete, overlaid with even louder *krang!* sounds of metal on metal, and six flashes of light from the jeep's passenger side, where an Indian man holds something that looks like a stick, as sparks fly from the taxi's engine, which sputters and dies.

It takes Danielle a moment to put together what has just happened. A gun. They shot the taxi, destroyed its engine. For a moment she is so stunned, by the shots, the confirmation that they have been lured and trapped by armed assailants, that she doesn't know what to do. Then she realizes. She has to run.

But it is too late. 'If you move, we will shoot! Stay where you are!' a voice orders. A familiar voice.

Nobody moves; the gunfire has paralysed them all. The jeep reverses, turning ninety degrees, aiming its headlights straight at them, as Danielle tries, her mind overwhelmed by what is happening, to place that voice.

The taxi door opens. Danielle gasps, afraid they will shoot Laurent for disobeying their orders. Then he takes one staggering step out of the car and collapses groaning on to the ground, and she whimpers with horror. One of the bullets aimed at the car hit Laurent. He has been shot, shot and hurt, hurt badly.

A figure steps out in front of the jeep, silhouetted by the headlights, holding a gun. 'Danielle Leaf,' a voice says. 'I told you we would meet again.' The voice of the man at Kishkinda, the man who interrogated her, and struck her with the lathi. Vijay.

12

Keiran stands with his hands up as the Indian men approach, trying to process the situation, think of a way out, an elegant hack. But there is no solution and no escape. If he runs he will never make it into darkness, not if they are willing to shoot, and they have shown that willingness already. If he could somehow knock out the lights – but he can't do anything without being knocked out or shot himself. He is furious at himself for not insisting they turn around the moment he noticed they were going in the wrong direction. If he dies here, it will be his own fault.

The leader of Kishkinda's men, they must be Kishkinda's, is taller, thicker and better dressed than the others, and carries a gleaming automatic pistol instead of a revolver. And he knows Danielle. This must be the man who captured her before, who Laurent thinks is Vijay from the Mumbai office. That's something. A chance, however small, for some social engineering.

'Vijay,' Keiran says. 'Good work.'

The man's expression flickers, confirming his name, and he stops. 'Who are you?'

'I'm your only hope of surviving the next seven days.'

Keiran isn't sure exactly where he's going with this, but at least he has Vijay's undivided attention. 'Who are you and what the devil do you mean?' Vijay demands.

'You've been betrayed. Kishkinda sold you out. After you do this job they're cutting you loose. I have proof.'

Vijay relaxes. Something Keiran has said has given the bluff away. 'If he says another word,' Vijay directs one of his men, 'shoot him dead.' Then he says something in Hindi, and two of his men start around the car, presumably to fetch Laurent. Vijay digs into his shoulder bag and unearths a large, clanking pair of handcuffs that look as if they belong in the Middle Ages.

There is a clunking sound from the other side of the car, and a gasp of pain. Keiran grimly realizes it is Laurent, wounded, being forced to his feet. But then it is followed by a single gasped word in Hindi, and another clunking noise.

Keiran looks over at the shot-up taxi. The headlights illuminate this side clearly. The heads of the two Indians who went to collect Laurent are no longer visible above the car. As if both of them have disappeared into the patch of shadow, on the other side of the vehicle, where Laurent fell.

Vijay barks two sharp Hindi words, turns, aims his gun at the taxi. He repeats his order. There is no reply. Keiran's heart fills with hope. Maybe Laurent was not wounded after all. Maybe his stumble and groan were only a ruse.

His suspicion is confirmed when Laurent's face appears above the edge of the taxi, behind a revolver held two-handed. He fires four times before any of Kishkinda's men react.

The jeep's headlights wink out. Showers of sparks tumble like fireworks from the shattered fluorescent lights. Then darkness covers them all like a thick blanket, and everyone is blind.

Keiran doesn't hesitate. They don't have much time, Kishkinda's men may have flashlights. He has already picked out his escape route. He reaches blindly for Danielle, grabs her arm and pulls her along with him, towards the jungle. Instead of running, he walks on the gravel as silently as he can. She resists at first, scuffing the gravel, but then catches on. There are several gunshots behind them, each of which causes Keiran to twitch with panic, despite his reminder to himself that you never hear the bullet that hits you.

It is only fifty paces to the end of the car park, but the walk seems to take hours. Then he feels vegetation beneath his feet. He leads Danielle into the jungle, still walking, they dare not run until they are out of earshot, heedless of the leaves and branches that slash at his face and arms, the muddy inconsistent footing, the fetid mosquito-filled air. Better malaria than murder.

'These fucking mosquitoes,' Danielle whispers.

'Don't slap them,' Keiran says, his voice low. 'They might hear you. Just accept it. And don't whisper, whispers carry farther than a quiet voice.'

'How long have we been out here?'

Keiran checks his watch. 'About thirty minutes.'

'Jesus. That's all? It feels like it should be the day after tomorrow already.'

Keiran nods. The last occasion on which time crawled so slowly was that night in the car park, the night Angus saved his life. He hopes Angus and Estelle got away as well. And Laurent.

'We're just going to sit here all night?' Danielle asks.

'We don't have much choice. We don't dare start shouting for help, and we're not likely to find our way back in this dark. I've never been anywhere this dark. You can practically drink it.'

After a moment Danielle says, 'I didn't hear any shouts. Of people being, you know, hurt. Did you?'

'No.'

'Maybe everyone got away.'

'Maybe.'

'I'm sure Laurent got away,' she says, trying to convince herself. 'He wasn't really hurt.'

'No,' Keiran agrees. 'You don't get shot and then knock out two men with guns, not unless you're fucking Superman, not in real life. And I saw him for a moment before he shot out the lights. He looked fine.'

'Then he's fine. He must be fine. If we got away, he must have got away.'

'It was a smart move. Shooting out the lights is exactly what I would have done.'

'High praise,' Danielle says.

'I certainly think so.'

'Does this mean you don't think he's a jerk any more?'

'What makes you say that?' Keiran asks, surprised.

'Keiran. How can you be so smart and yet so dumb? It was painfully obvious, and not just to me. You do know you're completely socially transparent.'

'No. Actually I didn't know that. But yes, I have new respect for Laurent. He's not a prat after all. Conditional on us all escaping this mess with our lives.'

'Mess is the right word. I'm covered with filth.' The terrain is not so much jungle as swamp.

'You'd rather be covered with your own blood?'

'Don't be an asshole.'

'Sorry,' Keiran says.

'Are you seeing anyone right now?'

He blinks. 'No. Not for a while.'

'It shows. You're more human when you're dating. Sometimes I didn't know if I was your girlfriend or your anthropologist liaison with the outside world.'

After a moment Keiran says, stung, 'I don't think this is really the right time for this conversation.'

'Sorry. I don't know where that came from. Stress.'

'Forgiven. But for the record, it's been four years since you really knew me. Do me a favour. Don't assume I'm the same man you used to know. People change.'

'Even you?' Danielle asks.

'Even me.'

'Change why? To what?'

Keiran's reflex is to change the subject, dodge the question, maintain his privacy and mystique. But he feels closer to Danielle than almost anyone else on earth. Which itself, he realizes, is a damning statement; they broke up years ago and since then have spoken only every few months. He has plenty of hacker friends, co-conspirators, but they would never dream about asking about Keiran's inner life.

'I guess I finally accepted I'm a human being,' he says, making a half-joke out of it. 'We're social animals. No sense denying it.'

'You were lonely,' Danielle says.

Keiran flinches at the word. 'No. I just figured most of the rest of my species seemed to value a considerably greater depth of social interaction than that in which I was accustomed to participate, and . . .' He stops, takes a deep breath. 'Maybe I was lonely. Maybe I just got old. I don't know. It doesn't make any sense. I have lots of money, a lucrative and occasionally interesting position, plenty of friends. Hacker friends, chemical friends, maybe not the cream of the social crop, but I get invited to plenty of parties. And one day about six months ago I realized I was profoundly unhappy. Not depressed. Just unhappy. I didn't know why. It was a problem, so I tried to logically analyse it, come up with a rational solution, but that just didn't work. And I realized I couldn't talk to any of my friends about it. Not one. We'd just never had those kinds of friendships. I was seeing this woman, but that was just . . . I certainly couldn't talk to her. Eventually I decided something had to change. Probably me.'

'Change how?' Danielle asks.

Keiran shrugs. 'I don't know exactly. Rejoin humanity. It sounds so fucking stupid when I say it. Like I said, the problem isn't susceptible to rational analysis. Let's say I need to integrate, instead of partitioning, my intellectual and emotional selves. And my mental and physical dichotomy while I'm at it. How does that sound?'

'It sounds like you have a lot of work to do,' Danielle says, amusement in her voice.

'I'm so glad you find this funny,' Keiran says sourly. 'You know, I've never talked about this to anyone before. I probably still wouldn't have if I wasn't on E.'

'And running for your life,' Danielle says. 'Fear tends to lower your inhibitions. Trust me. By now I ought to know.'

'Is that why you're with Laurent?'

'I'm with Laurent because he's the most truly good man I've ever met. Why are you here? What's a crypto-libertarian like you doing helping out anti-corporate activists like Angus and Estelle? Did that change too?'

'No,' Keiran says. 'I have not lost my mind. Their politics are still idiotic counter-productive bullshit. I'm here because I'm paying back a debt.'

'Must be a pretty big one.'

'Life-size.'

'What is it?' Danielle asks.

'Keiran hesitates. He suddenly wants to unburden himself, to tell Danielle the whole awful story of what happened three years ago in the car park. 'I don't think I can honourably answer that question in Angus's absence. At least not without his explicit blessing.'

After a moment Danielle says, 'Fair enough.'

'Sorry.'

'No. I understand. I am glad you're trying to change, Keiran. You're not a bad man. You've got real potential.'

'Thank you so much,' Keiran mutters. He isn't used to being patronized.

'Assuming, of course, we manage to live through the night.'

The night seems to linger an unnaturally long time, as if an eclipse has swallowed the sun, but eventually shapes begin to slowly define themselves, emerging into existence as if they have just been created from the primordial darkness itself; leaves silhouetted against the sky, long blades of grass floating on muddy puddles, some kind of airborne insect the size of Keiran's thumb. As dawn begins to stain the eastern sky, Keiran and Danielle move south, where they must inevitably encounter the road. It doesn't take long, though they fled through the thick brambles for what felt like a long time last night. Keiran suspects that in fact they went in circles.

The abandoned road divides the jungle like a river. They look both ways several times, like paranoid children, before stepping out of cover and on to its smooth black surface. Both of them are covered with scratches and mosquito bites. Keiran goes west, which he thinks will take them away from the petrol station, but as they round the bend they see it before them. Clearly they were more disoriented last night than he knew. The station is abandoned, the ruined taxi still next to the pump, as if waiting for a petrol delivery. The jeep is gone. After a moment's deliberation they approach cautiously. No one else is visible. The site seems to have been abandoned for decades.

Keiran approaches the taxi and opens the passenger door. The clunk as it opens sounds oddly forbidding, as if it might cue an ambush, but nothing happens.

'What are you doing?' Danielle asks.

'Looking for identification. I'd like to know how they found us.'

The taxi's interior, like that of virtually every vehicle in India, is decorated by a picture of Krishna and a protective statuette of Ganesh, both garlanded with fresh flowers. Keiran opens the glove compartment, which is overflowing with papers, cassettes, *bidis* and other debris. Much of the writing on the papers is Devanagari script, but some seems to be English.

'I'm sure he was just paid to look for us,' Danielle says.

Keiran shakes his head. 'No way. He just happens to be waiting for us, and his friends just happen to be ready to follow two minutes behind, at three in the morning? They knew we were at that party. They might have been following us all week.'

'How?'

'Maybe you didn't escape from Kishkinda after all. Maybe they let you escape. Maybe you were followed.'

'That's crazy.'

'Got a better idea?' Keiran asks. And then he sees the piece of paper with five words scribbled on it.

'No way,' Danielle says, behind Keiran. He is only dimly aware she is speaking at first, as he processes the repercussions of the fifth word. 'There's no way they let us escape. Trust me. There's no way. We weren't followed.'

'No,' he says distractedly. 'No, you weren't.'

'What?'

'You're right. You weren't followed.'

Danielle pauses. 'It's not usually so easy to change your mind.'

Keiran shows her the piece of paper.

'Angus, Danielle, Estelle, Laurent, LoTek,' she reads. 'So they know our names. No surprise if you're right and they've been following us.'

'No. They know your names. They know my *handle*. Did you ever tell Laurent about LoTek?'

'No.'

'You're sure? You're absolutely sure?'

'Believe it or not,' she says wryly, 'your hacker name four years ago really never came up as a topic of conversation.'

A branch snaps. They both freeze, then look up, and see Angus, Estelle and Laurent emerge from the jungle. All of them are scraped and scratched and filthy, and Estelle, limping on a twisted ankle, leans on Angus. Danielle sprints to Laurent and he lifts her off her feet with a hug.

'Look at this,' Keiran says, brandishing the telltale piece of paper.

Angus and Estelle do so; Laurent and Danielle are still too wrapped up in one another. 'In the taxi?' Estelle asks.

Keiran nods grimly.

'What do you reckon it means?' Angus asks.

'It means,' Keiran says, 'disaster.'

They wait on the gravel near the edge of the jungle, half shielded by the corner of the incomplete petrol station, hoping for a friendly vehicle to appear but ready to escape back into the forest if necessary.

'I didn't tell anyone,' Angus says for the second time. 'Not even Estelle. Not that I wouldn't have, but it just never came up, I always just used your name.'

Estelle nods her corroboration.

'Yes you did. You told someone. You had to.' Keiran knows this is true because no other explanation makes sense.

'Wait.' Angus winces. 'The foundation.'

'The *foundation*? And who the fuck are they when they're at home?' Keiran demands.

'Our funders. I told them in an e-mail that I'd brought the notorious hacker LoTek onside. And that, my friend, is all you will ever know about them.'

'Guess again. Someone in your foundation told Kishkinda.'

'No. That's ridiculous,' Angus says, shaking his head. 'Kish-kinda is their arch-enemy. They're no more likely to pass on information than me.'

'Then there's a spy in their midst.'

'Impossible. Only one person would have read that e-mail, and if he was secretly on their side, believe me, there is no way we would ever have gotten this far.'

'They knew my handle. Nobody knew I was working with you, and knew my handle, except for you, Danielle and your foundation man. You didn't tell anyone. Dani didn't tell anyone. It's him, or . . .' Keiran pauses as a new, maybe even worse, possibility occurs to him.

'It wasn't him,' Angus says, in a tone that brooks no dispute.

'Then you've been hacked.'

A moment's silence. Then Estelle says, 'What?'

'Of course,' Keiran says, a note of wonder in his voice as all the pieces slot into place. 'That's how they ambushed Jayalitha. That's why that roadblock was waiting for Dani. They've been reading every e-mail you send and receive. That's why it's taking me so long to crack their system. Their security's top-notch because they've got a pet hacker to harden it.' It is terrible news, but he smiles, pleased to have solved the puzzle.

'How can you be sure?' Laurent asks.

'Because it's the only answer that makes any sense.'

'Car!' Danielle warns.

It takes another second before Keiran can hear it. They all tense, ready to flee into the bush. Keiran wonders how fast Estelle can run on her twisted ankle. But the vehicle that comes into view is not a jeep filled with Kishkinda's men, but a very welcome bus, and one relatively unoccupied by Indian standards; Estelle even gets to sit. It takes them twenty minutes to get back to Calangute's dust, heat and noise. Keiran's opinion of the place hasn't changed, he still feels it should be nuked at the first available opportunity, but he has to admit he is glad to be back.

*   *   *

'You haven't just been hacked,' Keiran says scathingly as he descends to the kitchen, where the others are eating a full English breakfast. 'You've been *owned*. Your machine was a zombie. There was a key logger and a packet sniffer storing everything you typed, every message that went in and out, FTPing them nightly to an anonymous server.'

After a moment Angus says, 'I take it that's bad?'

'Very. I've cleaned it up. Wasn't easy. This P2 is a slippery bastard. Writes brilliant code, too. Elegant. Whoever he is, he's very, very good.'

'P2?' Estelle asks.

'The hacker on the other side.'

'How do you know his name?'

'His handle,' Keiran says, 'and I know it because he went and bloody well signed his code, didn't he? Talk about chutzpah.'

Laurent looks quizzical. 'Handle?'

'Online name. A hacker tradition. And sensible precaution, against identification by the authorities, and identity theft by your fellow hackers. It's like the old myths. These days, people who know your true name really do have power over you. Whether they know it or not.'

Angus and Estelle give Keiran you've-gone-slightly-mad looks, but Laurent nods thoughtfully.

'You didn't send or receive the address of this house via e-mail, did you?' Keiran asks Angus.

The Scotsman shakes his head. 'Booked it over the phone. Friend of a friend.'

'But you have checked e-mail from here. That's a risk.'

Estelle looks at him, worried. 'They could track us down just from that? Just from checking e-mail from inside this house?'

'It's unlikely. But it is possible if you don't use a secure SSH connection. Just. They'd have to hack the uplink, though, and the people who run satellite ISPs are not newbies, so we're probably safe.'

'Probably,' Danielle says. 'That's so comforting.'

'The universe doesn't do "safe". Especially for us here and now. Angus, you need to cancel that "secondary base of operations" plan. Sooner we all get back to Europe the better.' He smiles. 'I'd stay and be a tourist, but I can't take the gunplay.'

Nobody else gets the reference. Keiran sighs and says, 'Can you bring me some breakfast? I've got work to do.' He turns around.

Estelle blinks. 'What kind of work?'

'Teaching this P2,' Keiran says, 'that LoTek is *not* to be fucked with.'

He climbs the stairs, enters his room, closes the door, sits down in front of his laptop and opens the door to another world.

Keiran first used a computer in 1981. He was five. Four years later his parents gave in to his incessant whining and bought him a modem to accompany his Commodore computer. He unwrapped the modem, connected it and dialled into a Bulletin Board Service for the first time on Christmas Day 1986, ten days before his father left his mother for the last time.

When he was thirteen, the year his sister was first arrested, Keiran's teachers began to realize that he was more than merely very bright, that he was a once-in-a-lifetime student. A maths teacher took him to a university computer laboratory, where he connected to the Internet for the first time. It was in 1992, at age sixteen, shortly after his mother's death, that he first used the World Wide Web, which at the time was an engineering curiosity that consisted of a few thousand sites, almost all of them universities, connected to a de facto hub in Switzerland.

He has never lost his sense of wonder at what the Internet can do. At what it *is*. Keiran sits at his laptop and strikes keys; the resulting electrical signals travel around the world, amplified and transformed, converted to radio signals and back to electricity, through an incredible jumble of interconnected cables and wireless antennae and orbiting satellites; and only seconds later, a hard drive spins in Dakar, a monitor flickers to life in Los Angeles, sound emerges from a speaker in Kathmandu. The

Internet is like a second nervous system, enormously more powerful and more diffuse than the one that commands the muscles of
his body, and every machine connected to it is both appendage
and sensory organ. Being online is like being superhuman. The
difference being, of course, that Keiran's body is only his own,
while the god-body of the Internet is shared among anyone who
can afford access. Most people are cripples, barely know how to
twitch a finger, take a breath. But Keiran is an acrobat.

As is P2. That much is already clear. Keiran feels invigorated,
to have an actual adversary. He has been battering at the walls of
Kishkinda's corporate computers for weeks now with no measur-
able result. Now he knows why. There is a champion inside those
walls, repelling his every assault.

An unknown champion. Nobody on the black-hat IRC channels, no blogger, no search engine, has ever heard of a hacker
named P2. He examines the traces left on Angus's computer. The
key logger and packet sniffer are off the shelf, common hacker
tools, available to anyone who knows how to use Google;
tracking them back to P2 would be like trying to trace a generic
Phillips screwdriver to a particular hardware store. The zombie
code, however, is unique. This is the program that ran constantly
and invisibly on Angus's computer, and connected to a 'zombie
server' on the Internet at regular intervals to communicate,
essentially saying to P2 every day, 'I am here, master, and this
machine is yours, ready to obey your orders!' along with 'Here is
everything Angus typed, read, e-mailed or saw on the Web today!'
It is the smallest, least detectable zombie code Keiran has ever
seen. And there is no record of it ever having been used anywhere
else.

The only clue is the zombie server itself. And that must be
approached with caution. Keiran has only two current advantages
over P2. One of them is Shazam, his secret weapon. The other is
surprise. P2 doesn't yet know that he has been discovered, and
reaching out to his zombie server in the wrong way could trigger
an alarm. Like a Tom Clancy submarine hunt, when active sonar,

emitting a loud ping and seeing how it travels and echoes through the dark water around you, may help you track down your quarry, but also warns the target of the hunt.

Keiran tries passive listening instead. He does a search on the zombie server's IP number, its unique thirty-two-bit identification code. As he suspected, it too is a zombie. By day, it is a mild-mannered print server at a small Silicon Valley copy shop; but at P2's command, it becomes a conduit through which P2 rules his 'botnet', the collection of machines secretly controlled by his zombie program.

Keiran can tell by the zombie code that P2's botnet is elegant and secure; encrypted communications, multiple fall-back servers, a secure log-in protocol. He wonders how many machines are under P2's spell. Some hackers command multiple botnets of tens of thousands of computers. Or even more. Shazam, which to all intents and purposes is Keiran's botnet, is more than seven million machines strong. But not even Shazam can help Keiran track down P2, not with the sparse available data. His opponent remains invisible.

Keiran shuts down his computer and rubs his bleary eyes. Four hours have passed since he entered the room. He has a vague memory of Estelle bringing him breakfast, and himself eating it one-handed while typing with the other. But he hasn't learned anything tangibly useful yet. First round to the enemy.

After a much-needed nap, Keiran returns to the Internet. DHL's website reports that Danielle and Laurent's fake passports have left Los Angeles, arrived in Dubai and should arrive at the local DHL office tomorrow morning. Danielle and Laurent still haven't said where they want to fly to. He goes downstairs to get an answer. Angus sits in a chair, reading documents in a black binder; Estelle is in the bath, soaking her wounded ankle; and Danielle and Laurent are gone.

'They went to the beach,' Angus says.

Keiran stares at him. 'The beach? Angus. We're trying to hide.

None of us should leave the house until it's time to go to the airport.'

'Come on, mate. Have you seen that beach? Five thousand sunburned whiteys. They're safer there than they are here. And we needed some shopping. The cupboard is almost bare.'

'So they took a taxi. Because hiring a driver for the week is morally wrong. A decision which already nearly got us all killed. If I were Kishkinda, I would go to every taxi driver in this city with our pictures.'

Angus stiffens. He clearly hadn't considered that possibility.

'From now on,' Keiran says, 'certainly until we leave the country, I'm in charge of security, because you clearly do not understand the meaning of the word. You or anybody else. I expected better of Laurent. He's a soldier.'

'I gave them Estelle's mobile. I'll give them a call.' Angus draws out his phone.

'No you fucking well will *not*,' Keiran says savagely.

Angus stops and looks at him. 'Why not?'

'Because mobile phones are the least secure communication device ever devised. If Kishkinda has an in with the company, they might triangulate your location and theirs. That's not likely, but mobile conversations are totally insecure, foreign roaming phones are easy to pick out, and they have an expert hacker on their side. You call and ask them where they are, and there's a non-zero chance P2 listens in.'

'Ah.' Angus looks at his phone as if it might explode in his hand.

'I'll go and look for them. On foot.'

'What about the airport?' Angus asks.

'What?'

'If they know we're here, they know we might leave the country. How do we know we won't get stopped at the airport?'

Keiran smiles. 'That's better. Now you're thinking like a hacker.'

'Well, what are we going to do about it?'

'You're going to trust me to take care of things. Now, I'm off. If I'm not back in three hours, do yourself a favour. Get out of the country by any means possible.'

The walk to Calangute takes longer than Keiran expected. The enclave of walled, expensive houses north of the tidal river is larger than it seemed from inside taxis. Furious guard dogs howl rabidly as he walks past featureless gates. The interiors of these properties may be perfectly manicured, but outside their walls it is still India; weeds fight their way through cracks in the uneven road, and the dirt on either side is stained with betel juice, sprinkled with glittering crumbs of shattered glass, cigarette butts, torn plastic bags, dog turds. The whitewashed concrete tunnel that bridges the river is so cracked and crumbling that Keiran would be reluctant to cross it in a heavy car. Cows stare at him as he emerges on to the far side of the river and begins to walk south.

A pair of child beggars approach and he waves them off. They chase after him, mewling pitifully and tugging at his trouser legs, until Keiran feigns an intent to strike them and they scramble away to find another mark. He keeps walking. By a tree by the side of the road, a young woman with very dark skin nurses her baby. Her red sari is tattered, and her face is lined and gaunt despite her youth. She can't be out of her teens. She stares at Keiran as he passes as if he is a ghost. He expects a plea for money but she says nothing. He walks for another ten paces, trying to pretend she does not exist. If she had asked for money it would have been easy to keep walking and forget her. But her silent, otherwordly despair is somehow haunting.

'Why not?' Keiran mutters to himself. He could have died last night. Somehow that is a justification. He doesn't know exactly why this needs justification. He turns around, withdraws his wallet as he approaches the young woman, peels out five twenty-pound notes, and offers them to her.

She stares at him uncomprehendingly at first, then slowly reaches out and touches them, as if to ensure that they and he are real. Her expression does not change but her eyes come to life, stare at him searchingly. He presses the money into her warm hand. She holds the notes loosely and he wants to take her hand in his and close it over them, try to impress upon her that they are important, they can change her life. He suddenly realizes the likely futility of the gesture. She's probably never seen British pounds before in her life. She might not even realize that they're money. Even if she does, where will she go to change them to rupees? She will surely be cheated, stolen from. He should give her rupees, but he doesn't have enough to matter to her. He should go and change the money himself, come back and give her nine thousand rupees instead of a hundred pounds, but he can't bring himself to do it, to further bridge the gap between himself and this woman, this encounter is too heartbreaking already. Instead he just says, lamely, 'It's money.'

After a moment she inclines her head to the side. She understands, he can see it in her eyes. She may be ignorant but she isn't stupid. Maybe she can use it. Maybe this is the moment that will save her ruined life. Maybe it won't change anything. Maybe her life is fine and she is just wearing old clothes and sat to rest on her way back home after a hard day – although this doesn't seem likely. Keiran doesn't want to know. It is already too much to treat her as a human being; actually caring about her would be unbearable. He turns and walks away quickly, strangely numbed by the encounter, almost insensate, and twenty steps later nearly collides with Danielle and Laurent as they walk the other way, oddly distant from one another for a couple usually so inseparable. Laurent carries plastic bags full of groceries.

'Hi,' Laurent says, surprised.

'Oh. Hi.'

'How much did you give her?'

Keiran shrugs and looks away, like a teenager. He can feel himself blushing. 'What are you doing here?' he demands.

Laurent says, 'Went to the beach, went shopping, decided to walk back.'

Danielle doesn't say anything. Her expression is distant. She hardly seems to have noticed Keiran.

'Come on,' Keiran says. 'I was looking for you.'

'That was a good thing, what you did,' Laurent says.

'Come on,' Keiran repeats, angry now, at having been seen and patronized by Laurent. He leads them back towards the house. On the way he makes a point of ignoring the woman in the red sari.

'To India,' Angus toasts, with a glassful of Kingfisher beer. 'In all its beauty and madness.'

Laurent lifts his glass. 'Mother India,' he says simply.

They look at Danielle, but she is lost in sullen thought and says nothing.

'A fine balance between hope and despair,' Estelle says, quoting something.

Keiran wishes she hadn't said that. It makes him think of the woman he gave money to in the throes of his earlier moment of madness. 'Goodbye and good riddance,' he says gruffly, and drains his glass. The others follow suit, Angus giving Keiran an annoyed look before he drinks.

'So what's the schedule tomorrow?' Estelle asks.

'We pick up the passports at nine,' Keiran says, 'get to the airport at ten, which is the same time three honking great tour groups arrive. It'll be easy to lose ourselves in that paleface crowd. Hopefully by then Danielle will have some idea where she wants to fly—'

'Will you please *shut up about that*,' Danielle says angrily.

Keiran looks at her, surprised. 'All right. Sorry.'

Danielle shakes her head, clearly overwrought. Competing emotions play on her face, none of them good. Laurent reaches out an arm to her, but she shrugs it off angrily, gets up and stalks upstairs. Angus, Estelle and Keiran look at each other uncomfortably.

'I'm sorry,' Laurent says. 'Excuse me. I'll go and talk to her.' He stands up, and as if on cue all the lights go out.

A bewildered few seconds pass before anyone reacts.

'Fucking hell,' Keiran says.

Then Estelle's voice: 'There are candles in the kitchen.'

'No, there's a generator,' Angus says. 'In the crawl-space underneath.' The house is built on stilts a few feet above ground level, as with most sensible construction in tropical areas prone to rainy-season floods. 'It's supposed to come on automatically if the city power goes out. Give it a few moments.'

'It's not working,' Keiran says. The generator would have chugged into life already if it was going to. Electric switches don't operate with a fifteen-second delay.

'The owner swore up and down everything worked,' Angus says, exasperated.

There are scrabbling sounds in the kitchen, then a match flares, illuminating Estelle in profile. It dies out as she opens a cupboard; then another comes to life, is perpetuated as a candle. Estelle returns to the table with two candles and candle-holders.

Footsteps descend the stairs. 'Now the power's out?' Danielle asks angrily, as if this is the fault of someone present.

'Let's hope it's just a power cut,' Laurent says. 'Not the bad guys.'

Keiran nods. 'I was just thinking that.'

'Jesus, I just can't wait to get the fuck *out of here*,' Danielle says shrilly.

The next sound is that of glass shattering and tinkling against the hardwood floor. Keiran feels a shard ricochet off his foot. Like the onset of darkness, the crash is so unexpected that everybody freezes for an instant. Keiran thinks at first that someone has knocked a glass over. But the sound was too loud, there is too much broken glass gleaming on the kitchen floor in the suddenly flickering candlelight, and he can taste cool fresh air, coming from the huge jagged hole that has just materialized in the big window above the sink.

'Oh, shit,' Keiran says, barely aware that he is speaking.

A pale oblong shape sits amid glass shards on the hardwood

floor. A rock, a paving stone from one of the walkways that leads through the exterior gardens. Someone threw it through the window. They are under attack. Their assailants are already through the exterior walls, they have cut the power, must be only moments away from breaking into the house itself.

Outside, all the neighbourhood dogs begin to howl.

13

Danielle feels frozen, like on the awful mornings she has sometimes when she wakes up fully conscious but unable to move for long minutes, as if all she can do is stand here at the base of the stairs and watch, as if carved out of bronze, unable to act or defend herself when the men outside invade the house, to this maddening, coruscating soundtrack of howling dogs.

'They're outside, they're right outside,' Angus says, standing up. There is a crash, and a bolt of fear hits Danielle, but she does not even flinch, even involuntary motion seems beyond her. It takes her a moment to understand this new sound was only Angus's chair falling behind him.

Then Keiran leans forward and blows out both candles. In the darkness she can move again. As if it was the light which paralysed her. She takes a step just to prove to herself it is possible, and freezes again. She does not know what to do.

'What are you doing, we can't see!' Estelle says urgently.

'The light will give us away,' Laurent says, his voice reassuringly low and calm. 'We have to be invisible. Stay quiet, low voices. Don't panic. If we panic we are lost. The front door, is it locked?'

'Yes,' Keiran says. 'I locked it when we came in.'

'Then we have a minute at least.'

'To do what?' Danielle asks.

'Prepare to be invaded. We need weapons, a place to barricade ourselves.'

'Knives,' Estelle says. 'I'll get the knives.'

'Careful,' Angus says. There are grating sounds as Estelle steps on the broken glass, her feet protected only by thin flip-flops, moving through the kitchen by feel.

'Wood,' Danielle says. 'Everything's wood. They'll burn down the house.' She walks gingerly through the darkness towards the other voices, arms feeling in front of her. She cannot see anything, walls or furniture, the darkness is absolute.

Keiran says, 'They would have already.'

'They still want us alive, I think,' Laurent says. He alone does not sound terrified. 'They want to frighten us out. Or they wouldn't have thrown that stone. Outside we are easy prey. Inside, a house in darkness is dangerous territory for everyone, even if they are armed and we are not.'

Danielle feels her way towards him as he speaks, her groping hand touches his shoulder, grips it as if it is a life-saving rope. He puts his hand over hers.

'They may *prefer* us alive,' Keiran says, 'but I bet this time they'll settle for dead.'

A sudden intake of breath from Estelle.

'What is it?' Angus asks, alarmed.

'Cut myself. That's all. Glass. Nothing major. Here are the knives.' More crunching noises. Estelle carefully distributes kitchen knives in the darkness. Danielle winds up with the saw-toothed bread knife. She thinks this is crazy, the enemy surely has guns, these knives will be more dangerous to them in this darkness, but at least it feels good to have some kind of weapon in her hand, even a bread knife. It takes the edge off the bubbling panic that threatens to overflow and swallow her whole.

'Upstairs,' Keiran says. 'The master bedroom.'

Laurent nods. 'Yes. But first, everyone quiet a moment. Maybe we can hear them.'

But they can't hear anything over the dogs, howling as if to warn of the end of the world.

'Never mind,' Angus says. 'Let's get upstairs. Be careful.'

They join hands, forming a line, Angus in the lead, Laurent at the back. The procession to the master bedroom, which would take ten seconds in the light, stretches to a full two minutes in the darkness. Danielle feels a little better when they are upstairs, as if a flight of stairs makes them safe. The dogs finally start to quieten down.

They all sit on the bed. Danielle and Laurent still hold hands. There is enough light to discern the windows from the walls. To the south, across the river, they can see the city lights of Calangute, and to the west they can see the running lights of distant ocean-going ships. On this side of the river, the head-lights of a single car are visible, traversing the winding road that leads past the house, and a few other houses in the area are still lit, presumably those that also have back-up generators. It's clear that power to the whole area has been cut.

Angus draws out his mobile phone. Its screen glows bright green in the dark. 'No signal,' he reports.

'They must have jammed the local cell antenna,' Keiran says. 'Very thorough of them. Land lines carry their own power, but they'll have cut that too.' He lifts the telephone beside the bed. There is no dial tone. 'Yes. Cut the power, cut the phones. Then what?'

Nobody answers. Danielle wonders why they bothered coming up here. The master bedroom's door is solid wood, it's only a short hop from the window to the roof of the veranda, and the en suite bathroom's door locks, but none of this will do them any good. As if huddling in the bathroom behind a locked door, then making a final stand with kitchen knives, will make any difference to the outcome. Danielle realizes that this is very likely the room she will die in. Unless they find some way out.

'We have to get out of here,' Danielle says. 'We can't just wait for them.'

Angus says, 'She's right. They may not want to come in, but they will when they know we're not coming out. Or they'll just burn the house with us in it. As they did with Jayalitha.'

Keiran says, 'I'm going downstairs.'

'What for?' Danielle asks.

'Look and listen. We don't know enough to make a plan.'

'Do we have any flashlights?' Laurent asks.

'Flashlights?' Angus asks, his voice puzzled.

'Torches,' Keiran translates. 'I've got a little Maglite in my room.'

'I brought matches and candles up here,' Estelle says.

'Good,' Angus says. 'There are more, and torches, downstairs in the closet off the TV room. Behind the toolbox.'

Keiran stands. 'I'll bring them back. How do I get into the crawl-space?'

Angus says, 'I think there's a trapdoor under the stairs. But they're down there. They cut the generator power.'

'They probably won't have stayed down there. I might take a look.' He tries to sound casual, insouciant, but Danielle can tell by his uncharacteristically high voice how frightened he is. 'Back in a jiffy.'

Nobody says anything as Keiran leaves the room.

The waiting is almost unbearable. They can hear men outside now, at least several of them, moving through the garden, talking in low voices. Danielle almost wishes they would just do something, smash down the door, throw in a Molotov cocktail, as long as it ends the waiting.

Estelle says, 'I still think we should shout for help. Somebody's bound to hear us.'

Laurent shakes his head. 'That will force their hand. They'll burn us if they see help coming.'

'What are they *waiting* for?' Danielle asks.

Nobody answers.

'I wish I knew why I was going to die,' she says bitterly. 'I've never done anything to them. If they read your e-mail, they know that. I've got nothing to do with whatever you do. Why was I on that list in the taxi?'

'Because they're afraid of you,' Laurent says.

She manages a tiny black-comedy laugh. 'Afraid of me. Right. A billion-dollar company that apparently owns all of India is scared of me. Why exactly?'

'Because they think you know something. Or have something.'

'What something?'

She feels his shrug. 'My only guess is, something Jayalitha found.'

'Angus,' Danielle says after a moment, 'why did you send me to Jayalitha?'

'I didn't send you,' he says. His voice sounds guilty. 'I told Keiran we needed to get her passport to her and Keiran suggested you could do it. I thought it would be safe. We didn't have anyone else in India. We don't really do work on the ground, not like Laurent's group does.'

'So what was Jayalitha doing for you?' Laurent asks.

'All the evidence she was collecting, we were going to use it in lawsuits, create litigation risk for the company, the threat of jail for its officers. And then go after them extra-legally at the same time. The more ways we hit them, the more doubts we raise in their minds, the better. But the evidence was nothing new, villager testimony, pictures, documents smuggled out of the mine. You know that, you worked with her.'

'Worked with is a strong phrase,' Laurent says. 'She was fiercely independent. She never reported having found anything exceptional to you?'

After a moment Estelle says, 'There was that weird phone call.'

'Right,' Angus agrees. 'But that was nothing. She said so herself.'

'What phone call?' Laurent asks.

Angus says, 'Jayalitha found something one day. I don't know what. Not long ago, the same day I posted her passport to Danielle, maybe three weeks ago. Seems like a past life now. Jaya called me on the phone, which she never did, left a voice mail saying she'd found some very strange evidence, documents, she was going to e-mail me a transcript. But then the next day she sent an e-mail telling me that the evidence wasn't real, she'd made a mistake. She didn't mention it again. Not that she had much chance. The e-mail after that was the last I ever heard from her.'

Danielle leans forward, suddenly interested. 'If it was from her.'

'What?'

'They hacked your e-mail, remember? Maybe she did send that transcript. Maybe they deleted it and faked new e-mails from her to cover up. You can't trust anything that she did or didn't e-mail you. Kishkinda controlled your mailbox the whole time.'

Angus takes a moment to absorb this revelation. Then he says, 'Fucking hell.'

'Maybe she did find something,' Laurent says.

Estelle says, 'My God. She must have. Something major. That must be it. That must be why they're after us. Even if they know about the foundation, they can't be scared of that, not yet, we haven't *done* anything yet. They think we have what Jaya found. Or we might. They don't know what she said to you on the phone, she might have told you, or stashed copies somewhere, and it's so dangerous they can't take the risk. And then we flew right here to India. Right into the tiger's mouth, like Keiran said. Jesus. We couldn't have made a bigger mistake.'

'What could it be?' Laurent asks. 'To frighten them so much. Already they're poisoning, murdering thousands of people, brazenly. What could she have found?'

Silence falls, interrupted by noises, footsteps coming up the stairs. Danielle tenses, tightens her grip on the bread knife, but it is only one man.

'I've got bad news, worse news and one faint little shred of hope,' Keiran says, re-entering the bedroom. 'The bad news is there's at least a dozen of them surrounding the house. The worse news is they've got both guns and jerrycans of petrol. The little shred of hope is, I don't think they realize we can get into that crawl-space underneath from in here.'

'Doesn't do us any good,' Angus says. 'They'll see us coming out.'

'Unless they're distracted.'

'By what?'

'Well,' Keiran says, 'I do have one idea. I warn you now. It's going to sound completely mad.'

It seems crazy to Danielle now that seconds before the paving stone smashed the kitchen window she was on the verge of telling Laurent that tomorrow she would go to America without him. She didn't want to leave him; she was just convinced that the future would be disastrous, that it was better, awful but better, to leave him now. Like cutting off her arm to spare her life. Now, though, as men who want to kill her mill about outside the besieged house, any future at all, disastrous or not, sounds wonderful.

She was so worried about the future. She has always been so worried about the future, unable to choose just one of the thousand different paths available to her, because they are only available so long as she keeps her life at a crossroads – choosing just one will destroy the other nine hundred and ninety-nine. She has lamented growing old, because that too walls off those roads one by one, prunes the branches of her decision tree. Now it seems she will never get to make a decision at all. She will die without having ever chosen a road to see through to the end. Or a man. Men have always been another way to sample life's options, test roads without travelling them herself, try out new lifestyles like new clothes.

Laurent isn't like that. Their pure electric bond cannot be so casually discarded. If they leave Goa together, go to Paris or even to her Manhattan apartment to live together, that choice means sacrificing all other choices. And that thought was terrifying, until the stone flew through the kitchen window and taught her once again a lesson she should already have learned. What fear really is, and how ridiculous and pathetic it is to worry about the distant unknown future.

Danielle leans over to whisper in her lover's ear, 'If we get out of this, will you come live with me?'

'Of course,' he says.

They kiss. Her lips are dry with fear, but Laurent seems relaxed, confident, as if Keiran's insane plan is bound to succeed.

They are back on the ground floor, clustered around the trapdoor that leads into the crawl-space below. Above them a radio squawks in loud staticky Hindi, noise to cover the sounds of their escape attempt. Keiran has already descended. Angus and Estelle go next. Boards creak as they descend, and there is a muffled grunt as Angus bumps his head. Danielle closes her eyes. They do her no good in this darkness, and the act seems to accentuate the rest of her senses. She crouches down, feels with her hands along the floor until they make contact with the uneven wooden edge of the trapdoor. She moves closer, sits on the edge, her feet dangling into the emptiness beneath. For a moment she feels as if she is on the verge of a bottomless abyss, that if she descends she will fall for ever.

But it is less than four feet to the rough dirt beneath. The crawl-space smells of metal and gasoline. Keiran has turned on his Maglite and aimed it at the ground. The dirt swallows most of the yellow pool of light, but enough spills out that Danielle can make out the shapes of the others, and of the circular concrete pillars that support the house. The crawl-space is surrounded on all sides by a wooden-plank wall. There is no apparent exit, but one must exist. Keiran, more than six feet tall, is bent almost halfway, standing next to some kind of machine, maybe three feet square in profile, a curved oblong shape, with pipes and wires visible in silhouette. The generator. Of course.

Keiran passes something to Estelle, who passes it to Angus, who offers it to Danielle. A plastic canister, heavy, full of liquid, stinking of gasoline. She hesitates a moment before lifting it up to Laurent, who takes it and walks slowly away. She hears the boards creak as he pads upstairs.

Estelle sits on the ground, covers her face with both hands and breathes deeply, moaning a little with each exhalation.

'We have to hurry,' Angus says urgently, kneeling behind her, hands on her shoulders, trying to comfort her. 'She's claustrophobic.'

Not a good place for it, Danielle realizes as she moves away from the trapdoor, crouched in a half-squat. The walls are far away, but the grid of columns and the darkness would make this space seem close and tight even without the four-foot ceiling. It somehow reminds her of the labyrinthine corridors of her recurring nightmare.

'We must be out of our fucking minds,' Danielle says, mostly to herself.

Footsteps on the stairs, descending. Laurent. The smell of gasoline intensifies, becomes overpowering. Danielle starts breathing through her mouth. Then he is at the trapdoor, lowering himself down into the crawl-space.

'Matches,' he says, breathing hard.

Estelle has the matches.

'Estelle, love,' Angus says, his voice quiet, 'I'm sorry. We need the matches.'

For a moment Danielle is afraid she is too far gone, but Estelle nods, slowly, reaches for her pockets, every movement slow and consciously controlled, raises a shaking fist and opens it to reveal a box of matches. Angus takes them and gives them to Danielle, who couriers them to Laurent.

'Get ready,' he says. 'Danielle, Keiran, opposite corners. Keiran, switch off the light. It'll be redundant soon enough.'

Danielle tries walking in a squat, but soon drops down to hands and knees and crawls, much faster in this space. Behind her Keiran is headed to the opposite corner. Their job is to rove along the interior walls, looking through cracks and knots in the planking, and find out if and where their assailants cluster when the house begins to burn.

She hears a match being struck. Then light flickers behind her.

She looks over her shoulder and sees Laurent crawling to a third corner, illuminated by firelight through the trapdoor.

They don't know how much time they will have. Laurent dumped almost all the gasoline on the top floor, leaving only a thin trail down the stairs for the flames to follow, so the house should burn from the top down. Eventually it will collapse in on itself. The plan – hope, really – is that the men who surround the house will be taken aback by their quarry apparently burning themselves to death, and an opening will appear in their cordon. Failing that, maybe, just maybe, they can hide in this crawl-space long enough for the Calangute fire department to come.

She can hear the crackling noises of fire now. It lights up the space around the house. Through a knot-hole she sees an Indian man standing in the garden not ten feet away from her, carrying a massive revolver, gaping up at the burning house. After a moment he turns and walks quickly away, rounding the corner of the house and disappearing from her view. Danielle crawls quickly along the wall he has just vacated, looking for others, but seeing none.

She moves halfway back towards the trapdoor. She can already feel heat on her face, and the air swirls as if there is a draught, funnelling towards the trapdoor, feeding the flames. 'This way,' she says. She repeats it louder, in a near-shout, to be heard over the crackling flames. 'This way! It's clear!'

Keiran scurries towards her. 'They're all on the other side, by the front door!' he calls out. He keeps going, joins her, followed quickly by Laurent. Angus coaxes Estelle into moving too, although Danielle sees that she crawls with her eyes closed.

Hoping desperately that she is right, that there wasn't a man left she didn't see, Danielle leads them to the wall she has identified as safe. Now all they need is a way to get through it – but there, glinting in the flickering firelight, a brass hinge, and another, a section of the wall that folds inwards, secured by two latches that open easily. The doorway is stiff at first, the dirt has accumulated around it, but once Laurent and Keiran coax the first inch of movement from it, the rest is easy. They pour out of the crawl-space. Outside, the trees and bushes of the garden cast dancing shadows in the bright firelight. The burning house doesn't seem real, it looks like a model, a Hollywood prop. A huge pillar of smoke rises into the night. The flames have already consumed the entire top floor and the heat is intense. No one else is in sight.

They run, and it occurs to Danielle as they do so that now they have to leave the estate, with its high walls topped by broken glass – but the gates are open, and no one is watching. A jeep is parked in the driveway. They sprint through the gates and on to the open road.

Danielle's new passport is so convincing she would be fooled by it herself. Laurent's French passport seems a little flimsier, but maybe they are in the real world too. He seems pleased by the quality.

'Your friend does good work,' he reports to Keiran, as he riffles the pages.

'Mulligan's attention to detail is unmatched,' Keiran agrees.

'Come on,' Angus says. 'Last taxi ride.'

Airports seem unreal to Danielle at the best of times. Today, sleep-deprived, still dirty despite their attempts to wash up in a posh café's bathroom, trailing an odour of wood smoke that won't go away, having escaped what seemed like certain death for at least the third time in the last two weeks, it feels like a video game, part of Grand Theft Auto: Kishkinda.

Their arrival at the airport is contemporaneous with that of three huge tour groups full of sunburned Europeans. They line up at the Emirates ticket desk to buy tickets to Dubai. Once there they will be safe, and from that airport they can fly anywhere in the world. Angus and Estelle look terrified as they approach Indian customs, afraid that they will be stopped and taken to the police, but Danielle is relaxed. These sour-faced bureaucrats will do only what their computers tell them to; and in this, as in all technical matters, Keiran is completely reliable. Their passports are stamped and they are waved through to the gate area, where all five of them sit in a tight group, utterly comfortable with each other, as if they have known each other for years. Cheating death twice in two nights will do that to a group.

'Where were you thinking of going?' Estelle asks Danielle.

She shrugs. 'New York, I guess. But—'

'Don't,' Estelle says. 'Come with us. Work with us.'

'I'm sick of these bastards,' Angus says savagely. 'I'm sick of being hunted. I'm sick of running. You should be too. It's time for us to start hitting back.'

Keiran nods.

'We have a plan,' Estelle says. 'You can help us. Come with us to Paris.'

Danielle looks at Laurent.

'Yes,' he says. 'We should go with them. It's time for you to make the decision.'

'What decision?' she asks, bewildered.

'To help. To stop sitting on the sidelines. To stop reacting. To build a better world. You and I, together. With them. All of us.'

Danielle opens her mouth without knowing what she is going to say. She is distantly aware that this is one of the moments on which her whole life hinges. She wants to say yes. But a voice that won't shut up tells her the idea of joining an admittedly criminal group devoted to fighting enormously powerful corporations, and risking her life even more than she has this last month, is not just stupid but actually insane.

But is risking her life so much more insane than wasting it on one of the empty, plastic existences in which most of the people she has ever known immure themselves? Is the life on offer really that different from that lived by those brave people, those heroes and heroines, who volunteer for Amnesty International and Médecins sans Frontières in war zones like Afghanistan? Danielle thinks suddenly of the cell-phone ads she saw in Goa's villages. *An IDEA can change your life.*

Changing her life sounds like a very good idea. She has done it so many times before. But she is sure, somehow, that this time it will stay changed.

'Yes,' she says, to a chorus of smiles. 'All right. Yes. What the hell. Let's change the world.'

II Europe

Paris

1

'Danielle,' Françoise says, her voice grim, 'I am sorry to bother you, but we have a problem, a big problem.'

Danielle looks up from her computer and steels herself. 'What?'

'It is the accommodations. We have too many people coming from outside Paris, already hundreds more than we expected. We have no room for them, not even in the warehouse, we simply cannot keep more people there.'

'I'll talk to Estelle. We'll rent another warehouse.'

'There is no time. They arrive in only five days. We will be violating the law already, keeping so many people in one space. The owner of our warehouse will pretend not to see, but we have no more friends who will be so willing. I do not know what to do. These people, many of them cannot afford their own rooms, not in Paris, and we promised all of them accommodations. I know they say money is no obstacle but surely we cannot pay to put thousands of people up in hotel rooms.'

'Maybe not,' Danielle admits, though she isn't so sure – the mysterious foundation's fountain of wealth seems to be inexhaustible. 'Let me think.'

As she ponders she distractedly runs her fingers through her hair, which has grown to page-boy length in the last six weeks. An idea hits. 'How many volunteers do we have here?' Danielle asks. 'A hundred?'

'Nearly.'

Not enough. 'And how many more in Paris who signed up for the newsletter?'

'Nearly two thousand.'

'Send an e-mail to them all. Ask them to volunteer to put up a guest for two or three nights. Have them send in addresses and phone numbers, we'll make arrangements to route the out-of-towners to the volunteers' places somehow.'

'It will be chaos,' Françoise says, offended by the notion. A short, curvy, curly-haired fashionista, Françoise is a finicky detail person; exactly what Danielle needs in her translator and right-hand woman, but sometimes infuriating.

'Isn't it already? Just send the e-mail . . .' Danielle hesitates. '. . . and forward all the addresses and phone numbers to me. And the e-mails of the overflow people. I'll match them up.'

'You have no time for this.'

'Neither does anybody else. I'll make time. I'll have Estelle help.'

Françoise shakes her head. 'You are an amazing woman, Danielle, but I fear you will die young of exhaustion.'

Danielle looks at her. She tries to remember whether anyone she wasn't sleeping with has ever called her an 'amazing woman' before. She doesn't think so.

'I will send the e-mail,' Françoise says hastily, apparently mistaking astonishment for stern disapproval. She turns and leaves Danielle's bedroom/office.

Danielle wants to bask in Françoise's praise, but she has no time. She returns to her computer and the sprawling Excel spreadsheet entitled *La Défense 25 Apr* that has taken over her life. With a sigh she creates a new page. In the past six weeks Danielle has learned more about Microsoft Excel than any well-adjusted human being would ever want to know. She never realized until she tried it that activism was so like accounting.

But someone has to do the detail work, and there is so much of it to do. They need thousands upon thousands of people in La Défense on what she has been thinking of as The Day. When she, Laurent, Angus and Estelle decided, six weeks ago, to stage a protest at the International Trade Council's annual meeting in La

Défense, Danielle thought it was just a matter of sending out an e-mail to the world's activist groups, telling them where and when, then sitting back and watching them stream down the street on the day.

But no. Angus and Estelle have a web of contacts in the global justice movement around the world, friends in Paris able to recruit dozens of volunteer aides, phone numbers for hundreds of organizations, lists of thousands of supporters' e-mail addresses; they are willing to spend a sum of money that impresses even Danielle, daughter of millionaires; but you still have to give people a reason to come, and six weeks' notice isn't much, and the International Trade Council is not a sexy target. A simple invitation will not do. This protest needed marketing, and then, after the marketing succeeded beyond all hopes, it needed organization.

None of the other hundreds of loose-knit groups that make up the global justice movement joined the call for a demonstration. Some of them might pause to criticize the ITC in passing, in speeches and literature, but their rage-on-the-streets ammunition was conserved for bigger targets like the G8 and the WTO. By itself that should have doomed Danielle's protest before it began. The conventional wisdom, among the movement, was that a single voice calling for action would never be heard. But they have proved that wisdom wrong, and Danielle gives herself some credit for that. It was Estelle's idea initially, of course – *If we build it they will come* – but it is Danielle who has worked twelve-hour days for six straight weeks.

Since their first week in Paris she has hardly seen Laurent except to crawl into bed beside him. Protests of this size require logistical organization on the scale of a military invasion. Except that armies do what they're told, and the international global justice movement consists of people deeply sceptical of all authority. Organizing more than five thousand people, orchestrating the myriad of groups they belong to, is a profoundly complex and difficult task. But Danielle is good at it. She has never been quite so good at anything before. Between the ordered productivity she learned in law school, and her years of dealing with the same counter-culture types who make up the global justice movement, she is perfect for the job. And she enjoys it. All the endless niggling details, the hassle of translating everything to and from French, every crisis *du jour*, every roadblock – they are a new chance to get something done, something she believes in.

If only she could be left alone to simply do her work. But as the protest has grown, and other groups have become involved, the steering committee has become a battleground. Danielle sighs and begins to order her thoughts and evidence for the committee, where once again, she is sure, she and Estelle will have to defend everything they have done against the jealous cows who wish they had done it instead.

'We've examined your preliminary list of speakers,' the grey-haired woman who has become Danielle's *bête noire* says, 'and we thought it would be worthwhile to discuss it further until we reach a consensus.'

Dr Laura Sayers. American-born, Yale-educated, French resident, author of several academic books about the language of economic inequality, and the chairperson of Accat, a French organization whose full unacronymed name Danielle can never remember, but which has a membership of forty thousand dues-paying members and thus considerable economic weight in the perpetually underfunded global justice movement. Dr Sayers is also the de facto spokesperson for the seven members of the thirteen-person steering committee who are both offended by and opposed to the very idea of Danielle's protest in La Défense.

'Of course I'm open to a quick discussion,' Danielle says, smiling brightly. She leans back and looks out of the window. The steering-committee meetings are held around a table in a spacious room with a timbered ceiling, in an old warehouse along the Canal St-Martin in Paris's 18th *arrondissement*. Through the dozen westward windows she can see across the canal to another warehouse, this one so dilapidated that few of its windows have not been shattered. There are barges parked on the bank of the canal, and a few trees onshore, leafy with new growth. Danielle looks at the trees and affects an air of not really listening. She learned this looking-out-of-the-window trick from a fellow law student who used it to infuriating effect in a law-school show trial.

'Frankly, Miss Leaf, of course we understand that you're unaccustomed to organizing anything on this scale—'

'Danielle works with me,' Estelle says, an edge in her voice, 'and I have put together dozens of protests. I helped organize a million people in Hyde Park, Ms Sayers. Seven thousand is pocket change.'

'*Dr* Sayers, please, for the sake of accuracy, and attention to detail, and of course we understand that you young women are very well meaning, but I think attention to detail is just why you should be willing to consider a greater share of assistance in the organizational efforts on the part of Accat and the other groups represented here. To say nothing of the perception, the unseemly appearance, of two Americans running a protest here in Europe.'

'You'd rather it was three?' Danielle asks drily.

Dr Sayers winces. 'Please, Miss Leaf. I do not consider myself American, that's only an accident of birth, and more to the point I am by no means putting my name forward. What I am saying is that your organizational techniques seem to verge on autocracy rather than consensus. Take this list of speakers, for instance. It's unprecedented to simply come in with a list of speakers and ask us to accept it. As the facilitator, I must remind you that the accepted behaviour is to allow all members of this committee to nominate and vote on the names, rather than dictate to us who we will and will not hear. That flies in the face of the notion of consensus.'

Middle-aged faces nod sober approval. Danielle smiles sardonically. She knows Dr Sayers is no more interested in consensus than Stalin was. Danielle wishes that when the committee first formed she had known enough to veto Dr Sayers's acclamation as facilitator, a role the older woman has been trying hard to transform into agenda-setter, chairperson and dictatrix ever since. At least the ridiculous position of vibes-watcher has been abolished, ever since Irina, the meek Italian woman who held it, burst into tears and fled the room during a previous battle between Danielle and Dr Sayers.

'Of course we would have preferred to do it that way, but you do understand that the protest will take place in,' Danielle glances ostentatiously at her watch, 'one hundred and eighteen hours. We simply don't have time to take suggestions, assemble a list and then get in touch with people and see if they can come.'

'But this list is ridiculous. Are you seriously suggesting that we give Silas Warren a full fifteen minutes?' Dr Sayers demands. 'He's no more than a thug.'

'Diversity of tactics should necessarily imply a diversity of speakers,' Danielle says smoothly. It is amazing how quickly the right lines come to mind now, as if she is an actress with a little earpiece that gives her exactly the right words, the coded language of angry diplomacy. Six weeks ago she stuttered when talking to Dr Laura Sayers. Now she treats her adversary across the table with something like contempt.

' "Diversity of tactics".' The grey-haired woman says this as if she wants to spit. 'Code for black blocs. Code for violence. Code for smashed windows and smashed faces and all the worst, wrongest kind of media attention. Miss Leaf, I have no time, none whatsoever, for your "diversity of tactics". I move in the strongest possible terms that we expel Mr Warren from the agenda, and further that we make it clear that this protest has no time for the black blocs and, further, if any turn up, we as organizers will do our best to prevent them from attending and will help turn them over to the police if they do appear.'

Danielle looks over at Estelle, who is sitting absolutely motionless with the rictus smile on her face that means she's on the verge of eruption. Danielle represses a wave of irritation – she likes Estelle very much, but can't she control herself around these useless old biddies? – and intervenes quickly before Estelle can say anything.

'Of course, we respect your personal views, Ms Sayers,' Danielle says, her voice honey on treacle, 'but as a representative of Accat you're presumably here to represent its members and the desire to participate in this protest that many of them have expressed. Naturally if you feel that your personal views conflict with your duties to the extent that you can no longer continue on this committee, we will understand.'

'You'll understand? You'll *understand*?' Dr Sayers demands, getting to her feet. Danielle smiles inwardly. Victory. 'Young lady, you don't understand the *first thing*, not about how the movement works, not about our goals, not about the need for *ethical* and *non-violent* means, not about anything that I have devoted my *life* to! All you want to do is come to France and wave your dollars around and put ten thousand people in the streets for the sake of your own vanity. It's publicity hounds like you two who will destroy this movement, destroy any hope we have of making a better world, just so you can see yourself on CNN and tell yourself how important you are! Well, you won't, we won't let you get away with it. We are not for sale!'

Danielle looks out of the window again and tries to seem embarrassed for Dr Sayers. It isn't hard. After a moment the old woman sits down, breathing hard.

'Dr Sayers,' Danielle says, her voice soothing, 'I understand you're passionate about the movement, but I don't think out-bursts like this are productive. Why don't we get back to the list of speakers? As you say, I think it can benefit from discussion.'

Danielle and Estelle have chosen the names on the list with care. Danielle's policy is that steering-committee meetings should be held not to reach decisions, but to ratify decisions she and Estelle have already made. The committee has to be tossed a meaty bone once in a while, however, lest its representatives withdraw their support. Silas Warren has always been intended as just such a bone. Danielle is tempted, though, to push her point and keep him on the agenda, just to prove how wrong Dr Laura Sayers is. Maybe she isn't for sale, but the past six weeks have shown that the thousands en route to Danielle's protest most certainly are. Not for money, not exactly, but for something arguably even more tawdry: convenience. Despite the lack of interest and even opposition of every other activist organization, Danielle and Estelle have been able to convince an expected seven thousand people to converge on La Défense five days hence with only six weeks' notice, simply by making it easy and cheap.

Flood the streets with the foundation's money, organize everything in advance, so that all the protesters have to do is show up. Market it as a most-expenses-paid weekend in Paris, plus a communal festival with thousands of other fellow travellers, culminating in a Monday protest. And to the dismay of the global justice movement's aristocracy, its dues-paying masses have jumped at the offer. Despite their numerical supremacy on the steering committee, when faced with Estelle's money and the protest's popular support, all Dr Sayers and her supporters can do is try to limit the scope of what they see as a disaster.

'It's almost a shame, what you've done,' Keiran says. He is putting more memory into Danielle's too-slow computer as she fills him in on the steering committee goings-on. She hasn't seen him in almost a month, he's been in London at his day job, but with only four days to go until the protest, Keiran showed up at the Gare du Nord's Eurostar terminal labouring under a duffel bag full of sharp and heavy objects. 'I mean aesthetically. I'm glad you've got the protest going, you've done a wonderful job, but it makes me fear for the future of humanity.'

'What do you mean?'

'I'm fascinated by your so-called global justice movement. It's very like the Internet. Distributed decision-making. It isn't a single movement, it's like a huge primordial agglomeration of cells, each one some individual group. A dozen people calling themselves Brummies for Africa or some such. Different sizes, different locations, often rather different directions. But through relentless communication they become a functional organization. The cells spontaneously self-organize into a single being to perform a particular action, then disintegrate once again into a thousand separate elements. Right?'

'More or less,' Danielle says cautiously.

'Growth from the grass roots. Distributed hierarchies. Wave of the future. The protest movement works almost exactly the same as the open-source movement, or the Internet itself. But then you come along, and all this dispersed decision-making goes by the wayside as half the cells in Europe run for your beautiful image of a romantic little weekend waving placards in Paris. You're like a cancer. You've taken this wonderful little bottom-up self-constructing network and squashed it into a top-down hierarchy with a jackboot made of money.'

'Piss off,' Danielle says, a little angry. 'That's not true. What gets Dr Sayers's panties in a knot is that we're not following their hierarchy. We're giving the grass roots a choice, and they're choosing to follow us. How is that not democratic consensus? And besides, we're getting something done. Something really valuable.'

'You've really got into this protest, haven't you?' Keiran says.

Danielle hesitates. She badly wants this protest, her protest, to succeed. She wants newspapers and TV coverage around the world to show pictures of thousands of people denouncing the International Trade Council, even shutting the meeting down. It could echo, this protest, she really believes that. If done right, it could change the whole movement, show that they shouldn't be saving their efforts for the high-profile WTO and G8 meetings, that they should be hounding every meeting, every get-together, every photo-op among that conspiracy of the rich called the global free market. Make them hide behind barbed wire and in remote Swiss castles, make it clear that ordinary people will not accept their venality any more. If her protest goes well, then maybe, just maybe, it could set an example for activists around the world.

'I'm getting something done,' is all she says. 'I really don't think Angus and Estelle could have done this themselves. Estelle keeps talking about how she helped organize a million people in Hyde Park, but honestly, the scale of this thing seems totally beyond them, and they have no idea how to deal with the other groups. I thought they were supposed to be the experts.'

'There is some disjoint between how Angus and Estelle portray themselves and how they really are.'

'What do you mean?'

He snaps the lid of her computer back into place and sits on her bed. This tiny room, wooden floors and ceiling, brick walls, is undecorated except for her computer desk and chair, a metal filing cabinet so full of papers most of its drawers will not close, and the perpetually folded-out sofa-bed where she sleeps on those nights she can't make it back to Laurent and their apartment in the 11th *arrondissement*. The single window looks across a narrow street on to a brick wall.

Keiran says, 'Angus and Estelle spent years in the black blocs. The types who show up at protests with body armour and clubs, and not as a fashion statement. They never dealt much with the mainstream non-violent groups. You know where Angus grew up? A housing estate outside Glasgow. One of the poorest places in Europe. Get him drunk enough and he'll drop those fancy words and that posh Scottish accent and turn into an Irvine Welsh character. Estelle grew up in an Alabama trailer park. When she was twenty-one she married a forty-four-year-old British geologist researching exotic rock formations. Call me unromantic, but I think that was "getting out" more than "love". They're both very smart, obviously, they read a lot of books, they talk a good game, but neither of them ever finished uni. They don't work well with rich, educated, upper-class people. You do better. Not surprising.'

'Estelle told you all that?' she asks, knowing the answer.

'No.'

'Do you spy on me too?'

'No.'

'I'm supposed to believe that?'

'I've been tempted,' he admits. 'Right after you dumped me I thought a half-dozen times about breaking into your e-mail. But I never did.'

'I suppose you want a medal for it,' she says tartly, but she believes him and is relieved.

'No. No medal. A little trust would be nice.'

Danielle wordlessly acknowledges his point.

'Please don't get too hung up on this protest,' he says. 'When it's over, if everything goes well, you're on your own, you understand that? I'm through. If you want to stay with this lot it's up to you. I won't be watching your back any more.'

'Watching my back? Keiran, stop treating me like a lost little girl. I'm not just "staying with this lot". I'm setting directions here. I'm the one doing things. We're going to have seven thousand people at this protest, famous speakers, TV coverage – did you know the *New York Times* is sending a reporter? Six weeks ago this protest wasn't a gleam in my eye.'

'Six weeks and, what, a hundred thousand euros ago? For that kind of money I should hope you get some attention. There would always have been a protest here. Conferences like this are to protesters nowadays what butcher shops are to dogs. And protest is a national sport in France. It's just bigger than it would have been, thanks to you and the money. I'd love to know exactly who this foundation is that doesn't blanch at spending six figures on a one-day smokescreen. Maybe it's from some rich saint who died and left her money to a better world. Maybe not. You'd better start asking some questions yourself.'

'You *asshole*.'

Keiran looks at her, perplexed. 'What?'

'I've never worked so hard in my whole life. Never. I've stared down rooms full of PhDs, I've made arrangements for thousands of people, I've solved ten million problems that could all have shut the whole thing down, I've done something amazing here. And you stand there and tell me it was just money, it was nothing.

Fuck you. And it's not just a smokescreen. Not to me. It's something good in itself.'

'Dani, don't get me wrong—'

'I can't believe I ever wasted four months of my life on you.'

'Oh, come on. I'm sorry,' Keiran says, a perfunctory apology. 'I suppose I've been insensitive again. I'm sure you've done a wonderful job. But please keep your eye on the prize. You know perfectly well the International Trade Council has nothing to do with Kishkinda. Except their terrible misfortune of scheduling their annual meeting right next door.'

2

'*Au nom des frères Islamiques*,' Laurent says into the microphone, '*nous avons cachée une bombe dans la Tour EDF. Elle va éclater dans quinze minutes.*'

'Perfect,' Keiran says.

Laurent looks at him. 'You understand French?'

'Enough to know a bomb threat when I hear one.' Keiran replays the recorded message. 'You sure that's an Arabic accent?'

'I served in the Foreign Legion. Trust me. And you in turn are sure they will not recognize my voice?'

'Just listen.' Keiran taps keys, feeds the sentence Laurent has just recorded through an anonymizing noise filter, and plays it back. The result is scratchy and unrecognizable.

'Good.'

'You've studied the floor plans? And the plugs?' Keiran asks. 'Don't want you getting lost in there. And it'd be a shame to get you all the way in and then have you screw things up.'

'I don't screw things up.'

Keiran nods. 'Good. Neither do I. But Angus does. Keep a sharp eye.'

'I will. I don't suppose you have learned anything further about who we are truly working for?'

Keiran is glad he is not the only one who wonders this. 'Sorry. I have no idea who the real Hari Seldon behind this foundation is. But I am *very* curious.'

'A man like you, I would expect to be able to find things out.'

'Even I need some kind of starting point. Give me one thread, a name, an e-mail address, and I'll unravel their whole silicon curtain, but we've got nothing.'

Laurent says, 'If I happen to find such a thread . . .'

'Send it my way. Even after I'm gone. I'll be happy to give it a tug, free of charge.'

Keiran and Laurent nod shortly at one another, a quick look of mutual respect, then depart Keiran's room. In the kitchen, they find Angus ladling sauce on to plates full of spaghetti. Danielle and Estelle are sitting at the table, which is adorned with wine bottles and a cheese-and-fruit plate.

Danielle is speaking intently into her mobile phone. 'Don't bother calling a repairman, Françoise, it's too late. Just go to a copy shop and do it yourself. Well, find one! There has to be one open late somewhere in Paris. Yes, I'm sure they can find their way, but the one-sheet gives them the schedule, phone numbers, all the information they need. Françoise, I know they need you there, but this has to be done. Françoise—'

Laurent plucks the phone from Danielle's hand and switches it off.

Danielle stares at him as if he has just struck her. 'What are you *doing*?'

'Come back to us,' he says. 'It's too late to make any more preparations. Let Françoise handle things. Everything will work out tomorrow, I promise. Your protest will be fine. Now let's sit and have dinner and talk.'

'He's right,' Keiran says.

Danielle aims a dirty look at him, clearly still annoyed at whatever it was Keiran said out of turn a few days ago, but Laurent puts his hand on her shoulder and she thaws and smiles. 'OK. Sorry. I'm just stressed.'

'We all are, hon,' Estelle says as Angus brings the food to the table. 'Tomorrow's a big day for all of us. You have to run the show, I have to make a speech, these three have to . . .' Her voice trails off.

'Save the world?' Angus suggests.

'Exactly.' Estelle tastes the sauce. 'Darling, this is *exquisite*.'

'And they thought you kept me around for my striking good looks.'

'You're all ready for tomorrow?' Keiran asks. 'You've studied the floor plans, the plug types, you know the maximum distances . . .'

Angus sighs. 'Keiran. Mate. It's all fucking memorized. Leave it be, let it settle. Tonight let's just have an evening of civilized discussion. Please.'

'All right.' Keiran decides to do something nice for Danielle. Raising his wine glass, he says, 'To tomorrow. And to Dani for making it happen.'

Angus, Estelle and Laurent echo the sentiment. Danielle awards Keiran an embarrassed smile as she sips her wine.

'You've done a bang-up job,' Angus agrees.

'Thanks. I made a lot of mistakes, but at least now I'll know for next time.'

'There might not be a next time as such,' Estelle says. 'You've done so well with the protest I think in future we'll rope you in for the important stuff.'

Danielle cocks her head. 'Important stuff? The protest isn't important?'

'Well, it's a vital part of the plan, of course, but in itself it'll never be the answer,' Angus says. 'Protests are useless.'

Estelle clears her throat loudly in disagreement. Danielle smiles gratefully at her.

'Are you forgetting how we met?' Estelle asks.

'Ah,' Angus says. 'There is that.'

Estelle explains, 'We met at a protest. Our first date was in a holding cell. We both wore plastic handcuffs. It was very romantic.'

'To clarify,' Angus says. 'Other than matchmaking for lovelorn anarchists, protests are useless. That was the chief insight that brought us here. All those people sleeping in the warehouse, they're not here to get results. They know there won't be any results. They join because it makes them feel good. And that's very nice but doesn't actually accomplish anything. Protests only work when you get a million people out in the streets every day for weeks. Anything smaller is useless. Estelle and I spent years trying to shame companies into acknowledging that human beings are more than a fleshy shell with money inside waiting to be squeezed out. And of course this was a complete failure. Because companies don't feel shame, and most people are useless, selfish cunts. So we moved on to direct action, black blocs, violent protests, destruction of property, trying to physically shut companies down. But that doesn't work either. It worked once, Seattle 1999, but that was all we got. After that they were ready for us, and the police are on their side. The G8 and the WTO meet behind razor wire now, and big businesses are so distributed that it's hard to find a vital point – shutting down a single office does nothing. The black blocs get plenty of media attention, but that's only because what the TV audience really wants to see is someone's skull get split open. They won't actually care about why the black bloc is there in the first place. The proles are the problem, not the solution. Protests are useless. So how do you fight a massive transnational corporation?'

Nobody replies. Keiran hopes somebody will. He thinks he knows what Angus and Estelle intend to do with the access and information he will give them if tomorrow's plan succeeds, but he'd very much like confirmation. They've never actually explained their goals, at least not to him, but on this nervous night before the protest and the raid, they seem to have relaxed their instinctive need-to-know secrecy.

'We finally found an answer,' Angus says. 'Or it found us. The answer is, you don't want the media, you don't want the masses, you want management. That's how you take out a corporation.

You go straight after the men in suits. Scare the bastards, intimidate them, hurt them if you have to. Make them resign. Make them think twice before they market powdered milk with insufficient nutrition as a good replacement for breastfeeding, not because they'll feel bad about killing babies, they won't, but because they're afraid we'll come after them and their colleagues. Their families if we have to. That's what we do. That's what we're doing tomorrow. We could get a hundred thousand people on the streets of La Défense chanting "Death to Kishkinda!" and they'd sit up there and smile. But when we start following them home and knocking on their front doors, they'll change their tune, but fucking quick.'

Danielle looks as if her spaghetti sauce is made of vinegar. Keiran winces. He is glad to have his suspicions officially verified, but his toast has backfired. Danielle does not want to hear that the demonstration she has spent so much time and sweat on is useless except as a front. But no one else seems to notice her expression; Angus and Estelle are too carried away by his words, and Laurent is paying close attention to them.

'That's the ground war,' Angus says. 'To my mind, Estelle and I have a slight disagreement on this, the ground war is less important. Or not less important, but it's like modern militaries, before you can even fight on the ground, you have to win in the air. Except our air war is the information war. I use that word advisedly. Let's not fool ourselves, people have died, they murdered Jayalitha, this is a shooting war. You have to know everything about the enemy, and control what the enemy knows.' He nods at Keiran. 'That's you, you're our air war. Except it's a bit of a dogfight with this P2 about.'

Keiran nods.

'So why Kishkinda?' Laurent asks. 'Did you suggest it to the foundation, or they to you?'

'Kishkinda are first because they're an easy target.'

Keiran blinks. 'First?'

'We're not going to stop with them. We're here to build a whole better world, one dead evil company at a time. Maybe we'll fail, but that's the ultimate goal, and we're entirely serious about it. Kishkinda are first because they're vulnerable. If we intimidate enough of their management into resigning, destroy enough of their information, and maybe harass the mining operations themselves, we'll make that mine uneconomical. It's barely profitable as is. We can drive them bankrupt. We've got the tools, we've got the time, we've got the money.'

Laurent raises his eyebrows. 'Your foundation gave you enough money to wage war on a billion-dollar company? And another after that, and another after that?'

'More of a loan, really,' Estelle says. 'We pay them back by winning. If we do, Kishkinda stock will plummet. The foundation shorts that stock and makes millions. Which in turn builds a war chest for the next target.'

Laurent whistles with admiration.

Estelle says, 'I hate to use the terms of the enemy, but our war, our better world, has a very sound business model.'

'The revolution will be self-financing,' Keiran says. 'That's beautiful. That's *elegant*. I wish I'd thought of it myself.'

'Can we maybe stop talking business and just eat?' Danielle asks sourly.

Keiran returns to his food. He turns the scheme over in his mind as he eats, admiring it. Angus and Estelle are right. This is exactly how you fight a major corporation. Until now he has assumed that their task was quixotic, that they would never be more than a sharp stone in Kishkinda's shoe, but now he realizes, if tomorrow's raid goes well, there's an outside chance that they might actually win, that these few determined people could drive a billion-dollar company into collapse. Asymmetrical war. Like the 767s that felled the World Trade Center. Which isn't such a bad analogy. After all, even if they don't intend to hurt anyone, the people sitting around this table are, quite literally, terrorists.

3

Danielle wakes early and nervous. This is it; this is The Day. The sky is still grey with impending dawn, but Laurent is already up, sipping an espresso and reading *Le Figaro* in the corner of their room. He always rises before dawn, he blames the military for it, and stays up past midnight. Laurent needs less sleep than any other human being Danielle has ever met.

'Morning,' he says, a little surprised. '*Un café?*'

She half smiles. 'I don't think I'll need it today. I'm wide awake.' Awake and tense. She wants to throw herself into work, occupy the butterfly farm in her stomach with something productive, but today there is no more work; the mechanism of protest is grinding away, and it is too late to oil any more gears.

'Maybe you need a little physical distraction,' he says, his voice inviting.

She shakes her head. 'Not today.'

He nods.

'I'm sorry,' she says, taking it as a faint rebuke. 'I know I've been all distant and busy. I never thought I'd turn into one of those women who spend all day at the office and turn down sex because they're too distracted by work. It just happened. But it'll be over tonight.'

'Don't worry. It's all right.'

And it is, too, she can feel it. On paper, she and Laurent should be a disaster. She moved to a strange new city with him after knowing him for only two weeks of desperate mutual peril. Then she all but disappeared from his life to devote herself to work; in the last six weeks they have spent almost no ambulatory time together, and have slept in the same bed only on those three or four nights a week she made it home from the warehouse. By rights they should have drifted apart. Instead she feels, beneath the giddy madness that still comes over her sometimes when she looks at him, a quiet certainty that all will forever be well between them, that the ordinary rules of relationships do not apply, their bond somehow strengthens even when they are apart.

That doesn't mean she wants him to be absent. She aches to spend more time with him, as during their first week in Paris. Danielle cannot think of a happier week in her life. The others returned to London, Keiran to his job, Angus and Estelle to confer with the foundation, and Laurent and Danielle had this apartment and the city to themselves. That first week here, exploring the city by day and each other by night, going on long walks down streets full of so many gorgeous wonders Danielle does not believe they could ever be stained by ordinariness, staying up for dizzying all-night marathons of sex and conversation until they fell asleep murmuring in each other's arms at dawn, then waking tired but oh so eager for another perfect day to begin – that first week was bliss. For him too, she knows it – she still shivers when she thinks of Laurent's racked, halting voice when he finally told her about his past, and the way he picked her up and spun her around as if she were a weightless prop later that day, giddy with pleasure, atop the steps of Montmartre, with all Paris stretched out before them like a magic carpet of delights. She has been in love before, but never like this, never so painless, so uncomplicated, so perfect.

What he does today could put him in jail for many years. But somehow this doesn't worry her; somehow she is certain that he and Angus and Keiran will do their jobs perfectly and safely. It is the protest she has orchestrated which makes her nervous. The inside of her skin seems to itch with anxiety. She feels no anticipation. She just wants today to be over without anything going horribly wrong.

Keiran checks into the Sheraton La Défense using his real name. No harm in it. Nothing he does from here will be traceable back to him. LoTek's Law: *Always be invisible.* He can't get caught unless one of his four co-conspirators turns on him. And no fake ID is likely to help him then.

The bellhop is a little rough with Keiran's duffel bag. Keiran can't blame him, it's full of heavy boxes, but its contents are delicate. He tries to remember his A-level French, to think of the right words – *soyez doux* perhaps? – but he settles for English. 'Be gentle, please. Those are valuable. *Très cher.*'

The middle-aged bellhop gives him a long-suffering look and, Keiran is sure, deliberately scuffs the bag against the wall as he brings it into the suite. Which is lovely – elegant, stylish, spacious, and with a spectacular view of La Défense, the extraordinary complex of skyscrapers and vast concrete plazas, an almost comic-book cliché of hyper-modern metropolis, on the western outskirts of Paris. Keiran's room is twenty-two storeys above Esplanade Charles de Gaulle, the hundred-metre-wide pedestrian walkway three storeys above street level that runs for more than a mile, lined by the glass-and-steel spires and arcs of dozens of towering futuristic buildings, up to the mind-bendingly massive Grande Arche de la Défense. The International Trade Council's annual meeting will begin in four hours, at the hangar-like CNIT building, on the same side as the Sheraton, halfway to the Grande Arche and directly across the Esplanade from the EDF skyscraper.

It takes him the better part of an hour to set up his equipment. The Sheraton has high-speed Internet access, but he sets up a mobile connection as well. *Always have back-up* ranks just behind *Always be invisible.* Two state-of-the-art laptops connect to four large flat-screen monitors. Keiran opens a secure shell into the La Défense security system, which he spent the better part of last week hacking into. He opens feeds from the security cameras to his monitors, switches among them, ensuring that they all work. Between the access he has, and the distraction of the protest, today's exercise should be as safe and painless as modern dentistry. A good analogy, Keiran decides. Even modern dentistry can get a little bloody.

He wonders whether P2, wherever he is, has any idea what Keiran is doing right now. He strongly doubts it. Everything he is doing is secure, encrypted, connected through anonymous cut-outs. But P2 more than anything else is what worries him. The police he can handle. But being outhacked would be the end.

Keiran straps on his telephone headset and clicks a few keys, switching between channels, checking that all the encrypted phone connections are functional and clear. Sitting with the headset on, and four grainy video images flickering before him, he feels like Dr Strangelove in the war room, or, he searches for a more flattering analogy, some kind of space pilot, ready to fly his orbiter into action for the first time.

'Well now,' he says into the headset, to Angus and Laurent. 'In the words of Gary Gilmore in the electric chair, let's get it on.'

The crowd looks insignificant set against the skyscraper canyon of the Esplanade. Danielle stands at the back of the stage and tries to count. A cold chill settles into the base of her stomach. A few thousand at most, no more, and that's counting hundreds of curious passers-by. It is already 1 p.m., the protest is officially beginning, the ITC meeting kicks off in another hour, and there aren't nearly enough people. The demonstration looks like a random clump of people in the vast pedestrian plaza that is the Esplanade. The media pit is all but deserted. There are several television cameras, but only one is being manned. Scores of police in riot gear stand behind temporary steel barriers erected between the demonstrators and the CNIT building, looking deeply bored. Her protest is a disaster. Danielle has failed, failed utterly, and her failure endangers Laurent. She wants to cry. Or run away. She doesn't dare look over at Dr Sayers or Estelle, both of whom stand amid the other organizers on the temporary stage, arms folded.

Their first speaker, a tall African woman, comes to the microphone and begins. Her French is passionate and heavily amplified. Danielle doesn't understand a word. The speaker's image glows brightly on the thirty-foot-high projection screen behind her, but from Danielle's extreme angle, right next to the lower corner of the screen, all she can see are flickering lights, abstract art.

Françoise comes over. Danielle doesn't want to talk to anyone. She pretends to be engrossed in her copy of the protest agenda.

'She's marvellous,' Françoise says, pleased. 'She's so powerful. We should have scheduled her for later, when the crowd is full. The cameras would love her.'

Danielle turns to look at her, but Françoise is already on her cell phone, talking to someone. *Later, when the crowd is full?* She looks up again. There are more people on the Esplanade. The crowd is being fuelled by a constant stream of figures emerging from the Métro station below. And there, coming from the east, from the end of the Esplanade – a hundred more, at least, dressed all in white. As they approach a ripple of conversation washes through the crowd, and signs of life appear in the media pit, another camera is brought to life and turned on the hundred men in white – *masked* men in white – who march into the crowd and assemble in neat rows. The rest of the demonstrators give them plenty of space. The police are suddenly no longer slouching; rather, they too are arrayed in carefully spaced rows, or in furious conversation with their radios.

'Are those who I think they are?' Danielle asks Françoise.

Françoise clips her phone to her belt. 'Yes. The Wobblies.'

The largest and most organized of the black blocs, despite the ironic colour of their uniforms. Danielle had nothing to do with organizing them; that she left up to Estelle. Who has come through. And more people are coming, hundreds more, dozens every minute. The Esplanade is beginning to fill. And there is another group of fifty masked people, another black bloc, this one uniformed in the appropriate colour, a dark patch clearly visible in the otherwise crazy-quilt crowd. Danielle isn't sure how she feels about this. She hadn't really been concerned by the notion of black-bloc violence. She has never trusted police, and if these gendarmes' decision to serve an unjust system extends to fighting this backlash against that system, then they are responsible for their own fate. She had imagined it as an almost gladiatorial battle, black blocs versus cops with an audience of peaceful protesters. For the first time she realizes that the battle lines are not so easily demarcated, and ordinary demonstrators might get hurt.

'Starting to get a little crowded out there,' Estelle says, approaching, her words fast and thinly voiced, her Southern accent more apparent than usual.

'Yeah. I was getting worried.' Danielle tries not to notice that Estelle holds the pages of her speech with trembling hands.

'Fucking stage fright. Crazy, isn't it? Angus might go to jail for the rest of his life today and here I am worried about talking to all those people out there. Half of them won't even understand a word I say before it gets translated.'

'Where's Angus?'

'Over there. By that statue.'

Danielle squints. By a metal statue in front of the EDF Tower, one of the art installations that dot the Esplanade, she sees two men standing. She is too far away to see their features but recognizes their body language. Angus and Laurent.

'I said yes, by the way.'

Danielle looks at her uncomprehendingly. 'What?'

'Yes. To his proposal. I'm going to marry him. Even if I have to do it in some jail in Marseilles.'

'Wow. Wow! That's wonderful!'

The African woman's voice rises to a crescendo, the climax of her speech. The crowd roars its approval.

'I'm glad I'm going early,' Estelle says. She looks very pale. 'I think I'm going to be sick. Do me favour. If I puke onstage, turn off the big screen. Please.'

'You'll be fine,' Danielle assures her, trying to express a conviction she does not feel.

The African woman floats back to the organizers' tables on a wave of raucous applause. Dr Sayers begins introducing Estelle in fluent French. Danielle is sure her friend is being damned with the faintest of praise. She checks her watch as Estelle steps forward to the microphone as if walking to a firing squad. Half an hour until the first ITC attendees are expected. Estelle is meant to speak for all that half-hour. When she finishes, Keiran's plan will go into motion.

Keiran switches back to the view on the statue. The pixillated but recognizable figures of Laurent and Angus are both dressed in the kind of grey coveralls you might see on a factory worker. Angus's hair is tied back in a relatively respectable ponytail. Both of them wear latex gloves and mobile-phone earpieces. These, combined with seeing them on a screen, make them look like movie characters, celluloid Secret Service agents. They stand on the periphery of the crowd, where it thins into sparseness. The view is from a high angle, a camera mounted several storeys up, and beyond the crowd Keiran can see the line of gendarmes in riot gear, standing at attention now, ready for something to happen.

Another screen displays the monstrous glass and chrome of the EDF Tower itself, a narrow skyscraper aimed edgewise at the Esplanade like the prow of a massive ship. About halfway down, its front edge tapers into an overhang, as if a shard has been excised from the building with a huge curved blade. Ten metres above the ground, a metal disc twenty metres across protrudes horizontally from the tower like a massive steel frisbee stuck in its side, sheltering the main entrance.

The reason Keiran is here, the real reason the seven thousand people down below have been brought here, is that the Tour EDF's sixty-eighth, sixty-ninth and seventieth floors are occupied by Kishkinda SNC, the corporation that co-owns the Kishkinda mine along with the government of India. Kishkinda SNC is a public company, shares traded on the Paris Bourse, but forty per cent and effective control are held, through a bewildering web of interlocking offshore holding companies, by a British mining giant called Terre PLC. The shadowed nature of Terre's arms-length control protects them from any legal responsibility, so long as they can show that management decisions are in fact made on the seventieth floor of the Tour EDF. The truth of this claim is one of the mysteries Keiran hopes to resolve today.

He clicks at his keyboard. One of the monitors flickers to the image of a parking-garage camera, capturing a half-dozen dark sedans as they disappear into the maw of the garage. He connects to Laurent's earpiece and speaks into the headset. 'The lambs are nearing the slaughter. I reckon things are about five minutes from heating up.'

Laurent acknowledges. Keiran stands, full of nervous excitement, goes to the window and looks down. Before, during the speeches, the crowd looked like iron filings drawn to the magnet of the stage; now it seems a single amorphous organism, pressed against the line of steel and green that is the barricades and the gendarmes. He knows from the security cameras that most of the protesters are wearing jeans, hemp robes, tie-dye shirts, colourful counter-culture garb. But several knots of fifty or more are dressed all in black, and there is one tight group of more than a hundred in white jumpsuits. These patches of uniform colour, clearly visible from twenty-two floors up, are moving through the crowd to the police barriers. The other demonstrators part before them like the Red Sea for Moses. The general mass carries colourful homemade signs and banners supporting an incoherent panoply of causes, from African debt relief to abortion rights to the Palestinian cause; but the black blocs wear gas masks and body armour, and carry clubs and crowbars, and they are nearing the barricades.

Time for the bomb threat. Keiran's laptop screen is full of green-on-black ASCII characters, the colour chosen, tongue in cheek, to echo the *Matrix* movies. A blinking cursor on the bottom line awaits his next command. Keiran clicks a few keys; a line of text out of all proportion to the number of keystrokes swells across the bottom of his laptop; and all the text on the screen scrolls upwards one line.

The two-digit return code informs Keiran that all went well, that the threat he recorded from Laurent last night has just been conveyed via an untraceable voice-over-IP connection. As far as the French police are concerned, a man with an Arabic accent has just phoned them and informed them that a large bomb will level the Tour EDF within the next fifteen minutes.

The police react with impressive speed. La Défense's security systems report that the Tour EDF's fire alarm is triggered less than two minutes after the phone call. When the first of the International Trade Council representatives sets foot on to the plaza of the Esplanade, ready to brave the hundred-metre journey behind police barricades between the car park lot and the CNIT conference centre, office workers are already spilling out of the Tour EDF's atrium like water from a ruptured pipe.

The crowd surges towards the barricades. Most of them can't know that the ITC delegates have arrived, but even without sound Keiran can tell from the pictures, by the protesters' hate-contorted expressions, by the way they shout and shake fists and banners with new intensity, that some kind of vibe, some primal blood-lust, has run through the mob's collective mind, told them that battle is at hand. Even those who would never participate in violence, even those who ordinarily deplore it, are swept up in the collective wave of rage. This, Keiran realizes, is the real secret of the black blocs. If they worked only for themselves, they would be powerless to affect anything; but those armoured men with clubs are the crowd's id, the expression of its dark and secret desire for blood.

The Wobblies strike first, the group in white, best organized and most violent of the black blocs. They leap the waist-high barriers with military order and precision, attacking the gendarmes all at once. The riot police have only a few seconds' warning before the raging but peaceful protesters suddenly melt into an armed and armoured mass of a hundred organized troops. They bend before the wave. The battle is medieval, clubs and shields, and the tactics medieval as well – it could almost be a scene from *Spartacus*. As the first blows are struck, the demonstration's background noise of raucous cries and chants swells into full-throated roars and screams, a deafening wave of primal noise from seven thousand throats that carries up twenty-two floors and through the Sheraton's thick windows, so overwhelming that it makes the gendarmes falter. Then a smaller black bloc hits them, supporting the Wobblies, and the police line breaks, and the black blocs are running loose through overturned barricades, and the battle has degenerated from ranked troops facing one another into swirling knots of violence. Keiran sees on-screen a gendarme wielding his riot shield two-handed, smashing the edge of it on to the helmeted head of an opponent down on one knee. He sees two Wobblies kicking a fallen policeman so hard that blood splashes on to the concrete from his cheek, peeled open by a steel-toed boot. He can hardly believe that what he is watching is actually taking place just twenty-two storeys below.

Keiran connects his headset to Laurent again. 'The window of opportunity has been smashed open,' he says. '*Go.*'

He switches to the camera aimed at Laurent and Angus. Surrounded and ignored by the hangers-back and outliers of the protesting crowd, they strip off their coveralls, revealing green police uniforms underneath, and make their way towards the Tour EDF, Laurent in the lead. Even uniformed it takes them a little while to fight their way upstream through the men and women in conservative dress who are adding to the chaos on the Esplanade.

'Perfect,' Keiran says. He switches to the camera with the best view of the stage, just to check on Danielle and Estelle. His eyes narrow, then widen, and in a very different tone he says, 'Oh, bollocks. Shit. *Fuck.*'

4

Danielle gapes open mouthed as a riot swirls around the stage. She can't believe how fast it has happened. The moment the police lines broke, the demonstrators became a mob, a whirlpool of violence and chaos, and an eddy current has already surrounded them. The stage was placed not far from the police barricades, a media move, to ensure that TV cameras would capture the menacing ranks of gendarmes in riot gear looming behind the speakers. That placement now seems like a major mistake.

Small knots of police battle black-bloc members all around the stage, while around them a frightened mêlée of protesters try to get out of one another's way. Clouds of light-coloured smoke rise from the Esplanade, mostly where the crowd is thickest. Tear gas, Danielle realizes. A darker cloud of smoke is visible closer, between the stage and the police lines, and pale flames flicker beneath. Danielle recognizes the smell. Burning gasoline. Some of the black blocs must have brought Molotov cocktails.

The smoke-smeared scene by the barricade line looks like a vision of civil war. Police with their backs to a wall, gas masks making them look like giant menacing insects, fire into a crowd of protesters with bullets Danielle devoutly hopes are rubber. The gunshot sounds are lost in the roar of the crowd. A half-dozen black-bloc members, in gas masks of their own, regroup, shouting at one another, one of them on a cell phone, apparently waiting for instructions. A dozen police surround a pair of wounded comrades, one with a visibly broken leg, bent at a sickening angle, the other a small woman with blood-soaked blonde hair, weeping and covering her eyes with her hands, affected by the gas after her mask was torn off. Civilian protesters with useless rags tied around their eyes, their cheeks awash with tears, stumble blindly around, moaning with pain, arms extended and groping like zombies in a horror film, colliding or tripping and tumbling hard to the ground. A woman in a peace-symbol T-shirt sits wide legged on the concrete with a comical expression, as if she has just remembered something amazing, clutching her stomach and trying to breathe. Danielle thinks of the lathi she was struck with in India and winces with sympathy.

'We need to get out,' Estelle says. Danielle didn't notice her appearing. Almost everyone on the stage has clustered in the middle, in front of the big screen, as far away from the fighting as they can get. Danielle has stayed in the back corner, looking for an opening in the brawl, an avenue of escape.

She nods. Just beyond the edge of the stage, maybe five feet in front of her, the tops of their heads level with her feet, two men in black with crowbars and body armour exchange blows with two gendarmes armed with clubs and plastic shields. She can hear the grunts as they swing their weapons. She can't believe they are actually trying to hurt one another. Far easier to believe it is some type of paintball game or medieval times re-enactment.

'We just have to wait, it'll cool down,' Danielle says.

Estelle shakes her head. 'I mean before the tear gas hits. We're no use if we're blind. It's drifting this way.'

Danielle looks over her shoulder. The crowd has been thickened by the thousands flooding out of the Tour EDF, many of whom have been swept up in the confusion of the riot. The cloud drifting towards the stage isn't so much a colour as a visible shimmer, like heat-warped air on a hot summer day. A wave of humanity flees before it, many people clutching their faces as if they mean to tear their eyes out. When the front line hits the stage it shudders as if struck by an earthquake. Danielle realizes to her horror that people are being crushed against the stage's scaffolding as others climb desperately over them and on to the stage.

'*Now*,' Estelle says sharply. The four warriors have moved twenty feet away. There is another whorl of chaos on the other side, a half-dozen ordinary protesters with no weapons or armour clawing and kicking two gendarmes barely able to keep their feet in the chaos, but there is a little space between them. Danielle vaults down, lands on all fours. Estelle does the same, stumbles but rights herself, and they join the escaping protesters, a panicky throng, half blinded, keening with pain and terror. About twenty seconds after joining this mob, Danielle realizes it was the worst thing they could have done.

*   *   *

'Where are you?' Keiran asks.

'Mostly there,' Laurent answers.

'And about fucking time,' Angus says hoarsely. He is in good shape, but not like Laurent, who doesn't even seem to be breathing hard despite having just climbed sixty flights of stairs. 'What about the real bomb squad?'

Keiran scans the automatic transcription of the Paris police radio channel that overlays one of his monitors. 'On their way. But there's absolute fucking chaos outside, you've got plenty of time.'

So far the plan has worked perfectly. Angus and Laurent are probably the only people still in the Tour EDF. They will have plenty of time to pick their way through Kishkinda's offices and do their work, while outside the real police are stymied by the ongoing riot. Even if something goes wrong, Keiran should have plenty of notice – all Angus and Laurent have to do is get out of the building and they will quickly be lost in the mob.

'Sixty-five floors. The power's still on,' Laurent warns.

'Not for long. They'll cut the power soon. Standard procedure for a bomb threat.'

'What about the cameras?' Angus asks, alarmed. 'We walked right past them in the lobby. They can't know our faces.'

'Relax,' Keiran says. 'I own the cameras. You were never there.'

'Sixty-eight,' Laurent says. 'Here we go.' The sound of the stairwell door opening. And then, 'There it is. Looks fucking solid.'

'Send me a picture,' Keiran says.

He switches one of his screens over to the incoming signal from Laurent's camera. It takes a little while to download; encrypted wireless connections are slow. It resolves, line by line, into a picture of a double door, solid wood, with the Kishkinda logo in its stylized font above. There is no visible handle, just a flat white panel next to the door, a card reader, and a numeric keypad above it.

'What if they don't cut the power?' Angus asks.

'Then we're fucked, aren't we? But they will.' Keiran knows from hacking into the manufacturer's system that the door will open in case of power failure, to prevent people being trapped by a fire.

'You can't switch it off yourself?'

'I didn't have time to hack Paris's power grid. Even if I could, they've got a back-up power system only the fire department can shut down remotely. That system's a closed loop, no physical connection to the Net, hacker-proof.'

'So what do we do?' Angus asks.

Keiran opens his mouth to say, 'You wait,' when the screen he is using to monitor the La Défense security system flashes with updates. No signals are being received from the Tour EDF.

'Somebody turn out the lights?' he asks.

'Yes,' Laurent says. 'Flashlights on. The door opened. You were right.'

'Of course I was right.'

'We're in.'

'Good. You know what to do. Send me a picture of anything you're not certain of.'

The backpack Laurent carries is full of small plastic devices cunningly crafted by Keiran's associate Mulligan, the American known affectionately to the hacker world as Einstein with a soldering iron. These devices are bugs. Angus and Laurent will plug them into computers, between existing keyboard or network connections. These bugs will then track and recall every data packet that enters or leaves that computer, and every key typed by its user. Each one has a tiny Bluetooth transceiver that allows it to communicate with other bugs like it within roughly ten metres. The resulting ad hoc bug network will record all information going through the computers they feed off, then anonymously send this information to Keiran twice daily via a wireless base station that will also be hidden in the office. Even a hacker as skilled as P2 will never detect them without actually looking behind the machines in question, and computer security zealots are almost invariably software oriented, disinclined to dirty their hands and minds with hardware.

Laurent and Angus don't seem to need help; their muffled conversation is one of brief and confident expressions. Keiran hopes they are picking the right computers. They have only enough bugs for maybe a dozen machines. He has to rely on them to do their work correctly. He switches back to his views of the protest-cum-riot outside, hoping to find Danielle and Estelle, but the stage has half collapsed and he can't see them anywhere in the smoke-filled maelstrom.

'Keiran,' Angus says, his voice crackling with tension. 'The power's back on.'

Keiran blinks. That he hadn't expected. He looks back at the police-scanner transcription. It takes him a moment to mentally translate the written French. 'Right. Crap. Their bomb squad's at the tower, they can't reach the front so they've gone around the back. They turned on the power so they can open the emergency exit, it's got an electric lock too. You'd better get going. They'll be on their way up in a moment.'

'We can't.'

'What?'

'When the power came up the door locked again.'

Keiran takes a moment to parse that sentence. He swallows, opens his mouth and realizes he has no solution. He never even considered this possibility. Their only way out is the emergency exit – and that opens on to a stairwell full of one-way doors, a staircase that the real Parisian police are already ascending. Angus and Laurent are trapped *inside* the Kishkinda offices, the police are on their way, and Danielle and Estelle are somewhere on the Esplanade, lost in the riot. Keiran stares blankly at his computer. He has no contingency plan for this. He doesn't know what to do.

5

The mob has panicked. A human tide sweeps Danielle back and forth, lifting her bodily off her feet for fifteen or twenty seconds at a time. Arms jab painfully into her and are replaced by new ones. Fingers clutch desperately at her for purchase. She feels herself step on someone who has fallen, stumbles and almost joins them, but the press of the mob saves her, delays her plunge long enough that she can grab a shoulder and pull herself upright. Then the tear gas hits, she doesn't know from where – the police must have fired canisters at them. It feels as if acid has been poured into her eyes. Sobbing, she rubs her eyes with one hand, she knows it doesn't help and may harm but she can't stop herself, and tries to use the other to maintain her space in the solid, seething crowd of blinded, terrified humanity. Somebody grabs at her head, but their fingers slide out of her hair. A violent current of flesh carries her along, propels her shoulder into someone's face hard enough that she feels and hears their nose break. Then something hard, an elbow, hits her on the back of her head. Dazed, she drops to her knees, and a hand smacks her in the face hard enough to bruise, she flails about, tries to pull herself up but pulls someone else down instead. She manages to get to her feet again, back into the press of bodies, hellish but better than being trampled. All she can hear is screams. Her eyes feel aflame, and she is coughing and sobbing, she doesn't seem to be able to breathe enough, there isn't enough oxygen in the air, and there are hands and bodies all around her, crushing her, she scrabbles furiously but can't break free, all she can think about is her need to breathe, but she can't, she can't move at all, then the crowd shifts and she gets half a breath, the air here is mostly tear gas, it's like breathing white-hot poison but that's still better than breathing nothing at all, but the crowd has surged back, she is being crushed again, caught between two opposing currents.

With a violent, spasmodic effort, Danielle somehow dislodges herself, steps into a miraculously uninhabited niche amid the crowd, and takes a mercifully deep breath of almost clean air. And she is swept up in the crowd again. There is no use fighting. She will go where it takes her. She holds her arms over her head to protect it, learning from the previous blows. Then she stumbles and almost falls, because the crowd is no longer propping her up, she is once again responsible for standing unaided, and the people around her are dwindling away, and the air is clear and fresh. Somehow she has broken free of the riot, it has spat her and those around her out and surged back whence it came.

Danielle stumbles away from the screams and clouds of gas, weeping so heavily she cannot see, and bumps into something hard. It takes her a moment to identify it as the same metal statue Angus and Laurent lounged against earlier, what feels like hours ago, when the protest was still a peaceful assembly. She leans back against it, lets herself slide to a seated position on the ground, and weeps until the last of the fiery tear gas has been washed from her eyes, until her nausea and dizziness subside enough that she can stand without wavering.

The mixed smells of tear gas and burning gasoline are still so pungent that her eyes water and her nose throbs, but at least she can see. If it weren't for the statue she would have no idea where she is; the gas and smoke have merged into a thick fog that limits visibility to maybe fifty feet in all directions. The ambient human noise reminds her of a football game or hockey match, the sound of a crowd at some violent and highly emotional sport when a disputed or dirty move has gone uncorrected. A few people mill about her in little clusters, protesters all, frightened and angry. Almost everyone has pulled their shirts up over their faces, and Danielle follows their example. She is surprised by how well she can see through the thick cotton.

Her senses are so heightened by adrenalin that the tugging sensation in her pocket makes Danielle start as if someone has just kicked her. But it is only her cell phone. Her vision is still too blurred to read the number. She answers.

'Danielle,' Keiran says. 'Where are you? Are you OK?'

'I guess,' she manages. Her gas-choked voice sounds like someone else's. 'I'm on the Esplanade.'

'Where's Estelle?'

'I have no idea.'

'Listen,' he says, 'we have a problem.'

'What?'

'This isn't a secure connection. Do you understand?'

It takes her a moment. 'Yes.'

'Our friends need help. They're trapped in the place they went. They can't get out. But they need to get out very soon. Understand?'

For a moment she thinks he means Estelle. Then she goes cold with understanding. Angus and Laurent are trapped in the Kishkinda offices. 'Yes.'

'I need you to go to the door they're stuck behind.'

'Me? The . . . the main door? And do what?'

'I'll give you the key. To open the door.'

'Oh,' Danielle says, remembering that Kishkinda's door is opened by an external keypad. 'OK. I can do that. What's the key?'

'I'll have to call you back. I don't know yet.'

'You *don't know yet*?'

'Just go,' Keiran says. 'Call me back when you get there. Hurry. Our friends can't stay there much longer, you understand?'

Keiran types with furious speed. Angus and Laurent don't have much time. There is still a faint hope that the police will turn the power back off again, but they haven't yet, and that means it's not likely. Instead, the Paris bomb squad is doing a floor-by-floor sweep of the tower. And they have dogs. Angus and Laurent can probably smash their way out, and Keiran supposes that is better than being arrested right now, but once Kishkinda realizes their office was broken into, the game is all but up. Their security will quadruple, the police will start looking for clues, and despite all their precautions there's a good chance they'll find something: a hair, a fingerprint, a Handicam shot of Angus and Laurent entering the building in uniform. In this day of DNA analysis and ubiquitous cameras, the only way to be certain of avoiding discovery is to ensure nobody knows a crime has been committed. *Always be invisible.* But if Keiran can't get the security door's override key code in the next ten minutes, their invisibility is dead.

He still has a chance. He had already hacked into the corporate network of Krull Security, the company that built Kishkinda's security door, when he determined that the door would open when the power went out. Now all he needs is the factory override key used by the manufacturer if their clients forget their codes, or if the authorities need to execute a stealth search warrant. It will be somewhere in Krull's corporate network. There is still a chance.

His beachhead on the Krull network is, as is so often the case, a machine running Shazam. This gives him the permissions of an ordinary Krull employee, but Keiran needs more, he needs *root* – the access level that makes him God, permits him all things, gives him the power to access anything on Krull's network. Shazam can't give him that. There is no time for social engineering. He has to break in the hard way; with an exploit.

There are many ways to hack into a computer. You can social-engineer a user into giving you their password, often by simply calling them, claiming you're the help desk, and asking. You can take advantage of users who fail to change factory default passwords. You can steal passwords by installing a hidden camera, or a key logger; by tricking users into giving it away via a phishing or man-in-the-middle attack; or simply by watching them type it. You can dupe users into downloading a program that gives them access, an e-mail attachment that claims to be a nude picture of Britney Spears but is actually a virus, or a program like Shazam that is useful but also a Trojan horse. Or you can do it the hard way, the most effective way, without the user being involved at all; by finding and using tiny little flaws in one of the basic programs running on a machine. An exploit attack.

Keiran connects to his beachhead computer, calls for a view of its network. Far away, in San Jose, California, disk drives spin in the Krull office, network information is assembled, and this information is parcelled out in thousands of packets, each of which is sent on a journey across the Internet, directed by a chain of thirty routers scattered across North America and Europe, before they reach Keiran's laptop and are reassembled into a diagram on his screen. It all takes less than a second. Keiran looks at the resulting network map and sees that its hub, Krull's main data server, is a machine called LOCKBOX. He uploads a basic hacker toolkit to his beachhead and initiates a port scan of LOCKBOX.

A port scan is basically an interrogation: LOCKBOX is asked 'Do you run this program? How about this one? Or this one? Or this one? Or—' Ten seconds and sixty-five thousand such questions later, a list of the programs that LOCKBOX admits to running appears on Keiran's laptop. He knows exploits for most of these programs – but all have been patched. Part of the ongoing war between hackers and software companies; the former find exploits, and the latter release fixes, or 'patches', as soon as they are aware of the need. But keeping security patches up to date is a time-consuming and complex job, and companies are often very slack about it. Keiran hopes that this is true of Krull as well. He opens up his box of exploits, selects those that might penetrate Krull's software, and begins to try them. It is like finding a door with a dozen keyholes, any of which will open the door, and having keys for all of them, but not knowing whether any of them will work.

The seventh lock, a buffer overflow in Microsoft NetMeeting, has not been patched by Krull since its key, the exploit, was discovered three months ago. The door opens. Keiran is root on LOCKBOX. He glances at his watch. Ten minutes have already passed since he sent Danielle into the Tour EDF. And he still has to figure out Krull's database structure and find out where the door-key code information is held.

The good news is that this isn't hard. The database is well designed, structured in much the same way Keiran would have done it himself. It takes him only a minute to find the factory override code for the door behind which Angus and Laurent are trapped. The bad news is that the ten-digit key code has been encrypted into 256 characters of gibberish. And he has only a few more minutes before the riot dissipates and the bomb squad reaches Kishkinda.

His headset rings. Keiran switches windows and checks the caller ID. Danielle. He answers.

'I'm there,' she says. She sounds exhausted. 'Sorry I'm late. The doors were locked. I had to get a black bloc guy to smash the glass. Then the elevators were all locked down, I had to take the stairs.'

Keiran takes a moment to check that he is still filtering the building's security systems. Yes: as far as anyone looking at its security cameras knows, the door remains unbroken, nothing has moved in front of the cameras since the building emptied, and there is no one inside but the bomb squad. But anyone looking at these pictures – and Keiran strongly suspects this list includes the police – will soon start to wonder why the cameras in the lobby don't show the riot outside. Another deadline.

'Just a moment,' he says.

Keiran can tell by the 256-character size of the encrypted gibberish that the key code has gone through a relatively weak encoding process known as a 'hash function'. A single modern computer, if it was given a few years to work on nothing else, would be able to break it by the brute-force technique of running every possible ten-digit number through SQL Server's hash function. Keiran has a few minutes, not a few years. But he knows the hash function SQL Server uses – and he has several million computers at his disposal. Shazam. His botnet.

Keiran hesitates for a moment. He has rarely used Shazam's full capabilities before. Every time he does, there is a chance, small but non-zero, that someone will notice the extra network traffic and begin to understand Shazam's true nature. But right now that risk is tiny compared to the alternative.

Another call. Angus. 'Mate,' the Scotsman says in a fierce whisper, 'we can hear them on the stairs right below us, they've got fucking *dogs*, we have to get out *now*. We're going to break the door with a fire axe.'

'No!' Keiran says, alarmed. 'No. Trust me. I'll have you out in forty seconds.' His fingers are flying over the keyboard even as he speaks. He has written software to use Shazam for this kind of parallel computation before, against a future need. Today's future need.

Keiran composes his command and hits ENTER. Instructions fly out from Keiran's laptop to the global Shazam network. His command ripples through the Internet like a tidal wave. Around the world, on seven million different computers, the Shazam program takes a break from its usual pursuit of uploading and downloading stolen music and video files, and devotes itself single-mindedly to cracking the key code. In homes and businesses and universities and government offices, computers suddenly devote all their processing power to running several thousand ten-digit codes through the hash function they just received, and reporting whether the result matches that found in Krull's database. Between them they try all ten billion possible combinations in thirty seconds.

'Danielle,' Keiran says, after the single successful computer reports back to him. 'Listen carefully. You get one chance to get this right.'

Danielle enters the code into the keypad, her finger trembling a little. She has the presence of mind to cover her finger with a scrap of paper from her pocket, thinking of fingerprints. She enters the tenth digit. The lock releases with an audible click, the door opens, and Angus and Laurent are there, dressed in police uniforms. Angus's face is drawn with tension. Laurent seems more relaxed, but when he looks at Danielle, his eyes widen.

'Are you all right?' he asks.

She shrugs. She must look awful, covered in soot, with devil-red eyes and matted hair, her face bruised and bloody and smeared with tears, limping and exhausted in torn clothes. 'I'll live.'

'Chat later. We have to *go*,' Angus says, his voice humming with near-panic. He pushes past Danielle towards the stairs. Laurent stops long enough to close the door behind him, takes Danielle's hand and leads her after the Scotsman. He has to let go after the first couple of floors, they can't descend rapidly while holding hands, but she appreciates the gesture. Danielle almost falls, once. Laurent, ahead of her, hears her stumble, turns quick as lightning, ready to catch her. She clutches at the banister and manages to right herself. They exchange a quick grin and continue to run downstairs as fast as they can.

They go out the same way she came in, through the window smashed by a black-bloc man with a huge pipe wrench. Danielle shivers at the thought of the encounter. Clad all in black over body armour, wearing a gas mask, the man looked like an alien from a sci-fi movie. Danielle asked him in desperate English to break the window, then mimed it, since he clearly didn't under-stand a word. Danielle isn't sure whether that was because he never learned English or he was too far gone in primal rage to understand anything other than his mother tongue. His snarls as he smashed the glass were pure animal. When he finished he turned to Danielle, wrench held high, and she is sure that for a moment, drunk on bloodlust, he had thought of smashing her face as well. Instead the man had let out a yodelling howl and raced back into the crowd, looking for something or somebody else to destroy.

In the ten minutes since, the riot seems to have cooled into a kind of stand-off. The police are arrayed on the northern edge of the Esplanade, the rioters to the south by the Tour EDF. Smoke-and gas-obscured no man's land lies between them, strewn with overturned barricades. About a hundred protesters, most of them black bloc, are chained to metal fences behind the police with plastic zip-tie handcuffs. Windows have been shattered along both sides of the Esplanade. The protesters shout and chant. The remaining black bloc members are in the front of the crowd, snarling fury visible on the faces of those without gas masks.

It occurs to Danielle that somehow, incredibly, she is the architect of all this.

Everyone who intended to flee has got away by now. But despite the tear gas, clubs and rubber bullets, at least a thousand, probably more, have remained. When Danielle, Angus and Laurent emerge from the Tour EDF, the people around them, civilian protesters all, dressed in tie-dyed hemp or sober business wear, turn to stare at the two newcomers in police uniforms with expressions of shock and rage.

'We need to go,' Laurent says. 'By now even the pacifists must have their blood up.'

He leads the way. Angus and Danielle follow. The people around them watch with angry expressions, not sure how to react to their sudden appearance. The crowd thins out as they approach the fringe, populated by bystanders keeping their distance from the action. Danielle thinks they have got away. Then two twenty-something goateed men, dressed in jeans and black T-shirts, eyes red with tear gas, step into Laurent's path.

Without breaking stride, Laurent spins on one leg, kicks high with the other, and his foot comes around in a wide arc and knocks one of them senseless. Before the first man even hits the ground, Laurent punches the other in the stomach so hard he topples over and falls sideways, clutching his gut, his mouth open in a stunned O. A shocked gasp comes from all around them, followed by furious, dismayed shouting. Laurent grabs Danielle's hand and pulls her after him, running hard, pushing people out of their way, shoving between them or spinning around them like an NFL running back. Angus has to sprint to follow. The vengeful muttering around them intensifies, and Danielle is sure they will be chased and beaten, they are outnumbered a hundred to one.

Then the voices around them falter, become doubtful and afraid, as does the roar of the crowd in the distance. Danielle looks up. They have almost detached themselves from the protest now, they are right on its eastern edge, next to little sculptures of gnome-like heads set in banks of terraced plants. Ahead and to her left, she sees a tide of uniformed police with riot shields and gas masks emerge from the car park entrances on the northern side of the Esplanade, rank after rank of them, heading towards the crowd with a slow, unanimous, unstoppable gait. Danielle is crazily reminded of *Star Wars* storm troopers. Then she hears chunking noises from the police ranks, sees metal canisters fly overhead, land in the crowd. More tear gas.

The first man this marching wall of police encounters shouts at them desperately in French. They club him to his knees and handcuff him. The wall of gendarmes swirls and re-forms around the small knot formed by this event. They don't even slow down. They march straight into the demonstrators, squeezing the crowd against the buildings on the south side of the Esplanade, the Tour EDF and the Quatre Temps shopping centre. As the gendarmes force the last dregs of the crowd to disperse, Danielle, Angus and Laurent flee south towards the Sheraton. All she feels is relief.

Keiran opens the door. Danielle, bruised and battered, stands there, leaning on Laurent, who, like Angus beside him, is apparently untouched by the riot.

'No offence,' Keiran says to Danielle, 'but they let you in looking like *that*? This is a five-star hotel. Their standards are clearly slipping.'

'Don't,' she warns him, her voice dangerous. 'I'm not in the mood.'

He nods apologetically. 'Come in.'

They enter. Danielle sags on to the couch, and Laurent sits next to her. Angus remains standing. 'Where's Estelle?' he demands.

Keiran says, 'She's fine. A little bruised, is all. I just talked to her. She's trying to find her way here. The police have shut down the demonstration zone, she's on the other side, by the Grande Arche.'

Relieved, Angus sits.

'You did good work, all of you,' Keiran says. 'Excellent work.'

They nod. Keiran bites back a sigh at their lack of reciprocation. He just ad-libbed a feat of near-superhuman hacking, saving them from certain incarceration, and they take it as no more than their due.

'Did it work?' Laurent asks.

'Seems to have done. The network is alive and reporting, all our little listeners accounted for. We won't get any actual information from it until tonight's update, though.'

Angus says, 'Once we clean up we should go back to the apartment.'

'We can't stay here?' Keiran asks, looking around at the luxury hotel suite. 'This is *proper*.'

'Sorry,' Angus says. 'The foundation's pockets are not bottomless. Even if they were, I'm sure they could find better things to spend money on than your outrageous room service bill.'

'Name one.'

'World peace,' Laurent suggests.

'I'll take the room service.'

'Sometimes, Keiran, I think you are not a true believer,' Laurent says, amused.

'I'll believe anything you like for five hundred a day plus expenses. Now give me a hand packing my gear. And be gentle. It's very sensitive. Like me.'

'What's the plan for tomorrow?' Danielle asks.

'With any luck,' Keiran says, 'tomorrow we crack Kishkinda open like a walnut.'

6

'So, in short,' Angus summarizes, 'we have nothing.'

'We have quite a lot,' Keiran says. He looks around the dining-room table at the others. It is very quiet, as if the whole 11th *arrondissement* is listening to his report. 'We have access to their internal corporate network. That's not nothing.'

'But it gives us nothing.'

'We have home addresses and phone numbers galore. You wanted to go after the suits? Now we know where they live.'

'But nothing *culpable*,' Angus says angrily, as if it is Keiran's fault. 'No evidence that Kishkinda is knowingly dumping toxic chemicals.'

'I found plenty of documents which seem to indicate that they're not. I mean, half of them are in French, maybe you can correct me, I've only got an A-level and two years of uni,' Keiran is being sarcastic, 'but these seem to claim that as far as Kishkinda knows, they're not dumping anything, and the soil and groundwater samples *they* take have chemical levels well within international standards.'

'Don't be an idiot. Of course they have documents like that. You think they make the real ones available to everyone in the company? No. Only a very small group know the truth.'

'Like who?'

'Like the CEO,' Angus says. 'Gendrault. What do the files on his machine say?'

'I told you. We don't know. We only have his password. Which is "chevalier", incidentally. Think he fancies himself as a knight? Or he's hoping for a gong? He's got a British passport too, if I recall.'

'If you have his password, why can't you read his files?' Estelle asks.

'Because they're paranoid bastards, aren't they? They use SecurID tags. Little key-chain things that generate a new six-digit number every minute. In sync with their server doing the same thing. You have to enter both his password and his current SecurID number to log in as him. Or any of the other top management.'

'Fucking hell.' Angus shakes his head. 'We break into their office and plant bugs and we *still* don't have their passwords?'

'We've got their home addresses,' Estelle says. 'That's a start. But we wanted their details, schedules, security plans.'

'What I wanted was culpable evidence,' Angus says. 'Not that I expect the police would actually arrest anyone from a major company. But if we could create litigation risk for them, that would weigh heavily on their share price.'

'You sound like you're planning a takeover,' Danielle says.

Angus nods. 'If we had the money we would. Take it over and shut it down. Easiest solution. But driving them bankrupt works just as well.'

'Listen,' Keiran says, 'I did find something interesting.'

They look at him.

'There's a stack of encrypted documents on their network server, in a directory called "Project Cinnamon". And not your standard shite Microsoft password protection. Serious public-key encryption.'

'Can you crack the codes?' Danielle asks.

Keiran half laughs. 'No way. Your National Security Agency couldn't decrypt this if you gave them a decade. These files are *secure*. That is, until someone on one of our bugged computers reads them. When they enter the pass phrase, our lovely little bugs will remember every word they type.'

'It could be weeks before anyone reads those files,' Angus says. 'Months.'

Keiran nods. 'A lot of hacking is waiting.'

'We don't have that kind of time. What about their e-mail? That's what we wanted most. Can we read that?'

Keiran sighs. He doesn't like being the bearer of bad news. 'Sorry. The Exchange database file is encrypted. Not like Project Cinnamon, but we'd need a SecurID code, again, to read a given person's mail. Or root access to read everyone's.'

'Root access,' Laurent repeats. 'Who has that?'

'Gendrault, presumably. The CIO, definitely.'

'CIO?' Estelle asks.

'Chief Information Officer,' Keiran says. 'Or CTO, Chief

Technical Officer. I don't know the French equivalent. Anorak-in-chief, essentially. We have his password too. And he must be easier to get to than Gendrault. If we can get our hands on the CTO's SecurID for a minute . . .' Keiran lets his voice trail off into pregnant space.

After a moment Laurent smiles. 'My friend, you are thinking far too small.'

Keiran looks at him quizzically. 'Not something I'm often accused of. How so?'

'The CTO's little security device would maybe be useful. But not as useful as the CTO himself. It will be he who set up their security, no? He will know where all the encrypted bodies are buried. He must. It's his job to keep them safe.'

'Sure,' Keiran says, 'but even root access won't let us decrypt those files, and I don't think he's likely to up and tell us the pass phrases.'

'That, *mon ami*,' Laurent says, 'is where I disagree.'

'What do you think?' Estelle asks Danielle.

Danielle doesn't know what to think. On the one hand, it's Laurent's idea, she doesn't want to say anything against it, but on the other . . . 'It seems so . . . drastic. Breaking into their office is one thing, but this . . .'

Estelle nods. 'Keiran?'

Keiran shrugs. 'It's the logical extreme of social engineering. I'm sure it will be very effective. I want nothing to do with it.'

'We won't know what you need to know,' Angus says. 'You'll have to be there.'

'Angus, mate. I agreed to help you, and you agreed—'

'I know what I agreed. We need you to be there. You won't have to do anything but ask questions.'

Keiran shakes his head. 'I don't like it.'

'I'm not asking you to like it. I'm asking you to be there.'

Keiran doesn't say anything.

'Angus didn't want to be in that parking garage,' Estelle says quietly.

'*Fuck*,' Keiran says. 'What are you two, a double act? All right. But this is the end. No more. I use whatever you get from this, find whatever I can, and then I'm done, I go home, and, no offence, but as far as I'm concerned, we never see each other again except maybe to hoist a few pints and talk football. Am I being perfectly clear?'

Angus nods. 'Transparent.'

The apartment falls silent for a moment.

'I don't like it either,' Angus says. 'But it's effective. And this is war. And this man's not bloody innocent. Not with his job. At best he's wilfully ignorant.'

Estelle says, 'This is extreme.'

Angus looks at her, taken aback. 'Are you saying we shouldn't do it?'

'No. I'm saying this is extreme. What if something goes wrong?'

'If you actually do this,' Keiran says darkly, 'and something goes wrong, we're all behind bars till our teeth fall out.'

Estelle nods her acknowledgement of this truth, and pauses, visibly deliberating. Danielle looks at her, hoping that she will say she is opposed to Laurent's suggestion. Then Danielle won't have to decide whether she wants to fight the idea or not. Estelle's opposition will effectively be a veto. And surely gentle Estelle will say no to something this extreme.

'This is war,' Estelle says. 'Think about Jayalitha. Not just that they murdered her, and murdered her family, but remember why. She knew something. She found out something important, something that scared them so much they had to kill her. We have to find it too. We can't afford the luxury of being squeamish. We're the only hope of thousands of dying children. I wish there was some other way, but there isn't. We have to do this.'

*   *   *

Their Paris apartment is near the eastern edge of the 11th *arrondissement*, working-class Paris, half blue-collar whites, half African immigrants, both maintaining an uneasy truce that consists largely of staying out of one another's way. Danielle loves it fiercely. She loves the smell of *boulangeries*, the buzzing Wednesday and Saturday markets held along the wide median of Boulevard Charonne, the galleries and statues and architectural treasures around every corner, the quiet rubber-wheeled Métro and the glorious art deco signs that indicate its stations, the effortless style of French women, even though they always make her feel frumpy. She even speaks a little of the language, thanks to America's East Coast upper-class quirk of studying French rather than far-more-useful Spanish in high school.

She had been to Paris before, as a backpacker, and liked it well enough but was frustrated by crowded hostels, rude French service, long lines at the tourist-soaked Louvre and Eiffel Tower and other obligatory tourist stops. She thought it over-hyped and overcrowded. But here, away from the theme-park city centre, she understands that living in Paris, more than anywhere else in the world, means living surrounded by beauty. It already feels almost like home.

Two days after the La Défense protest, Danielle and Laurent leave their apartment for what starts as a short walk and turns into an epic journey. To the vast roundabout of the Bastille, then along Rue Rivoli, past chocolatiers and creperies and music stores and smoky little bars, until they reach the Gothic majesty of the Hôtel de Ville. There they cross the Seine on to Ile de la Cité, pass Notre Dame, and continue into the Latin Quarter, Danielle's favourite district, between the Seine and the Sorbonne, full of students, artists, bookshops and cinemas. After a long walk through the Jardins du Luxembourg they continue west along the Seine. Danielle feels as if she is walking in a movie set, surrounded as she is by vast architectural wonders: the Eiffel Tower perching spider-like ahead, the Musée d'Orsay and Les Invalides to her left, the Louvre and the Tuileries to her right, and the dark Seine coursing between them as it has for centuries. Since setting out she and Laurent have hardly talked, just walking companionably, sometimes hand in hand, in a silence which she knows she must eventually break.

Danielle takes a deep breath and says, 'Laurent?'

Laurent looks at her.

'Your plan? I don't know about it. I just don't know.'

He nods, slowly. 'I could sense your hesitation.'

'It's not that I don't think it will work. I don't know if it's the right thing to do.'

'It's the wrong thing,' he says. 'But less wrong than doing nothing.'

'There has to be some other way.'

'There probably is. But the other options are slow. Children are dying, Danielle. We don't have the luxury of time.'

'Then . . .' She hesitates, knowing she is about to take the most cowardly road. But she can't abide any of the other options. 'Then I don't want to be there. I'm sorry. I just . . . I can't, I don't have the stomach for it. I'm sorry. I'm really sorry. I don't want to be involved.'

Laurent nods again, thoughtfully, as they walk past the gleaming dome of Les Invalides, Napoleon's tomb. 'Let's take a little detour,' he suggests.

He leads her halfway to Les Invalides, then veers left, to the Musée Rodin. The museum itself is expensive, but entry to the gardens is only one euro. Near the entrance, above a field of gravel, a vast iron sculpture looms. Danielle recognizes it. Rodin's masterpiece, the *Gates of Hell*. Two iron gates, in which tortured human forms lie half suspended. Above them, a man sits with his head resting on his fist, contemplating the world. *The Thinker*. The larger, more famous version of that statue is some fifty feet behind them, but that piece was only a study for this masterwork.

'You have to come,' Laurent says.

'What?' Danielle asks.

'You have to join us for this. I'm sorry. I don't want to demand. But I have to. You're . . .' He hesitates.

'What?'

'I don't yet really believe in your commitment,' he says finally, not meeting her gaze, his voice low and rasping. 'To us or to me. There. I've said it. I feel like you might drops us, drop me, and go back to New York at any moment. I'm not sure you want to be here. I'm not sure you want to be with me. I need you to be present for this so I know I can believe in you.'

'I . . .' Danielle stares at him. She is appalled by his demand, but she also feels horribly guilty, that she has been so distant, allowed Laurent to grow insecure, to doubt her. She wants to rush to comfort him.

'I love you,' she says. 'I'm not going *anywhere*. You understand that?' She grabs him, pulls his head down to her, kisses him roughly. 'You can believe in me.'

He smiles, but wanly. 'And I love you. But can I believe in your commitment? Not just to us, but to our cause? Fighting for a better world, whatever the cost, whatever the consequences for ourselves? Because if you can't believe in that . . .'

He leaves it unsaid.

'I do believe,' she says.

'Whatever the cost? Whatever the consequences?'

'What you're talking about makes us no better than them.'

'I know. That's what I mean. We disgrace ourselves by even talking about it. Part of the cost I'm talking about isn't capture or jail. The cost is having to do awful things.' He gestures at the *Gates of Hell*. 'We don't have the luxury of just sitting and thinking. We have to go through those gates. And if you believe what we're doing is right, you have to join me.'

She looks at him, realizes she is softly shaking her head, makes herself stop.

'You're willing to let it happen, as long as you're not there,' Laurent says. 'You just said so. But I'm sorry. That's not good enough.'

Danielle closes her eyes. She thinks of the children with warped faces and deformed limbs in that village near Kishkinda, of their bright eyes. She thinks of her hopes for the protest, how she thought it might change the world, and of her sickened relief when it ended.

'All right,' she decides.

'You're sure? You're certain?'

She nods slowly. She feels his fingers on her chin, turning it up towards him. He kisses her. She realizes she is crying, and she presses herself into Laurent's iron arms, leaning against his unyielding solidity, trying to melt into him, letting his kisses take her doubt away.

Jack Campbell, Chief Technical Officer at Kishkinda SNC, is surprisingly easy to kidnap. His modern, minimalist fourth-floor apartment is in a building with security cameras and electronic locks; but he is single, and drinks heavily on weekends, and is all too eager to join a tiny but very pretty American girl with purple-streaked hair and black velvet gloves for a nightcap at her home. He is too drunk to be suspicious when his new friend 'accidentally' gives the taxi the wrong address, then leads him on a five-minute walk through the dark alleys with which the 11th *arrondissement* is replete.

Campbell is so drunk he sways and staggers as he walks. His first hint that all is not well comes when a masked and gloved Laurent appears out of a shadowed nook and knocks him dazed and sprawling with a single punch to the solar plexus. By the time Campbell has any idea that this is more than a simple mugging, he is handcuffed, blindfolded, gagged, and in the back of a rental Citroën, seated between Estelle and Laurent.

Angus drives. Campbell moans through his gag a little at first, but a few elbows to the gut from Laurent cure him of that habit in a hurry. Danielle sits in the passenger seat, eyes wide, heart racing. Everyone else seems cool and matter-of-fact, professionals at work, but she is terrified. She is in the midst of committing a serious crime. They have beaten and abducted a man. And there may be worse to come. Danielle hasn't done anything herself, won't do anything, but she doubts that will mean much to the authorities, going along will be seen as conspiracy, almost as bad as committing the crime herself. She has somehow, without doing anything other than following her heart, become a criminal. She supposes she was already that when they broke into Kishkinda's offices, but that felt more like a college prank than a violation of the law. This is different. They have hurt this man already. This is violent crime.

She doesn't understand how Angus can drive so coolly. Every car they see looks at first like a police car, every pedestrian seems to be staring suspiciously at them. She cannot even imagine what she would do if the police were to stop them now. Would she panic and crumble? Or would she be calmly alert until the crisis passed? Except it wouldn't pass. If the police stop them now, Danielle's life is to all intents and purposes over.

7

No one is in the alley behind their building, or seems to be watching, as Angus and Laurent hustle Campbell out of the car, to the back stairs and up to the apartment. Even an insomniacal nosy neighbour would not see enough to provoke a phone call to the police. Or so Danielle hopes. She follows the men upstairs as Estelle parks the car. When she enters the apartment she feels a little bit better. They are safer now. Discovery is unlikely. They still have to get him out of here, when they are finished, but at least they can pick and choose their own time to do so.

They sit Campbell down at the kitchen table, his hands still trussed behind his back, a dark scarf still wound around his eyes, the ball gag purchased at a sex-toy shop still filling his mouth. He makes a low noise deep in his throat as Laurent expertly ties the chain of his handcuffs to the back of the chair and produces their victim's key-chain, anchored by a small black lozenge with the SecurID logo and a liquid-crystal screen that displays six numbers. Laurent drops the lozenge in front of Keiran, who sits on the other side of the table, laptop before him, looking as if he has eaten, and swallowed, something disgusting. After a moment Keiran types the SecurID number into his laptop.

'Listen,' Angus says in a harsh whisper, 'we're going to ask you some questions. If you answer them fully and truthfully, you will not be hurt. Understand?'

Campbell doesn't move.

'*Understand?*'

Campbell nods. Laurent unclips and removes the gag.

'What the *fuck* is this?' Campbell demands, his voice rising into a shout, his words slurred. Laurent quickly pinches his nostrils shut and reapplies the gag as Campbell breathes in.

'Marvellous,' Keiran says. 'Bloody excellent. Our subject is too drunk to think. Well done. Full marks.'

'Sorry,' Estelle says. 'He was already half kettled by the time I walked in.'

'I'll sober him up,' Laurent says.

Keiran snorts. 'I don't think black coffee is going to do the trick.'

Laurent takes Campbell's nose firmly between his thumb and forefinger and gives it an abrupt, forceful twist. There is an audible snapping sound. The strangled remains of a scream escape Campbell's gagged mouth. He writhes so violently that Angus has to lean on his chair to prevent him from falling over, and blood begins to pour from his nose. The other four people in the room stare aghast at Laurent.

'Bring a towel,' he says to Danielle. 'Move! We don't want his DNA everywhere.'

Moving numbly, she obeys. He presses the towel to Campbell's face, keeping the blood from seeping on to the table.

'Wait for the blood to clot,' Laurent says. 'He'll be sober enough by then.'

'Fucking hell,' Angus says quietly. He seems a little shaken. Estelle, standing next to him, does not.

Laurent looks at him. 'If you don't have the stomach for this we should stop now.'

'No,' Angus says. 'No, I'm fine. That was . . . unexpected. That's all.'

The next few minutes seem to stretch out for aeons. No one has anything to say. The rasping as Campbell breathes sounds like that of a dying animal. Keiran looks as if he wants to throw up. Danielle feels the same way. Interrogation, what they called it before it happened, was one thing. Torture is another. But they have come too far now, taken too big a risk already, to even think of stopping.

'All right,' Laurent decides. 'We'll try this one more time. Are you going to be loud?' he says into Campbell's ear. 'Bear in mind you have two hundred other bones in your body.'

Campbell gingerly shakes his head.

'Are you certain?'

Campbell nods. Laurent removes the gag. Campbell breathes deeply and gratefully through his mouth.

'You'll answer our questions, won't you?' Laurent says.

'Yes.' It is more a moan than a word.

Laurent looks at Keiran.

'Project Cinnamon,' Keiran says. 'We need the pass phrases.'

'What pass phrases?'

'To open the documents,' Keiran says, exasperated.

'I don't . . . I don't have them. They've all . . . Mr Gendrault, the CEO, he's the only one who knows the passwords.'

Danielle sags with disappointment.

'I've read your CV,' Keiran says harshly. 'You're a professional. Do you really expect me to believe that you let the CEO, and only the CEO, encrypt those files without creating a back door just in case he forgot his password down the road?'

Campbell doesn't say anything.

'Do you need further encouragement?' Laurent's voice is dangerous.

'Just a minute,' Campbell says, his voice raw. 'I don't . . . it's hard to think. Yes. Yes, there's a back door.'

'What is it?'

'PGP encryption. The phrase is Double Nickel Override. Nickel was my dog's name. When I was just a kid.'

'We don't fucking care about your dog,' Angus growls, as Keiran types furiously.

'Got them,' Keiran says.

'What are they?' Estelle asks, coming to look over his shoulder.

A minute passes as Keiran and Estelle scan the documents.

'No,' Keiran says. 'These are takeover documents. Letters of agreement, minutes of negotiations, financials, balance sheets. Kishkinda management is in secret takeover talks with some other company, behind Terre's back. Zulu Fields. South African, I presume. Interesting. But nothing like what you're looking for.'

'Who are you?' Campbell asks, confused now. 'I thought . . . You're not from Terre?'

Angus slaps him, and Campbell rocks back and moans. 'Stop fucking around,' Angus growls. 'We want the real files. The real Kishkinda files. The real groundwater reports. The real health studies. Accounts of which thugs and politicians you pay off, and how much. We want everything.'

'What are you talking about?' Campbell asks. He actually sounds angry. Alcohol has watered down his fear. 'We don't do that. We don't pay bribes. No more than every company in India does. There's only one set of groundwater reports. There are no secret files. I know the whole network, I'd know if there was. That's a lie spread by ignorant fucking anarchists like you. We don't poison people and we don't pay anyone off.'

'Believe me, sweetheart,' Estelle says, 'you're not doing anyone any favours by lying. Least of all yourself.'

'I'm not lying. We're clean.'

'Maybe,' Angus says, 'just maybe, you actually believe that. But I think you're in this shite up to your neck. And you think we'll kill you if you tell the truth. But we won't. Tell us and we'll let you go. That's a sworn promise.'

'There's nothing to tell. There are no hidden files.'

Angus looks across the table. 'Is that true?'

Keiran shrugs. 'I've downloaded their e-mail archive, but it'll take days to go through. And if I do find anything it will probably be encrypted.'

'He'll tell us now,' Laurent says. 'Won't you?'

'I can't. There's nothing to tell.'

'Keep him quiet,' Laurent says. He walks to the sink, takes a large porcelain bowl from a cabinet and begins to fill it from the tap. Danielle looks at him with horror. She just wants this to be over.

'I'll tell you anything,' Campbell says desperately. 'I'll answer anything. I'm not lying. I can't point you to something that doesn't fucking exist. *Please!*'

'Quiet,' Estelle says, smacking Campbell lightly on the back of the head, almost as if he were a disobedient pet.

Her victim cringes. 'Please,' he repeats, quieter but no less passionate. 'It's true. We're not hiding anything. Or if we are I don't know anything about it. Please. I want to help you. I just can't.'

'You want to help us,' Laurent says, coming back with the mostly full bowl of water, putting it on the table in front of Campbell. 'An unlikely story.'

'What are you doing?' Angus asks.

'A little incentivization. Don't worry. It's harmless. No permanent marks, so long as you're careful. And I'm always very careful.' Laurent smiles. Then he grabs the back of Campbell's head and shoves his face down into the water.

Campbell tries to fight, but his neck muscles are no match for Laurent's strength. The others watch and do not move. Campbell's desperate writhing starts to subside. Danielle opens her mouth to say something, she doesn't know what, when Laurent pulls his head out of the water, allows him two deep wheezing breaths, and shoves it back in. Campbell kicks his feet pathetically against the floor.

'Other people waste their time with knives, thumbscrews, fire, electricity, genital torture, you name it,' Laurent says, speaking slowly and distinctly. 'All you really need are restraints and a bowl of water. It doesn't even leave a mark.' He allows Campbell another breath. 'People say drowning is one of the worst ways to die. Of course, you have to think, how would they know? But that's what those who almost drown always say. That it was the worst experience they can imagine.' Another rattling gasp of breath. 'Most people have no idea how painful long suffocation can be. Most people can't take more than a couple minutes. Dunk them a few times and they're yours for life. But you, my friend, you seem like a hard case. You'll be here for quite a little while. Maybe you have already decided to tell me everything, but I won't even ask you for a good, let's say, five minutes.' Two breaths. 'When I do ask, just remember, if you get the answer wrong, you'll get another ten minutes of this. Maybe I'm doing you a favour, you know? Helping you kick your oxygen habit.' A breath. 'People say physical interrogation doesn't work, but you know what? They're not usually the same people who have experienced it.'

'Stop it,' Danielle whispers. 'Stop. Laurent. Please stop.' She knows he is acting, she knows it is tearing him up inside to do this, it has to be, he cannot really be the icy sadist he seems right now, he's just trying to intimidate Campbell, but she can't sit silently and watch any more torture. This has to end.

'No names!' Laurent says angrily.

'Stop it. You have to stop. You'll kill him.'

'He's perfectly safe. I've done this before.' He pulls Campbell's head out of the bowl for two more breaths, then plunges it back into the blood-clouded water.

'I'm not part of this,' Keiran says. He folds his laptop and picks it up. 'I'll be in my room.'

'No,' Angus says. 'Keiran, mate, we need you. No one else understands the technical side of things.'

'Look at yourself. I should fucking give you up is what I should do.' Keiran stalks into his room.

'We don't need him,' Laurent assures Angus, as he continues asphyxiating Campbell. 'Believe me, this man will be more than willing to spell it all out.'

'Please stop,' Danielle begs. 'Please. We can't do this.'

'I know how you feel,' Estelle says quietly. 'But we can't let ourselves feel sorry for men like him. He knows who he works for. He knows they deliberately let thousands of people die for their profit margins. He's not even wilfully ignorant, he's worse than that. There's a legal phrase, "depraved indifference". Don't feel sorry for him. Remember that he's a monster. He's the worst kind of monster, the kind that gets to go to parties and talk about his work and pretend he's a normal human being.'

'What if you're wrong?'

'You've been to those villages,' Angus says. 'You think it's coincidence that every village around the Kishkinda mine has cancer rates a thousand times those of the average Indian population?'

Eventually Laurent says, 'I think he's ready,' and pulls Campbell's head out for good. Campbell spends thirty seconds coughing up water, his body convulsing as if with powerful electrical shocks. Then he vomits into the bowl and hangs limply in his chair, all strength gone, every slow and laboured breath a moan.

'Tell us where the hidden files are,' Laurent says.

It takes Campbell a few moments to muster an answer. 'I don't know,' he says, his voice so wheezy that Danielle has to strain to hear. 'Please. I don't know anything. I'd tell you if I did. I'd tell you anything. I don't know. Please. Please.'

Laurent clenches his fist in Campbell's hair and looks at Angus. 'More?'

'No,' Danielle demands. 'No. You have to stop. *He doesn't know.*'

Angus looks at Estelle, who slowly shakes her head.

'No,' Angus says. 'Let's get him out of here.'

*   *   *

Danielle is already in bed when Laurent returns. In bed but wide awake. She twitches with dismay when he reaches over and rests his hand on her shoulder. She doesn't know how to react, whether to push him away, or pull him to her so they can try to help each other forget.

'I was so sure,' he whispers.

She can't keep her back turned on the man she loves any longer. She rolls over to look at him. His eyes are wide and vulnerable. 'Sure of what?' she asks, her voice harsh.

'That he knew something. I was so sure he was a monster I turned into a monster myself. I can't believe I did that.'

'You said you'd done it before,' she says.

'Yes. Twice, in the Legion. To men I'd seen kill with my own eyes. But Campbell didn't know anything. He was innocent. And I . . .' His voice trails off. He rolls on to his back and covers his face with his hands.

'You thought you were doing the right thing.'

He shakes his head. 'You told me to stop. You told me again and again. And I wouldn't listen. I was so sure.'

She takes a deep breath. 'Listen to me. You made a mistake. We all made an awful mistake. And you . . . you did turn into a monster. I was . . . I was scared of you in there, you understand? Not just frightened for you. Frightened of you.'

'I'm sorry. Danielle, I'm so sorry, so sorry.'

'I know you are.' She moves closer, rolls on top of him, so she is resting with her head above his, their eyes just inches apart. 'And it can't ever happen again. You understand that? Not *ever*.'

Wide eyed, he nods. She closes her eyes and breathes deeply with relief.

'You made a mistake,' she says. 'So did I. Well, if there's one thing I've gotten good at, it's making mistakes. I bet you don't have my experience. So let me tell you. You know what you do with mistakes? You learn from them and you let them pass. We don't pretend it never happened, but we don't pick at it either. We let it scab over and heal. That's what we're going to do. Understand?'

He nods again. She kisses him.

'I don't deserve you,' he says, his voice warm but oddly distant. He sits up a little and looks at her as if he is seeing her for the first time. 'I don't. I truly don't.'

'In the words of Clint Eastwood,' Danielle says drily, 'deserve's got nothin' to do with it.'

She kisses him with a passion she does not really feel. He doesn't move. She takes his right hand and puts it on her breast, then takes his left and kisses it, takes his thick fingers into her mouth, presses herself against him until she can feel him reacting. He frees his hands and grabs her, pulls her against his hardness as he kisses her harshly, and she sighs, feeling herself react to the inevitable tug of desire, letting herself disappear in it. Her hips start to move almost involuntarily against his. He opens his mouth to say something.

'Don't,' she whispers. 'Don't say anything. Let's forget about everything. At least until tomorrow.'

'I'm going back to London today,' Keiran says, over morning coffee and *tartines* at the Brasserie de la Reine. He does not look directly at anyone else at the table save for Danielle, who gathers she has somehow escaped his wrath, perhaps by protesting, however feebly, last night. 'I'm done.'

'I understand,' Angus says. 'But we need you to teach whoever we get to replace you. Give them the files you've found, the network access, everything.'

'I'll send you a CD. I'm *done*. I'm leaving Paris today.'

'We all are,' Estelle says.

Danielle looks at her. 'What?'

'We've got everything we can get here. We're all going to meet with the foundation, back in London.'

'The foundation,' Keiran says scornfully. 'And what can they do for you?'

'Give us direction,' Angus says.

'You don't need direction. You need to have some fucking sense knocked into you. You say you want to help the world's poor and you wind up torturing an innocent man. And you're still trying to justify it. You don't know fuck-all about the poor and down-trodden, you just want to fight the powers that be, because you love being a romantic outlaw. You say businesses exploit the Third World, and that's why its people are so pitiable and deprived. You stupid, selfish cunt. The Third World is hopelessly poor and sick and ignorant because it's been hopelessly poor and sick and ignorant for ever, and its governments are corrupt sociopathic kleptocracies. Free trade, big business, capital invest-ment, globalization, all the things you hate, those are the *only fucking hope* of the people you say you want to save. What's really going on is that *you're* exploiting the poor, the sick, the slaves, you exploit them as your excuse to fight the only force that has a real fucking chance of helping them. You make me sick.'

'Keiran, mate—'

'Don't call me mate. Our friendship is over. Is that clear?'

After a moment Angus nods. He looks as if he has just been punched in the gut.

'I'm on the three p.m. Eurostar. Pick a different train. I'm going to pack.' Keiran downs his espresso and leaves the brasserie. Angus and Estelle look at one another.

'The foundation,' Laurent says. 'At last. I hope they're worth the wait.'

London

8

Danielle has not been to London for years. After two months in Paris it seems ugly, dirty, dark, unfriendly. They walk from Waterloo station across the muddy Thames. Even at night the Circle Line is overcrowded and running late. They have to push their way through a crowd to get themselves and their luggage on board, and are rewarded with glares from other passengers that simultaneously condemn and look right through them, as if they are both evil incarnate and do not exist. Estelle has booked a short-term two-bedroom flat just south of Euston station. The flat is small, the furnishings wilted and impersonal, the beds lumpy and creaky. Danielle wishes they could have stayed in Paris.

They meet the foundation's representative the next morning in a temporary office near Green Park, grey-blue carpet and fake wood panelling and a conference phone in the middle of the oak conference table. It reminds Danielle of the office in Bangalore where she worked, once upon a time. The foundation is personified by a lean, wolfish, white-haired man named Philip. Faded tattoos are visible beneath the sleeves of Philip's blue button-down shirt. His business-casual dress is entirely at odds with his taut body language and alert expression. Danielle gets the same kind of impression she did from Laurent at first, that he is constantly holding himself back from physical action.

'You've done excellent work,' he assures them. 'Bloody excellent. Don't let anyone tell you different. And don't get cold feet. I can see that you might. Don't let it happen. You're saving lives. You're making the world a better place. The worst thing the money bastards who run the world have done is set things up so this is the only way they can be overthrown. They figure, people who aren't willing to do the hard things can't touch them, and the people who are willing, they *are* them. We have to be the third way. We have to be hard men with hearts of gold. I don't like it any more than you. But that's the way the game is rigged. It's the only way to possibly win.'

'Spare us the inspiration,' Angus says. 'Motivation is not our problem. Our problem is we stuck our necks out and didn't find anything.'

'Of course you did. You broke their system wide open. If this Campbell doesn't say anything . . . You say you don't think he will?'

'I think we put the fear of God into him,' Laurent says. 'Or at least the fear of us.'

He actually sounds amused. Danielle looks at him and wonders where the recent remorseful, self-doubting Laurent went.

'He promised to say nothing and to resign next month,' Angus says.

'And you believe him?' Philip asks.

'He was passionately convincing,' Laurent says.

'He might change his mind.'

Angus says, 'He seemed impressed by our detailed knowledge of where his sisters and his sainted mother live.'

'We wouldn't,' Estelle says quickly, seeing Danielle's expression. 'It's a bluff. But he doesn't know that. He's got good reason to take our threats seriously.'

Philip looks at Danielle with a concerned expression. 'Danielle Leaf, yes? You're the recent volunteer?'

Danielle nods. Philip looks at Angus.

'We trust her completely,' Angus says firmly.

'Well,' Philip says. 'Of course we trust your judgement. And you are Laurent Cinq-Mars of Justice International?'

'I am.'

'You and your organization have impressive CVs.'

'We try,' Laurent says. 'And who are you?'

Philip pauses. 'How much do you know about the foundation?'

'Almost nothing.'

'That's the way we prefer it. I'm sure you understand. We don't even have a name. Security through obscurity. But in broad strokes, we are a group of activists who have come together, aided by a number of wealthy supporters who believe in our cause but feel that their role is to support rather than take the risks that we take, in order to be a counterbalance to some of the world's more egregious examples of corporate exploitation.'

'You talk like a vice-president,' Laurent observes.

'I've been a vice-president,' Philip says. 'I've also been a convict, a drug addict and a punk musician, if you're questioning my bona fides. I've spent months sleeping rough. I've broken bones at demonstrations. I've negotiated million-pound contracts. The foundation is not some fly-by-night group of freaks and misfits with a single "sugar daddy", to use your lovely American phrase. We are a thoughtful and professional group. And we think it behoves us to sound thoughtful and professional.'

Laurent nods, satisfied.

'So,' Philip says, 'to continue. However convincing Mr Campbell may have sounded, we agree that it's best that you stay out of France for the foreseeable future. Losing Mr Kell is regrettable, but he has agreed to perform knowledge transfer to our chosen replacement, yes? Or at least intends to document everything?'

Angus nods.

'Mr Kell isn't himself a disclosure risk, is he?' Philip asks. 'I gather he's leaving because he's become disenchanted—'

'No,' Angus says shortly. 'Keiran won't talk.'

'Well then. We're still in a favourable position. We have no smoking gun, but our plan never called for one. We have full access to everything Kishkinda knows. Pulling you out of France on a precautionary basis means we can't move against their management there. But we have developed a new strategy based on the information you uncovered. Specifically, that Kishkinda is in takeover talks.'

Angus looks at Philip quizzically. 'What does that have to do with us?'

'Terre,' Philip says. 'They own forty per cent. Effective control. It's time to move up the food chain and go after the big dog. We need to show them, and this Zulu Fields outfit, that owning the Kishkinda mine is not worth the risk. If we convince Terre to shut down the mine, the battle is won. And Terre is based right here in London.'

'What are you suggesting?'

'A few visible actions, a few heart-to-heart conversations with Terre's senior management, and they will crumble.'

Danielle knows what that means. More violence. Kidnapping or mugging Terre's management, threatening them and their families with worse if they don't leave the company.

'We'll know when it's working,' Philip continues. 'We'll see it in the share price. We'll make owning Kishkinda uneconomical. And nobody else will want to buy it and risk the same thing happening to them. They'll have no choice but to shut it down. The City and Wall Street will demand it.'

'Sounds lovely,' Angus says. 'Let's return to the world of specifics and details, shall we? What exactly would you like us to do next?'

'We need to announce to the world that Terre is under assault, and make it clear that Kishkinda is the cause. Something public, to make the City take notice. But nothing drastic. An obvious but unexercised option of violence. The specifics?' Philip shrugs. 'Your bailiwick. Do whatever you think is right.'

'This is a whole new kettle of fish,' Estelle says sceptically. 'Kishkinda was one thing, but Terre . . . How big are they again?'

'Eight billion pounds of revenue in the last year,' Philip says. 'They're an elephant. Once roused they'll be enormously dangerous. That's true. But they're also slow and clumsy. A little group like you can dance around them as long as you need to. So long as you're careful. Remember, they're a business. Your job is to be a thorn in their side that it is cheaper to have removed than to destroy.'

'And they have an office in London?' Laurent asks.

'Yes,' Philip says. 'Hammersmith.'

For weeks, Danielle's image of the future ended with the protest, as if it were an opaque wall at which the road of time ended. But now they have left Paris she finds herself once again contemplating what is to come. She doesn't really want to. The distant future has always frightened her. She has lived her life in increments of a few months – a new boyfriend, a new project, a new place to live. Part of what terrified her about law school was the way it made her future stretch out visibly for years; passing the bar, articling, years as a junior lawyer at some firm, a bland red carpet paving the way to being old. She has been content not knowing where she will be, what she will be doing or who she will be with six months from now. Long-term plans seemed like stagnation.

But now that she has found a man she wants to spend her life with, the future terrifies her even more, because she can't imagine, or doesn't want to, what it could possibly be. Her voice is thin with trepidation when she brings up the subject that night.

'What's going to happen to us?' she asks.

Laurent lies on their bed reading the *Guardian*, wearing only jeans, his tattoos lurid against the pale flowered bedspread. He looks at her quizzically. 'What do you mean?'

'I mean, all this. What we're doing. What are we doing?' she asks.

The question isn't entirely rhetorical. When she first came to Paris, the idea of fighting Kishkinda seemed like just and noble revenge for having been captured, beaten, pursued and nearly murdered by the company's thugs in India. Breaking into their headquarters to uncover whatever explosive secret had got Jayalitha murdered, and organizing a huge anti-corporate protest to cover the break-in, that had been both reasonable and rewarding. But kidnapping and torturing a man Danielle is now sure was innocent – and now this new, equally disturbing plan, one intended to damage Kishkinda's share price rather than unearth

Jayalitha's secret – have made her wonder. Are Angus and Estelle and their foundation just flailing about at random, trying to attack Kishkinda by any means they can, with no real strategy? She wants revenge, she wants to help Angus and Estelle, and the children poisoned by Kishkinda, but surely there must be some limit to how far she and Laurent will go. When will they have to say enough and dissociate themselves from this war? Or are they, perhaps, already past that point?

'Are we just going to keep going?' she asks. 'Keep on breaking the law in the name of a better world until we get caught and thrown in jail? Even if we win, what happens next – we go on to the next company?'

'No,' Laurent says.

'You don't know how glad I am to hear you say that.'

'No, when this is over, when Kishkinda has been stopped, you and I will go to New York. I will do work there, peaceful work, legal work, for Justice International. You will too, if you like. We won't join Angus and Estelle in their endless war.'

'How does JI feel about you doing it now?'

He shrugs. 'They've been busy in India, getting our people out of jail. Their blood is boiling. Anything I can do to hurt Kishkinda, they support. But this kind of destructive activism, it isn't what we do, not usually. When I left the Legion I never intended to go to war again. But I suppose sometimes your war finds you.'

'So when this is over we move to New York,' Danielle says. She wants this to be very clear.

'Yes. Maybe soon. I think our next action might be decisive.'

Danielle swallows. While no one will actually get hurt, the 'next action' he and Angus and Estelle have been talking about is in some ways far more drastic than kidnapping and torturing Jack Campbell.

'I don't want to sound like a stuck record,' she says, 'but I don't know about our next action either.'

Laurent puts down the newspaper and cocks his head at her inquisitively.

'It's so *major*. If we get caught, we'll seem like . . . I thought we were going to be subtle. Invisible. Like Keiran always says.'

'Keiran isn't with us any more. This time circumstances call for a frontal attack, not stealth.'

'I don't think we should do it,' she says. In her nervousness it comes out with more hostility than she intended. 'Something else, maybe. But not this. It makes me feel like I did before we . . . before Campbell.'

'Come on,' Laurent says, smiling thinly. 'It'll be a valuable learning experience. I'll teach you how to build a bomb.'

'I really don't want to know.'

'You never know when it might be useful.'

'You think this is funny?' Danielle asks, appalled.

Laurent shrugs. 'Black comedy. I'm sorry.'

'You should be. Jesus. We're talking about . . . how can you fucking *joke*?'

'It's my way of dealing with being angry at you.'

At first she doesn't know what to say to that. She sits at the end of the bed and looks at him. She feels cold and frightened. 'Angry at me? At *me*? For what?'

'Because you're acting like a tourist. Sometimes I wonder if you are a tourist. Everything you do. Just visiting, trying things out, moving on. You've never belonged to anything. You've never given yourself to anything. Or anyone. You've never committed yourself to anything enough that your actions have real consequences. And then you wonder why the world seems so meaningless. So you run back to your daddy's bank account and find some new thing to try to make yourself happy. You try being with me, you try being political, working for a better world, and then you find out it doesn't happen overnight, it requires years of hard work, and doing things you don't enjoy, and we can't have that, can we? You're not willing to make sacrifices. You don't even know how.'

'You're talking about building a *bomb*,' Danielle says after a moment. 'And you're angry because I won't support that?'

'It's no more a bomb than a movie prop. It won't go off. It's performance art. You know that. But you think it's awful. No, you think it's beneath you. Like maybe you think I'm beneath you.'

'*What?*'

'Maybe I'm just your man of the hour. A little excitement, a little military revolutionary fun, but soon it's time to move on, isn't it? Is that what you've been working up to? Is it time to run back to Daddy and find a nice corporate lawyer to marry? If so, just tell me now and walk away. Please. Tell me now. It will hurt less.'

'No,' Danielle says. 'No, no, no, no, *no*. I love you. That hasn't changed. That won't change. Jesus, Laurent, if you believe anything I've ever said, believe that. Please.'

'I want to.'

'Then do. God. How long have you been thinking this?'

'I've been worried I wasn't worthy of you since the day we met,' he says.

'Well, stop worrying. That's . . . that's an order.'

He smiles faintly, warming her heart. The fight, and it wasn't much of a fight, is over, and they have passed through it OK. 'Yes, ma'am,' he says, and snaps a salute.

She doesn't want to risk anything further. But she has to. 'I love you, but we shouldn't do this.'

'I'll tell you what,' Laurent says after a long moment. 'We will do this. But if it doesn't work as planned, if anything goes awry, then you and I will follow your instincts, give up and move to New York.'

'We won't be going anywhere if we get caught,' she says harshly. 'Except jail and the front page.'

He nods. 'Yes. But we have to give them this one last chance, this one last risk. We owe them that much.'

She doesn't want to. But it sounds so reasonable. She nods helplessly.

*   *   *

A bomb, Danielle learns, consists of four elements. The case that contains it, in this instance a gleaming metal suitcase. The secondary explosive, which makes up most of the bomb's bulk and power. Here, fuel oil and the common fertilizer ammonium nitrate, mixed to the consistency of mud, cut to the size of bricks and baked in an ordinary oven until it feels like bread. Touch a match to secondary explosive, and it will puff into flame so quickly your eyebrows are unlikely to survive the encounter, but it will not explode; only a shock wave from some initiating explosion can detonate it.

This detonation is the job of the primary explosive, which Laurent assures them can also be made with the spoils of a shopping trip to a supermarket and a hardware store, but in this bomb consists of industrial blasting caps supplied by the foundation, triggered by twelve volts of DC power. The blasting caps are connected to the last element, the trigger. Bombs can be triggered remotely, by mobile phones; automatically, by cheap alarm clocks; by motion, with the aid of a mercury switch; or directly, by simply completing an electrical circuit, hopefully from a considerable distance. There can be a fifth element: shrapnel, ball bearings or nails packed around the secondary explosive, designed to shred any soft material – such as human beings – unfortunate enough to be close to the device when it goes off. But this bomb includes no shrapnel. There would be no point. It is not intended to ever explode.

Laurent orders Angus, Estelle and Danielle out of the garage while he attaches the trigger. In order to be convincing, the bomb has to look potentially lethal, as if the trigger were erroneously connected. Laurent wants as few people as possible around during final assembly, in case of a slip of the hand. Danielle waits on the street outside the garage, located beneath a railway line in an industrial area of south London, watching for oncoming trains. If one appears, they are instructed to shout and warn Laurent before it rattles overhead and causes his entire workplace to shake dangerously. Other than that risk she is not worried for Laurent. He has built the device with such confidence, such total lack of fear, that the odds of his hands slipping seem like those of a Tour de France winner falling off his bicycle on a dry, flat road. One thing she has learned in the last hour is that successful bomb-making is more about steady hands and confidence than any elaborate chemistry or engineering. If anything it is frighteningly easy.

Laurent appears in the grimy brick doorway a few moments later, smiling. '*Fini!*' he calls out. 'Safe as houses. Come in.'

The open suitcase looks as if it has been filled with children's mud cakes, into which two small discs have been pressed. These blasting caps, which look like ceramic rather than high explosive, are connected via two sets of wires to a cheap alarm clock taped to the secondary explosive with duct tape. It looks completely amateurish, like some sort of high-school science experiment.

'If it exploded,' Danielle asks, 'what would it do?'

Laurent considers a moment. 'We'd get smeared all over the walls. But the walls wouldn't be there. This place is made of brick, they'd fly fifty metres. Probably open a ten-metre hole in the railway line.'

'Just from that?' Estelle asks.

'Just from this.' Laurent closes the briefcase. 'Let's go make our delivery.'

'Need a hand?' Angus asks.

Laurent shrugs. 'It's not too bad.' He hoists the briefcase. All the others flinch.

'Don't worry,' he says, smiling. 'It's not dangerous. I've wired it so it looks like the real thing, but you could hit this with a sledgehammer and it wouldn't go off.'

'If you say so,' Estelle says, unconvinced.

Laurent lets go of the bomb. It slams into the ground with a loud metallic *clunk*. Danielle gasps; Angus twitches; Estelle cries out.

'Satisfied?' he asks.

'Prat,' Angus mutters.

'Now you won't be afraid of it on the way over,' Laurent says.

*   *   *

Assembling the bomb was easy. Depositing it at Kishkinda's London offices, and calling it to the attention of the media, is more challenging. A single overlooked hair can provide the police with DNA evidence. London is full of thousands of closed-circuit cameras; they would certainly be captured on camera en route to Terre, and if their car is ever associated with the bomb, the police might track down such footage, or witnesses might remember them. Phone calls made to alert the media and authorities to the bomb's presence can be easily traced to a specific location if from a land line, and a fairly small region if from a mobile phone, and cameras and witnesses at those sites are also a concern. Danielle has never appreciated how many pitfalls modern criminals face.

Criminals and terrorists. She realizes, en route to the suitcase's destination, that 'terrorist' is, somehow, exactly what she has become. Their reluctance to use extreme violence does not exclude them from the label. Their objective is to terrorize Terre's management.

Terre's office is in Hammersmith, but their destination is on the other side of the city; a deserted building on a quiet street in north London with no onlooking cameras. Angus parks their Vauxhall with tinted windows, another exhibit of the foundation's largesse, across the street. Laurent carries the suitcase to the steps outside the building and leaves it there. Danielle watches him, trembling nervously. If anyone sees her in the next thirty seconds, she will likely be jailed for life.

Laurent comes back towards the car, walking with exaggerated jauntiness; she emerges and joins him on the pavement, and they walk away. Danielle reminds herself to look casual, forgettable. There is no one in sight but she is icily sure some old biddy is watching them from behind a window. Her heart thunders in her chest. Her legs feel fluttery, she is certain she is walking with visible weakness. She is sick with fear.

'No more,' she says breathlessly. 'I can't do this any more. Never again. This is the last time. I'm sorry. I just can't. No more.'

Laurent nods. 'I agree.'

'Why us? Why did we have to go walking? Why do we have to make the phone calls? It's safe for them. They're in the car. They just have to sit and make sure it happens. Why did you say we would do it?'

'It's sensible. I'm sorry. His dreadlocks, her purple hair, they would stand out. We have a better chance of going unnoticed.'

Danielle relaxes a tiny bit when they have gone a few blocks. She may still be doomed, but if so, at least it has already happened, the awful waiting is over. Laurent takes out his mobile phone. Purchased for cash days ago, untraceable. He dials a number and waits briefly.

'A-1 Courier Service?' he asks, hamming up his French accent. 'Yes. I'd like a courier to come pick up a package. The recipient's name is Terre PLC, 26 Paddenswick Road, London W6 0UB.' He gives the address of the deserted house they have just left. 'The name of the sender is the Kishkinda Liberation Front. Yes. Thank you.'

He turns off the phone and puts it away.

She looks at him. 'Kishkinda Liberation Front?'

He shrugs. 'A little insouciance. We can almost skip phoning in the official bomb threat. The police will figure it out from that alone. It will leak to the newspapers, the City will go haywire, their shares will plummet. All from those three little words. And one bomb.'

'Let's just go,' she says.

Then there is an intensely bright flicker of light behind them. For a fraction of a second Danielle mistakes it for a camera flash.

9

The noise and the shock wave hit like a wall falling on them, the air itself pulsates, not like regular noise, but as a force tearing at her ears. She doesn't hear anything after that, doesn't hear the sounds of buildings crumbling, cars flung into one another like children's toys, alarm sirens. The shock wave forces Danielle on to her knees. What she remembers most is seeing it ripple down the street like a gust of wind. The shock wave moves at six hundred miles an hour, the speed of sound – it takes only a fraction of a second to pass through her line of sight, but she swears afterwards that she saw the storm front of the explosion advance like a hurtling wave, shattering windows all the way down the street.

It actually takes a few seconds, stunned, deafened and on her scraped knees, for her to associate what has just happened with the bomb they built earlier today.

Laurent helps her to her feet, takes her hand, leads her on, walking away from the blast. His shirt is torn and there is blood on his arm from some kind of shrapnel. Danielle follows him robotically, in shock, unable to think, her legs marching by themselves. The world is soundless, as if someone has pushed the global MUTE button. They pass ambulances and police cars racing the other way, sirens flashing. They keep walking. Her knees hurt. She looks down and sees they are bloody – the material has been scraped off her jeans. The world seems to be moving too fast around them, she doesn't have time to react to any sensory stimuli. People, old people and mothers mostly, are standing out in the streets or in their front gardens, talking to one another with concerned expressions, on their mobile phones, looking back past Danielle and Laurent. A couple of them approach, meaning to help, but Laurent waves them off and they keep walking. They mustn't be noticed, mustn't be remembered, mustn't be caught. Danielle knows this but can barely remember why. A crackling buzz in her mind, overwhelmingly loud, drowns out all attempts at coherent thought.

She isn't sure how far they've walked when she begins to emerge from her cocoon of shock. Miles, she thinks. Her feet ache. So does her head. Her skinned knees have clotted over but bloodstains dangle like tongues on the shins of her torn jeans. Her ears ring as if she carries a fire alarm with her, but at the edge of her perception she can hear the noises of the city, traffic, pedestrian chatter. They are in a more built-up area now, a busy street with a few stores, a Boots pharmacy, a newsagent, a post office, a café. A red double-decker bus passes. The people all around act as if nothing has changed, as if the world has not ended. She tugs on Laurent's hand to make him stop and turn to face her.

'I need to sit down,' she says. She knows from the vibrations in her throat that she is speaking loudly, but she can barely hear herself.

He nods. They enter the café. The furnishings are cheap uncomfortable plastic, the plates and cutlery old and chipped, the stink of grease pervasive, the service malevolent, the decor non-existent, but it seems like a sanctuary. They order bacon sandwiches and cups of tea. The fat old woman behind the counter gives them a sharp mistrustful look, but Danielle suspects she does that with everyone. It is a great relief to sit on the plastic chairs. The sandwiches taste like ashes.

'Maybe they . . .' she begins, and then stops. She can't think of a maybe.

Laurent shakes his head violently. 'Not here.'

She nods. It doesn't matter. Angus and Estelle must be dead. Danielle cannot even imagine how they might have survived the blast. The thought seems curiously unreal, as if it is not they who died, just their characters in a video game. Angus and Estelle can select NEW GAME and pop back into this world untouched any time they like.

Only minutes after returning to the apartment Danielle realizes she has no recollection of how they got there, of any time between the café and now. Laurent goes straight to the shower without saying a word. She slumps on to the couch in front of the television. After a moment, not allowing herself to think about it, she takes the remote and turns on Teletext, the BBC's archaic pre-Internet system of textual news updates. The crude white letters on a black screen are like time-travelling back to the 1980s. The lead story is BOMB IN NORTH LONDON – FIVE DEAD.

She can't bring herself to select the story and read more. She clicks the television off. She vaguely knows she should cry, tear out her hair, wear sackcloth and ashes, but it all still feels so unreal. And besides, her hair isn't long enough to tear. For some reason this thought produces a ghostly smile which immediately prompts a stab of horrible, unspeakable guilt. Danielle tells herself that she just participated in the accidental murder of five people, including two good friends. It sounds ridiculous. She is very tired. She decides to go to sleep. In her heart she really believes that when she wakes up all this will somehow be over, erased, forgotten like a nightmare.

For a moment when she wakes she doesn't remember what has happened. Then it hits her and she moans as if struck, curls into a fetal ball, unable to deal with the enormity of it all. Her whole body is shot through with icy shivers. Her mind keeps recoiling from the idea and then returning to it again, as if picking at a scab. Breathing hard, she sits up. Laurent is sitting in a chair, staring dully at her. She rushes past him to the bathroom and throws up. Eventually she takes a shower. It doesn't make her feel clean. She scrubs angrily at her skinned knees, making them sting like fire. When she comes out, wrapped in a towel, Laurent does not seem to have moved, but there is a newspaper on the bed in front of him, the *Evening Standard*. BOMB KILLS FIVE is the headline.

She sits on the bed and reads. The dead have already been identified. Angus, Estelle, an old woman, a young mother and her infant daughter. Danielle cries out loudly when she reads that last. Seventeen others were wounded but are expected to recover. The article calls Angus and Estelle 'anarchists with a history of violence'.

'We probably shouldn't be here,' Laurent says. His voice is devoid of life. 'I don't think Estelle booked this place in her real name. But even so. They might be able to find it.'

'What happened? How could this happen?'

'I guess I fucked up. Maybe, when I dropped it on the ground, to prove how safe it was . . .'

Then, incredibly, Laurent begins to giggle.

'Laurent,' Danielle says, when the giggling continues. 'Stop it. Stop it!' She stands up and shakes him. His laughter deepens, his whole body shakes, tears begin to roll down his cheeks. Frightened, Danielle takes a step back and slaps him hard.

The laughter stops as if she has flicked a switch. He stares at her with red eyes. 'Thanks. I needed that. I'm sorry. I don't know where that came from.'

'Don't do it again.' She feels as if the ground has dropped away to a steep angle. The one thing she had thought was bedrock was Laurent's stability.

'I won't,' he promises.

The telephone begins to ring. Both of them jump, then stare at the phone as if it too might explode.

'I'll get it,' she says. Maybe it is the police. She almost hopes so. At least this would be over. She deserves to be captured. She deserves to be jailed. They both do.

'This is Philip,' a hoarse voice says. 'What the fuck is going on?'

'This is not a setback,' Philip says. 'This is fucking *catastrophic*. The police connected the bomb to Kishkinda. The papers are full of speculation that Angus and Estelle didn't act alone, they had no history of bombs. They're looking for you. And us.'

They are again in the foundation's rented boardroom near Green Park. Somehow a day and a night have passed, somehow time has not stopped. Danielle's night was spent in endless non-sleep, dipping into the pool of unconsciousness for only minutes at a time, then waking and nervously expecting a knock on the door – the police have come, they have tracked their phone calls, or their walk down the street away from the bomb, or the manufacturer of the metal suitcase, or their intrusion into the Paris offices. Each time Danielle woke she thought of Angus and

Estelle, the new mother and the infant girl, and howled softly with anguish. Beside her, Laurent slept soundly.

'Five people dead, including Angus and Estelle,' Philip continues. 'Seventeen wounded. Millions of pounds of damage. Every police officer in London trying to track the bomb. And Paris as well, now they have found the bugs you planted. The purpose of this meeting is to officially inform you that the foundation is temporarily disbanding. We strongly suggest you leave the country. If you are arrested, and to be honest at this point we consider this quite likely, I *very* strongly suggest you do not breathe a *word* about us. We have friends and ears in unlikely places high and low. Ministers' offices and prison cells. We can't afford to have our existence investigated and testified to. We will not be destroyed by your colossal mistake. We will ensure our invisibility. By any means necessary. Do I make myself *perfectly clear*?'

'Transparent,' Laurent says.

Danielle nods.

Philip takes a deep breath and forces himself to relax. His face sags and suddenly he looks old and weak. 'Go home, both of you,' he says. 'Go back to America.'

Danielle bursts out crying in the middle of yoga class that afternoon. She has to be helped out of the room. She takes a long shower in the changing room and manages to keep her tears in when she leaves the building, at least until she is out in the Primrose Hill sunshine. It is a thirty-minute walk back to the flat. She cries all the way. At an intersection halfway there, she is nearly struck by a car, and after leaping to safety she almost wishes she hadn't.

'They're going to catch us, aren't they?' Danielle asks, sitting in her chair, staring down at the street outside, clogged with London traffic and pedestrians. A curdled haze of cloud hangs over the city.

'Not likely. We'll be gone tomorrow.'

'Running away isn't going to help. Everyone in the world is looking for us.'

'How will they find us?' Laurent asks.

'I don't know. Something. Some little clue.'

'No.' His voice is assured, steady; there is no sign that yesterday's crazy giggling fit ever happened. 'You know why most criminals are caught? Because they're stupid. Or they panic under pressure and make flagrant errors. Don't believe what you see on television. TV police win because it's what people want to see. The truth is most police and security services, even the elite, even the FBI and MI6, aren't as bright and well trained as they'd have you believe. Smart people who don't panic can run rings around them. You wouldn't believe the damage a single determined, competent person could wreak on a country like this, if one of us really tried. They won't catch us. They count on mistakes. We didn't make any.'

'You made a pretty fucking big one, didn't you?'

'Yes,' Laurent says. 'I did. And in wars mistakes kill people. And I'm sorry for them. I'm terribly sorry. If I could trade my life for theirs I would. But I can't. Neither can you. So stop acting like you want to be caught. You think they should catch us, don't you? You think we deserve it.'

'Don't we?'

'No. Our intentions were pure. Our objectives were noble.'

Danielle half laughs. 'Pure. Noble. We *killed* people. Have you read about the ones who lived? One of them will never walk again.'

'What can I say?' Laurent shrugs. 'It's horrific. It's no more horrific than what's happened to the brain-damaged children in Kishkinda, or the ones who will never walk, or Jayalitha and her children. Remember what you told me about making mistakes? You move on. We will move on to New York. We will heal. It will be slow, it will be painful, but I promise, we will heal. And it *wasn't you*. It was me. It was my mistake. I'm the killer. You did nothing wrong, you have no responsibility.'

'I could have stopped you. Or left you.'

She lets the last sentence hang in the air.

'Don't leave me,' he says, confidence suddenly drained from his voice. 'Please. Not now. Please. If you've ever believed anything I've said, believe this. You're the only woman I've ever met who might save me.'

She turns and looks at him. 'Save you from what?'

'Myself,' he says. 'Come with me to New York. Please. We'll put all this behind us. It will all be over, all of it, for ever. I swear.'

Laurent has gone out for a long walk when her phone rings. Danielle stares at it for a long time, lets the rings fill the empty space of the room a half-dozen times, knowing in the cold centre of her heart that the caller bears bad news. She fears the unknown so badly she can hardly bear to make it known. But she forces herself to answer.

'Danielle?' A familiar voice, but one she is too distraught to place immediately. 'Is Laurent there?'

'Who is this?'

'Keiran.'

'Keiran?' She blinks. 'What do you want?'

'Is Laurent there?'

'No.'

'Good,' Keiran says. 'You should come and meet me. Right this minute.'

'What? Why?'

'Come alone,' Keiran says. 'It's about Laurent. I've found out who he really is and what he's doing. What he's really doing. I have to tell you. It's . . . appalling.'

10

Keiran arrives fifteen minutes early at their agreed destination, a Starbucks on the south side of the Thames, between Blackfriars Bridge and the ominous tower of the Tate Modern. He feels nervous. Not just because he is exhausted, has been at his computer non-stop since hearing the news of the bomb. Keiran doesn't want to let his cloak of invisibility slip like this. This is a public place, it should be easy to get away and lose himself if he needs to, but that doesn't make him feel safe. Not with what he now knows about Laurent. Danielle is in love with him, she might have told him. This isn't safe. But it's necessary. He knows her well enough to know this has to be done in person.

He orders a black coffee and sits with his back to the wall. He sees Danielle approach, on the pedestrian thoroughfare perpetually buzzing with hundreds of people that is the South Bank of the Thames. She looks pale and weak. Her smile when she sees him does not reach her eyes, and when she enters, she pauses for a fraction of a second to look around the Starbucks. Her nervousness alleviates his; an equality of fear.

She orders a chai latte and sits across from him.

'Thanks for coming,' he says.

She nods acknowledgement.

He reaches into his leather jacket, draws out a manila envelope and gives it to her. 'Have a look.'

Danielle opens the envelope and spills its sheaf of A4 paper on to the wooden, coffee-stained table. The first page contains two black-and-white pictures of a young Laurent, height markers behind him. Mug shots. His hair is up in a black mohawk but he is recognizable, staring angrily into the camera, then looking to the side, his jaw clenched. The name on the small chalkboard he holds reads 'SYLVAIN BRISEBOIS'. She stares at it for a moment, then starts on the next three pages, his criminal record. She reads intently. Her hands begin to shake.

'He probably told you his real name was Patrice,' Keiran says.

Danielle doesn't react.

'After what he did he had to get two false names. One from stealing a dead child's birth certificate. Security in Quebec was non-existent until 2001, anyone could walk into a church registry and steal an identity. Just like *Day of the Jackal*. The Foreign Legion demands a government ID when you join them, before they give you a new name, and he couldn't give them his real one. Not when he was wanted for rape and murder. From what I can gather he was associated with a biker gang in Montreal, the Rock Machine. But never actually a member. There's been a war on between them and the Hell's Angels for years now. Hundreds dead, bombs, shootings, bars burned, people disappeared. Sylvain disappeared too. Age twenty-two. Then Patrice appeared, for maybe a month. Then Laurent turned up at the Foreign Legion office.'

'I knew all this already,' Danielle says. He knows she is lying. 'So he grew up fucked up. That was years ago. He's different now.'

'If you say so.'

'What do you care about what he used to be?'

Keiran says, 'I don't know if you've been reading the news, but Kishkinda and Terre have been going through some interesting times lately.'

'Very funny.'

'We had quite an amazing run of bad luck as soon as Laurent appeared on the scene, didn't we? We get run out of India moments after he turns up, we smash and grab their Paris office and watch him torture a man for no gain, then a bomb goes off and kills Angus and Estelle. Look at the next report.'

The next document is highly technical, carefully formatted, full of numbers and medical-sounding terminology. It is twenty-three pages long. Some of the jaw-breaking words are grouped under headings with Indian-sounding names.

'It may not mean anything to you,' Keiran says, 'but—'

'No, it does,' she says slowly. 'It's like some of the documents they processed in the Bangalore office when I worked there. One of our clients was this big Hartford insurance company. It looks like an analysis of medical claim reports. Is that it? What does this have to do with anything?'

'Not quite. The people in this study were receiving medicine, not making claims. A drug study. A human trial.'

'Where did you get this? Some pharmaceutical company?'

'Almost. Drugs tested on humans, yes. But not by a pharmaceutical company. No. By Laurent's outfit. By Justice International.'

'Justice . . .' Danielle stares at Keiran for a long moment, eyes wide. Then she shakes her head. 'That doesn't make any sense. Where did you get this?'

Keiran sips his coffee before answering. 'I hacked in. And it wasn't fucking easy.' It would have been impossible without Shazam. Justice International's network security is invulnerable but for the single instance of one of their employees using Shazam to steal music from the Internet. 'I couldn't figure out why they ran such a tight ship. Until I got inside and saw P2's name on the firewall. Justice International is performing drug trials on the people sickened by Kishkinda. Is that clear enough? They're not trying to help them. They're not trying to shut down Kishkinda. What they do is test experimental drugs. Which, judging from that report, are often counterproductive. Sometimes lethal.'

'Why would they do that?' Danielle asks.

'Because they're being paid. Quite a lot. Six hundred thousand dollars materializes in their bank account on the first of every month. Not bad for a virtually unknown volunteer organization.'

'Who would pay them? What for?'

'Any drug company who wants to avoid petty little ethical concerns about drug testing. They spend lorry-loads of money every year on research that never goes anywhere because it fails human trials ten years down the road. If they test out their drugs on the quiet like this, as soon as they get out of the lab, before they've done any animal testing, if they secretly know in advance which drugs in their pipeline will be winners – that's worth *billions* to them. Billions every year. They're much bigger than Kishkinda or Terre. Kishkinda is a pimple on the face of a major pharmaceutical, that's how big they are. So they pay off Justice International with petty cash to find populations of sick people, cut off from civilization enough that the rest of the world will never know, and test a whole fucking cornucopia of new drugs on them. There're *dozens* of reports like that one. Most of them encrypted. I rescued that one from an automatic back-up that didn't get cleaned up, but from the file names, we're talking a lot of drugs here.'

'This is crazy. Laurent works for them.'

'That's my point.'

'No,' Danielle says. 'No.'

'Yes. He didn't join Angus and company to help. He joined to infiltrate and sabotage. To make sure they didn't find out the truth. And he used you to get in. First he led them to us in India, made sure they scared us out of the country, then he probably made sure we didn't find anything in Paris, and now every police force in the world is looking for you. From the moment he turned up, it's been nothing but disaster.'

'I'm sorry. No. You don't know him like I do. That's not possible.'

Keiran shakes his head. 'Look at the last report.'

DEBRIEFING: 2 MAY

Met with Voice at tertiary time/location. He arrived late and was eager to leave. Had many aggressive questions about his remuneration and demanded that it be doubled and its schedule accelerated. Refused to speak to me at first until I agreed. Eventually accepted I had no authority to do so. I feel Voice has become erratic, untrustworthy, and excessively motivated by immediate gain. Furthermore, I believe Voice has become emotionally involved with his entry point to an extent that has clouded his judgement. While she remains ignorant of his real activities, at

least to date, he actually threatened my own
personal security (and that of the board) in
the event that any action, physical or
legal, were taken against DL. I strongly
recommend no further utilization of Voice
without some means of securing intensified
loyalty.

That said, Voice has been as effective as
ever. Has located home address of
foundation member Philip Tasker, and
photographed two other believed members who
met with Tasker. DNA samples and
fingerprints have been acquired and
dispatched for analysis. Initial working
hypothesis seems likely but not yet
confirmed. Have received word from P2 that
this new information should lead to sound
evidence of foundation's true identity.
Voice also suggested an extreme course of
action which, though it would likely result
in a near-term cessation of foundation
activites, I vetoed. Viz. the 'accidental'
detonation of a powerful explosive device.
While of course you may overturn my veto I
very strongly recommend against it.

'A smoking gun,' Keiran says.

Danielle's world is swimming around her. 'A fake. It has to be
fake.' It's a set-up. It must be. Despite the logic, the supporting
documentation, the way it all makes a sickening, dizzying sense,
Keiran must be lying to her. Or fooled. Except Keiran doesn't get
fooled, not by things like this.

'It seemed too convenient at first,' Keiran admits, 'but I think,
from where I found it and how, that it's real. Some idiot took an
encrypted message, copied its text into a Word document so it

213

would look nicer for his boss, and foolishly trusted Word's password protection. Some idiot named Vijay. Probably the same bloke we met in Goa. Before Laurent got us out of that mess oh so conveniently. When P2 finds out he'll probably have Vijay's head. All the security in the world doesn't help when your people are careless and stupid. And people always are.'

Danielle can hardly hear him. 'It's not possible,' she says, clutching at straws. 'You didn't see what they did to him at the hut, where they locked me up. They beat the shit out of him.'

'Convenient how it happened in front of the window. Convenient how there were lots of little cuts and bruises but nothing serious. Convenient how easily you got away after that. And it certainly happened to a man who we both know wouldn't let little things like pain and suffering stand between him and what he wants.'

Danielle can't find any words.

'I'm sorry,' Keiran says. 'I would have been convinced too. I was convinced. I liked him. I respected him. Justice International does enough real anti-globalization work that Angus and the foundation fell for it too. And he's a fine actor. But I don't have to tell you that. I'm sorry.'

'I want you to leave,' Danielle says savagely. 'Get out. Get the fuck out.'

'You don't believe me yet? I can take you to a computer, show you the files.'

'You could have faked them.'

Keiran nods. 'True. I could have forged all of this. Almost all. I don't know nearly enough about medicine to forge that drug trial document. But even supposing I did, why would I? If for some reason I wanted to make trouble I could just go to the police, tell them I thought he built that bomb. I don't need to go through this kind of charade. But more than that. It makes sense. You're smart. You know that. It makes too much sense not to be true.'

'Get out.'

'I'm sorry. I'm sorry I had to be the one to tell you. If you need anything, anything at all, call me, any time.'

On the way back to their flat, through London streets warped by tears, the way back to Laurent who is also Patrice and may also be Sylvain, her knight who may also be a traitor, Danielle tries to consider her options, to make sense of what she has just heard. It doesn't really matter whether she believes it or not. It will haunt her, gnaw at her gut, until she knows for sure. She has to know. And there is only one way.

11

Laurent is back in the flat when she returns, packing with military efficiency, folding his clothes so neatly the creases could draw blood, assembling his possessions so they inhabit the minimum possible volume in his pack.

'Where have you been?' she asks.

'A long walk down the Embankment. You?'

'The other side. South Bank.'

'We probably passed each other.'

'Are you going to take me to visit Montreal after we get settled in New York?'

He shrugs. 'If you like.'

'Visit your family?'

'Montreal's nice in summer. But the winters are brutal.'

'It's Sylvain, isn't it?'

He drops a shirt, and in that moment she knows it's all true.

'What's Sylvain?' he asks.

'Your old name. Your real old name.'

'It says Patrice on the birth certificate.'

'But it says Sylvain on *your* birth certificate, doesn't it?'

'Where have you been?' he demands. 'Who have you been talking to?'

'Why do they call you Voice? Is that your other name?'

He looks at her, this time genuinely puzzled. 'What? Who?'

'You don't know, do you? Justice International. That's what they call you in the reports they send back about you. Voice. I guess it's a code name. I don't know why they bother. They didn't give me a code name.'

'I don't understand what you are saying,' Laurent says, approaching her, his expression gentle and concerned.

'But why did you make the bomb? So it went off, I mean. They didn't want you to. Did you hate Angus and Estelle that much? Or did they change their minds?'

He puts his hands on her shoulders and shakes her gently. 'Start making sense. Please.'

'I don't understand how you could do it,' she says. 'I'm impressed – I mean, to live a lie like that, for such a long time, to betray all the people who trusted you, who,' she starts to cry, 'who *loved* you, that can't be easy. I guess you're real tough, huh? I guess you're so tough it doesn't mean anything to you.'

'I don't know what you're talking about,' he says. Convincingly. But not nearly convincingly enough.

'I know what you did.' She has to fight to get the words out of her sob-clogged throat. 'I know what you're doing. Drug tests at Kishkinda. Scaring us out of India. Setting us up. Tracking down the foundation. The bomb – you killed, you *murdered* Angus and Estelle. Cold-blooded murder. How could you? How *could* you?'

'Who have you been talking to?'

'What does it matter?'

'Danielle. Who told you all this? It's not true. Who told you?'

'Don't lie to me. Don't you think you've lied to me enough? You might as well stop now. Start telling the truth just for a little fucking variety, why don't you?'

Laurent grabs her by the arms, turns, making her spin with him, and pushes her back, forcibly sitting Danielle down on the couch. He releases her, pulls a chair up and sits very close to her, his legs inside hers, their knees touching, and waits for her cries to subside. He looks intensely worried, for her, not himself. She feels an urge to lean forward, throw her arms around him and weep on his shoulder, and the wave of shame and rage she feels at this, realizing that even now some part of her wants this liar, traitor and murderer to console her, helps strengthen her, moves her from despair to cold fury.

'Tell me who told you this,' he says quietly.

'I'll tell you the truth when you tell me the truth,' she says, spitting out each word.

He studies her for some time. Then he nods. 'That's fair,' he says, his voice low. 'The truth is I do owe it to you to be fair.'

'That's so fucking big of you.'

'You're going to be safe. I made sure of that. I won't let anything happen to you.'

She thinks of the debriefing report. *Voice has become emotionally involved with his entry point to an extent that has clouded his judgement.* He does care for her. At least a little. But not enough to outweigh the awful things he has done, not even close.

'How could you do it?' she asks. 'The children in that village. You never wanted to shut down Kishkinda at all, did you? You wanted them to keep going. So they could keep poisoning children for you to test drugs on. For money. Was that it? You did it for money? That was all?'

Laurent relaxes slightly. 'It was a deal with the Devil. We sacrificed that one place so we could help many more of them, all over the world, with the money we got. JI got millions of dollars a year. Above the costs of the trials. We've saved many more people with that money than Kishkinda ever killed.'

'You're talking about children's lives like they're poker chips. How much money did you get? You personally.'

Laurent tilts his head uncomfortably. 'Eighty thousand a year. US dollars.'

'Pretty good for a rapist and a murderer.' She is almost blinded by rage. 'Who were you working for? What company?'

'It isn't a company.'

'Then what is it?'

'I'll show you. In just a moment.'

'Show me? Show me what? Stop dancing around and just tell me the truth or I'll . . .' She doesn't know what she'll do. But she knows it will be awful.

'Who told you all this?' Laurent asks. 'Keiran?'

Danielle shakes her head. 'I'm not going to tell you.'

'Yes, you are. It must be Keiran. Who else knows? The foundation?'

'We've got proof. We'll go to the newspapers. We can shut you down.'

'But you won't,' Laurent says.

'Why not?'

'Who else knows?'

'Fuck you.'

'Danielle,' Laurent says, his voice raw, 'you have to tell me who else knows. Please. It's important. I don't want to have to hurt you.'

Danielle's mouth slowly opens but no words escape.

'Please don't make it necessary. Please tell me. Don't lie. I'll know if you're lying.'

'Hurt me? What do you mean, hurt me?' It had never even crossed her mind that Laurent might threaten her, that the repercussions of confronting him might include danger. They are lovers. They have lived together, struggled together, enjoyed countless hours of whispered intimacy in one another's arms.

'I have to know who else knows. And exactly what they know.'

'Or what? You'll break my nose? Tie me up and stick my face in a bowl of water?'

Laurent does not speak.

'My God,' Danielle says. 'You would, wouldn't you?'

'We can't be together,' he says rapidly, his Quebecois accent more pronounced than usual. 'Maybe I wish we could but we can't. Not in this world. Maybe in some parallel dimension we're perfect for one another. In this world we're impossible. That's the reality. We both have to live with it. Understand? I have to live in the real world. Not fantasyland. And you do too. So *answer the fucking question*. Who else knows?'

Danielle looks at him wide eyed. Then she says, 'Keiran. I think just him.'

'Yes. Good,' Laurent says. 'Do you know where Keiran lives?'

'No.'

'Well. P2 had better fucking find out fast. Stay where you are.' Laurent stands and walks into their bedroom. For a moment she thinks of running for it, fleeing the room, down the hall and down the stairs; he will pursue but on the streets, in public, surely she will be safe, and they are only a few minutes' run from Euston station, she can lose herself in those crowds. The idea feels crazy. But she is suddenly certain that it is the only way to save her life, that if she doesn't run, and now, she is a dead woman. She stands – and Laurent re-enters the room, wearing his jacket, holding a cell phone she has never seen before.

'I said stay where you are,' he says sharply.

Numbly, she sits again. Laurent selects a number on this phone and speaks to the recipient at some length in French. Then he sits again on the chair across from the couch, watching her carefully. She wonders whether she might ambush him, a quick kick to the groin – but no, that's insane, he's a soldier and a black belt in three martial arts, she doesn't have a ghost of a chance. A scream for help would last all of half a second before he silenced her. Her fate, one way or another, is sealed.

'What's going on?' she dares to ask.

'I can't answer that. I can only show you.'

'Show me how?'

'Wait,' he says.

'But—'

'Wait *quietly*.'

It is an order, a calm one, but phrased in a military voice she has never heard from him before. She swallows and tries to remain perfectly still, as if this will keep him from deciding to do her harm. She understands now that she knows too much. Melodramatic as it sounds.

Eventually a knock comes on the door: two short, three long, two short. Laurent stands. 'Downstairs,' he says.

He escorts her outside with a firm hand on the small of her back. There is a limousine waiting outside, its windows tinted. The light inside is dim and it takes her a moment after sitting on the plush leather seats to recognize the figure splayed on the seat opposite her, beneath the opaque partition that separates the passenger compartment from the driver. Keiran, swaying in his seat, looks straight through her; no spark of recognition seems to fire. His pupils are so dilated that they occupy most of his eyes.

Laurent sits next to her and closes the door. She looks at him. 'Where are we going?' she whispers.

'Far.'

12

Danielle doesn't recognize the airport, but knows from the brief duration of their limousine journey that it must be London City, near the docklands; Heathrow, Gatwick, Stansted and Luton are all much farther away. The limousine door opens on to the inside of a hangar, an enormous building home to three small jet aircraft. One of them is active, lit up. Stairs ascend to its yawning entry-way. Laurent escorts her up into the cabin. She expects bus seating like a regular airplane, but instead there are two tables with six plush chairs around each. A burly black man stands before the cockpit door and watches as Laurent sits her down at one of the tables. Laurent descends from the plane. Danielle looks at him through the window as he hustles Keiran up the stairs. Keiran leans on him the whole way, his jaw slack, drooling a little. Once Laurent has eased Keiran into his seat, the black man pulls a lever on the side of the aircraft, the stairs fold into the side of the plane.

As the engines begin to hum and throb, Laurent closes all the window panels. They latch shut, unlike on commercial aircraft.

'Where are we going?' Danielle asks. Her mouth is desert-dry.

'The less you say, and the less I say, for the duration of this journey, the better it will be for all of us. Understand?'

After a moment Danielle nods. She thinks of tales of Argentinian political prisoners, thrown out of airplanes from ten thousand feet above the Atlantic Ocean, a hundred miles offshore, to disappear for ever into the maw of the wild sea.

'Buckle up,' Laurent says.

Danielle attaches Keiran's seat belt and then her own. Keiran is breathing quickly and his shirt is damp with sweat. He is too drugged to be afraid like her.

The take-off is short and bumpy. Laurent reads the same Celine novel he has been working his way through for two weeks. Danielle is somehow insulted that he had the presence of mind to bring it with him. It diminishes what they are doing; her life is being changed, and is at real risk, she can feel it, but to him it is only another errand.

Danielle doesn't wear a watch, and Laurent took her cell phone before they left the flat. She cannot guess how long the flight lasts, her heightened emotional state distorts her sense of duration. Anywhere from one to three hours. She is relieved when the timbre of the engines alters, and the pressure change in her ears tells her that they are descending. She had not really believed he meant to drop them into the Atlantic. Surely there are easier ways to murder them and dispose of their bodies. And surely even the real, revealed Laurent is not such a monster as that.

The relief, and the end of the anxious waiting, outweigh her fear of what might await them, dungeon or gallows or boardroom, at their destination. She is almost impatient to land and disembark, on to an airfield that seems utterly deserted but for a helicopter that looks like some kind of gigantic insect. Green fields surround the hangar and single administrative building next to the runway.

The black man remains on the airplane. Laurent leads them on to the helicopter, occupied by a single pilot, blond hair spilling from the back of his headset. The passenger compartment consists of two fold-up padded benches facing one another, front and back. Keiran still seems dazed, as if he has just woken up. Laurent straps Danielle and then Keiran into safety harnesses. Keiran remains silent, but he is paying some attention to his surroundings now, as if there is a three-dimensional movie going on around him, and he dares not interrupt for fear of inciting the rest of the audience's anger.

'Listen,' Laurent says, his voice low and intense, 'I've pushed the decision of what to do with you up to a higher level. That's all I can do for you. I would prefer that you live, but when we get there, your fates are out of my hands. Do you understand?'

Keiran doesn't react. Danielle slowly nods.

When the pilot starts the motor the noise is overwhelming. The whole craft throbs with the engine's bone-rattling pulse. Danielle has never been on a helicopter before and the sensation is bizarre and overwhelming. She gasps when they lift off and the pit of her stomach drops nauseatingly away. Around them she sees endless green fields, dotted in the distance with little houses, villages. She sees mountains to the east, peaks emerging from a sea of clouds, their snowcaps stained crimson by the dying sunlight. They must be the Alps. And the glittering blue sea beyond the coastline ahead of them the Mediterranean. Are they going to Corsica? Africa? Can a helicopter, even one of this size, make it across the Mediterranean Sea? And why not just take the airplane?

The answer becomes apparent about half an hour later, when they swoop down towards a single discontinuity in the endless sheet of rippling blue. From a distance the ship looks tiny, a child's toy with a mainmast the size of a matchstick, but as the helicopter descends with graceful precision to the landing pad's giant X, Danielle realizes that the mast is more than a hundred feet high, and the ship itself half as long again. They have landed on the aircraft carrier of yachts.

*   *   *

Keiran is filled with a great lassitude, a blissful warm stupor. But the drugs are wearing off. He feels a part of what is going on now, rather than a spectator in a body belonging to someone else. His limbs react to his commands again; he fumbles with the safety harness but manages to disconnect it by himself. His memories of everything up to the helicopter ride are incoherent fragments, vague recollections of shock and terror as two men broke into his flat and overpowered him in a few fleeting seconds. It feels long distant, years ago.

The last thing he wants to do is stand, but he forces himself, totters off the helicopter with Laurent's aid. He supposes abstractly he should be terrified or furious, but the comfortable lethargy of whatever drug they injected him with is so overpowering that he can manage neither. He does manage an interest in his surroundings. He has never been anywhere so luxurious. Even the exterior surfaces of this mega-yacht, exposed to sea and sun, are polished and beautiful. The mast is of some dark alloy, probably titanium, and the massive sail a pale luminous grey.

The helipad is behind and level with the sail, on a building-like projection on the aft of the ship; they have to climb down a ladder to deck level. As Keiran waits for Danielle to descend, machinery goes into motion all along the mast and mainsail, ropes coil smoothly through burnished-metal pulleys, and the sail shifts a little to port, presumably to better catch the light breeze. Not a single other human being is visible on deck. Keiran realizes with something like awe that the sail is entirely automatic, run by actuators and solenoids and engines commanded by some computer within. He gapes for a moment at this shining array of conspicuous electromechanical consumption, wanting to know the details of how it works, wanting to see the software, before Laurent pulls on his arm.

Behind the helipad, at the absolute stern of the ship, a pair of WaveRunner personal water craft, the aquatic equivalent of motorcycles, are strapped on to the deck. As they pass an open door, he sees within an elaborate collection of scuba gear: tanks, hoses, spear guns. It occurs to Keiran that Danielle is an expert scuba diver. A fact that could conceivably work to their advantage – but not with a veteran soldier and lethal martial artist like Laurent watching their every move.

The yacht's interior is almost comically opulent. Light spills from golden candelabras and crystal chandeliers on to hallways lined with original art, Persian rugs on teak floors, rooms full of mahogany and ebony furnishings. Every surface gleams, every light glows; but for all its palatial luxury, the yacht feels cold, impersonal, a museum not a home. They pass a marble fireplace that could roast a horse; Keiran associates it with a metal tube that protruded from the aft deck above them.

They descend a spiral staircase whose sides are filigreed with stone carvings of hundreds of birds, each one unique, and whose marble banister is an endless chain of smoothly carved animals. It is like something out of a dream, as is the elegant white-haired man in tuxedo and tails who waits for them on the deck below. For a moment Keiran wonders whether this old man is who they have travelled so far to see. But no: he is only the hired help.

The septuagenarian butler leads them along a main hallway that runs down the centre of the ship like a spine, a hall of mirrors that rivals Versailles, its effect only slightly diminished by the airtight bulkhead walls that protrude every thirty feet or so, from which doors are ready to slam shut in the name of safety. Keiran feels slightly dizzy, partly from the drugs, partly the surroundings. The doors are covered with abstract, filigreed metal designs, one of them recognizable to Keiran as the Mandelbrot set, and have no handles or knobs; they open automatically in response to a touch. There are data jacks in all the rooms, and discreetly placed cameras in the corners of every ceiling. Keiran realizes with awe that the entire yacht is automated. Every system, every moving part, is controlled by an electronic nervous system whose intricate web runs the entire length of the ship, this automation reducing the necessary crew to a handful.

Keiran's mind begins automatically to connect dots. Even with sedatives still in his bloodstream, he can't not solve problems, it would be like looking at words without reading them. A yacht like this likely belongs to someone with a technical background, a scientific fetish, someone who trusts machines over people. Keiran knows that Jim Clark, the three-time dot-com billionaire, owns such a vessel. Not this one, Clark would probably be appalled by such ornate ultra-luxury, but Keiran feels safe concluding that their host is likely some kind of scientist or engineer.

They turn off the hall of mirrors into a room that feels slightly more lived in; carpets are disarrayed, doors are closed instead of flung open for display purposes. Keiran notices an antiseptic smell that reminds him of a hospital. The white-haired butler opens the double doors beyond this antechamber, and red sunlight floods the hallway.

The extraordinary room revealed beyond is at the absolute bow of the ship, a triangle about forty feet to a side. Its entire forward wall is a pair of single gigantic windows, one-way, Keiran is sure, which form the mid-section of the ship's prow. Its floor and other walls are barren grey metal. Through the windows, the sun is setting behind the intensely blue, wave-torn Mediterranean.

In the middle of this triangular space, there is a room within the room, an entirely self-contained bubble of transparent plastic that takes up most of the available space; the rest of the room is little more than a walkway around this bubble's perimeter. It is apparent from the way the plastic bulges that it is pressurized. A two-chambered airlock-like projection allows access. Inside the first chamber, a portable shower stall stands next to a rackful of white environmental suits, the kind that people who work in industrial-strength clean rooms wear.

Within the bubble, a single hospital bed is surrounded by banks of monstrous and extremely clean machinery. Keiran recognizes a rack of blade servers, but the rest are medical devices unknown to him. Two nurses in clean suits stand by the machines, one of them making notes on a Palm Pilot. Plastic pipes and electrodes extend from this machinery and into the man who lies in the bed. Only his head is visible, hairless and as wrinkled as crumpled newspaper. The hospital smell is overwhelming.

'Mr Shadbold will see you now,' the butler says.

'Jesus Christ,' Keiran says, beginning to regain his vim.

'No,' a cracking voice booms, seemingly from all around them. Keiran starts, then realizes it emerges from two pillar-like speakers planted on either side of the airlock. 'But I do hope to rise when the stone is rolled forth from my tomb. Walk around to the front.' The accent is South African. The voice is mostly whisper, eerily amplified.

Danielle looks at Laurent, who nods. Keiran leads the way around the bubble to the western extremity of the dome, and turns to look at the hospital bed. Their host looks only barely human. A ropy growth has erupted from his throat, and in places its livid grey-red mass has burst through ragged holes of dry, overstretched skin. It reminds Keiran of dissecting an animal in school when a teenager, the fleshy blobs of organs inside his frog. Traces of blood feather the white sheets near where the cancer actually emerges from his body. A plastic tube runs straight through this growth and into his throat, and shudders slightly in time with the rise and fall of his frail chest. Two more plastic tubes protrude from his ribcage and connect to the largest machine. Liquids pulse through both tubes, one pale blue and the other blood red. It takes a moment for Keiran to realize that this is in fact Shadbold's blood, circulating through the attached machines.

'I'm not as old as I look,' Shadbold croons. 'But Blair intends to kill me.' He raises a feeble hand to touch the horrific growth that envelops his neck, and winces. 'Meet Blair. Dennis Potter, the great television writer, when he had a cancer, he named it Rupert, after his arch-enemy.' He speaks with a strange cadence; eight or ten words, a brief pause, then more words, in time with the monotonous rhythm of the machine that breathes for him. 'I named my cancer after two Blairs. Tony and Eric. You know Eric better by his nom de plume. George Orwell. If not for the misguided socialism they represent, Blair would be eminently curable today. We have sacrificed progress for the brass calf of equality. Does that sound monstrous? Do I seem a monster to you?'

'You mean physically?' Keiran asks, kicking himself for it a moment later; usually he holds his tongue and analyses all possible responses before speaking, but his drug-addled brain has betrayed him.

Shadbold's papery chuckle hits some resonant frequency and reverberates horribly through the room. 'The sins of my flesh are indeed very great. Most of my organs have been externalized. Doctors tell me I should be dead. *But I'm not ready yet.* I built a billion-dollar empire with my bare hands. I won't die like this. Not yet. Not without a fight. Maybe not ever. I will walk again. Does that sound insane?'

'Shadbold,' Keiran says. 'I've heard of you. Basic patents, right?'

'Well done, Mr Kell. Yes. I was a scientist. An inventor. Now I am a patient. My friend Blair is slowly choking me. Metastasizing. Spreading through my body. The only reason I still live is that my doctors' medicines are years ahead of the rest of the world. You already know why that is.'

'Kishkinda.'

'Precisely. A month after any drug company dreams up a possible anti-cancer drug, we are already testing it. They might think of beginning human trials seven years later. It isn't hard to borrow their formulas. We have made incredible strides. I'm not as doomed as I look. There is hope. Testable, verifiable hope. I intend to walk again.'

Keiran looks away from the torn, desiccated ruin that is Shadbold's body. It is hard not to pity him.

'Democracy,' Shadbold says, 'that last refuge of the madness of crowds, declares it wrong to experiment on human subjects, but right to let them die in their own filth by the million, of poverty and curable diseases. Lest someone dare whisper the truth that all men were created unequal. If we hadn't let myopic visions of so-called human rights get in our way, poverty would be a dying nightmare, we would be on the brink of affordable immortality. But I digress. A dying man's privilege, to rage against the dying of the light. But what if I'm not dying? What if the new drugs we are testing now, what if they *work*? What if Blair is *curable*? What then?'

'You tell us,' Keiran says.

'Then I shall live. A thought which may turn your stomach. But so shall others. Think of that. Thousands of others. Millions. But if my work is discovered before it bears fruit, the tests will be stopped, political volcanoes will erupt, the scientific data will never be used – and all those who suffer from the same kinds of cancer I do, manageable cancers, *curable* cancers, will be condemned to needless death.'

Shadbold pauses. Keiran can't think of anything to say. The drugs in his bloodstream, this dreamlike place, this talking corpse animated by machines – it's all too much, too grotesque. He doesn't even feel afraid. All he feels is numb.

'I have brought you here to answer a single question,' Shadbold says. 'Answer it truthfully. If I do let you return to your world. What will you say about me and my work? What will you do?'

After a moment Danielle opens her mouth. Keiran shoots her a sharp look. They lock eyes for a moment, and then, thankfully, she shuts her mouth. For once Keiran is sure that he knows better than Danielle how to deal with another human being. If Shadbold still counts as human. Because Jack Shadbold too, in his own way, is a hacker. And this is a test. If they answer wrongly, they will not leave this ship alive.

'We don't know,' Keiran says calmly. 'And even if we claimed to, you could never trust anything we say under this kind of duress.'

Danielle gapes at him.

'But what you *can* be sure of,' Keiran continues, 'is that disappearing us will have complicated and unpredictable reper-

228

cussions. Danielle comes from money. Her family will investigate. And a half-dozen of the world's best hackers are close personal friends of mine. Then there's the foundation. You'd best consider all the consequences very carefully before you drop us into the Mediterranean.'

'Dying men don't care about *consequences*,' Shadbold says.

'How fortunate for us that you're not dying.'

And Shadbold's horrible laughter fills the room again. 'Oh, I do like you, Mr Kell. I would applaud, if I could.'

'I'm flattered.'

'I'm glad I agreed to see you before deciding your fate. I can deal with a rational man like you. You never believed in the fight, did you? You were only honouring a debt. I respect that. Debts must be paid, personal and business, contracts must be enforced. But you, Miss Leaf.' He pauses. Danielle tenses.

'You I only feel sorry for,' Shadbold says. 'It was your beliefs that led you astray. You were used, from the beginning, by all sides. I have a truth to reveal. Your precious foundation? Those noble battlers for the poor sick children of Kishkinda? We know who they are now. A front for Zulu Fields. They pretended to be activists and hired your friends to fight dirty for them so the share price would fall, make their takeover easier, make Terre willing to sell their shares cheap. Once they owned the mine they would have turned on you, exposed you, discredited your whole movement as a freak fringe of violent extremists. You thought you were a noble warrior for good. My poor child. From the beginning, nothing more than a pawn in a fight between kings, myself and Zulu Fields. I won. I always win.'

'You're lying,' Danielle says, aghast. 'That's not true. It isn't true.'

'No word a lie. Look into Zulu Fields' computers, Mr Kell. There's proof abundant.'

Keiran stands stunned. The foundation a front for a takeover attempt. It makes sense. It explains everything. And makes everything meaningless. Angus and Estelle died for nothing.

'I learned a long time ago that human nature is as reliable as sunrise,' Shadbold says, his voice weaker now. 'If you offer a rational human being both reward and punishment, both carrot and stick, he will almost without exception do what you want. I know both of you now. I know you will see things my way. Simple human nature. What do you have to gain, by speaking out? Nothing. What do you, and the rest of your benighted species, have to lose? So much. If you breathe a single word you declare war on me. I think you know now that there is no surviving that war.'

Keiran doesn't say anything.

'Henri,' Shadbold whispers. 'Take them away. I'm tired.'

Laurent doesn't come with them. He doesn't even say goodbye. Once Danielle and Keiran are strapped back into the helicopter's safety harnesses, her lover, her betrayer, the man who changed the course of her life, who led her into a doomed struggle for justice that has made her a criminal, vaults down on to the yacht and climbs down from the helipad without even looking at her. Danielle stares at his dwindling form, the long shadows he casts from the ship's deck lights, as the helicopter lifts away into the starlit sky above the Mediterranean. She doesn't feel anything at all. There isn't anything left. She feels empty.

The helicopter returns them to the airfield in France. The pilot gestures to the plane that brought them there, where the same man who accompanied them from London awaits.

'We don't have passports,' Keiran says, as the plane taxies to the end of the runway. 'I don't have any ID at all. Or money.'

'You will need no identification.' The man's voice is deep and booming, his accent foreign, African.

Danielle manages to doze off during the flight back. It isn't hard. She is so drained by fear and loss that remaining awake simply requires too much energy. She sleeps through the landing. When Keiran shakes her awake, she is dazed and clumsy, and has to lean on him as they descend. The limousine is waiting for them, a door open. They enter it without even considering other options. Soon they emerge in front of Monument station, in the City of London. It is night, and clumps of drunken overpaid bankers pass them, going home from their post-work pubs. Danielle is hit by a wave of molten fury when she sees them. She rages at their smug self-satisfaction, their lives of champagne and million-pound flats, their pretty blonde girlfriends whoring themselves out to live with money, because money, and the respect of people with more of it than you, is all that really matters. She wants to smash their faces until they bleed from nose and mouth and eyes, break their kneecaps with a hammer, squeeze their testicles until they cannot scream any longer. As quickly as it came, the fury is gone, leaving her weak kneed.

'Are you all right?' Keiran asks, worried.

Danielle nods. She thinks of the twisted, raging faces she had seen at the demonstration in Paris, especially among the black bloc. She understands their endless well of anger a little better now. The rage at people who have a life of peace and wealth and comfort and love, and do not deserve it, while you have been fighting all your life for what you believe is right, and you have none of those things, and you have been betrayed by everything you believe in, all the goodness you once thought filled the world.

'You can stay with me tonight.'

She shakes her head violently. 'No. No. I'm getting out of this fucking country. I'm getting my passport and going straight to the airport.'

'What are you going to do?'

'I'm going home. What did you think?'

'I mean about Shadbold,' Keiran says.

'I'm not going to do anything.'

'You think he's right?' Keiran pauses. 'Mengele. You know who he was?'

'I'm not a fucking idiot.'

'Sorry. You'd be surprised how many people don't. His experiments. Nothing of any actual scientific value came from them, but what if they had? Would it be right to use that knowledge? I suppose this isn't the same thing. It's the mine that causes cancer. Shadbold just tests drugs on the ones who get it. It's unethical, exploitative, but they're probably not much worse off than if he didn't. If he does find the cure for some cancer, will it have been worth it?'

'Who cares?' Danielle asks. 'I don't. Not any more. I tried caring and it didn't work. Fuck caring. I'm going home.'

'You're an inspiration to us all.'

'And fuck you too.'

'I suppose I earned that,' he says. 'I'm sorry.'

'What are you going to do?'

Keiran shrugs. 'Same as you. Nothing. He's right. It's awful, but something good might come out of it, and I'm not willing to risk myself. And he's too big for us to fight even if I wanted to. I'm going to go home and pretend that none of this ever happened.'

'Good.'

'You really think so?'

'I don't give a shit.'

'If you ever need anything,' Keiran says, 'anything at all. Danielle, I'm so sorry. If I can ever do anything for you, just call. I mean it. I hope you know that. I'll ring you in a couple of days, make sure you got home OK.'

'Don't bother,' Danielle says, and turns and advances into the London night, hot despairing tears in her eyes, moving quickly, fuelled by self-loathing, into the flow of ten thousand anonymous pedestrians on the South Bank of the Thames.

She returns to the flat she shared with Laurent, collects her passport and packs as quickly as she can, necessities only, holding each breath as long as she can, as if the very air might pollute her. A black cab takes her to Heathrow. She pays fourteen hundred pounds for a last-minute one-way ticket to JFK. Cheap at the price. Right now Danielle would sell her soul, if necessary, to get out of England and back to America as fast as possible. Not that she thinks anyone would be willing to buy.

III New World

America
Three months later

1

Danielle has rarely been so relieved to return to her apartment. Her feet hurt, her little black cocktail dress has been decorated with half a spilled Cosmopolitan, and the taxi that brought her home smelled of vomit. She totters into her building's foyer and waits for the elevator. Her apartment is only two flights up, but high heels, exhaustion and alcohol make those thirty-two steps seem like the Empire State Building. Once home, she leans against the wall to remove her shoes, and nearly knocks over the ornate wooden coatstand that once belonged to her grandparents. Collapsing on to her bed is a physical relief. She knows she must undress, shower and drink as much water as she can stand before allowing herself to pass out, but right now it is so good to close her eyes and just lie here. Even if she is all alone.

Her phone rings. She ignores it, lets it warble five times and switch to voice mail. But it rings again, five more times, and again, and again. She tries to tune it out. Even getting up and walking across the room to unplug the phone seems like an unbearable effort. But the sound bores into her brain like a barbed drill bit, and eventually she forces herself to her feet, steps to the glass table and, on impulse, angry now – who dares call her at 3 a.m.? – she answers.

'Who *is* this?' she demands.

At first there is no reply. She is about to hang up, thinking it a prank caller, when a woman's voice answers, accented and tentative: 'Hello? Is this Danielle Leaf, please?'

'Yes, what do you want? Do you know what time it is?'

'I am so sorry to call you at this hour. But it is necessary.'

'Necessary for what?' The woman's accent is Indian. A tele-marketer? If it is, Danielle vows, she will call the Better Business Bureau come morning.

The woman says, 'My name is Jayalitha. I was a friend of Angus McFadden. I believe, if you are the Danielle Leaf I seek to contact, you will recognize that name?'

Danielle takes a moment to digest this. Then she retreats to the bed, sits on it and says, 'Yes. I knew Angus.'

'Oh, thank goodness. Thank goodness.'

'What are you . . . Wait. Are you . . . Was I supposed to deliver your passport? To Kishkinda? Like, six months ago?'

'Yes.'

'You're supposed to be dead,' Danielle says.

'Yes. I am sorry. That was necessary.'

Danielle hesitates. She doesn't want anything to do with this. But she can't just hang up. 'Why are you calling me?'

'Please, Miss Leaf,' Jayalitha says. 'I know no one else in this country. I have no money left. I am here without papers or visas. I fear there are men hunting me. Please can you help?'

'This country?' Danielle now notices the absence of a trans-oceanic call's tiny but perceptible time-lag. 'Men hunting you? Where are you?'

'I am in the city of Los Angeles.'

'What are you . . .' Danielle pauses, not sure what question, if any, she wants to ask. She tries to collected her frazzled thoughts, but they won't stop unravelling.

'Please. My telephone card will soon empty. I beg you, Miss Leaf. You are my only hope.'

'Don't go confusing me with Obi-Wan.'

'I beg your pardon?'

'Shit,' Danielle says. 'Call me collect.'

'I am sorry? Collect?'

'Reverse charges. We call it collect here. Call me collect in ten minutes and I'll try to figure something out.'

Danielle takes advantage of the pause to have a quick shower, as cold as she can stand. She is drunk, but not too drunk to know that Trouble is rearing a monstrous and many-fanged head, and she needs to be as sober as possible.

'Where are you exactly?' Danielle asks, after accepting the charges.

'I am in Union Station, Los Angeles.'

'How did you get there without ID?'

'By ship. From China. It was a terribly long journey.'

'And you think there's someone after you?'

'Yes. I called Angus earlier today. I did not yet know what,' Jayalitha's voice falters, 'what happened to him. Someone else answered. Someone with a terrible voice. And then tonight I was pursued by two men. Perhaps they were just dacoits. Criminals. But I saw them moving through the station, seeking someone. When they saw me they gave chase. I barely escaped. I fear they may return.'

'Huh.' Danielle isn't sure she should believe any of this. 'How did you get my number?'

'From your parents.'

'My *parents*?'

Jayalitha says, 'I recalled your last name and that Angus described your parents as wealthy lawyers in the city of Boston. I used the Internet to find their telephone number. Miss Leaf, I am terribly sorry to bother you. It mortifies me to call you like this. But when I learned that Angus is dead . . . Please, Miss Leaf. I truly believe you are the only person in this world who might be willing to help me. Please. I beg you. Please help me.'

'Help you how?'

'Any way you can.'

'Well, uh, where are you staying? Maybe I can send you some money.'

'I am not staying anywhere,' Jayalitha says.

'You're on the *street*? In Los Angeles? You can't do that.'

'I have no choice.'

'You don't have any money at all?'

'I am barefoot, Miss Leaf. My pockets are empty. I have no jewellery. I have nothing but the clothes on my back.'

'Shit.' Danielle tries to think whether she knows anyone in Los Angeles. A few acquaintances, but no one she can call to pick up a strange homeless Indian woman in Union Station at night. 'Look, I'm sorry, I don't think there's anything I can do for you tonight.'

'Tomorrow. The next day. Anything, Miss Leaf. I beg you.'

Danielle shakes her head. 'Call me back in the morning, OK? I need . . . I'm sorry, but I'm falling over here, I need to sleep. When my head's clear I'll try to think things over. I can't promise anything. But call me back and I'll answer. Is that OK?'

'Thank you,' Jayalitha says passionately, as if Danielle has just promised her a million dollars and a special forces honour guard. 'Thank you, Miss Leaf.'

'Don't thank me yet. I haven't done anything for you.'

'You have given me hope, Miss Leaf. I thought I was lost.'

'Just call me in the morning,' Danielle says uncomfortably. 'We'll work something out.' But she can't imagine what or how.

The next morning's hangover is not too bad. Headache, malaise, waves of nausea when she thinks of eating, all easily dulled by codeine-fortified Tylenol. Danielle has suffered far worse, and recently at that. She tries to work out how many times she has gotten drunk in the last month, but gives up before the calculation is complete. She knows the answer will be depressing.

Maybe she should get a job. But she hates jobs. She could volunteer somewhere. But she hates people. It would be easier if she didn't have any money. Then she would have to get a job. She would have to struggle to get by. She would not go out almost every night with her false friends, the New York social circle she now inhabits; heartless men and women in their thirties with too much money and time on their hands, living an almost hysterically decadent existence of drink and drugs and clubs and parties and Hamptons weekends, as if the Black Death of age does not exist.

Danielle met them through a girl she knew in college. She was welcomed with open arms. This dissolute clan's numbers are constantly diminishing, their members lost to exodus, coupledom or parenthood, and people like Danielle – fresh blood, a new distraction, someone of the right age and inclination, willing to fill all their hours with empty pleasures – are always welcome. So long as they have money. And Danielle has plenty of money, without even going to her family. At least not directly. Citibank has loaned her four hundred thousand dollars, secured by her Manhattan apartment, which has nearly doubled in value since her parents bought it for her five years ago. The way things are going, she will spend it all in three years – but what does that matter? Three years are an eternity. And Danielle knows her parents will rescue her, if they have to, when that day of reckoning comes. She promised herself, once, when she went to India, that she would never depend on her parents again, but today that passionate oath seems ridiculous. Why should she care about self-reliance? Or, for that matter, anything else?

She sits in her apartment, reads the *Times*, and drinks two mimosas. The more she waits, the more Jayalitha does not call. Danielle wonders uneasily whether something bad has happened to her. She decides she will find some way to send the Indian woman some money. Maybe a thousand dollars. But that will be all. It is more than she deserves, after the way she has dredged up bad memories of Laurent and those two months of madness. That was only a few months ago, but Danielle had managed to make it feel so distant, so long ago and far away, until last night's phone call. Today those memories feel like a wound whose scab has peeled off before it has even begun to heal.

Eventually she decides to call Keiran. He might want to know that Jayalitha is still alive. Maybe Danielle can outsource her charity case to him. She has spoken only once to Keiran since their surreal abduction to Jack Shadbold's superyacht, a week after her return to New York, when she called and asked him to keep track of any police investigation of the bombing. Back then she was terrified of being hunted down, arrested, extradited. That fear has since withered away. Now the thought of actually being investigated and punished for her part, or more accurately non-part, in Laurent's actions seems ludicrous. Danielle knows she was completely irrelevant to Laurent. As she was to Angus and Estelle and their foundation. The same way she has been irrelevant to everything all her life. She has left no more trace on this world than a drifting butterfly. Pretty, briefly entertaining, but completely immaterial.

When she picks up the phone, the dial tone pulses rapidly, meaning she has voice mail. Danielle guiltily punches the code. Jayalitha must have called already, and Danielle slept through it without knowing. And indeed there are two messages of an automated voice asking whether she will accept a collect call. She hangs up, hesitates, and calls Keiran.

'Danielle,' he answers warmly. Her outgoing caller ID is supposed to be disabled, but she supposes that doesn't apply to hackers. 'How are you?'

'Fine,' she says shortly. She doesn't want this to become a personal conversation. 'Guess who called me last night?'

'Rin Tin Tin?' Keiran is clearly in one of his whimsical moods.

'Jayalitha.'

'And who's she when she's at . . . *Jayalitha*? But she's dead.'

'No. She isn't. Laurent lied.' Danielle winces. 'Go figure. She's in LA. Arrived on a boat from China or something, illegally. She must have been really out of touch, she didn't even know Angus was dead until she got there. She said I was the only one she could call.'

'It might have been an actress.'

'I don't think so. I think it's her. She says there're men chasing her.'

'Chasing her? Why? How do they know she's there?'

'I don't know.' Danielle's guilt at having missed the previous two phone calls intensifies as she realizes Jayalitha may have been running for her life while Danielle slept. 'Apparently she called Angus and someone else answered. With a terrible voice, whatever that means. Then two guys turned up looking for her but she got away.'

'Wait a moment,' Keiran says, his voice suddenly taut. 'She rang Angus, someone else answered, and then she rang you?'

'Yeah. Weird, huh?'

After a moment he says, flat and businesslike, 'I'll ring you back. Lock your door. If anybody knocks, call the police.'

'What the hell—'

'I'll call you right back.' He hangs up.

Keiran's warning is ridiculous. His hacker and drug-culture background has made him paranoid, that's all. Nobody is going to come after Danielle in her 16th Street apartment on a bright Sunday afternoon. Nobody can possibly have any reason to. The phone rings. Danielle jumps, scolds herself for being skittish, and answers.

'This is MCI,' a robot voice says. 'Will you accept a collect call from . . .' and then Jayalitha's voice, identifying herself.

'Yes,' Danielle says.

'Miss Leaf. I am sorry to trouble you again.'

'It's no trouble,' Danielle lies. 'How are you?'

After a pause, Jayalitha says, 'I believe I have been worse. And yourself?'

'Hung over,' Danielle says, and quickly kicks herself for complaining about a hangover to a penniless, homeless, friendless illegal refugee. 'Never mind. Is there any way I can send you money?'

'I am afraid I know nothing about how such things work in America. Will my lack of papers make it difficult?'

Danielle sighs. 'Yes.' She has never used Western Union, or poste restante, but she can't imagine them not requiring ID.

Her phone beeps. Call waiting. 'Just a minute,' she says, and switches over.

Keiran says, 'Someone's been paying for Angus's phone.'

'What?'

'His mobile number. Someone paid to keep it active, and forwarded all calls to an untraceable VOIP gateway. I hacked into Virgin Mobile's phone records. He's received exactly one call in the last two months. From Union Station, Los Angeles, yesterday.'

'So she's telling the truth,' Danielle says.

'Then the truth is bad news. Someone keeps Angus's phone alive, then answers in an anonymized voice? Must be a hacker. Must have a reason to go to all that effort.'

'What are you talking about? What reason?'

'Think it through. They've been waiting for her. They knew she was alive. Angus's phone was bait for when she rose from the dead. They traced the call, now they know where she is, and they're after her.'

'They who?'

'P2. Laurent. Shadbold. Justice International. Who else?'

Danielle grunts at the sound of Laurent's name. 'Why?'

'Because she knows something she shouldn't,' Keiran says. 'Something big. Come on, Dani, think. That's why she had to pretend to be dead for the last six months. That's why she's in trouble. That's why she *is* trouble.'

'What do you mean?'

'I mean, if I was P2, I'd take a look at what other numbers she called with that phone card. And I'd come across a very familiar name.'

'Me.' Danielle sits down hard on her couch. She feels the world whirl sickeningly around her, as if she has had too much to drink already. If Keiran is right, the mere act of answering her phone last night was disastrous. They won't know Jayalitha didn't tell her anything.

'Exactly,' Keiran says.

'They wouldn't really. Would they?'

'Wouldn't really what?'

'Do anything,' Danielle says softly.

'Predicting the behaviour of psychotic dying billionaires is not my speciality. I suppose it depends on what exactly Jayalitha knows. Did she tell you?'

'No. I've got her on the other line right now.'

Keiran thinks for a while.

'Whatever it is, it must be important for them to go to all this effort to catch her,' Danielle says, thinking aloud, beginning to realize how much trouble she might be in. She feels dizzy, as if she is on some kind of carnival ride that won't stop, is spinning out of control.

'Not just important. Dangerous. To them. And by logical extension, her as well.'

'And now me too.'

'And now you,' Keiran agrees. 'Tell her to get away from Union Station before it's too late. And then – maybe I'm being paranoid, but I think at the moment paranoid is good. You get out of there too.'

'Out of where?'

'Your apartment. New York. Go someplace you can't be found for a while. Actually . . . Wait. Any chance you could get to Los Angeles?'

'Are you serious? Won't that just get me into more trouble?'

'She needs help,' Keiran says. 'Angus and Estelle would have wanted us to help.'

'So go there yourself.'

'I will. But I can't go today. And she needs help now.'

'I'm starting to think I do too. I'm going to call the police.'

'And what? Tell them the whole story?'

Danielle thinks for a moment. 'Maybe not.'

'If Shadbold really has gone on the warpath, the only thing your NYPD can do for you is draw the chalk outline around your corpse.'

'Thanks. That's so comforting.'

'Just get out of there. Go to LA. Get Jayalitha to meet you.'

'Why? If we've got our own problems, why do we have to worry about her? Can't we just send her some money? I mean, I'm sorry for her, but she's Angus's friend, not mine.'

'I want to know what she knows,' Keiran says. 'Don't you?'

2

Danielle is accustomed to domestic flights with United or American, on airplanes that smell faintly rancid, staffed by harried stewardesses who charge passengers five dollars for the privilege of headsets so they can listen to bad movies projected on to stained screens. She is a little overwhelmed by JetBlue's leather seats, cheerful staff and individual TV screens with thirty satellite channels. Danielle finds herself wishing she had never dropped out of school, had gotten her degree instead and joined JetBlue when they were young. She could have made herself part of something constructive. Instead of fleeing to Los Angeles to rescue a woman she has never met.

On the flight she reads *The Famished Road*, which only accentuates the sense of fatalism that has crept into her since leaving her apartment, a feeling that she has been suddenly swept up into one of the river of time's inexorable rapids, and no longer has anything to do with the determination of her fate. There is no exit, no escape hatch; all she can do is tread water and hope to be carried into calm water again.

The landing proceedings pass in a blur, and then she is outside in Los Angeles' bright summer sunshine. The ellipsis that is LAX is centred around a building that looks like a UFO on stilts. A restaurant, if she recalls correctly. As she waits for the Avis van to arrive, a handsome man with a craggy jaw tries to talk to her. She ignores him, suspicious that he might be assigned to follow her. When they reach Avis, and he rushes to be the first to get a vehicle and drive away, she realizes he was just an actor trying to pick her up. A useful reminder. Even if there is a conspiracy, not everyone is part of it. Just because they're after you doesn't mean you're not paranoid.

Los Angeles' Central Public Library is a large, austerely pale building located on the good side of downtown, steeply uphill from Skid Row, easy to find thanks to the landmark pyramid that tops its central tower. Danielle enters twenty minutes before it closes. There are plenty of poor and homeless people in the reading rooms, but only one barefoot Indian woman. She is younger than Danielle expected, early twenties at most. Her skin is very dark, almost black, her features strong and aristocratic, high cheekbones and deep-set eyes. Her long hair has clumped into greasy hanks, and her clothes, jeans and a loose black shirt, are stained and thickly wrinkled. Her body language is rigidly composed, almost military. She would be pretty if she were not so gaunt and drained.

'Jayalitha?' Danielle says from behind her.

The Indian woman looks up from her 1999 Fodor's guide to LA. 'Miss Leaf?'

Danielle nods.

'You came,' Jayalitha says incredulously. Her smile lights up the room. 'Oh my goodness. I did not allow myself to believe you might really come. I scarcely allowed myself to hope. Oh, thank you, Miss Leaf. Thank you so much.'

'Call me Danielle. Please. Let's . . . let's get you some food, OK?'

'Please.'

They cross the street to the Westin Bonaventure hotel and its panoply of restaurants. Danielle intends to take her somewhere nice, then realizes Jayalitha's lack of footwear might be a problem. She is saved by Jayalitha's gasp of desire when she sees the Subway logo. One vegetarian sub and large Coke later, the Indian woman is visibly blissful.

'I hardly remember the last time my belly was full,' she says.

'Shanghai, perhaps. A month ago. There were Subways in Bangalore. There was one in a shopping centre on Brigade Street I frequented whenever I visited the city.'

'I used to go there,' Danielle said.

'Oh, yes, you lived in Bangalore. I used to go there and try out American foods. I always wanted to go to America. And now,' she looks around, 'it was an evil road, but somehow, here I am.'

'Here you are,' Danielle agrees. 'Come on. I've got a hotel. By the beach.'

It's a twenty-minute drive down the Santa Monica Highway to the Cadillac Hotel, a moderately priced Art Deco hotel right on Venice's boardwalk, where Danielle once spent a week with Jonas DeGlint, one of her nicer Crazy Years boyfriends. Jonas was neurotic, needy, a bad guitarist and worse songwriter who believed himself the second coming of Jimi Hendrix, but he stayed away from hard drugs and was always good to Danielle, and her memories of the Cadillac are fond ones.

She parks on Rose Street. Jayalitha is half asleep in the passenger seat. Danielle wanted to watch the sun set over the Pacific, but it is already dark; she wanted to buy Jayalitha sandals, but the stores have all closed. She supposes one more barefoot night won't kill her. The Indian woman hardly needs shoes anyhow, she has half-inch calluses on her feet.

'You must be tired,' Danielle says, when they arrive in their room, small but clean, with two double beds.

'Exhausted.' Jayalitha's eyes drift from Danielle to the bed as if magnetically compelled. 'I know we must speak. But if it is possible to sleep first . . .'

Danielle knows she has to find out what Jayalitha knows, why she fled India and has stayed quiet for the six months since, but she also knows the subject is poison. She is reluctant to bring it up now, when Jayalitha is so childishly happy to be fed and given a place to sleep. 'Go ahead,' Danielle says. 'Take a shower, go to bed. We'll talk in the morning.'

*　　*　　*

The ringing phone startles them both awake. Danielle crawls to the edge of her bed and gropes for it, dazed by sleep. The room is lit only by starlight and the glowing red digits of their alarm clock. It takes her four rings to locate the phone by sound.

'Yes?' she answers.

'Danielle. It's Keiran.' The connection is terrible, his voice sounds fuzzy. 'They know where you are. You have to get out of there.'

'What?'

'I'm serious.'

Danielle shakes her head to clear it. 'How . . . how do you know?'

'I have a tracer on P2's VOIP gateway. I can't listen in, it's encrypted, but I know he just called your hotel. Presumably confirming your presence. Then he called two other Los Angeles numbers. I think he's sending people after you.'

'How . . . how could they have found us?'

'P2 must have cracked every hotel in the city,' Keiran says. There is something like awe in his voice.

'What are we supposed to do now?'

'You're supposed to run.'

'Where can we go?'

'We? You found her?' Keiran asks.

'Yes. She's right here with me.'

'Good. Where's a good place to meet, near the airport?'

'The airport,' Danielle says, and tries to think. 'There's a building in the middle. A restaurant. Looks like a flying saucer.'

'I'll be there by noon. Your time.'

'Noon?' Danielle looks at the clock. It is 3.05 a.m. 'Where are you?'

'Five miles over the Atlantic. Listen. Don't make any phone calls. Don't use a credit card. Take out as much cash as you can and move right away. I think this P2 can trace most anything. Banks, government, maybe even military, it's fucking mad what he can do.'

Danielle swallows. 'All right.'

'Don't pack. You don't have time. Just leave.'

The man behind the Cadillac Hotel's desk gives them a bewildered look when they emerge from the elevator shortly after 3 a.m. In no mood for conversation, Danielle sweeps past him and leads Jayalitha outside.

Across from them, there is a small line of shops boarded up by graffiti-tagged metal canopies. The boardwalk and beach are about twenty feet to their left. The beach is wide enough, and the night dark enough, for them to be unable to see or hear the ocean. To their right, Dudley Avenue, a narrow pedestrian thoroughfare, climbs east from the Cadillac for two hundred feet before it reaches Pacific Avenue, busy by day but now deserted. About a third of the way there, it intersects with an alley that runs parallel to the beach, called Speedway. East of Speedway, Dudley is lined on both sides by small houses, their gated properties obscured by near-jungle.

The breezy night air smells of the ocean. There is no one else in sight. Danielle leads the way east, towards their car, parked on Rose Street a few blocks away. They are halfway to Pacific Avenue when they hear an engine purr behind them, a car turning on to Speedway. They duck into an open gateway and watch the car stop in front of the Cadillac. A police car. Danielle watches, her whole body prickling with goose bumps, breathing deeply, as a uniformed police officer emerges.

She is tempted to rush to the officer and ask for help. But she doesn't. During the Crazy Years, when at any given time she was probably carrying drugs or technically in contravention of several bylaws, and frequently got hassled and moved along by intolerant uniformed tyrants, she developed a powerful avoidance reflex towards police. To this day, when she spots a police car, it is like seeing a shark passing by. She just watches as the cop enters the hotel. A minute later, a light flickers in the window of the room they so recently inhabited.

248

Maybe the police, like Keiran, knew they were in danger. Maybe the police *are* the danger. She thinks of the Rampart scandal, when a cabal of a dozen crooked LAPD officers was unearthed, amid dark hints that they were only the tip of an iceberg of corruption. It's very easy to kill someone, if you're a cop. You don't even need to leave the scene of the crime. Just walk into the hotel room with the skeleton key the night manager gave you, shoot your victims dead with an untraceable weapon, then call in your discovery of a murder scene, thanks to the anonymous tip phoned in half an hour ago.

'Let's go,' she whispers. Jayalitha nods. She seems alert, nervous, but not terrified. Danielle is glad of that. She too is frightened but not panicky. If she had nothing to do, if she had to wait and hide, that would be different; but as long as there is a course of action – find the car and meet Keiran at the airport – she can bury her fear beneath activity.

They go to the end of Dudley, walking very fast now, cross Pacific, go the half-block north to the corner of Rose, and start east towards Main Street, only two blocks from where their red Dodge Neon is parked at Rose and 3rd – but Danielle stops after a few steps and stares. There is something blocking the street near their car. Another car, double-parked right by their rental. The street lights are dim but she can make out a telltale girder shape above the vehicle. Another police car.

She freezes for a minute, then grabs Jayalitha by the hand and takes two quick steps backwards, trying to get back around the corner on to Pacific, out of sight. But she is too late. The searchlight mounted atop the car blazes to life, almost blinding them from three blocks away. Danielle and Jayalitha turn and run. Behind them, the car growls into life; tyres squeal as it leaps towards them.

On impulse Danielle takes a chance, keeps running down Pacific, south past Dudley to Palermo Avenue, the next pedestrian walkway, and then westwards towards the beach. She knows from her previous tenure at the Cadillac that the streets around here are open, hard to hide in. Their best bet is the lightless beach. Hopefully their pursuers will go the wrong way – but as they pelt down Palermo, the searchlight illuminates them from behind, casting their hundred-foot shadows against the pale pavement and the golden sand beyond. Danielle keeps running, to the beach, and Jayalitha follows. They veer on to Venice Boardwalk, sprinting diagonally away from the light, shadowed from it by buildings that by day contain colourful T-shirt stores, pizza stands, rental bicycles and tattoo parlours, but by night are as bleak as a prison wall.

Danielle keeps going, over the boardwalk, across a patch of grass, and briefly along a bicycle path shaped like a sinuous river. They stagger a little when they hit the soft sand of Venice Beach, easily two hundred yards wide. 'Keep going,' Danielle pants. She has half a plan now. But they need to move fast, get away from the street lights, and her lungs and muscles are burning from exertion, the last few months of drink and dissolution have not been kind to her nearly-thirty body – and now *another* pair of headlights is coming at them from the north, along the beach. For a moment Danielle sags and slows, defeated; this car is still distant, but if it is hunting them and has a searchlight, there is nowhere else to run.

But no, she realizes, this is the beach patrol, who rove the sand all night to ensure that the homeless do not sleep here. Danielle isn't sure whether they are technically police or not, but they are probably not out to get her. She can go to them for help – but then what? Then the police chasing them will arrive, and take them into custody, and she is horribly certain that if she lets this happen, neither she nor Jayalitha will ever make it to any police precinct. Instead they will be driven on a one-way journey to one of Los Angeles' many lonely and dangerous streets, where their bodies will be discovered come morning. She keeps running. She thinks she hears, behind them, over the ocean's gentle roar, the sound of boots slapping against the boardwalk, of men racing towards them.

3

The sand firms beneath their feet and slopes downwards; they have reached the high-water mark. The moon has set or is hidden behind cloud, but starlight and the ambient light of the city reveal whitecapped waves before them. To their left, a spit of sand projects into the sea, ending at a long perpendicular wall of stones, a breakwater that caps the spit like the crossbar on a capital T.

An appalling thought hits Danielle as they reach the waterline. 'Can you swim?' she asks, her voice low.

'No,' Jayalitha says.

'Shit.' Danielle halts for a moment, then decides they have no choice. 'We're going into the water anyway. Stay with me and be quiet.'

Jayalitha doesn't argue. Danielle takes her hand and leads her into the water. Jayalitha gasps with the shock of transition. The water feels painfully cold, although Danielle knows it should be near sixty-five degrees. It is probably horribly polluted, Venice is full of drains that lead straight to the ocean, but plenty of surfers risk it, and besides, if she gets out of this fix with only an incurable skin rash, Danielle will consider herself very lucky.

The beach drops down more steeply than she hoped; they are only thirty feet from the shore, where the secondary waves begin to crest, when Jayalitha can go no farther without submerging her head.

'OK,' Danielle says, 'turn around.'

They see two flashlights, scanning back and forth across the sand, flickering up and down as those who hold them approach at a fast run. Jayalitha squeezes Danielle's hand tightly. Danielle, standing behind her, holds her zipped-shut purse with her other hand, equally tight. If this works, and they somehow get out, they will need money. They rock back and forth in the surging water, endlessly finding their feet.

'Our hope is that they will not find us here?' Jayalitha whispers.

'Yes.' Danielle looks to their right, at the breakwater at the end of the protruding spit of sand. If they can get to the water behind that high, unclimbably slippery wall of rock, they will be invisible. 'This way,' she whispers, and begins to edge towards it. It is only a hundred feet away but their pace, walking through the sea, is incredibly slow. She hopes the ocean floor does not drop any lower en route. She hopes they can make it there before their pursuers think of the water as a possible hiding place. She thinks of footprints, they must have left footprints, and freezes with terror for a moment – but then relaxes. Venice Beach is so busy by day that the sand is riddled with thousands of footprints, it will be nearly impossible by flashlight to work out which are freshest. Unless the tide is going out. Then theirs will be the only ones leading into the water. She adds 'tide coming in' to the list of her desperate hopes.

The two flashlights have separated now, at the water's edge, one going north and one south. Danielle considers making a run for it while they're both moving away – but no, too chancy, best to head for the breakwater, past which they cannot be seen, and wait for them to leave. She wonders how long they can hold out in the water. Sixty-five degrees is plenty warm enough to swim in, but simple biology dictates that the body can't maintain its necessary ninety-eight degrees for ever when soaked in liquid so much colder.

'Breathe hard,' Danielle whispers, thinking of yoga classes, *pranayama* lessons. 'Try to warm yourself.'

'Yes,' Jayalitha says. 'I understand.'

They are almost at the end of the breakwater now – but the ocean floor is descending again, too low for Jayalitha. And the flashlights are coming back, converging on the beach before them. They will just have to hope to stay here unseen. Snatches of conversation between their pursuers, two men, are audible between waves.

'– around here somewhere. They didn't just vanish. Maybe—'

'– It's not like we can call for back-up. They're on foot. Let's get back to the vehicles, maybe some street kid saw—'

'– Wait. Wait a minute. Maybe they're in the water.'

Danielle goes rigid with fear. Then both flashlights rise and rotate towards the ocean. One of them sweeps straight towards them.

'Take a deep breath,' Danielle whispers to Jayalitha, 'and trust me.' She thrusts her right arm into the loops of her purse handle, threads her arms under Jayalitha's, and pulls her down into the ocean.

Jayalitha squirms violently at first. Danielle tightens her grip, and Jayalitha stiffens, then goes limp. Danielle kicks as hard as she can, trying to propel them past the breakwater, but her legs keep hitting Jayalitha's, impeding their progress, and when she must come up for air they are next to the wall of rock but not yet past it. Two circles of light criss-cross the dark water, hunting them. Jayalitha gasps loudly for air, and Danielle is afraid she might be heard. She fills her lungs and pulls Jayalitha underwater again. She can tell they are past the breakwater by the way the surge of the sea strengthens, and for a moment she feels triumphant – until a wave catches them and flings them straight into the wall of rock.

The breakwater is made of stones the size of washing machines. Danielle's head hits one of them, just behind her right ear, so hard that she sees stars, sudden explosions of false light that fog her vision for a moment. A jagged edge scrapes painfully across her lower ribs. Somehow she manages to keep hold of Jayalitha. As the wave retreats, pulling them back out into the water, Danielle flails with her feet, propelling them out and away from the breakwater. Her vision slowly clears. The next wave is not as strong, it rushes them towards but not quite to the rocks, and with its ebb Danielle manages to get them far enough away from the breakwater that she thinks they are safe. If treading water for two, while bleeding, dazed and being pursued by corrupt police officers, counts as safe.

The breakwater's invisibility works both ways. There is no way of knowing whether their pursuers are waiting for them on the beach. They might have gone already, or they might have heard Jayalitha's gasp and be willing to wait there until dawn. There is certainly no way Danielle can hold out that long. At first, kicking so frantically that her legs start to cramp, she fears exhaustion will soon force them back on to land. But when she relaxes a little, understanding that they are buoyant enough to stay in place with less work, her legs begin to loosen and grow accustomed to the rhythmic paddling motion that keeps them afloat.

'Are you OK?' she asks, keeping her voice very low.

'I think so,' Jayalitha says. Her voice is high and weak, she is still breathing fast, but at least she has managed to force herself to relax into a floating position, with Danielle holding her firmly from behind. 'Do not let me go. Please.'

'I won't,' Danielle promises.

Time passes. Danielle has no idea how much. She can't let go of Jayalitha to look at her watch, and her sense of duration has been stretched like a rubber band by imminent peril. It feels like hours. It almost feels as if she has spent her whole life treading water in this cold ocean, trying to ignore the pains in her side and skull. But surely it can't have been more than twenty minutes.

'How are you doing?' she asks.

Jayalitha starts at the sound of her voice. Then she says, her voice trembling with cold, 'I am sorry, Miss Leaf. I am very sorry for the trouble I have brought on you.'

'Let's worry about apologies when we get out of this.'

'Yes.'

'And call me Danielle.'

'Yes, Danielle. You may call me Jaya. If you wish. My friends do.'

'Jaya,' Danielle says. 'OK.'

'I am very cold, Danielle.'

'Join the club. I'm fucking freezing.'

Danielle can feel herself starting to weaken from the cold. A crippling headache is growing inside her skull, and she thinks she may be bleeding quite a lot from the wound on her side, which hurt like fire even before it was invaded by salt water. But she knows she has to hold out here as long as she can. It is not until her teeth begin to chatter that she gives in. Her legs are stiff and lethargic, and when she feels a cramp starting to tighten in her left thigh she starts to wonder whether they will make it back to the beach at all – but the cramp's vice grip loosens before it grows unbearable, and she manages to navigate them around the break-water and back into the shallows. No flashlights are visible on the beach. Jayalitha moans with relief when her feet find sand. Danielle realizes that the whole miserable experience must have been five times worse for her.

The beach is deserted. The night breeze feels like an arctic gale, and both of them shiver violently, teeth chattering like machine guns, as they cross the beach towards the boardwalk. Danielle tries to think. They can't go to their car, it has somehow been found by their enemy's hacker, P2, whose abilities leave even Keiran awestruck. Maybe via the tracking device rental compa-nies put in their cars now. Regardless, they need to get to the airport. She looks at her watch. Thankfully it is waterproof. Eight and a half hours to go before Keiran arrives.

She wishes she were in New York, where twenty-four-hour diners adorn practically every intersection. She doesn't know of anywhere here that might be open. They dare not return to the Cadillac Hotel. They can walk busy streets and try to hail a cab – but those are the same streets their pursuers are most likely to patrol. The smart thing is probably to stay on the beach until dawn. Except they are so cold and drained that hypothermia will become a real concern.

'We can't be the first people ever to die of hypothermia in Los Angeles,' she mutters. 'That would just be too embarrassing. It's *July*, for God's sake.'

'I beg your pardon?' Jayalitha says.

'Nothing. I think we have to take the chance.'

The chance pays off. The first vehicle they see at the intersection of Main and Brooks is a taxi with an illuminated call light. Its aged Middle Eastern driver casts a weary, seen-it-all eye over their two drenched figures, and as soon as Danielle demonstrates their ability to pay with two sodden twenty-dollar bills, and agrees to an extra ten in exchange for soaking his back seat with salt water, they are en route to the airport. Their driver even turns the heat up to maximum at their request. Halfway there, passing a Wells Fargo branch, she remembers Keiran's warning, and they stop long enough for her to withdraw five hundred dollars from its ATM.

LAX never closes, but at four in the morning it definitely slows down. In the Tom Bradley International Terminal, at the western tip of the airport's ellipse, the only open establishments are a few food stalls on the departures level. Haggard, exhausted people mill about in small groups, argue with airport staff, sit on plastic chairs and stare dully at the monitors. Danielle and Jayalitha, wearing new Los Angeles T-shirts and sweat pants, ugly but dry, sit at a table in front of Sbarro's Italian Food. Their wet clothes are piled on a spare seat. Sbarro has only pepperoni slices and Coke left for sale, but after freezing herself silly in the Pacific to escape probably murderous cops, this tastes as good to Danielle as truffles and Château Latour.

'Our friend's going to be here in eight hours. We just have to kill time until then. He'll be able to help us.' Danielle is not at all sure of this but tries to sound confident.

Jayalitha nods. 'Tell me,' she says. 'What happened to Angus? It was not clear to me, from the Internet. The newspapers said he was killed by a bomb he manufactured, but I did not think he would ever do such a thing.'

'No,' Danielle says. She swallows. She knows she owes Jayalitha the whole story, but she isn't yet ready to admit her own culpability. 'He was murdered.'

'Because of me.'

'No. No, not because of you.'

'Yes. I assure you. Because of me.' Jayalitha closes her eyes, then says something, several somethings, in a fluid Indian language that does nothing to disguise the pain in her voice. Danielle expects her to weep, but when Jayalitha opens her eyes, they are cold and hard as diamonds. 'He was a very good man,' she says. 'He deserved to live a long life.'

After a quiet moment Danielle asks, 'How did you know him?'

'I was seventeen,' Jayalitha says. 'He was travelling in India. I had run away from my parents, I was working in a hostel in Kerala, cleaning rooms. Angus saw past what I did, he treated me like an equal. Most travellers, they are good people, but that idea never occurs to them. We stayed up very late several nights, talking, talking about everything. After he left we stayed friends. That too is very rare. He supported me in everything I did. He worked so hard, all his life, to build a better world. He deserved to live to see it.'

'I'm sorry,' Danielle says inadequately.

'But who of us receive what we deserve?' Jayalitha glances at her left hand for a moment. 'It is I who should be sorry, Miss Leaf. Danielle. I have brought you into this as well. I fear I will have ruined you too before the end. It seems I ruin everything I touch.'

Jayalitha does not wear any rings, but the mark of one worn for years is etched around the second finger of her left hand. 'Were you married?' Danielle asks softly.

'I had a husband. I had two babies. They too are dead.'

'Jesus God.'

'Everyone dies,' Jayalitha says harshly.

'How old are you?'

'Twenty-two. I married when I was eighteen.'

'My God,' Danielle says.

'Life is different in India.'

'Yeah. I noticed. But still. Jesus. We must seem like overgrown children to you.'

'Sometimes. Yes. Does it matter?'

'I guess not.' Danielle shakes her head. 'This is all so crazy. There are policemen probably trying to kill me. I'm in Los Angeles with you. Two days ago my biggest problem was I was drinking too much.'

'You can go back to New York. Maybe they will leave you alone.'

'I thought of that already. No offence. But no. They'll assume I found out whatever it is that's so poisonous they have to kill everyone who knows. What is it? What do you know? Why are they after you?'

4

'Holy fucking Christ,' Keiran says.

'Yeah,' Danielle agrees.

It takes him a moment to digest what he has just heard. Danielle looks past him, out of the windows of the Encounter Restaurant, the *2001*-themed restaurant in the Jetsons-esque building at the heart of LAX, a flying saucer supported by swooping, curving pillars. She was a little disappointed to learn that the restaurant did not revolve, but the view is still spectacular, a vista of the airport and its dozens of jumbo jets lined up like children's toys, the blue Pacific just beyond.

'You're certain?' he asks Jayalitha. 'You're absolutely certain?'

'I could not bring the evidence with me. But there is no doubt.'

'It makes sense. Christ. It all makes perfect sense. How did you find out?'

'I suspected it first one night when my husband and I found our way into the mine,' she says. 'We overheard a meeting of four of the senior managers. They began to discuss the protests and media coverage of the tailings. They were furiously outraged.

They said these were all terrible lies, they knew of no such thing, they followed all international safety standards. They had no reason to be lying. They did not know we were listening. My husband and I began to wonder if perhaps they might not be speaking the truth.'

'And they were.'

'They were. The Kishkinda mine is entirely innocent.'

'I don't understand how they can do it,' Danielle says. 'There're so many people involved. How could no one find out until now?'

Keiran shakes his head. 'That part I understand. It's like a coding problem. Encapsulating information. Hiding it from those who don't need it. The people on the ground, they truly think they're giving out medicine, vitamins, vaccinations, and then being very thorough about documenting their patients' medical conditions. The researchers only know that someone else does the experiments, and this is the data. They only need a few trusted intermediaries, to put labels on bottles and send the data to the doctors. A half-dozen, if that. And you don't become a billionaire without accumulating a Filofax full of people who will keep their lips sealed shut.'

'People like Laurent,' Danielle says, remembering the deformed and dying children in that Kishkinda village of the damned, and Dr Lal's black case, bulging with medicines and vaccines supplied by Justice International. She wants to throw up.

'People. Using the word loosely. Psychopaths happy to induce cancer in *thousands* of people, with poison dressed up as medicines and vaccines, then test experimental drugs on them and blame it all on the mine next door. While the world's anti-capitalist activists eat the cover story up without ever considering other options that don't fit their preconceptions. They must try out new carcinogens as often as new medicines, to induce the kind of cancer Shadbold has more reliably.'

'Outsourcing,' Danielle says. 'He's outsourced dying to India.'

Keiran nods. 'In a way it's brilliant.'

'You say brilliant, I say fucking monstrous, let's call the whole thing off.'

'I doubt it's just Kishkinda,' Keiran muses. 'They must have other sites. Africa, Bolivia, anywhere life is cheap. I wonder how many people are murdered for every month they add to Shadbold's life. Probably hundreds.'

'We have to tell someone. We have to expose him.'

'Of course,' Keiran says. 'Except, we can spread it as an ugly rumour, that's a start, but it would certainly help if we had some actual evidence.'

'I'm sorry,' Jayalitha says. 'I was very fortunate to escape only with my life. I had to bury the evidence.'

Keiran turns to stare at her. 'Evidence? What evidence? Buried where?'

'Documents. I gained access to Justice International by subterfuge, and managed to abscond with documents that confirmed our suspicions. I could not take the evidence with me when I escaped. I buried them in Kishkinda.'

'Where?'

Jayalitha hesitates. 'I do not think I can explain the location. I could only show you.'

Keiran nods. 'How did you escape? How did you get here?'

'It was very difficult.' She pauses, remembering. 'They burned down my house. With my family in it. I was like an animal. Somehow I made it to Bangalore. I had friends there. I had to flee, I was pursued by the police, the government, everyone. My friends took me to Calcutta. Then to China, across the mountains. That took a very long time. In China I had no more friends. I did not dare contact anyone. That was how they found us, my e-mails to Angus. I sent an e-mail to him, telling him everything I had found, but I suppose they destroyed it before he read it. I thought in America I would be safe. I made my way to Shanghai. Then I had to find a way to cross the ocean. Then a way to pay. I speak only a very little Chinese. It was very difficult. It was such a long journey.'

'God,' Danielle says, inadequately. She cannot even imagine the perils and obstacles of a voyage like that, the constant terror of discovery, months of solitude in unthinkably alien places, struggling even to be understood, haunted by the burning memory of your murdered family, desperate to cross half the world so you might begin to be safe, and begin to have your revenge. But she hasn't found safety in America. Quite the opposite. She stares at Jaya, only twenty-two, with mixed awe and pity.

'You're hurt,' Keiran says to Danielle. 'Your side.'

'Huh?' Danielle looks down at her pink Los Angeles T-shirt, through which a thin crescent of blood has seeped. 'Oh. The rocks. It's not so bad, it's pretty shallow. Never mind that. What are we going to do? Can you rent a car here?'

Keiran considers for a moment. 'That's chancy. P2 might get into immigration records and see I just landed. I'm going to ring a friend of mine who lives here. Fellow hacker. He'll put us up while we work out what to do. I have some ideas about that, but we can talk those over once we're secure.'

'Are you sure you can trust him?' Danielle asks.

'I've known Mulligan twelve years. I trust him absolutely. Eat up. I'll buy a phone card and ring him from a pay-phone. Until further notice, we are living the anonymous lifestyle.'

A taxi takes them north from LAX, along the 405 towards the San Fernando Valley where Mulligan lives.

'What's Mulligan's real name?' Danielle asks.

Keiran looks at her. 'Why?'

'I just like knowing who I'm about to meet.'

'I don't actually know his birth name. He just uses his handle.'

'What is a handle?' Jayalitha asks.

'Online name,' Keiran says. 'Choosing your own clearly artificial handle for public use is part of hacker culture. Like leetspeak.'

Jayalitha looks bewildered. Danielle represses a sigh. Once again Keiran has entirely failed to understand his listener; Jaya has no idea that 'leetspeak' means hacker slang. Neither would Danielle if she hadn't once dated Keiran.

'Why did your friend pick Mulligan?' Danielle asks.

'Better ask him yourself.'

'What is your handle?' Jayalitha asks.

Keiran looks at her for a moment, then says, 'Not many people know both my handle and my birth name. LoTek. Capital L, capital T.'

'Why did you choose that?'

'If they think you're technical, go crude. If they think you're crude, go technical. I'm a very technical boy,' Keiran says cryptically. Any further explication is interrupted by a beeping that emerges from his windbreaker. He draws out something that looks like a slightly overgrown Palm Pilot.

'Danger hiptop,' he explains. 'I'm never without a processor. The beep means I have urgent e-mail from a trusted source. Don't worry, this can't be traced to me.' He pokes at a few keys on the miniature computer. Then his eyes widen and his face grows grim.

'What is it?' Danielle asks.

Keiran looks up at the taxi driver and shakes his head. 'It's from Mulligan. Our situation has escalated. I'll explain when we're there.'

When the driver, who had only been told 'the Valley', turns off the freeway and asks for specific directions, Keiran tells him to go to Laurel Canyon and Victory Boulevard. Then he makes them walk a long block back to Coldwater Canyon.

'Why couldn't we just get out where we were going?' Danielle asks, slightly exasperated; her legs are very tired, her headache has been dimmed with Tylenol but her side still hurts.

'Security. I don't like it either. I have to lug this backpack around.' Keiran's possessions are jammed into a large Lowe Alpine backpack, and they are heavy enough that he is sweating by the time they arrive at the Starbucks that is their destination.

He walks in, takes a table without even looking around, and puts his Danger 'hiptop' in the middle of the table.

'Is he here?' Jayalitha asks, as she and Danielle sit.

'I don't know. I've never met him before. He'll know us by my hiptop.'

'You've never *met* him?' Danielle asks incredulously. 'How can you trust him?'

'Don't get so hung up on meatspace,' Keiran says dismissively. 'Mulligan is solid. I'd stake my life on that. In fact, I rather think I'm doing just that.'

'Not just your life.'

Keiran shrugs. Danielle decides resignedly that help from someone trusted by proxy is better than no help at all. As Keiran goes to the counter to order drinks, she opens the California section of the *LA Times* someone has left on their table and scans the headlines, looking for something interesting and diverting.

What she finds is appalling.

'Oh my God,' she breathes.

'What is it?' Jayalitha asks.

Danielle looks around, suddenly terrified, but no one is paying any attention to them. She slides the newspaper over to Jayalitha and indicates an article headlined 'UK Bombing Suspects Reported In LA'. Above the headline are two photos, grainy and passport sized, but recognizably of Keiran and Danielle.

'Oh my goodness,' Jayalitha says.

Danielle reads the article and learns that she is wanted not only for the London bombing, but also for the murder of Kishkinda's chief financial officer at a conference in San Francisco two months ago. Keiran returns. When he sees what she is reading he nearly spills the drinks.

'Fucking hell,' he says. 'Turn that over. He didn't tell me it was in the papers.'

'You knew?'

'That was the e-mail in the taxi.'

'I've haven't . . . This is crazy. I haven't been to San Francisco in *years*. I didn't even know their CFO was dead. How can they—'

'Shadbold,' Keiran says. 'Trying to catch and discredit us simultaneously. Why hunt us down themselves when they can get the FBI to do it for them?'

As Danielle tries to absorb the information that she has suddenly become a felon wanted on federal charges, a man rolls up to their table in a wheelchair. Goateed and near-spherical, with dark eyes hidden in his round head like marbles sunk in butter, he wears a tent-like black T-shirt two sizes too big even for his horse-like girth. His legs emerge from black shorts and end at mid-thigh, in grotesque flipper-like protrusions of boneless flesh that Danielle has to look away from.

'LoTek?' he asks.

'Mulligan.' Keiran leaps to his feet, apparently entirely unfazed by the discovery that his friend is wheelchair-bound and legless. 'We should move. Right now.'

Mulligan doesn't argue. They follow him to his battered Ford Taurus. Fortunately no one in Starbucks seems to have registered their presence; or at least, no one is looking at the physically normal people. It takes Mulligan almost a minute to lever himself from his wheelchair into his car. He breaks out in a thick sweat, and wheezes with exhaustion, but waves off all offers of help.

Mulligan drives them through the vast, endless blocks of strip malls and suburbs that form the San Fernando Valley. He does not use the steering wheel at all; rather, he drives with what looks like a video-game controller, plugged into the steering column, held in his lap.

'Is that what I think it is?' Keiran asks.

'Yeah,' Mulligan says. 'Built the interface myself. Can you believe there's been no fundamental vehicle control improvements since Henry Ford? Fuckin' cultural inertia, man, it'll be the death of us all. The steering wheel is *nineteenth-century*. But this PS2 controller, ergonomic geniuses put millions into its design, it's the obvious choice.'

Danielle is unconvinced. Mulligan's driving is highly erratic. 'Is it legal?' she asks.

Mulligan shrugs. 'I unplug it if I get pulled over, pretend I was using these.' He gestures at paddles attached to the steering column. After a moment Danielle realizes they are intended for use as brake and accelerator.

It takes them fifteen minutes to reach Mulligan's large bungalow in the heart of Encino. His property smells of orange trees, reminding Danielle of family holidays in Florida when she was younger. From the ungroomed back yard, a sliding door opens automatically. Past the entryway, a hallway takes them past a filthy kitchen, then a filthier bathroom, to a sequence of several cavernous rooms full of metal racks and shelves, on which computer carcasses and the gutted remains of unidentifiable electrical devices are piled. It looks like a madman's museum of dead machines. There are several workbenches, festooned with tools that range in size from microscopic screwdrivers to welding torches. There are also a half-dozen computers in working order, plus a dozen Microsoft XBoxes stacked atop one another, all wired together.

Everything is low, all the shelves and benches thigh-high so that Mulligan can easily access them; Danielle feels a little as if she is visiting Lilliput. The whole building smells of metal, plastic and chemicals. There are posters of implausibly endowed and gravity-resistant women, most of them from American and Japanese comic books, and a few fold-outs of naked women, clearly from porn magazines considerably less classy than *Playboy*. Jayalitha looks shocked by these.

'Sorry,' Mulligan says, turning red and pulling the pornography from the walls as he wheels past. 'I didn't realize you were female. LoTek didn't specify.' He glares at Keiran, who shrugs.

Danielle knows, from dating Keiran years ago, that hackers can generally be divided into two groups: lean, black-clad, tattooed and pierced counter-culture rebels, and social-outcast ultra-geeks. Keiran floats somewhere between the two categories. Mulligan clearly belongs to the latter.

The only vaguely domestic part of the building is the far corner, where a large overstuffed leather couch and love-seat are arrayed around an Ikea table, in front of a huge flat screen that hangs on the wall. The floor here is occupied by old pizza boxes, some of them empty, cans of Jolt cola, pyramids of books and magazines, crumpled papers and clothing, and a spaghetti tangle of wires, almost entirely obscuring the faux-Persian rugs which are a welcome change from the bare concrete of the rest of the place. A Sharper Image Ionic Breeze air purifier in the corner is coming out the loser in its eternal battle.

'This is it,' Mulligan says. 'I guess you'll be staying here a while, huh?'

'Yes,' Keiran says firmly, despite Danielle's doubtful expression.

'Where do you sleep?' Danielle asks.

'In here.' Mulligan opens a wooden door obscured by the shadow of the stack of XBoxes, and reveals what was once a wine cellar, now occupied by a futon illuminated by a single dangling light bulb. The sheets, blanket and pillows are black. The concrete walls are unadorned save for a bar bolted to the wall that helps Mulligan get to and from the bed.

'That's your bedroom?' Danielle asks, unable to disguise the horror in her voice.

'Sure. I go in and sleep, I get up and leave, why decorate?'

'Let's play *Changing Rooms* later,' Keiran says. 'We've got some big decisions to make.'

Danielle finds it hard to concentrate on what Keiran is saying. She is wanted by the FBI. The idea sounds too unreal to take seriously. She had nothing to do with that bomb, except for falling in love with the man who made it. She is completely innocent of the San Francisco murder. This has gone too far. She is sorry for Angus and Jayalitha's family and everyone else, but her whole life could be ruined by this. She should walk to the nearest phone, call the police and turn herself in. Surely the FBI will understand, the charges will be dropped, the truth will set her free.

Except. Maybe she isn't, technically, innocent. She knew that a bomb was being made; she thought it was never intended to go off, true, but she was still an accessory, to that and to the Paris break-in. And turning herself in must be exactly what Shadbold wants. He's responsible for this, that's obvious, he and Laurent must have leaked evidence pointing to herself and Keiran. If he can't silence them by killing them, he can destroy their credibility, and ensure they get locked up. And continue to murder thousands of people. He wants her arrested, and by itself that's a good enough reason to run as long as she can. Because it means they are dangerous to him, somehow, while they are free.

But if she won't turn herself in, what can she do? Her bank accounts and credit cards will be frozen. Her picture will be studied by police officers across the country, and by newspaper readers, maybe even television watchers – the UK bombing made headlines around the world, and wanted criminals always make for a juicy news segment. And who can she trust? She suspects her friends and family would all turn her in, telling themselves it was for her own safety, for her own good, no matter what Danielle might say. She can't trust anyone not in this room.

Part of her is terrified. The prospect of being pursued by both a vengeful billionaire and the FBI is overwhelming. Part of her just wants to flee, go home, escape by any means necessary, fly back to New York or her parents in Boston and take her chances there. But the more Danielle considers her situation, the angrier she gets. Shadbold and Laurent have already used and discarded her like a rag. Now they are hounding her again. In the last twenty-four hours of terror and misery she has been pursued, bruised, bloodied, nearly drowned and frozen, and now falsely accused of mass murder in the eyes of all the world – all for nothing more than the sin of knowing too much, trusting too much, and wanting to help people. She is sick of running. She wants revenge.

'Let's face it,' Keiran is saying. 'If we run and hide, we're doomed. We could own every police computer in America and still just delay the inevitable. We have to go with the Napoleon doctrine. Our only defence is a good offence. We have to show that Shadbold was behind that bomb. And incidentally the murder of several thousand Indian peasants. Not that I expect the world to care much about that part.'

'I can try to take you to the evidence I buried,' Jayalitha says doubtfully, 'but surely returning to India will be disastrous for us all?'

Keiran nods. 'Quite right. We can't risk that while their cyberspace superman P2 is out there tracking our every move. But I'm wondering now if he might actually be their weakness. If we can get to him, find out how he can do what he does, maybe we can use that to break them open.'

'Get to him how?'

'With luck we can get the men who chased you at the beach to tell us where he is.'

Danielle stares at him. 'The men at the . . . are you *crazy*? Those were *cops*. What do you want to do, go to their homes, knock on their doors and ask them questions? That's insane. Our pictures are in the newspaper. If we go outside, we'll be arrested.'

Keiran and Mulligan exchange a look.

'I think you underestimate our capabilities,' Keiran says.

'What capabilities?'

'Don't wanna brag,' Mulligan says unconvincingly, 'but if there are twenty better hackers in the world than LoTek and me, I'd be real surprised. I don't think you quite grok what we can do. Believe me, your buddy Shadbold has fucked with the wrong hombres. Never mind the feds. It's not like TV. They're not really that scary. Actually they're pretty dumb. I guess LoTek's right, if you just ducked off the grid they'd get you in the end, but we can keep them off your back for, I don't know, months at least.

They've wanted me for ten years now, and they still don't even know my name.'

'They know mine already,' Danielle says.

'That's OK. We'll get you a new one.'

She blinks. 'What?'

'LoTek and me both got a few spare identities on the shelf. No females, but I'm sure we can make one up for you. You'll have to change your look in case they eyeball you.'

Keiran runs his fingers through his hair. 'Not just you. I intend to develop the world's most sudden case of male-pattern baldness.'

Danielle looks from one of them to the other, trying to work out whether they're serious. Both of them are smiling.

'Are you enjoying this?' she asks, incredulously.

'Well,' Keiran says cautiously, 'don't misunderstand, I wish it hadn't happened. But given that it has, I have to admit, on the run from the FBI, it does have a certain ring to it.'

'The legend of LoTek lives on!' Mulligan intones. 'Well. Hopefully. Unless you, like, die and shit.'

Danielle looks at Mulligan's tarnished mirror, so low on the wall she has to squat to see her face, and hardly recognizes herself. She supposes that's the idea. The picture in the paper was her passport photo, taken when she had short hair. She has let it grow since then, into a bob – now a very blonde bob. She looks around. The tub and toilet bowl are scaly and stained. The floor is covered with old dirt and new tufts of hair, the latter thanks to Keiran's newly uncovered scalp. And Danielle's hair is now the shade of platinum blonde she associates with fake breasts. Well, no one ever said running for your life was dignified.

She emerges into the living room and sits on the couch. Jayalitha is curled up in a tattered sleeping bag, dead to the world, and Mulligan has gone somewhere to buy food and electronics. Keiran sits in front of one of Mulligan's computers, his face bathed by flickering LED light.

Danielle is reminded of the night she first met him, four years ago, at a noisy party in Oakland. She went upstairs to use the bathroom, and on the way back saw light gleaming in a dark room. A man working at a computer. Something about the scene had intrigued her, the man's dark solitude while a party throbbed below, and she had gone in and struck up a curious conversation. It wasn't until he accompanied her out of the room a half-hour later that she realized he was tall and good looking. And amazingly Keiran still is, despite his newly shaved head, despite the years of abuses and deprivations, junk food and drugs, he has put his body through. He is blessed with looks, health, superhuman brains. Everything comes naturally to Keiran except human understanding.

He glances at her. 'Nice hair.'

Danielle sighs. 'Same to you. I feel like a walking escort service ad. You really think this will stop police from recognizing us?'

'No. But it might slow them enough that we get a head start. The idea, remember, is that they never see us in the first place.'

Danielle nods.

'How are you doing?' Keiran asks.

She pauses. The question is uncharacteristic of him. 'I don't know,' she says. 'Scared. Dizzy. Angry. Stressed. I'm tired of it all already. Like, I just want the whole situation to be over, one way or another. How are you?'

'Mostly angry. Not just at him. At the system that lets it happen. If people actually cared about a few thousand dead children in India, there would have been real investigations, Shadbold would have been found out and stopped long ago. But nobody really cares.'

'Why do you?'

He looks at her, surprised. 'What do you mean?'

'You're not exactly a people person. What do you care about children in India?'

'I'm not . . .' Keiran pauses. 'What Shadbold's doing, that's . . . it's a crime against humanity, not just people. I believe in humanity. To quote our murdered Scottish friend, I believe in a better world.' He smiles sourly. 'I like the *idea* of people. It's the individual instances I have problems with.'

'Because we're all so stupid.'

'You're not stupid?'

'Compared to you I am. Compared to you almost anybody is.'

'I used to think so. But, you know, lately I've begun to wonder.'

'If you're so smart, why ain't you rich?' Danielle asks sarcastically.

'Not rich exactly. More like, why aren't I doing something with it? Why aren't I . . .'

'Happy?'

'Not that,' Keiran says quickly. 'More like, if I'm so smart, how come it's taken me thirty years to work out that utter contempt is maybe not the best default standpoint to take when dealing with other human beings?'

Danielle half smiles. 'Yeah. I kinda wish you'd figured that out when we were dating.'

'Well, you helped put me on the road, if that's any consolation.'

'I'm flattered.'

'Was I a bastard to you?' Keiran asks. 'When we dated? I'm sorry if I was. I tried not to be. I truly liked you.'

Danielle shrugs. 'You were a boyfriend. Better than some, worse than others.'

Keiran looks deflated.

'I did like you too,' Danielle says hastily. 'You were different. There wasn't any bullshit about you. I liked that.'

Keiran nods. They look at each other.

'What did you owe Angus?' Danielle asks. 'What did you have to pay back? I know you said you couldn't explain without his blessing, but . . .'

'But he's unlikely to come back from the grave to OK it now,' Keiran says.

'Yeah.'

'Angus and Estelle, wherever they're buried, I'll bet you they're organizing the whole graveyard. Holding skeleton meetings, assembling communiqués, issuing strongly worded corpse grievances. We demand better flowers and fewer maggots. Or maybe they're marching on the Pearly Gates with protest signs and gas masks. End the Cloud Nine Discrimination! Equality and salvation for all!'

Danielle smiles wanly.

'My sister,' Keiran says. 'She owed these three insane Albanians a lot of money. For drugs, I don't know what kind. They took her up to the top of this empty car park in Birmingham, told her she was out of chances, broke her cheekbone with a hammer. She called me. Middle of the night, I was just coming down from acid, I hardly recognized her voice. It had been years. Half her face was broken, she was sobbing, it took me ages to understand her. She said I had to bring money, six thousand pounds, and if I wasn't there by dawn, or they saw the police, they would drop her off the roof.'

'I didn't know you had a sister,' Danielle says softly.

'I don't. To all intents and purposes. She was,' he hesitates, 'damaged. From birth, I think. But I stupidly decided to help, called Angus, woke him. Between us we had the money – I was paranoid hacker enough to keep a few thousand around, and he'd collected dues for some protest he was organizing. I'd known him less than a year, but he was round my flat five minutes later, all his money in the glove box, to pick me up and drive me to Birmingham. It should have been simple, right? The money for the girl. I remember getting out of the car holding six thousand pounds in a Tesco bag. My sister looked like she'd been hosed down with her own blood. Up until then I had wondered if it was a ruse, if she was part of it. But no, there really were crazy Albanians. Kids, teenagers, tweakers, strung out on crystal meth. They decided the money wasn't enough, they wanted our car too. They didn't have guns, no one has guns in Britain, but they had knives and hammers. They grabbed me, I tried to fight, they hit me on the head, I fell down. It seemed pretty apparent by then that they weren't planning to let us get away alive. Angus could have just driven away. It wasn't his problem, his sister. But that was Angus. Always fighting other people's battles.'

Keiran falls silent.

'What happened?' Danielle asks.

'He ran us over,' Keiran says. He smiles faintly at the memory. 'We were all in one tight group, that was their mistake, they never thought he'd run us down with me and my sister there too. Sideswiped us like a fucking stunt driver, knocked them all over. Cracked two of my ribs and hairline-fractured a tibia. Not that I noticed until the next day. I don't remember exactly what happened after that. Concussions fragment your memory. I remember picking up a knife and stabbing one of them. I was snarling. Like a dog. Everyone was. It sounded like a dogfight. I remember Angus coming out of the car with a crowbar, and one of them hit him with a hammer. After that it gets hazy. Like a nightmare. The whole night was like a nightmare, but instead of waking up, it just kept getting more real, and more awful. Somehow we won. They ran away. Angus's arm was broken, I was the only one who could drive, so I drove us to casualty with a concussion and a broken leg. Still on acid – good thing too, dulled the pain. And while they were examining Angus and me, my sister vanished with the money. I don't know how she made it outside. She'd sprained her ankle badly. Must have had some drugs left on her.'

'What's her name?' Danielle asks.

'Doesn't matter,' Keiran says brutally. 'She's not dead yet. I check coroners' reports sometimes. I couldn't find her even if I wanted to, she lives completely off the grid, with crusties and squatters. Doesn't matter. She might as well be dead. But she isn't. Neither am I. That's what I owed Angus.'

'God,' Danielle says.

A long silence falls.

'All right,' Keiran says. 'Let's get back to business.'

'Right,' Danielle says, very briskly. 'Business. You were going to give me a new identity, right? Enrol me in your own personal witness protection programme? Go on, then. Show me what you got.'

5

Keiran has to admit that on some level Danielle is right: part of him is glad to be pursued by the law. He has spent years hacking into dozens of corporate and government systems, but he has never been able to justify actually using his access before. It has always been too risky. Every abuse of a compromised system might be noticed and somehow be tracked, could be the mistake that leads to his downfall. But now he has an excuse to flex his virtual muscles, use all the dormant authority he has accumulated over the years, and the exercise of raw power feels good.

First he needs anonymous money. Easy enough. He occasionally advises a group of Russian credit-card hackers on technical matters; in exchange, he has access to their 'platinum list' of high-limit, high-volume credit-card numbers, the kind for which a single hundred-dollar charge is likely to go unnoticed. Hacked from some upscale travel agency in Chicago, apparently. He uses thirty such credit cards to rent a nearby post office box, then purchase and post to that box four anonymous Virgin mobile phones, two hundred dollars' worth of phone cards and twenty cashier's cheques for a hundred dollars apiece.

After money, identity. In the space of forty minutes, he arranges for three brand-new Social Security cards and California driver's licences to be mailed to the post office box he has just rented, in the names of Sarah Crawford, Julian O'Toole and Parvati Rumanujan. Keiran and Danielle's new licences feature photos from Mulligan's digital camera that display their new looks, touched up to look entirely unlike the pictures in today's newspaper. He goes back to the Russian credit-card list and throws in a secured MasterCard for each of them, with thousand-dollar limits, in the same false names.

'Aren't you worried they could find the mailbox?' Danielle asks, when he explains the outcome of his cyberspace pillaging. She has been sitting quietly beside him the whole time, shoulder-surfing, although he doubts she or any other non-hacker could have followed a tenth of the work he has just done.

'They don't know to look for it. And we have to make sure it stays that way. Remember, no phone calls home, no checking e-mail, don't even visit any of your favourite websites. We're only omnipotent for as long as we're invisible.'

'If you can do this, why haven't you ever just taken ten million dollars from some bank and retired?'

Keiran shakes his head. 'Taking money is a violation of LoTek's Law. Always be invisible. Creating a new identity is invisible hacking. If you do it right, no one will even notice. But stealing an identity, or stealing money especially, that's very visible. I could probably steal a million dollars a week from social security if I wanted to. Maybe I could break into a bank. Maybe not, they're a lot sharper about security than the government. But even if I did, money is a zero-sum game, there is no way to steal significant amounts without being noticed. More than a few hundred dollars will trigger their alarms, alert their forensic accountants, get them angry. And once they're angry, they *will* track you down. Once they start they usually win. Authorities are stupid, but they're very big, very resourceful, very persistent. If they find out I exist they'll squash me like a cockroach. But if you don't even know you have roaches, you never call the extermi-nator.'

'It's scary that you can do this,' Danielle says.

'Good. Because right now we need to be frightening.'

'I can't believe all these systems are so insecure that anyone can break into them.'

Keiran smiles. 'Not just anyone.'

'Sorry. I didn't mean to imply you were mortal.'

'Not what I meant. I have a secret weapon. Shazam.'

Danielle looks at him. 'I've heard of that. I've used it, I had it on my computer in Bangalore. It's a program for downloading music, like Napster or iTunes, right?'

'In a way. But Napster had central servers, and a business, and an address that record companies could send their lawsuits to, so they got shut down. Shazam is just a piece of software. People install it, and it looks around the Internet until it finds other computers with Shazam. It can be used to share anything, but yes, almost always music. It's very popular. More than seven million copies in active use. It's free and open-source, so people can look at the software themselves and see that there's no hidden agenda, no spyware, nothing that will take over your computer. And it works. Most open-source software usually doesn't quite. I'm very proud of it.'

'You hid something in it.'

Keiran nods, pleased. 'A tiny little buffer overflow, obfuscated inside one of the trickiest and dullest parts of the code. Anybody can look at it, but in all these years nobody's analysed it in enough detail to find the bug. Like Shadbold said when he let us go. You can rely on people to do things. It would take a great programmer several very tedious hours to analyse that piece of code and find the bug, and none of them can be bothered to waste their time like that.'

'And that little thing lets you take it over?'

'It's like a tiny lock, with an insanely complicated key, which opens up their whole computer to me. I can own any box that runs Shazam. And you'd be amazed where it runs. Seven million copies. Police stations, the ATF, the White House, foreign militaries, you name it. Secretaries and IT grunts around the world use it to steal music from the Internet on work time. And then I use it to steal their machines. Places with seriously organized IT security ban it and make the ban stick, but you've worked in offices, you know how often those rules are followed in the real world. Maybe one company in ten actually enforces them.

Kishkinda being one of them. Not a single instance running there. But there's one machine on the Justice International network that proved very useful indeed.'

'And once you've got access you can turn around and get me a driver's licence and social security card just like that? It's that easy?' Danielle asks.

'No. Shazam is just a beachhead. I have to work out what to do with the access, where their databases are, how to break into the rest of their network, how their home-grown programs work. It isn't easy. When I broke into Social Security, two years ago, it took me three weeks at fifteen hours a day to work out how to issue a new card and fix the audit trail to fool their safeguards. But once that work's done, well, today I could fill a city with people that don't exist.'

'How long has Shazam been out there?'

Keiran pauses to think. 'Almost five years. To tell you the truth, it'll be obsolete soon, it's already being replaced by BitTorrent and the like.'

'You never told me about this when we dated,' Danielle says accusingly.

He looks at her incredulously. 'You can't be serious. We're talking about the hacker Holy Grail here. I've never told *anyone* except a few of my hacker friends. Mulligan, George, Klaupactus, Trurl. Everyone else just thinks I'm naturally godlike. You're the first non-hacker I've ever told. You should be flattered.'

'I'll try to remember,' Danielle says, but she sounds mollified. 'So if your Shazam network is so great, why can't you stomp this P2 guy?'

Keiran opens his mouth – and closes it again. He is not accustomed to being pitted against a superior hacker. But he has to admit that truth. He could have tracked Jayalitha's phone call to Danielle; he tunnelled into America's major phone companies years ago, and has at least read-only access to most of their corporate databases. But he could not have worked out overnight which Los Angeles hotel she was in. On Keiran's advice, Danielle had showed up at the hotel without making a reservation, and yet P2 had found her. She couldn't have been followed, or he wouldn't have waited until midnight, or bothered calling her hotel to verify her presence. P2 must have broken into the rental-car company's tracking system, located Danielle's car, and then literally hacked into every one of the dozens of nearby hotels.

It seems like a little thing, compared to creating new government identities, but hacking is a time-consuming art. It can take Keiran days or even weeks to crack a new network, even with Shazam's seven million machines on his side. P2 found Danielle in a few short hours. Maybe he just got lucky – but three months ago, when Shadbold's thugs kidnapped him from his London flat, they were sent there by P2, who found Keiran in a matter of minutes despite Keiran's many paranoid precautions.

Those two extraordinary feats cannot both have been luck. The only logical conclusion to draw is that Keiran is outmatched. Either P2 has been around for ever, and has a finger in every electronic pie on the planet, or he knows some extraordinary new exploit that gives him the power to immediately hack into virtually any system. For safety's sake, Keiran has to assume that P2 has at-will access to every computer, database, network and satellite in the known world. Other than Shazam.

'Let me put it this way,' he says. 'I might have the Holy Grail, but P2 appears to have a direct line to God himself.'

'Great. Just great. When does my new ID get here?'

'A few days.'

'We're supposed to stay here until then?'

'No,' Keiran says. 'We need more to work with if we're going to catch P2, and we need it fast. This hunt is sure to be a major time sink. You remember the corrupt police who chased you last night?'

'Like I was about to forget,' Danielle says drily.

'Well, tonight we chase them.'

6

He looks at Mulligan. 'Are we ready?'

'Record away.'

Keiran raises the microphone to his lips and affects a French accent. 'This is Anna Fiche-Toi, personal assistant to Jack Shadbold.' He pauses for a moment. 'I apologize for not going through the usual channels, but this is a matter of some urgency. Danielle Leaf and Keiran Kell have been seen at a movie theatre and will be on the Third Street Promenade in Santa Monica in thirty minutes. You are instructed to be there to intercept.'

He nods at Mulligan, who types a few lines.

'Anna Fiche-Toi?' Danielle asks.

'Anna Fuck You, loosely translated.'

'You don't sound like an Anna.'

'He does now,' Mulligan says. 'Listen.' And his computer plays back Keiran's speech, the pitch adjusted up at least two octaves, the voice obviously filtered. It sounds more inhuman than female.

'You're sure you want to come?' Keiran asks Danielle and Jayalitha. 'We don't need you. And if there's trouble . . .'

'If there is trouble I am sure it will find us regardless,' Jayalitha says.

'Fair point. Let's take our toys and go spring a little ambush on the bad guys.'

Getting into his car again costs Mulligan a half-pint of sweat. Danielle can see why he rarely leaves home. In his apartment, before his computer, Mulligan is a master of the universe. Why go to a gruelling physical effort just to become an object of pity?

'Try not to get pulled over,' Keiran says as Mulligan swings the car clumsily out into night-time Valley traffic, wobbling between lanes. 'Might be hard to explain how you happened to pick up two wanted terrorists and one illegal immigrant.'

'Sorry. It's been a while,' Mulligan says.

Jayalitha gasps and Danielle grabs the seat in front of her as the car skids into a last-second-decision left turn.

'You don't say,' Keiran says drily. 'Also try not to get us killed. Killed is bad.'

'You wanna drive?'

'I would if I could, but I seem to have too many legs.'

Danielle's jaw drops at the insensitivity of this comment, but Mulligan chuckles and says, 'Those damn legs gonna get you in trouble someday.'

'They already have,' Keiran agrees.

'You oughta get them removed. I know a doctor.'

'I was saying just the other day I wanted to lose a few stone.'

'That's brilliant. The Amputation Diet! We'll sell millions. Make Atkins look like a chump.'

'You're both sick,' Danielle says, amused despite herself.

'It's not us,' Mulligan says. 'It's the fuckin' rest of the world.'

The Third Street Promenade is an upscale open-air shopping mall, a pedestrian thoroughfare in Santa Monica only a few blocks from the sea, decorated with elaborate fountains and dinosaur topiaries, entertained by buskers, lined by stores vending all the famous brand names of American commerce. It is a very popular place to shop, wander and meet. This is only partly because of its laid-back luxury. In southern California, where the unwritten law is 'drive or be dogmeat', easy parking is a draw in itself, and Second and Fourth Streets, which bracket the Promenade, boast a half-dozen inexpensive parking garages.

'All right, Mulligan *mi amigo*,' Keiran says, from the roof of the largest such garage. No other cars are on the roof; it is nearly 9 p.m., on a weeknight, and there are plenty of parking slots available on lower levels. 'Go forth to Starbucks and send our enemies my sweet whispered words of love. And try not to be obvious.'

Mulligan glares. 'Go teach your grandmother.'

He rotates his wheelchair and speeds it towards the elevators, his closed laptop in a carry-case where his calves would rest if they existed.

'All right,' Keiran says. 'Back in the car.'

They wait a long half-hour before Keiran's hiptop beeps. He glances at it and shows it to Danielle and Jayalitha. 'These men look familiar?'

The danger hiptop's screen displays a picture of two men, both middle aged, one lean with hawk-like eyes and greying temples, one plump, balding and moustached. 'Yes,' Danielle says immediately. 'It was them. On the beach. Right?'

'I think so,' Jayalitha says hesitantly. 'It is hard for me to distinguish white men.'

'It's them. I'm sure of it,' Danielle says.

'Good.' Keiran taps a reply into his hiptop. A minute later it beeps again and he grins triumphantly. 'Excellent. They have been Bluesnarfed.'

'That's it?' Danielle asks after a moment.

'You were expecting fireworks? Remember LoTek's Law. That was about as spectacular as I hope to get.'

'Perhaps you could explain?' Jayalitha asks after a moment. 'I do not fully understand.'

'Well.' Keiran hesitates. 'Crash course in hacking. You remember I went looking for our friend P2 online, didn't find him but did find the phone gateway he's using, and the fact that he'd called two Los Angeles numbers. That's why I called you at the hotel.'

Jayalitha nods.

'So. What do we want? Information about the opposition. What do we have? Phone numbers. What do we do? Look up their names and addresses, right? No dice. Their phones are anonymous. But I think to myself, what kind of phones? We can look that up, because every time you use a mobile phone, you tell the network your phone's serial number. Ironically this is to prevent stolen phones from being used. We hacked into the mobile phone company's database, looked up their call records, and discovered, to our joy, that theirs are flashy new Nokias with Bluetooth. Meaning they're equipped with special radios that let them talk to other phones and computers within twenty feet. So you can update your address book from your computer and so forth. Bluetooth is a communications protocol. You know what communication means? Communication means vulnerability.'

'How very male of you,' Danielle says, amused.

'Very funny. Our good friend Mulligan's laptop speaks Bluetooth too. And it has been sitting in its case for the last hour running a program we wrote that plunders any Bluetooth phone within range. The moment they walked within twenty feet of him, he pillaged their call records, address books, text messages. And these are the anonymous phones our on-the-take friends use to talk to their secret masters. Surely they have been given a phone number to use when they do catch us. If so, we have that number right now.'

'Well, good,' Danielle says. She has never seen Keiran so excited.

'We've only just begun. They're walking down the promenade, looking for us. When they walk back up, we move on to phase two.'

'What's phase two?'

'Social engineering, with a side order of Bluebugging, and a real-time VOIP trace for dessert. Much more exciting. Hold on to your hats. We're going to ring our friends down there and have a little chat.'

'You're going to *call them*?' Danielle asks.

'Terrible shame to acquire their phone numbers without bothering to use them, no? But what makes it interesting is that they're going to ring us too. And they won't even know it.'

A moment later his hiptop beeps again, then rings. Danielle hadn't realized it was a phone as well.

'Here we go,' Keiran says. He answers the hiptop, gives it to Danielle and says, 'Listen. Don't push any buttons.' Then he draws out his own Virgin Mobile phone, dials, pauses, and punches more numbers into the phone.

Danielle puts the Danger hiptop to her ear and hears a warbling ring. It sounds distant. Then a gruff voice, equally distant, says, 'Yes?'

'Good evening,' Keiran says in front of her. 'My name is Keiran Kell. I understand you're looking for me.' Danielle nearly drops the hiptop.

'The fuck?' a man's voice hisses in her ear. 'It's him. It's Kell.'

'Kell? The fuck? What does he want?' a second male voice asks. Both voices are familiar, from the beach, last night.

'What do you want?' the first voice asks.

Danielle works out what is going on. The two cops are back within range of Mulligan. He has caused one of their Bluetooth phones to secretly call Keiran's hiptop number, while Keiran calls their other phone. Getting a phone call from someone's pocket without their knowledge is as good as planting a listening device on them.

'I want you to pass a message to your employer. We want ten million dollars in my Cayman Islands account by midnight to-night, or we release evidence of what Shadbold is doing.' Keiran hangs up.

'What was that all about?' Danielle asks, then twitches with dismay, worried that her voice might emanate from the phone on the other end of the hiptop's connection. But the voice on the hiptop, repeating what Keiran has just said, does not falter.

'Don't worry, they can't hear you,' Keiran says. 'Mulligan connected that phone to one of our VOIP gateways. That records the conversation and pipes the output one-way to the hiptop.'

'You want money from them?' Jayalitha asks.

'Oh, good Lord, no. I don't even have a Cayman Islands account. The Caymans are so five years ago. No, the idea is to make them ring their secret masters right away.'

'Quiet,' Danielle says. 'I think they're calling them now.'

'Here,' Keiran says. He takes the hiptop and adjusts one of the controls on its side, turning it into a speakerphone.

'Sorry to bother you, but Kell just called us,' the man says. 'That's right. He called us.' He summarizes Keiran's demand, then says, 'All right,' and in a different tone, 'We're supposed to wait a moment.'

'Come on, Mulligan,' Keiran says, quietly but intensely. 'Do your thing.'

'What's going on?'

'Ever seen a film where the police try to make the villain stay on the phone long enough to trace his call?' Danielle nods. 'Well, that was always risible shite. As if phone companies could make a phone ring without knowing where it was. But this is almost like those films. I guarantee you that number they rang went through a VOIP redirector before it reached P2. Just like we're listening to them through our gateway. Mulligan's sitting in Starbucks right now trying to hack into their redirector before this conversation ends. If he's good enough and fast enough, we find out where P2 physically is. But if they hang up first, anonymous redirectors don't keep records, all those packets will be lost like tears in the rain.'

'How poetic.'

'*Blade Runner*. Cyberpunk icon. Come on, darling,' he says to the hiptop, 'give me some good news.'

The hiptop beeps as if to answer. Keiran scrolls to his e-mail and grins with triumph. 'We have a physical phone number. We have a location.'

'He's a block away from us right now?' the hiptop exclaims.

Keiran, Danielle and Jayalitha stop and stare at it for a moment.

'Parking garage at Fourth and Arizona,' it says. 'Let's move.'

'Oh, fuck,' Keiran says hoarsely. 'Fucking shit *bollocks*. He tracked us too. What is he, fucking omniscient? Must have triangulated the mobile signal. We need to be going right now.' He takes two steps towards Mulligan's car.

'Can you drive that?' Danielle asks, thinking of Mulligan's PlayStation controller, and the back-up hand-paddle accelerator and brake.

'Shit. Probably not. Shanks's mare. Come on, the stairs. No, the elevator.' He starts towards the exit. Jayalitha follows.

Danielle does not. Instead she looks over the wall of the parking garage, down into the alley between Third and Fourth Streets, and sees, from seven storeys up, two men sprint up the alley towards the garage. They are not uniformed, and the street lights are far too dim to recognize faces, but it has to be them.

'Stop,' she says urgently. 'It's too late. They're already here.'

7

Keiran tries to imagine a plausible escape route. None is obvious. The parking garage's interior is laid out in a giant helix, like New York's Guggenheim Museum. Elevators and stairs descend from the north-east and south-west corners of the building. Both corners will surely be watched. Mulligan's car is parked on the western edge of the roof. Keiran can probably hot-wire it, but he cannot drive it well enough to escape the police. The garage is much taller than any other buildings around them, ruling out any escape to a connecting rooftop. The street lights of Santa Monica wink red and green seven sheer storeys below, and there is nothing above them but the night sky. Keiran shakes his head, as if he might dislodge a moment of genius. *Think outside the box.* There must be some hack, some unexpected action, some lateral leap of logic that can save them. But nothing comes to mind. They are boxed in.

'We could call back-up,' his hiptop says. 'Seal the place, have them arrested.'

'I want that bonus,' the other voice says, his voice muffled but decipherable. 'Stay here and watch the exits. Show your badge, get the attendants to help. I'll go up top and work down. If they get past us, then we call it in. They won't get far, Santa Monica's crawling with squad cars.'

'Shit,' Danielle mutters. 'Shit shit *shit.*'

'Come on,' Keiran says. He doesn't know how to get out, but he knows that if they stay where they are they'll be captured immediately. 'The stairs.'

'They'll see us.'

'We're not descending all the way. Give me that.' He takes the hiptop from her as they begin to descend, and switches off the speakerphone.

They have gone down only one level when they hear the elevator ding on the roof above them. They freeze for a moment. If their pursuer takes the stairs immediately, they are caught. But they hear his boots moving away. Obviously he plans to walk the garage's helix from top to bottom, checking under cars and other hiding spots, hoping to flush them out to the ground floor where his partner waits. He is unaware that his prey know they are being hunted.

'We can just go back up top in a moment,' Danielle whispers, as Keiran leads them out on to the third floor.

'No,' Keiran says. 'Then they call back-up and we're not murdered but we're definitely arrested. We have to get out before they give up on finding us. Except I have no idea how.'

'The lights,' Jayalitha suggests. 'If there is a wire we can find and sever. In darkness they will never see us.'

Keiran stops in mid-step and turns to stare at Jayalitha. 'That's brilliant. The lights. Of course.'

'How? Find the fuse box? It'll be locked,' Danielle says.

'The rather large fuse box.' Smiling now, he takes out the Virgin Mobile phone again and punches a long series of numbers into it, establishing a secure connection to Mulligan's mobile phone.

'Yo,' Mulligan answers.

Keiran says, 'We got hacked and tracked. We need darkness and we need it ten seconds ago.' He hangs up immediately.

'What do we do now?' Jayalitha asks.

'Same thing we've been doing all night. Pray that Mulligan's as good as I think he is.'

The seconds ease by, much more slowly than Keiran would like. The elevator they stand next to dings, and the shock causes him to nearly swallow his own tongue, but it contains only a young couple, who give them curious looks before returning to their car and driving off.

Keiran still has his hiptop to his ear. A few seconds after the couple's car disappears down the helix, he stiffens; the other officer, the one who stayed at ground level, has told the attendants to start asking outgoing drivers if they have seen a white couple and an Indian woman.

'We have to move to the other stairs,' he commands. Danielle and Jayalitha look startled, but there is no time to explain. They are midway across the parking garage when they see the hawk-faced man begin to descend the strip of pavement that leads to them from Level 4.

Their pursuer is closer than they are to the north-eastern stairs. And when he sees them, he starts to run.

'Police officer! Don't move or I'll shoot!' he shouts.

They run. They are almost at the south-western stairs when the other man, the fat man, appears in the open doorway, crouched in a shooter's stance, the barrel of his gun levelled at them. It is animal terror more than thought which causes them to go from sprint to halt so rapidly that Keiran stumbles and nearly falls.

'That's far enough,' the fat man growls. 'Hands behind your head. Against the wall.'

Keiran and Danielle look at one another. There is nowhere left to run. Keiran is coldly certain they will shoot if they need to. Slowly, they interlace their hands behind their heads and proceed to the wall next to the elevator. The fat man and the hawk-faced man are behind them, approaching, handcuffs jingling in their hands, when five miles south of them, in Scattergood Power Station on Manhattan Beach, a false alarm triggers an emergency shutdown, and all Santa Monica blacks out.

Jayalitha, Danielle and Keiran, who have spent the last minute praying for exactly this eventuality, react first, sprint along the wall to the stairs during the few seconds it takes their pursuers to react to the shock of blindness. That is all the head start they need. Their non-uniformed pursuers do not have flashlights, and the darkness in the garage is total. Keiran somehow manages to take the stairs in the darkness at a dead sprint, three at a time, without falling. Once at ground level, they can see a little; the major streets are eerily illuminated by car headlights. The city's darkness is powerfully unnatural. It feels as if they are at a midnight auto rally in a desert ghost town.

'This way,' Danielle says, and leads them north. They pelt across Wilshire Boulevard into a residential zone that has so little vehicle traffic at this hour it is almost entirely blacked out. They zigzag for several more blocks before stopping, all of them panting with exhaustion.

'This won't last long,' Keiran warns. 'They've seen how we look now, they'll get the Santa Monica cops on to us. We need to get out. Or hide somewhere until the lights go on and Mulligan can get the car and pick us up.'

'Hide,' Danielle says. 'Shit. I don't know this area too well.'

'The beach is near,' Jayalitha says.

Danielle smiles thinly. 'Yes. Getting to be a habit. We can even try last night's trick again if we have to.'

But thankfully that isn't necessary. Ten minutes after the city lights reignite, Mulligan picks them up by the Santa Monica Pier and drives them north through Pacific Palisades to Sunset Boulevard.

'Oh, crap,' Mulligan says, when they are heading east on Sunset.

'What?'

'Don't look around, but there's a cop behind us.'

Keiran swallows. He sees the following black-and-white in Mulligan's side mirror. They drive in complete silence for the next few minutes. Keiran closes his eyes and tries to pretend the silent tension does not exist. Being pulled over would almost be better than this waiting. But Mulligan drives with unusual precision, and their follower eventually veers off on to a different route.

'Jesus fuck,' Mulligan says. His entire body is glistening with sweat. 'This is why I don't leave the house. The real world's too fucking uncontrollable.'

Mulligan feels better when they are back safe in his apartment. 'Not a bad night,' he says. 'Snarfed their phones, tracked their boss, shut down half of LA for twenty minutes, and got away clean. Beats watching TV.'

'We broke LoTek's Law with that blackout,' Keiran says darkly. 'They will look into why it happened.'

'They won't trace us.'

'The more we use Shazam like that, the more certain it becomes that someone finds out what it can do.'

'You know it's near its best before anyways,' Mulligan says. 'Everyone who's anyone uses BitTorrent now.'

Keiran shrugs. This is true, but he doesn't want to admit that his secret hacking weapon will soon be obsolete. 'I was hoping to wring a couple of years out of it yet.'

'Is it possible to eat something?' Jayalitha asks.

'Yeah,' Danielle agrees. 'If there's one thing I've learned this year, it's that fear makes you fucking famished.'

Mulligan orders a pizza while Keiran works to trace the phone number they have just acquired, and very nearly traded their lives for. It doesn't take him long; again, it is a Virgin Mobile number, and by now he knows their database as if he built it himself.

'Eureka,' Keiran says. 'The phone is anonymous, but it was last used in Las Vegas.'

'Vegas,' Mulligan says meaningfully.

Keiran and Mulligan look at each other.

'BlackHat,' Keiran says, smiling.

'Got to be.'

'We can't get there. Our ID won't arrive. I don't want to go naked.'

'He'll stay for DefCon,' Mulligan suggests.

'Of course. Yes. Perfect.'

'Explain to us lay women, please,' Danielle says, obviously

annoyed by their cryptic conversation. She stands and looks over Keiran's shoulder, as if the call records displayed there might explain everything.

'We know where he'll be this weekend,' Mulligan says.

'Where?'

'DefCon,' Keiran says. 'World's biggest hacker convention-slash-party. It's this coming weekend, in Las Vegas. All the hacking world's great and good turn up. Except hermits like Mulligan. If P2's already in Vegas, he'll certainly stay for DefCon. And I strongly doubt he knows we have his phone number. With only a little luck we can use it to track him down.'

'What are we going to do when we catch him?' Danielle asks.

'We will humbly request of him that he shares with us his hacking arsenal, and reveals all of Justice International's super-secret files.'

She gives Keiran an uneasy look. 'And what if he says no?'

'He will not say no,' Jayalitha says, her eyes flashing.

'But what . . .' Danielle begins.

'This is the man who led the Frenchman to my family. Who sent me into exile. Believe me when I tell you, if you bring him to me, he will tell us whatever we need to know.'

After a moment Danielle asks, in a near-whisper, 'The French-man?'

Jayalitha says, 'The man who burned my family in my house was a French soldier. That is all I know. But I will ask this P2 about him as well.'

Danielle turns pale and sits down hard on Mulligan's couch.

'What?' Jayalitha asks. 'Do you know of him?'

'Yes,' Keiran says bleakly. 'Laurent.'

SuperCheap Car Rental, located just a few blocks from LAX, rents elderly cars with tens of thousands of miles on them for cheap monthly rates. Danielle and Jayalitha are visibly nervous as they and Keiran stand in their office and use their brand-new driver's licences and credit cards to rent a car. Keiran is slightly perturbed as well, not from any fear that their ID might fail, but because the proprietors insist on photographing their customers. Although the thousands of tiny photographs that line the office walls imply that this is not special treatment.

'How can you be sure they don't track their cars?' Danielle asks as she gets behind the wheel of their new ride, a battered maroon Toyota Corolla with 75,000 miles on the odometer. 'If they find out we're using fake ID—'

'Simple economics,' Keiran says. 'Look at their office. Look at this car. It isn't worth tracking, and they couldn't afford it if it was. And our identities are not fake, they're false. They're just as good as a real person's.'

'Would it be possible to arrange a passport?' Jayalitha asks from the back seat.

Keiran shakes his head. 'Sorry. My magic is fickle. The passport office is still beyond me.'

Jayalitha nods. 'How long is the drive to Las Vegas?'

'Six hours,' Danielle says. 'Buckle up. I'm going to do it in five.'

8

Danielle has driven from Los Angeles to Vegas several times before, in the Crazy Years, but she is always amazed by the raw isolation of the desert in between. Once out of LA – and so sprawling is that city that it takes them ninety minutes to escape it – the only town they pass is Barstow, halfway. Two enormous casinos stand like Scylla and Charybdis at the Nevada border, for those gamblers who can't be bothered to drive the remaining hour to Vegas. The highway itself is wide and busy, a long smooth strand of civilization that occasionally knots itself into little roadside clusters of buildings that provide, as the signs say, GAS FOOD LODGING. But mostly the road traverses a vast trackless wasteland, the Mojave and Sonoran deserts, occupied only by cacti, Joshua trees, rattlesnakes, coyotes and the occasional desert hermit. Danielle wonders how many lives this pitiless desert swallowed before the age of the automobile. Surely thousands.

Las Vegas would be surreal anywhere. After a five-hour desert drive, their progress up the neon canyon wonderland called the Strip is nearly overwhelming. They pass a pyramid, a compressed New York City, a fantasyland castle, a gigantic green cube, an Eiffel Tower, a Roman coliseum, an erupting volcano, a pirate ship, all of them larger than life. Huge crowds flood the Strip like army ants. Traffic moves more slowly than pedestrians. The sun is setting as they arrive, but its shine is soon replaced by multi-coloured neon that will dazzle the throngs of drivers and pedestrians until dawn. Vegas never sleeps.

'I never imagined a place like this could exist,' Jayalitha says, eyes wide.

'Read the subtext before you get excited,' Keiran warns her. 'All hail the great god Mammon. Thou shalt have no other god before me. Sell thy father and thy mother. Covet thy neighbour's wife and donkey.'

'Don't be so cynical,' Danielle says. 'It's just a playground. Disneyland for adults.'

'More like a carnival of lost souls. Gambling is just a means of relieving the statistically incompetent of their money. The house always wins.'

DefCon is hosted by the Alexis Park Resort, a large hotel east of the Strip, across from the Hard Rock Café. It is almost unique in Vegas in that it has no gambling, not even slot machines. They originally claimed to be full when Danielle called, but Danielle knows that hotels always keep a few rooms in reserve in case of disaster or a VIP appearance. By the simple expedient of claiming that she was verifying a reservation, rather than arranging a new one, and then flying into feigned outrage when they reported they had no record of her previous booking, she managed to annex a superior suite for a standard price.

The heat hits Danielle like a slap in the face when she gets out of the car. It is night, but it is also July in the desert. It reminds her of India. She hurries into the plush and air-conditioned lobby. The lobby's ATM machines have already been hacked to display DefCon's happy-face-and-crossbones logo and cartoon pictures of geeks at computers. She makes a mental note not to use them.

There is a crowd around the check-in desk. Their most common features are thinness, paleness, multi-coloured hair, black clothing, tattoos, laptop cases, and a large number of flashy electrical accessories. There are more men than women, but the disparity isn't as great as Danielle expected, and the men aren't as social-outcast geeky as Mulligan. It is a subculture of anarchists more than rejects.

She and Jayalitha get the keys, return to the car park and escort Keiran to the room. He wears a black hood that conceals his face; Keiran is well enough known in the hacker community that the odds of being recognized are good, and Danielle is sure a few of his fellow hackers would be rather pleased by the prospect of reporting him to the FBI. As a result, he will have to spend almost all of DefCon in their room, and wear a hood if and when it is necessary for him to emerge.

The Alexis Park occupies nearly a square mile of space. Past the main building on Harmon Street that contains the lobby, restaurant and conference rooms, a walkway weaves its way through an outdoor common area a hundred feet wide and a quarter-mile long, decorated with swimming pools, palm trees and fake rocks. The guest rooms are found on either side of this central corridor, in two arrays of long, low, motel-like buildings. Their perfectly adequate suite is near the third and last swimming pool. Danielle and Jayalitha go out again, to get food from a Subway down the street. By the time they return Keiran has assembled the laptops and other gear loaned by Mulligan: computers, screens, antennae, black boxes and less comprehensible electronica, all interconnected by a spaghetti chaos of cables. The resulting nexus of computing power looks like the control centre for a mid-sized NASA mission.

Danielle watches Keiran and his total immersion in his cyberworld. It is bizarre, and awe-inspiring, and more than a little frightening, that he can do so much, create identities, shut down whole cities, from almost anywhere, with nothing but unparalleled knowledge and a few keystrokes. She wonders whether maybe the rise of the Internet, and this resulting age of interconnection, is a global disaster waiting to happen.

'So now we walk around and hope you call P2 when we're in sight?' Danielle asks.

Keiran frowns. 'I like to think the plan is slightly more sophisticated.'

'Doesn't seem like it.'

'Again we start with one piece of information. His phone number. Now, when a mobile phone is on, it constantly transmits its location to its network, so it can be informed of call requests. I assume P2 keeps his phone on in case of some Shadbold-related emergency. I'll hack into the local Sprint network, they're the Virgin Mobile carrier, and at any given time I should be able to triangulate his location to within about a hundred-foot radius. The same way he found us in that car park. When you two are confident you have a good view of everywhere he might be, I give him a ring. We won't get more than a couple of chances. Maybe only one before he gets suspicious and switches phones. So don't fuck up.'

'Your managerial style needs work,' Danielle says.

'Common side effect of misanthropy. It will most likely take me until midnight to own the Sprint network completely and figure out the triangulation. You two should spend that time figuring out the local geography. But watch out. Federal marshals come to DefCon too. Techie types, mostly, but a Russian bloke was arrested here two years ago just for presenting a paper.'

'Great. And you want me to walk around down there, with my picture on the Most Wanted list.'

'Don't exaggerate. We're not on the Most Wanted list. Not yet. And you look nothing like that picture any more. Believe me, the *federales* have plenty to distract them. Just don't attract attention. If you find anyone called Trurl or Klaupactus, bring them up here, they're trustworthy, I could use their help. Otherwise just stay quiet and get the lie of the land.'

The land in question is strange and unforgettable and costs eighty cash dollars to enter. The heart of DefCon is arguably the after-hours events in individual rooms, or the all-night-every-night pool party, but its public face, in the Alexis Park's convention area, is no less colourful. As Danielle and Jayalitha enter they pass the Wall of Shame, where the user names and passwords of those foolish enough to use unprotected wireless connections anywhere near the hotel are displayed on a huge scrolling screen. In a cavernous room next door, a banner proclaims that the 'War-Gamez Capture the Flag' hacking contest is in full swing; around it, a dozen teams of hackers hunch over their laptops, typing and talking furiously.

The hallways and meeting rooms are full of people wearing translucent green DefCon badges, their demography white and young, ranging from teens to mid-fifties but skewing heavily towards the former. Dress is mostly casual decrepitude or counter-culture black over punk hair and tattoos. Hiptops like Keiran's are present by the dozen. Two camera crews rove around, presumably filming for TV or documentaries. Jayalitha and Danielle make sure to give them a very wide berth.

They pass a talk on 'Bluetooth Vulnerabilities', which Danielle now feels qualified to talk about. A pretty teenage girl is giving out 'personal firewalls', which turn out to be condoms. In the Vendors' Room, the Jesus Phreakers and the Culture Junkies sell T-shirts and stickers with legends such as 'I read your e-mail' and 'Norton cannot protect you'. In another room, eight fearsome locks are lined up for a Lockpick Challenge; according to the leader board, the record time for picking all eight is less than a minute. Outside, a convoy is grouping for something called a 'Wi-Fi Shootout' that involves lots of vehicles with mounted satellite

dishes and people carrying elaborate homemade shotgun antennae that look disturbingly military. Danielle decides to stay
indoors for now, and blend in with the largest crowds.

'You know what I heard?' she hears a teenage voice say. 'I
heard fuckin' LoTek was here.' Danielle freezes for a moment,
until the voice continues, 'Someone said they saw him out by the
pool with this hot supermodel chick. Like, in your face, FBI.'

'That's fucking cool,' the acne-scarred kid's girlfriend says, as
they pass by, wearing matching black I SAW YOUR MOM ON THE
INTERNET T-shirts. Clearly just an unfounded rumour. If an
extremely unhelpful one. Keiran's hacker-scene living-legend sta-
tus doesn't make their life any easier, especially if the feds take that
rumour seriously and decide to, say, search the entire hotel.

'Idiots. LoTek would not *dare* show his face here,' she hears
another man say after the teenagers have passed, and looks over
to see a man of about thirty, with pale skin beneath a thick shock
of black hair, talking to a muscular bald man. The speaker's
accent is eastern European, and he wears an expression of sour
anger. 'He is not stupid. The marshals are everywhere, and never
mind what they say, they are looking for him, just as they are
taking pictures of us all, fingerprints, DNA, to go into their files,
which you can be sure they keep offline. Go on, laugh. You think
they are not?'

'It would be illegal and inadmissible,' the bald man points out.
Danielle notices that he wears a single brass knuckle on his right
hand; half decoration, half weapon.

'Of course it would. You think the police don't do illegal
things? These are hacker police. They bend the rules just as we do.
They circumvent imposed limits. They perform illegal acts to
secretly pave the way for their legal investigations. As they
should. The rules they work under are stupid. I hope they do
catch most of the people here and jail them for life. They would be
doing the world a favour. Script kiddies, wannabes, has-beens.
Take them away, who is left? Maybe ten of us. I myself will not
come next year. DefCon is a useless, pretentious waste.'

'You said exactly that last year,' the bald man observes, amused. 'I think I have a recording. But yes, I don't think we'll see LoTek this year. He won't risk jail just to defend the Lockpick Challenge title. He doesn't come to learn – no one here but the CDC, the Legion and maybe you and Klaupactus can teach him anything. He comes for the parties, and if he can't show his face, why risk attendance?'

'You say *maybe* me?' the eastern European man demands. 'LoTek is very good, yes. Overall better than me, I concede this. But George, I assure you, there are fields in which my knowledge far outstrips his. And your knowledge as well. As you well know. I hate your kind of false humility.'

'Of course you do. You hate everything.'

'Not true. It only seems that way because the world is so detestable. Is there some reason you feel the need to eavesdrop?' the eastern European man demands of Danielle and Jayalitha, who have slowly approached.

'It's just . . . we're looking for a man named Klaupactus,' Danielle says.

'We heard you speak his name,' Jayalitha clarifies.

The dark-haired man snorts. 'Spot the feds,' he says contemptuously.

The bald man looks at Jayalitha. 'No, I don't think so. They don't hire foreign nationals. And that's a real Indian accent, yes?'

'Yes,' Jayalitha says.

The bald man nods. 'I did a year of research in Bombay. What do you want with Klaupactus?'

'Him and Trurl,' Danielle says. 'We . . . we have a message for them.'

'This is Trurl,' the bald man says, pointing to his companion.

Trurl sighs. 'Tell me your message,' he says, his tone of voice indicating that he would like to get this interaction over with as quickly as possible.

'I am afraid the message is for your ears only,' Jayalitha says, and looks apologetically at the much friendlier bald man.

'Don't be ridiculous,' Trurl snaps. 'This man is one of the three people in this world I trust, and I will tell him your message the moment you give it to me. Please do not insult my intelligence by insinuating unnecessary inefficiency into this conversation.'

Danielle hesitates, and decides to take the risk; from what they heard, the bald man too is a friend. 'LoTek would like to talk to you.'

'Please,' Trurl says scornfully. 'Do not waste my time.'

'I'm not.'

Trurl and the bald man search the women's expressions for a moment. Then, his voice much less hostile, Trurl says, 'You must be joking.'

'You see anybody laughing?' Danielle asks.

'He's really here?'

'Come,' Jayalitha says. 'We will show you.'

'You have balls like bronze basketballs, my friend,' Trurl says as he shakes Keiran's hand. 'You know they are here looking for you.'

Keiran shrugs. 'Never mind the federal agents. We have bigger problems.'

'Oh? What problems?'

'People who play by no rules at all. Details are need-to-know. But I could use your help.'

'Klaupactus and I are at your service.'

'The handle P2 mean anything to you?'

Trurl frowns. 'I think so. Some script kiddie. Years ago. Hung out in chat rooms.'

'He's no longer a script kiddie. He's very, very good, he has access to tools like none of us have ever seen, and he's working for the bad guys.'

'I thought we were the bad guys.'

'No such luck,' Keiran says.

'That *is* a problem.'

'If you two could just start some social engineering. Mention his name a lot, see who seems interested. Try and lure him someplace tomorrow night. Then I'll ring his number, I've got that, and we'll see who answers the call of the vibrating pocket.'

'Then what?' Trurl asks.

'Then we buy a Taser from the back of some vendor's van.'

Trurl's eyebrows shoot up. 'You understand, when I say I will help, this does not include committing physical violence.'

'That's what Charlie has his angels for,' Keiran says, nodding towards Danielle and Jayalitha.

'Charlie doesn't watch it,' Danielle says sourly, 'his angels will test his Taser on him first.'

'I will bring Klaupactus,' Trurl says. 'I'm sure he will be happy to see you. Anything makes that fool happy.'

Klaupactus is a tall, athletic man in his thirties who looks as if he'd be more at home in a kayak or climbing a sheer rock wall than in front of a computer. Long dark hair and eighties-style stubble surround a perpetual smile. His accent is a weird combination of Romanian and Australian.

'This is bloody ridiculous!' he exclaims. 'As if you would build a bomb. You shouldn't hide from the government. You should attack them with a lawsuit. For tens of millions. Harassment, false arrest, libel, character assassination. I have lawyer friends who would be gagging to represent you.'

Keiran nods. 'I'll be happy to, once this situation is resolved.' 'Have you finished with the triangulation?'

'Almost. I have to write a couple of new utilities to map it on to the local GIS in real time. But I've already established the phone's location somewhere in the hotel grounds. Our friend P2 is definitely here. And he took a ten-minute phone call within the last hour.'

'Did you intercept the call?'

'Of course. But it was encrypted.'

Trurl raises his eyebrows. 'A secure anonymous phone?'

'Our opponents have enough money to buy this whole hotel and everyone in it.'

'Money,' Klaupactus says dismissively. 'You know what I say about money. Happiness can never be bought. It can only be stolen.'

'Very pithy. Now go find my arch-enemy for me, will you?'

'It will be a pleasure,' Klaupactus says.

'Pleasure,' Trurl mutters. 'I suppose at least it is a welcome distraction from the rest of these idiots.'

Danielle and Jayalitha steer clear of Trurl and Klaupactus when they venture out into DefCon once more: those two are trying to attract P2's attention, but Danielle, fearful of being recognized behind her mask of blonde hair and make-up, wants to avoid just that.

At about midnight, tired from the long drive and the overload of sensory stimulation, they return to the hotel room. Keiran is already asleep in a cot by his improvised science-fiction control centre. The three largest screens show top, side and front architectural plans of the Alexis Park grounds, with a reddish cloud that Danielle takes to indicate the possible location of P2's phone.

After a moment she realizes that the edge of this cloud intersects with this very room. Their quarry is somewhere within two hundred feet of them right now. Unfortunately some four thousand other DefCon attendees are as well. As she watches, the cloud shifts slightly; P2 is on the move. Maybe going to some party. Maybe hunting them just as they are seeking him. If he has overheard Trurl and Klaupactus talking about him, it is not a great logical jump to the conclusion that Keiran – LoTek – is here.

But she can't worry about that now. Danielle has too much to worry about, and she has to put it all away every night, or she will never be able to sleep. It isn't easy. She has learned that she has to exhaust herself every day, or she will be up for hours, sweating and tense, brooding about her possible futures, all of which are bad. But tonight she is too tired to worry. She closes her eyes gratefully and allows sleep to carry her away.

Keiran shakes her awake at four in the morning.

'Come *on*,' he says urgently. 'I've got a fix. I know where P2 is. You have to go and get him right now.'

9

'He moved,' Keiran explains. 'I set the scanner to wake me up if the phone left the hotel grounds. He's just down the street. Get up, come on, go!'

Ninety seconds later Danielle and Jayalitha, clad in sandals and pyjamas, are jogging down the hallway to the elevator bank. Danielle holds one of their anonymous cell phones. She does not quite believe that she is really awake. Except that dreams are never this uncomfortable; being shaken awake this early was almost physically painful.

'Remind me again why you can't come with us,' she says into the phone, annoyed. 'Just in case someone sees your precious face?'

'Believe me, I want to be there. But I have to stay here to monitor his activity and make the finger call. Let me know when.'

There is more activity on the street outside the Alexis Park than Danielle would have expected at four in the morning, even in Las Vegas. At least fifty people cluster, smoking and talking, around the twenty-four-hour 7–11 store down the street, at the corner of Harmon and Paradise. A group of a half-dozen passes them on the way to the store. From their chatter Danielle gathers that a big party has just ended; from their giggles, shining eyes and the way they gape at street lights, it's clear hallucinogens were involved. Two other groups pass them going back into the hotel. Their members seem very young. Danielle supposes old fogeys like herself, even those who took drugs in their youth, are mostly in bed by now. As she would very much like to be. She doesn't know whether she can pick out a single person answering a phone in this noisy, milling crowd, but she also doesn't know whether they'll get a better chance, either. She decides to go for it and opens her mouth to tell Keiran so.

'Bollocks,' Keiran says. 'He's back inside. He must have walked right past you.'

'Why the fuck didn't you tell us?' Danielle demands, turning around.

'It's not a real-time scan. Every thirty seconds.'

The two groups that passed them looked college-age, if that. Danielle wonders whether their fearsome nemesis P2 will turn out to be a pimply monomaniacal teenager. Both groups continue, their pace leisurely, through the main building and down the long outdoor walkway that winds past the Alexis Park's three swimming pools. Danielle and Jayalitha follow.

'He stopped,' Keiran reports, a minute later.

Danielle shakes her head. 'The people who passed us are still moving.'

'Then he's not with them. Or not any more. Where are you?'

'By the main pool.'

'Go back. Check the lobby.'

They return indoors. There are eleven people on the lobby chairs and couches; one group of four teenage boys, two couples and three lone men, one reading a newspaper and two more working on their laptops. She reports this to Keiran.

'All right,' Keiran says. She hears him take a deep breath. 'He has to be there. The phone might be silent. Keep a sharp eye. I'm going to connect.'

'He's doing it,' Danielle whispers to Jayalitha, who nods.

'Well?' Keiran asks, fifteen seconds later.

'Did you do it?'

'Yes. It rang. Someone answered. They didn't speak. I started talking and they hung up, they must have some code-word system. You didn't fucking see anything?' The frustration in his voice is palpable.

'No. They're not here.'

'Danielle,' Jayalitha says. 'The lavatories.'

Danielle turns and looks at the two doors, marked with the universal man and woman symbols, set in wood panelling. Of course. P2 stopped in to take a leak on his way to the pools.

'Come on,' she says, and she and Jayalitha barge into the men's room.

There is a man standing by the sink, young and pot-bellied, with wide Elvis sideburns. He looks at them with surprise and alarm.

'P2, I presume?' Danielle asks.

His surprise and alarm intensify. 'Huh?'

Jayalitha pushes past Danielle, grabs the man by his lapels and pulls him down to her height. 'Are you P2? Do you work for Shadbold? For Justice International?' Her voice is low but throbbing. '*Answer me.*'

'What the fuck you on, lady?' The man tries to separate Jayalitha's hands from his clothing. The attempt earns him a kneecap hard in the crotch. He doubles over, hands folded over his battered genitals. Soft gagging noises come from his mouth.

'If you move,' Jayalitha warns him, 'I will end your miserable life.' She crouches by the collapsed form. 'And if you are the one I seek, I swear to you, you will burn just as my family burned.' She pulls a mobile phone from his pocket and gives it to Danielle.

Danielle stares at Jayalitha for a moment. It is like seeing a kitten turn into a wolverine. Then, as the man writhes in gasping agony, and Jayalitha searches him thoroughly for any other, hidden phone, she turns her attention to the one in her hand. It is a Nokia, she knows its interface well. She quickly establishes that it last received a call more than an hour ago.

'No,' Danielle says. 'Not this one.'

Jayalitha looks up, past the urinals, to the stalls. One of the doors is closed.

'It is occupied,' she says. 'You must knock down the door. I will keep this man from leaving.'

Danielle swallows. The situation is both absurd and appalling.

But they have done too much to back out now. And besides, she reminds herself, she is already wanted by the FBI. She walks up to the stall. She hears fast, shallow breathing from behind it. Its occupant is afraid.

'Open the door,' she says.

'What the fuck is this?' A frightened, teenage voice.

Danielle considers kicking the door, but decides that sandal-clad feet are not right for this. There is enough space beneath the stall door that she could wriggle in, but she would leave herself vulnerable to physical repulsion, and it would be somehow undignified. There are no tools in sight; she will have to do it herself. She feels blood pounding in her temples.

'You do not move except to breathe!' she hears Jayalitha warn the man on the floor, her voice still harsh, as if he might yet turn into P2. He whimpers an understanding.

Danielle steps back to the wall, crouches, tenses her abdominal muscles, and charges the stall shoulder first. It pops open with surprising ease. She very nearly falls into the gangly teenager sitting on the toilet within, wearing shorts and a T-shirt. Something metal, the stall lock, rattles on the floor.

'Are you P2?' she asks, feeling ridiculous. At least he has already drawn up his shorts in anticipation of her invasion.

'I don't know what you're talking about.' His voice quavers.

'Give me your phone.'

He pauses for a moment. Then another thump and groan of pain from near the door. The other man must have tried to make a move. The teenager quickly draws his phone out and passes it over. It too has not been used within the last hour. He can't be hiding any other phone in his shorts, unless . . .

'Stand up and drop your pants,' Danielle orders. When she hears the words leave her mouth she very nearly starts giggling like a madwoman, and stops this only by biting her lip so hard she tastes blood.

The teenager stares at her. Then, slowly, he stands up and lowers his shorts. There is no cell phone concealed within.

Perhaps it was flushed away? But no, a quick glance reveals that the toilet has not been flushed, and no phone gleams within.

'Stay where you are,' Danielle commands. She drops the phone, kicks it to the far corner of the bathroom, walks back to the doorway, takes Jayalitha by the wrist, and leads her out into the lobby, just as a teenage blonde girl comes out of the women's room, babbling at high speed into her cell phone: 'And then she was all, like, Christina's a totally better singer than Britney, and I was like, duh, totally, *everyone* knows that, but it's not about the voice, it's about, like, the *style*.' She stops and looks at Danielle and Jayalitha. 'Uh, excuse me, ladies, I think you want *this* door, unless you're, like, totally desperate for male companionship.' She points at the women's room and smiles archly.

'We're fine,' Danielle says shortly, humiliated enough already without this bubble-headed ditz adding to it, and marches out of the main building, towards the pools and their room, before the men they have left behind come to their senses and raise a furore. Her face is red, and she feels weak, from confrontation comedown, embarrassment and a sick sense of disaster. They should have found him. They failed. And now he must know he is being traced.

They are just past the main swimming pool when Jayalitha grabs Danielle's arm from behind and pulls her to a stop.

'What is it?' Danielle asks.

'The other room. The ladies' room.' Jayalitha turns and rushes back to the lobby.

'The ladies' room? But why would he . . .' Danielle says, following, and then she understands.

He. That has always been their assumption. But they have no reason other than demographics to believe that P2 is a man. And P2 is, by all accounts, a truly exceptional hacker; and true exceptions are beyond statistics.

The door to the men's room opens as they approach. The two men they terrorized look out nervously, blanch at the approach of Danielle and Jayalitha, and quickly shut the door again. They proceed into the women's room. It is empty.

'The girl,' Danielle says. She can't believe it. The teenage blonde girl with her overdone white-trash-pop-culture spiel. She rushes out into the lobby. She is nowhere to be seen. But Danielle is sure. Dead certain. Something in the look the blonde girl gave them when she pointed at the women's room. A hint of triumph.

P2 is a teenage girl. And she knows their faces. And knows she is being chased.

'Well,' Keiran says. 'This is not good.'

'We know that,' Danielle says grimly.

'But it's not a total catastrophe. We had one piece of information. It's now useless, that phone's been switched off. And they'll be looking for us here now. That's bad too. But you did add to our store of knowledge.'

'How?' Jayalitha asks.

'You know what she looks like.'

That is true. Danielle tries to remember. Short, dirty blonde hair, probably natural, cut a little above her shoulders. Upturned nose, wide mouth, good skin, no jewellery. Maybe ten pounds over her optimum weight. She was wearing hip-hugger jeans, a tank top and sandals.

'The human brain is an amazing pattern recognition machine,' Keiran says. 'When it recognizes a face it does in a fraction of a second what computers require hours to manage.'

'Yes. We can recognize her. But she's not going to be parading around the hotel any more, is she?' Danielle asks, exasperated.

'Never mind the future. We have the past.'

Danielle looks at him, irritated by his typically cryptic comment, and then guessing its meaning. 'Cameras. The hotel has cameras. You can take them over.'

'Unfortunately, no. This is, after all, DefCon. The hotel cameras get pre-hacked weeks in advance. It scores major bragging rights. I don't know who owns them right now, but we probably can't risk asking them for a favour. But I do happen to know that our friends at 7–11 have moved to a central webcam security system in all their stores, so they can document hold-ups and shoplifting across the whole chain. And you know what that means.'

'Shazam to the rescue?'

'With luck. You two can get back to sleep. This will take me an hour or two.' He sounds eager. 'I'll wake you when I've got something.'

'That's big of you.'

'Oh, and don't forget, don't go out. Either of you. She saw you too.'

'What if *she* took over the hotel cameras?' Jayalitha asks.

'Then we're fucked. Sweet dreams.'

This time Danielle wakes to the smell of bacon and eggs. It is 9 a.m.

'I room-serviced breakfast,' Keiran says absently, as Danielle pokes her head into his room to see what is happening. 'Help yourself. I won't be a moment with this. I'm in their network like a snake in the plumbing.' But both Jayalitha and Danielle have showered, their breakfasts are devoured, and their mugs of tea almost empty, before Keiran finally grunts with triumph.

'Who would have thought 7–11 would have been such a nut to crack?' he demands cheerfully. 'If their head office hadn't been Shazam-crazy I never could have done it. No matter. Here's the video from across the street, from ten minutes before you left the hotel. Sing out when you see her.'

Danielle and Jayalitha peer at the slightly grainy footage. She isn't there. They watch intently, as if *Late Night 7–11 Camera* is the most fascinating reality TV show ever, as customers line up and pay for cigarettes, chocolate bars and Slurpees.

'There!' Jayalitha exclaims. Danielle echoes her. They watch P2 come through the door of the store, glance up directly at the camera for a moment, and then proceed to the counter, where she buys a pack of Marlboro Lights.

'I love that look at the camera,' Keiran says with satisfaction. 'Classic hacker instinct. Betrayed you this time, sweetheart, didn't it?'

'Betrayed her how exactly?' Danielle asks.

'Hopefully,' Keiran admits. 'This is conjecture. But think of it this way. You're P2. You come here for perfectly innocent reasons, to check in on the state of the hacking art, and then you find out that the dastardly fugitives your friends in LA were supposed to track down are here looking for you. And you're presumably rather annoyed by this turn of events. What do you do?'

'Get out of town,' Danielle says.

'No,' Jayalitha corrects. 'I would call for assistance to deal with the dastardly fugitives. I would stay in the city. But I would move to another hotel.'

Keiran nods. 'My guess exactly. And at some point, when you check into that other hotel, you will pass a cashpoint or step into an elevator. And you know what that means.'

'We can't sit here looking at all the cameras in Las Vegas,' Danielle objects. 'It would take our whole lives to find her.'

'Quite true. This job cries out for automation. Something like a powerful facial recognition program. I think I can dig at least two of those up at short notice. The one Klaupactus wrote is probably the best. It requires front and side views of the target's face, but conveniently we now have those.'

'You were just saying that computers take hours to recognize a face,' Danielle points out.

'Yes. And that's why they'll never imagine I can possibly do what I am about to do. Because they don't know that I have at my disposal the most powerful accumulation of computing power ever assembled on the planet.'

'Excuse me?'

'Shazam,' Keiran says. 'Seven million instances, remember. All of them at my beck and call. And this is just the kind of granular problem you can go massively parallel on. With seven million computers working on this problem, it'll be like every camera in Las Vegas is looking for our little blonde sweetheart and knows how to shout out to us if she walks by.' He sighs. 'It's a blatant violation of LoTek's Law, of course. I wrote the parallel processing code hoping I'd never have to use it. It will probably be Shazam's final blaze of glory. Seven million computer owners will start wondering what just happened to their suddenly very slow machines. Backbone administrators will start asking why global Internet traffic just spiked twenty per cent. But better that than some real-life Gil Grissom trying to work out what happened after our corpses are found out in the desert.'

'What if she left town after all?' Danielle asks.

Keiran nods. 'Then I'll have burned Shazam for nothing. It's a gamble. But what the hell. We're in Vegas. Let's roll the dice. Give me space, if you would. Operation Argus has now begun.'

Eight hours later, a beaming Keiran shows them footage of P2 checking into Room 1723 of the Mirage. According to the Mirage's records, her name is Sophia Ward, and she is nineteen years old.

'Come on,' he says. 'Let's go have a little chat with our angel of cyberspace.'

10

The crowd at the Mirage is very different from that at DefCon; older, Midwestern, conservatively dressed. In the lobby, dominated by an aquarium three storeys high crowded with colourful fish, Keiran checks in with his false ID. He smiles as he takes the keycard. He knows what the desk clerk does not: that the Mirage's check-in system, which Keiran now owns, recognized the name on his ID and, as per the instructions he programmed before they entered the hotel, has impregnated the magnetic strip on his card with a master-key code that will open any room in the hotel.

They walk through the damp air and palm trees of the lobby bar, then the whirling lights and burbling noises of the casino; like all hotels on the Strip, the Mirage is arranged so you can't go anywhere without walking through an enticing sea of gambling tables and machines. Banks of slot machines face men and women, mostly old, who push buttons like rats in a Skinner box. Even the people who walk the green baize floors without gambling move like extras in a zombie movie. Keiran is relieved when they reach the elevators.

They walk past 1719, the room they have just checked into, and stop outside the door to 1723. Keiran withdraws the gun from his pocket, sleek and dully metallic, densely heavy, delivered to their room this afternoon by Trurl. The Polish nihilist hadn't offered any information on its provenance, other than that it was untraceable, and Keiran hadn't asked. The weapon feels foreign in his hand. He used to go on shooting expeditions in the California desert with other hacker friends regularly, when he lived in Oakland, but until today he hasn't held a gun for four years.

Keiran looks to his right and left, to Danielle and Jayalitha, checking readiness. Danielle nods. Jayalitha tilts her head Indian-style. Keiran takes a deep breath. He secretly hopes that P2 – Sophia, if that's her real name – is out, the room is empty and they can find what they need to know by rummaging through her computer. He'd rather avoid actual physical confrontation.

He inserts the keycard. The little light above the card reader turns green. Keiran pushes the door open and enters 1723, which is a suite. The connecting door is half closed.

'You're early,' a voice says from the other room. A girl's voice, its tone eager and teasing. 'Maybe you found some reason to make good time?'

Keiran throws open the connecting door. P2 is lying on the bed facing the door. She wears black jeans, a white bra and a shocked expression that turns to a gasp of horror as Danielle and Jayalitha follow Keiran into the room. Eyes wide, she gapes at each of them in turn, and at the gun in Keiran's hand.

'You will tell us what we want to know or I will strangle you here and now myself,' Jayalitha says. Her voice is soft, almost a whisper, but allows for no doubt. 'You led them to my family. For you my husband was murdered. For you my children burned. You are no girl. You are a demon.'

P2 finds her voice, high and quavery. 'Please.'

'Cooperate and you won't get hurt,' Danielle says, parroting every cop show ever, playing good cop to Jayalitha's murderous cop. 'We believe you didn't fully understand what you were doing. Answer our questions and we'll leave you be, Sophia. Is that your real name? Sophia?'

The girl on the bed nods.

'Vocalize, please,' Keiran says. 'But not too loud.'

'Yes,' she says hoarsely. 'That's my name.'

'Why check in with your real name?' Danielle asks.

'I didn't think you could find me.'

'Well,' Keiran says, pleased, 'you're very good, but you're not omniscient.'

'Can I put on a shirt?' Sophia asks.

Keiran looks at Danielle, who nods. He takes a shirt hanging over a chair and throws it to her.

'Who were you waiting for?' Danielle asks, as Sophia puts it on. 'Your boyfriend?'

'Yes.'

'When will he get here?'

'I expected a couple more hours.'

'How could you?' Jayalitha bursts out. 'How could you condemn so many people to agony and disease? How could you be so cruel?'

'It wasn't me,' Sophia says, shocked. 'I don't have anything to do with it. That was all Shadbold. I just make sure he doesn't get caught. That's all I do.'

'Why?' Danielle asks. 'How much does he pay you?'

'It's not about the money.' Even frightened, she injects a hint of scorn into her tone when she says *money*.

'The tools,' Keiran suggests. 'He gave you a whole fucking arsenal to play with, didn't he? What have you got? Fundamental exploits?'

'Yes. But that's not why I help him. I wouldn't do it for that. Never. He's an awful man, I know that. But if they find him out, all his research will be cancelled, just thrown away.'

'Right. You're a humanitarian helping him out to speed the cure for cancer,' Danielle says sarcastically.

'My dad is dying,' Sophia says quietly. 'He has cancer. Just like Shadbold. Late-stage. If it wasn't for Shadbold's drugs he'd already be dead.' She looks at Jayalitha. 'I'm sorry for your family. I didn't order whatever happened to them, you know. I just tell him things I find out, he makes the decisions. I'm trying to save my father. And the rest of the world can fucking roll over and die as far as I care. That's all I know. I'm not going to let my dad die.'

'You foolish, selfish *witch*,' Jayalitha says.

'Let's steer the conversation back to constructive topics,' Keiran says. 'These tools he gave you. What are they?'

Sophia says, 'I don't know for sure where they came from. I think they're military.'

'*Military?*'

'Military, NSA, something like that. I can't imagine who else could have had them and not revealed them. We're talking fundamental exploits at the operating system level. Get me on to a network with these tools and I can own just about any machine on the planet.'

'You're going to show me these tools,' Keiran says. 'And burn me a copy. Then you're going to show us all the evidence that Shadbold, through Justice International, is poisoning thousands of people and then performing illegal pharmaceutical research on them. Anything less and we unleash her on you.' He nods towards Jayalitha.

Sophia swallows and shakes her head. 'I'll show you the toolkit. But I can't give you evidence. There isn't any. It's destroyed as soon as it's not useful any more.'

'You can point us to the scientists who design the studies,' Danielle says. 'And the ones who analyse the results. You can show us how they ship the cancers to India. You can tell us who collects notes from the field and sends them back. You can tell us enough.'

'No. No! I won't. My father . . .' She stops, has to visibly compose herself. 'What do you care? But I won't. Do anything you want to me. I won't betray him. I won't let him die.'

There is a brief silence.

'We'll start with the tools,' Keiran says, 'then discuss the rest.' He nods towards the laptop on the desk. 'You're going to log me in as root. Typing very slowly indeed.'

Sophia looks at him wide eyed. Keiran understands. Giving someone else root access to your machine is a wrenchingly personal violation.

'Now,' he snaps, and raises the gun towards her, feeling ridiculous.

He half expects her to laugh, but instead she pales, rises, walks over to the desk, wakes up her laptop – Debian Linux, as he expected – and slowly logs in as he watches. Her root password is a string of twelve gibberish numbers and letters. Keiran takes a moment to memorize it.

'Now what?'

'Sit back on the bed a moment.'

She obeys. Keiran sits at her laptop and disables her machine's wireless connection. He can't risk her somehow triggering an alarm. 'Now come back here,' he says, 'and show me what Shadbold stole from the military.'

'Holy Christ,' Keiran says, yet again.

'Yeah,' Sophia says. 'An undiscovered fundamental exploit in the Linux kernel.'

'Except it's not in the kernel per se, is it?'

'No. In the way GCC compiles it.'

Keiran and Sophia exchange a brief marvelling look. Keiran can tell that Danielle, who sits on the bed holding the gun awkwardly while he and Sophia work at her laptop, is not impressed by their professional camaraderie. But whether the girl next to him is evil or misguided, Keiran has to respect her.

It's clear she hasn't succeeded only because of the military-grade hacking weapons Shadbold gave her. Most hackers wouldn't understand how to use this attack suite, much less how its exploits work. Half a dozen fundamental Windows exploits, two in Apple's OS X, this one in the Linux kernel, and another, stunningly, in IBM's CICS mainframe transaction architecture, used by multimillion-dollar big-iron machines around the world. A clutch of Internet Explorer flaws, and one in Firefox that allow a web server to take control of any machine that visits its site. Remote root access to Cisco and Juniper routers. Subtle security holes in Oracle, DB2 and SQL Server databases. All together, a suite of exploits that give the knowledgeable user the ability to take over almost any computer or network on earth. Sophia has built a brilliant harness which automates their use; given an IP number, she can reduce almost any computer to servility within five seconds.

'You did this all by yourself?' he asks.

'I had to. I couldn't trust anyone else.'

'I'm impressed,' he admits.

'Enough of the love-in,' Danielle says sourly. 'Let's get to the important stuff.'

'Just a moment. I want a copy of this,' Keiran says. He draws a burnable CD from his day pack, inserts it into Sophia's machine and begins to burn a copy of her military attack suite. 'All right. Let's get to what you know about Justice International.'

Sophia stiffens.

'Just a moment,' Danielle says. 'Sophia.'

'Yes?'

'Your father. When did he get sick?'

'Three years ago,' Sophia says.

'How did you get into hacking?'

'Come on,' Keiran says sharply. 'We have no time to saunter down Memory Lane – her boyfriend's going to be here soon, and I'd very much rather not have multiple hostages.'

Danielle says, 'Keiran, *shut the fuck up.*'

Keiran considers his options and decides to follow orders.

'Sophia, tell us. Briefly,' Danielle says.

'All right. Well. The usual way, I guess. I was always good at it. I always won all the state math and computer contests. And was top five in the nationals. My dad worked at Xerox PARC in the seventies.' Keiran whistles, impressed; Xerox's Palo Alto Research Center was where modern computing was born. 'My mom died when I was young so he sort of raised me. Anyway, I got bored in computer class one day and started just playing around. This was in the early days of the Net, security was pretty slack. First I hung around in hacker chat rooms. I don't know, I was a kid, I thought breaking into stuff was cool. Anyways, I found this stupid implementation bug and hacked into the CIA. First I got arrested. Then they let me go, 'cause I was a kid and I didn't really do anything. There were a couple newspaper stories and everything. It was embarrassing. Anyway, then my dad got sick. I was hacking around looking for ways to get him better, maybe fund more research, and I found Mr Shadbold. He was doing lots of public research funding back then too. He took me to his boat.' Danielle nods. 'Oh, right, you've been there. Anyway, I started doing some technical work for him. And then one day he told me about this other secret project and how he needed to keep it secret. And I could tell right away it was the only way my dad might make it. When they diagnosed him they gave him six months.'

A phone rings, startling everyone. Keiran's mobile phone. He looks at it suspiciously. The LED read-out claims the caller is Trurl, but there's no guarantee that the call display hasn't been hacked. He pushes the answer button but says nothing.

'LoTek,' Trurl says. 'Remember I was keeping a back-up eye on your phone monitor? P2's phone came alive again, ten minutes ago, in the Mirage Hotel. I cross-referenced Alexis Park and Mirage bookings. The only intersection of the two sets is a woman named Sophia Ward, in Room 1723 of the Mirage.'

'Yeah,' Keiran says. 'No kidding. OK. Redundant, but thanks.' He hangs up.

'Who was that?' Danielle asks.

'Just Trurl. Telling us what we already know.'

Danielle nods. 'Listen,' she says to Sophia. 'Didn't you ever wonder how your father got sick?'

Keiran takes a sharp breath. He suddenly understands where she is going with this line of questioning.

'How?' Sophia looks at her as if it is the stupidest question imaginable. 'It's cancer. It's a random function. A protein un-folding the wrong way one day.'

Danielle opens her mouth to suggest something horrible—

—when something even worse occurs to Keiran. Pieces of the puzzle assemble in his head. According to Trurl, Sophia's phone just came alive. It wasn't Sophia who turned it on. Her phone is nowhere to be seen. Someone else has it, and turned it on. Someone in the Mirage. And that means . . .

'No,' he says, leaping to his feet. 'It's a trap. It's a fucking honey trap.'

'What?' Jayalitha asks.

'We were meant to come here, weren't we?' he asks Sophia. 'Just not quite so early. We were supposed to find your phone, not your face, weren't we?'

Sophia doesn't answer. Danielle and Jayalitha look stricken.

'We need to be leaving,' Keiran says, 'right now.'

The Mirage's elevators are located in an alcove off the main hallway. The three of them wait in that alcove on the seventeenth floor. Seconds crawl by. Keiran has to restrain himself from jabbing at the glowing call light again and again. Danielle, next to him, holds the gun concealed in her purse. Keiran holds Sophia's laptop under his arm. They have left the hacker prodigy unceremoniously bound to her bed and gagged with a pillowcase. They had to spend two precious minutes restraining her, lest she call security.

The elevator indicator chimes. The call light goes out. The elevator immediately in front of them opens.

Laurent looks out at them.

Danielle, Keiran and Jayalitha freeze for a fatal instant. Laurent does not. He takes one step towards them; the next step turns into a spinning kick that hits Danielle's wrist so hard the gun goes flying out of her purse and clatters against the wall behind them. He lands, spins the other way, and an elbow slams into Keiran's temple. Keiran topples as if hit with a sledgehammer. He barely feels himself hit the ground. He tries to get up, but his limbs flop uselessly, disobeying his commands. He can see and hear clearly, but can't seem to direct his arms and legs – it's as if he is trying to command a video-game character without knowing how the controls work.

From his supine position he sees Danielle, her face distended by fear and wrath, as if possessed by some desperate, primal force of destruction, an avatar of Kali or Durga. She opens her arms and literally leaps at Laurent. He ducks and spins, almost avoids her entirely, but she catches him with her left arm and wraps herself around him, pulling him awkwardly to the ground from behind. Out of the corner of his eye Keiran sees Jayalitha duck into the elevator. He tries to get up. Danielle and Laurent are tangled together only a few feet away, he has to help her. But he can't even prop himself up on an arm without falling back down again. All he can do is watch.

Danielle tries to bring a knee up into Laurent's crotch, but he has crossed his legs, protecting himself. She tries to head-butt him, ram her forehead against the back of his skull, but he is already moving, twisting like a snake in her grasp, and instead her head connects with his shoulder. Half dazed, she still holds him as if he is her only hope. Laurent grabs one of her fingers and bends it back viciously. Keiran hears the snap as her finger breaks. Still she does not let go. The elevator doors begin to shut.

Laurent gets to his feet, Danielle still half draped on him but sliding off now. He tries to intercept the closing doors, and Danielle wraps her arms around his waist and bites him through his shirt, like a wild animal. Laurent yowls with pain and arches his back involuntarily. Red blood seeps from the corners of Danielle's mouth. The elevator doors close, with Jayalitha safe behind them. Then Laurent brings his arm back sharply and hammers his elbow into Danielle's head with a sickening thunk. Danielle's whole body sags, but somehow, incredibly, she keeps hold of her opponent, until he grabs her by her waist, lifts her off her feet and slams her bodily down on to Keiran's fallen form.

The world goes dark.

Lazarus

11

Danielle doesn't want to wake. Dimly aware that reality is bright and cold and painful, she fights to stay in sleep's cocoon as long as she can, for ever if possible, that wouldn't be so bad, to spend her life in a coma's warm oblivion. It sounds better than waking and facing the world. The world is so much bigger and crueller than she.

But her body's demands for attention seep into her consciousness like blood into water. She is cold. Her head hurts. Her hand hurts. Her stomach is queasy. The whole world seems to be moving in a strange way, rocking sluggishly from side to side, like a slow continuous earthquake. The body cannot deal with these sensations by itself any longer. Attention must be paid.

It is the cold which eventually forces her into action. She gropes clumsily around without opening her eyes, hoping to find some blanket, and instead her fingers encounter the headboard of the bed she lies on, wood carved into some sort of elaborate pattern, whorls and ridges, like a relief map. It occurs to her to wonder where she is, and that is the end of sleep. Her eyes open and immediately shut. The incandescent power of the light above her seems to approach that of the sun. In her eye-blink of vision she saw that the room was tiny but luxuriously appointed, illuminated by a crystal chandelier in the shape of a painfully bright octopus, furnished with two small beds made of some kind of dark wood. The word *mahogany* comes to her unbidden. Both beds are entirely unfurnished, bare mattresses. A man sleeps on the other bed, someone she knows. The beds are hard against the walls with a channel maybe a foot long between them. The wall by her feet is slightly concave, and inset with a strange circular window, through which cloud-streaked sky can be seen.

She has to fight to call to mind the name for this type of window. Porthole. Yes. She must be on a boat. A very nice boat. With the man whose name eludes her. Her head and hand hurt very much, she knows this abstractly, and the motion of the boat makes her feel nauseous, but there is some kind of disconnect between her and her nervous system, she is aware of the pain and sickness without viscerally feeling it.

How did she get here? She tries to remember the last thing that happened to her, but the door into memory will not open. She casts about for any recollection at all. Jagged, kaleidoscopic images flicker through her mind. Her boyfriend Gavin, in college. Scuba diving on the Baja peninsula, in her Crazy Years. Riding a motorcycle through Hampi, in India.

That last is the key that opens the lock. Her eyes snap open and she takes a sharp breath as memory floods into her awareness. Kishkinda. Shadbold. The man who lies next to her is Keiran. The last thing she remembers is wrestling with Laurent. Clearly she lost.

Keiran is still asleep. No; unconscious. His breaths are fast and shallow, nothing like the respiration of deep sleep, and his body glistens with sweat. Like her, he wears only underwear and a T-shirt, the same black *You've Been 0wnz0r3d* shirt he wore in Vegas. Danielle makes herself sit up, swings her legs to the right, into the narrow crack between the beds. The carpeted floor is very soft. The air mostly smells like a hotel, but also, faintly, of salt, iron and diesel.

There is a three-foot gap between the heads of the beds and the door, which is solid wood, with an L-shaped metal handle protruding from it. She reaches out, turns the handle, pushes. The door shifts a little but is locked.

The middle finger of her right hand is grossly swollen, bigger than her thumb and almost purple. It dangles across her ring finger at a sickeningly unnatural angle. She remembers Laurent breaking it. It has not been set. She wonders how long they have been here. She is aware of the stream of desperate pain signals sent by that finger, but somehow they seem not to pierce her.

'Drugs,' she says aloud. Her mouth is so dry only a hiss comes out. She looks at her arm, sees a fresh needle mark. That explains the depth of her sleep, the slowness of her thoughts, her immunity to pain and thirst. But this sensory invulnerability will not last long. Her waking testifies to that. Soon she will be in terrible pain. Her skull hurts both externally, where Laurent struck her, and internally, where a devastating headache broods, waiting to erupt. She looks around for water. There is none. Not even a pot to piss in, not that her drug-calcified body will need that anytime soon.

She reaches out and shakes Keiran, careful to use her left hand. Eventually he twitches awake and his dilated eyes open. She waits for his addled stare to become awful comprehension.

'They got us,' she says.

'Yeah. What about Jayalitha?'

'I think she got away.'

'Where are we?'

'I think we're on a ship. His ship. Shadbold's.' Danielle gets to her feet, unsteadily, her balance would be tenuous even without the slow rise and fall of the floor beneath her, and looks out of the porthole. She sees no land, no other boats, not even any birds, nothing but sky and cloud and the vast furrowed sea, gleaming like steel in the midday sun, so enormously monotonous that it looks like a false background, something from a movie or video game.

'Your hand,' Keiran says.

Danielle looks down at it. 'Yeah. It's gonna hurt.'

'They could have set it.'

'I don't think our well-being is their number-one priority.'

Keiran rubs his eyes. 'I don't know how we're going to get out of this.'

'No.'

'I'm very glad I'm on drugs right now.'

'They're wearing off,' Danielle says.

'Don't remind me. Look.' Keiran points to a curved mirror set into a top corner of the room. 'One-way glass. There'll be a camera behind it.' He waves to it limply.

'I wonder why he didn't just drop us in the ocean,' Danielle says.

'I guess they still want something from us.'

'I'm cold.'

'Me too. Come here.'

They curl up on Keiran's bed, animals seeking warmth. It is barely big enough for both of them. Danielle cradles her wounded hand in her good one instinctively. It is hurting more and more. His breath is damp against her neck. Her headache is beginning to throb, in waves that seem to come in time with the motion of the ship.

'Maybe,' Keiran says, 'maybe Trurl and Klaupactus tracked us somehow. Maybe they can send some kind of help.'

'Don't be stupid.'

'It's possible.'

Danielle would shake her head, but it hurts too much. 'No it isn't. Don't be an idiot. No one's going to come. And they're not going to let us get away. Not this time.'

Keiran swallows. 'Yeah.'

'I sort of just hope they get it over with soon.'

'Don't say that.'

'It's true.' It is hard to feel frightened of death when she is in great pain, sick and miserable, bereft of hope. Life does not seem precious when it hurts this much.

'I'm sorry,' he says eventually.

'Don't be. I got me into this. Not you. I'm sorry they got you too. But I'm glad I'm not alone.'

'It's an honour to keep you company,' Keiran says, a faint hint of amused vitality entering his voice. 'Wouldn't have missed it for the world.'

They both fall silent. Danielle closes her eyes and tries not to notice how much she hurts. Amazingly she manages to drift back into sleep for a little longer. She is woken by Keiran detaching his limbs from hers, then slowly climbing over her.

'What is it?' she asks.

'Just looking around.'

He pushes the door a few times, provoking a dim rattling sound. 'Padlocked,' he mutters. He examines the porthole, probes the mirror in the corner, lifts the mattresses from the beds and looks at the riveted steel slats underneath. Danielle watches without comment. The drugs have worn off fully now. Her broken finger and ravaging migraine burn with white-hot pain, and her stomach is so uneasy from the ship's motion, and maybe the drug hangover, that she has to concentrate on breathing slowly and not throwing up.

'No getting out of here,' he says, sitting down on the other bed with an air of defeat. 'No lock on this side, much less anything to pick it with. Pity. I'm a two-time DefCon Lockpick Challenge champion. How's that for an epitaph?'

'Even if we got out . . .' Danielle says, and doesn't bother finishing the sentence.

'Yeah. We'd still be fucked.'

'Come back to—'

She stops. There are footsteps in the hallway, boots on metal, coming towards them. The sound of a key in a lock. The door opens. Laurent is there, along with two burly men in olive-drab uniforms without insignia, and a tall Indian man in designer finery. The same Indian man who imprisoned Danielle in that hut in Kishkinda, who struck her with the lathi and threatened her with worse, six months ago. Vijay.

'It's time,' Laurent says, his face a stern mask. He avoids Danielle's eyes.

12

They are marched, hands cuffed behind their backs, down a narrow side hallway, panelled in teak, in which alcoves display marble and alabaster antiquities. Then they enter the wide central hall of glittering mirrors and chandeliers which confirms Danielle's suspicions; they are once again on Shadbold's super-yacht, *Lazarus*. They ascend the marble staircase adorned by a bestiary of carvings, and emerge into a galley so clean and well appointed it looks like a TV set for a cooking show. The food smells make Danielle's stomach roil. Past the galley they continue into a small dining room, a whole wall of which is a single window that reveals an expanse of pale deck and the endless ocean beyond. The sunlight is bright and Danielle has to squint. Vijay and the two burly guards remain in the dining room; Laurent, Keiran and Danielle continue through another door into a small library, a room maybe fifteen feet square, lined by ornate bookshelves, with a mahogany table in the middle and four Aeron chairs.

Sophia is sitting in one of the chairs, her blonde hair pinned up into a bun, a Vaio laptop in front of her. She looks uncomfortable. There is a large jade bowl, full of water, in front of one of the other seats. Laurent guides Danielle to that seat, then Keiran to the one opposite. They sit without protest or comment. Laurent does not sit in the last seat; instead he moves to stand behind Danielle. She looks at the bowl of water and remembers the way Laurent interrogated that man in Paris, so long ago.

'This conversation will be easier for all of us,' Laurent says, 'particularly Danielle, if you are as forthcoming as possible.'

'Don't bother with the threats,' Keiran says tiredly. 'I don't care any more. I'll tell you whatever you want.'

'Very sensible of you. We only have three questions. Once you've answered them we'll helicopter you back to shore. On the understanding that you never speak of us again.'

Keiran says, 'Don't bother with the lies either.'

'The first question is technical. Sophia reports that you have access to some extraordinary computer network. You will tell her how to take it over.'

'Shazam,' Keiran says. 'Yes.'

Danielle looks at Sophia, and wonders whether her paleness means she is seasick or wrestling with her conscience. There was something she wanted to say to her. Of course. Keiran has begun a lengthy technical discourse, and Sophia has begun to tap at her laptop in response, but Danielle interrupts about thirty words in. 'You poor thing,' she says loudly to Sophia. 'You're so smart. But you were too close to it to see it, weren't you?'

Sophia stops typing. Everyone falls silent for a moment. And then, simultaneous with Laurent's sharp 'Don't waste our time', Sophia asks, 'What do you mean?'

'Your father,' Danielle says. 'It never even occurred to you to wonder, did it? First you make a name for yourself as a teen super-genius. Then your dad gets sick. Then you happen to stumble across Jack Shadbold, and he gives you a job, wins your loyalty, and puts you to work. Don't you see it?'

'No. See what?'

'That wasn't coincidence. Shadbold infected your father. With the same drugs he uses to give the people at Kishkinda cancer. So he'd have someone to use the military tools he found. Someone he could rely on to be as loyal as a dog.'

Sophia sits up very straight and stares at Danielle. 'That's insane.'

'You really think Shadbold's going to cure your father? No. He's no good to him cured. Your dad will be kept in great pain, on the edge of dying, for as long as Shadbold can, as long as Shadbold needs you, and then he'll kill you both—' and then a strong hand grabs Danielle's hair and forces her face into the jade bowl of water.

After the initial shock she gives up her instinctive thrashing attempt to escape and just goes limp. No point trying to fight. Her lungs begin to ache, as if they are compressed in an ever tightening clamp, and then they cramp with the agonizing need for breath, and she begins to fight again, she can't not, her muscles spasming almost at random, as the world goes dark around the edges, as her mouth opens up involuntarily to try to breathe water, her body betraying itself despite her fevered attempts to stay in control, the tiny part of her brain that can still think understanding that Laurent isn't just shutting her up, he's killing her, as simple and final as that, this is the moment of her death—

—but at the last possible second her head is pulled back up into the air, she can breathe again, two great rattling whoops followed by a coughing fit that sounds like an artillery fusillade. She breathed only a little water in but it takes a whole minute to get it all out, during which she isn't aware of anything but her lungs. By the time it is over she feels exhausted, her core muscles so worn from the coughing that she can barely sit up. Her chest aches with every breath as if her lungs are full of broken glass.

'That's enough out of you,' Laurent says. 'Understand?'

Danielle barely manages to nod.

'No,' Sophia says. 'Nice try, but no. You're not going to social-engineer me like that. Shadbold couldn't have done that to my dad. His drugs don't reliably cause the right kind of cancer in an individual. Let's get back to the subject.' She turns to Keiran. 'Shazam.'

'It wasn't just you,' Keiran says.

'What?'

'We did some research. There were a dozen young bright computer whizz kids whose parents fell sick or died in the same two-month period that year.'

Danielle knows Keiran is bluffing. They never did any research. But he might be right.

'Enough!' Laurent says angrily.

'Look it up,' Keiran says. 'You're being used. You've been used for years.'

Laurent takes two steps around the table, intending to punish Keiran.

Keiran says, 'Why do you think he's so desperate to shut us up?

It's because your boyfriend here knows it's true too. He knew all along.'

Laurent stops.

'But never mind,' Keiran says. 'What do you care, right? You want Shazam? I'll give you Shazam.'

He starts into his technical deposition again. Danielle understands none of it. But she can tell that Sophia isn't listening. She is lost in disturbed thought.

Laurent sees this too. 'Sophia, are you getting this?' he asks in a pointed voice.

Sophia looks at him for a moment before answering. 'I'm a little seasick,' she says. 'Can we do the other two questions first?'

'Seasick?' Laurent is sceptical.

'That's what I said. Seasick.'

He and Sophia exchange a brief hard look.

'All right,' Laurent says. 'Question two. Where is Jayalitha?'

Keiran shrugs. 'Fucked if I know.'

The flippant answer earns him a broken nose. Keiran's chair rocks back with the force of Laurent's punch, and nearly deposits him on the floor before it rights itself. Blood streams from his nose, drips down either side of his mouth like a gory handlebar moustache. Keiran, incredibly, smiles.

'Then where do you think she might be?' Laurent asks.

'I honestly haven't a fucking clue.'

Laurent shifts the bowl of water to Keiran's side of the table.

'Do your worst, mate,' Keiran says dismissively. 'You think we had a fall-back plan in case we got kidnapped? She's a ghost. After what she's been through, living on the streets will be a piece of piss. You'll never find her.'

'We shall see. Question three. Where is the evidence?'

Keiran looks at him as if he's crazy. 'What evidence?'

Laurent is on the verge of renewed violence, but Sophia raises a hand to stop him. 'I think I'm going to be sick,' she says quietly.

'What?'

'I think I'm going to be sick. I need to go outside.' She stands up, folds her laptop and walks out of the room. Laurent watches her go, a wary expression on his face.

'Relationship problems, Laurent, old son?' Keiran asks. 'Is the level of trust between you and your new lady love not what it could be?'

'Shut it.'

'Or what? You'll kill me?'

Laurent walks out of the library, after Sophia. They hear the door lock behind him.

'Find a lockpick,' Keiran hisses, the moment the door shuts. 'Quick. He'll send one of his men to watch us.'

They both stand up and begin looking around. But the room seems barren apart from the shelves, books, table, chairs and the bowl of water. Outside they hear Laurent issue some kind of command, and then boots, stomping towards them.

Danielle examines the bookcase. It is bolted to the wall, but will move a little back and forth. Wooden brackets protect the top and bottom of each shelf, preventing books from flying out in rough seas, and requiring them to be inserted and removed sideways. The only exception is the top shelf, larger than the rest, which is covered by netting that hooks into holes drilled into the shelf below. The hooks themselves are too large to be useful, but . . . 'There!' Danielle says urgently, seeing a folder full of loose papers behind the netting. 'There'll be staples. Or paper-clips.'

'Get it,' Keiran says, as he puts his back to the table and tries to shove it towards the door – but it too is fixed to the floor. The boots have almost reached them. Danielle gets up on the chair, manages to unhook the netting with her teeth, but the papers are too far away. The door opens. Vijay enters, looks curiously at Danielle standing on a chair, and Keiran with his back to the table.

'Sit,' he says. 'Behave.'

Defeated, for the moment, they obey.

'At least Jayalitha got away,' Keiran says.

'Yeah.'

'You are to remain silent,' Vijay warns.

Keiran looks at him scornfully. 'Or *what*? We'll probably be dead in an hour. What can you possibly threaten us with that isn't already going to happen?'

The Indian man has no answer.

'And they think we know where Jaya's evidence is,' Keiran continues.

'Should we talk about this—'

'Why not? It's not like we know anything. Good thinking with Sophia's father, by the way.'

Danielle shrugs dully. 'Too little too late. Probably.'

Keiran nods. 'Alas. Afraid we don't have much longer. If they knew we don't know anything about Jaya or her evidence, they would have just buried us in the desert instead of bringing us here. Where are we, incidentally?' he asks Vijay.

Vijay smirks.

'I asked you a question, you stupid fucking cunt,' Keiran says, and hawks a stream of bloody phlegm across the table into Vijay's face.

For a moment the sheer chutzpah of the act freezes both Danielle and Vijay with shock. Then Vijay is on his feet, rushing around the table towards Keiran, brushing past and nearly knocking over Danielle. Keiran runs, keeping the table between them. Vijay gives up on the Keystone Kops chase, jumps up on to the table with surprising nimbleness, and leaps at Keiran, who does not dodge, but lets the force of the charge carry him backwards into the bookshelf – the same bookshelf that holds the sheaf of papers. The force of the impact causes them to spill out into the room. Danielle, understanding now that this is method not madness, gets out of her chair, and as Vijay slams a fist into Keiran's solar plexus, and he collapses into a quivering wreck, she manages to squat down and liberate a paper-clip from the papers strewn across half the room.

Vijay stands and uses one of the fallen papers to wipe the spittle off his face. Danielle gets back into her chair, holding the paper-clip tightly. She hopes Keiran isn't too badly hurt to use it. The wind has been knocked out of him, he fights for breath for twenty seconds, his eyes bulging from his face, before he is able to draw in air again. An idea hits her. She stands up, leaving the paper-clip on her chair, and goes to kneel beside Keiran. 'Are you OK?' she asks, her back to Vijay, putting as much worry into her voice as she can. And then, as he looks up at her, she bends towards him and whispers: 'Take my chair.'

'Sit down,' Vijay warns. 'Now. Or I will end the love taps and a real beating will begin.'

Keiran slowly gets to his feet, his face liberally smeared with blood from his broken nose, totters to Danielle's chair, and sits, breathing hard. Vijay appears not to have seen the paper-clip. Danielle hopes Keiran won his DefCon Lockpick Challenges honestly and not by hacking the scoring system. Not that she can imagine how his escape from cuffs might possible save them. She stands, intending to take the nearest seat, but Vijay blocks her path. He closes his hand around her throat, not quite hard enough to block her breath, but firmly, as if he owns her. He steps close to her, keeping his legs inside hers, preventing a knee to the groin.

'Danielle Leaf,' he says. 'It is a pleasure to see you again. As I told you before, we have many more subjects to discuss.' His hand tightens. 'I hope we can spend some time before you depart. I have such plans for you.'

The door opens. Laurent is there. 'Let her go,' he says sharply.

Vijay obeys. He looks a little hurt, like a child whose toy has been taken away for some incomprehensible adult reason.

'Danielle,' Laurent says. 'Come with me.'

She doesn't want to, but has no choice. Wondering whether he will now simply push her off the edge of the boat, she follows him through the galley and out on to the deck again. The sun hurts her eyes.

'I'm sorry,' Laurent says.

She looks at him. 'What?'

'For what I did to you in there. I didn't intend it. I panicked. I thought I had to silence you and it was the only way.'

'That's what you're sorry for.'

'Yes. I regret the rest of what happened with us. But this was different. This was a mistake. What happened before was unavoidable.'

'And what happens next? Is that unavoidable too?'

'You will not be harmed further,' Laurent says. 'You have my word. You understand we cannot release Keiran, he is much too dangerous, but you will go free.'

'Right.'

'It's the truth. I realize you have no reason to believe me. That's fine. You don't need to believe me. But when you are released, you need to understand the necessity of not ever talking about this, to anyone.'

'What about when they come to arrest me?' Danielle asks.

'I can promise you that the FBI will soon realize that they erred in making you part of the investigation.'

'Sure.'

'As I said, it does not matter if you believe me now,' Laurent says.

'Why would you possibly let me go?'

'I'll be honest. In part in the hope that Jayalitha will contact you again. And because we have nothing to fear from you. You aren't a credible source. Anything you say will be called paranoia, with no evidence. But mostly it's an operational decision on my part. I think you deserve another chance at life.'

'That's big of you,' Danielle says.

'Ask yourself, why would I lie?'

'So you can use it as a carrot for Keiran. If he tells your pet hacker everything he knows, then I get to live.'

'That incentive for cooperation is an added bonus,' Laurent admits.

'Assuming your pet hacker doesn't turn on you.'

'She won't. I don't know whether your allegation about her

father is true. I agree it's plausible. But if Mr Shadbold does find a way to live, he will share his cure with all other victims, that was no lie. It will be his legacy. He intends to go from pariah to hero. Even if he changes his mind, Sophia will be able to steal the cure, as long as she stays within his organization.'

'Is that how she sees it?' Danielle asks.

'That's how I explained it to her. I think she agrees. It just took her a moment to adjust to the new understanding.'

'Doesn't she realize you're a lying fucking sociopath?'

'She knows I will lie to protect my loyalties,' Laurent says. 'As will she. In a way it's a more candid understanding than most relationships. Ours is a partnership of equals.'

'Two tigers, huh? Not like you and me. Not like tiger and mouse.'

'You are not a mouse.'

'No. If you're telling the truth, I get to be a lab rat in a maze. I spend my whole life with you watching everything I do, in case Jayalitha calls me or I start to make trouble. Is that about right?' Danielle asks.

'Yes.'

'After you tie Keiran to an anvil and drop him off this boat?'

'Operational necessity.'

'You're so casual. You're so fucking *casual* about it.'

'The inability to be casual about death is what prevents otherwise exceptional people from becoming great,' Laurent says. 'Such as yourself. We live in a world where the strong inevitably eat the weak. Great men and women accept this. Only fools deny it.'

'Great. Psychopath philosophy. As if my day wasn't complete.'

'Back to the library,' Laurent says. 'I would like you to be there while Keiran explains what he knows.'

Danielle hopes and even half expects to find Vijay unconscious and Keiran gone to work some evil technical wizardry on the ship. But when she returns to the room it is unchanged except that

Vijay has been exchanged for one of the burly khaki-clad white men, the spilled papers have returned to the bookcase and the blood has been cleaned from Keiran's face; he must have been escorted to a bathroom.

Laurent stays outside.

'Well?' Keiran asks. 'What did he say?'

Danielle doesn't want to answer. She knows that this is all part of Laurent's plan, to incite Keiran's cooperation with the lure of her survival, as well as the threat of turning her over to Vijay the sadist. Both carrot and stick. He must have learned that from Shadbold. But she isn't willing to lie to Keiran. She recounts her conversation with Laurent.

'You believe him?' Keiran asks.

'He's a liar.'

'That's not what I asked.'

Danielle hesitates. 'I do. But it might . . . I mean, of course I'm going to believe what might be a happy ending for me, right? I don't want you changing what you do because of anything he says, or . . .' Her voice trails off.

'True or not, I'm not leaving this ship,' Keiran says.

'No.' Danielle realizes that this is true. It is pure self-delusion to stake some kind of hope on a stolen paper-clip. Keiran will die on this vessel.

'I might as well give you a chance. I hope it's real.'

Danielle doesn't know what to say. She wants to cry.

Laurent enters, accompanied by Sophia, carrying her laptop. She sits next to Keiran. Laurent stands during the ensuing technical conversation, which makes little sense to Danielle, or apparently to Laurent or the guard. Both Sophia and Keiran speak in clipped, unemotional tones, one scientist to another, as if it is a conversation between co-workers, rather than the surrender of potentially world-shaking knowledge by a man who will soon die. Only about half their words are recognizably English. Keiran's cuffs are removed so he can take turns using Sophia's laptop, which she can tell makes Laurent uneasy. Their mutual technical

333

respect is obvious; Sophia makes little impressed grunts as Keiran tells her details, and Keiran nods as Sophia understands what he says, often before he even finishes his sentences.

'Sorry,' Keiran says after a good hour of this. 'I'm losing focus. It's been a hard day. I need to rest before we continue.'

'Continue?' Laurent asks. To Sophia he says, 'You said this wouldn't take long.'

Sophia shakes her head. 'I didn't know how much he had. It's not just breaking into systems, it's understanding them and using them once you're there. Keiran's been doing this for fifteen years. He's a walking encyclopedia. I could spend all week learning from him.'

'We haven't got a week,' Laurent says darkly. 'He's just stalling.'

'He's not. I've learned more in the last hour than in the previous six months. Give me two more days with him and we'll have fingers in every pie within five miles of the Internet. Seriously. This is amazing stuff.'

'Two more days.' Laurent considers. Danielle can tell he doesn't like this at all, is on the verge of just ordering Keiran dead on the spot.

'What have you got to lose?' she asks.

Laurent gives her a sharp look, but then nods. 'Back to their brig. Both of them. Twenty-four-hour watch. At both the door and the camera.'

The adrenalin that has fuelled Danielle all day drains away when she realizes both she and Keiran will live to see another. By the time they get back to the room they woke in, and their cuffs are removed, she is dead tired and her headache is so immense it clouds her whole mind. Thankfully, the beds have been outfitted with three-hundred-thread-count sheets, incredibly soft blankets and firm pillows. The luxury is surreal. But it is still a jail. It is still light out, and she can tell Keiran wants to talk, but Danielle doesn't think she is capable of conversation. She curls up under her blanket, closes her eyes and waits for sleep to wash the pain away.

It is night when she wakes. This is apparent only from the dark porthole; the fluorescent octopus above them still burns with eye-scarring brightness. Danielle feels immensely better, fully alert, her headache a damp throb rather than yesterday's stabbing agony, and her finger hurts only when she moves. She can tell by Keiran's breathing that he too is awake.

She might survive this. Keiran is surely doomed, but Danielle might be released. Maybe Laurent is lying. But maybe not. It is a tiny but golden strand of hope. *If you let me get through this*, she vows to God, the cosmos, whatever supernatural forces might be listening, *then I promise* . . . She comes to a mental halt. She isn't quite sure what to promise. To be good, as a five-year-old might? *To do good*, she decides. *To stop wasting my life. To devote it to something. A better world.* She doesn't know how, exactly, but maybe the how isn't so important.

She needs the bathroom. Danielle gets up, bangs on the door, starts to shout. Eventually the guard, his eyes red with sleeplessness, allows her out and into an opulent bathroom of marble and gold. He doesn't allow her to close the door, but she is beyond physical embarrassment, and he doesn't pay any attention to her anyway. She drinks water straight from the sink's solid gold tap. When the guard comes to escort her back, she briefly considers making a run for it, but gives up the idea as futile and meekly lets him lead her back to captivity, where she joins Keiran on his bed. He reaches out to her and they hold each other close.

'Do you still have it?' she whispers. She wonders for a moment about bugs, but her voice is so soft that it will surely be lost in the ambient noise of the sea.

'Yes. I practised. I can pick those cuffs in five seconds.'

'Then what?'

'I don't know exactly. But do you remember our last visit here?' Keiran asks.

'I guess.'

'You remember what's at the very back of the boat?'

After a moment Danielle stiffens with excitement. 'That's right. Those jet-ski things. And scuba gear.'

Keiran nods. 'Standard issue on all super-yachts.'

The personal watercraft are probably useless, Danielle doesn't know how to drive them and they have neither the time nor the circumstances to learn, but the dive gear is very much another story; Danielle is an experienced divemaster. 'Do you dive?' she asks.

'No. Never.'

'Shit.' She considers, and her hopes sag again. 'And even if we get out somehow, it takes a while to get scuba gear ready. There's no way we'd have that much time.'

'Unless there were some kind of distraction.'

'Like what?'

Keiran responds with a crooked smile. 'I think we can expect something interesting to happen tomorrow.'

'What? How?'

'When you look into the Internet, the Internet looks into you. This ship is online, there's a pair of VSAT dishes up top. I had to connect to Shazam to show our little friend the ropes. She doesn't know yet that Mulligan can track that. He knows where we are.'

Danielle frowns. 'So? What can he do?'

'Don't underestimate Mulligan,' Keiran says. 'If he throws caution to the wind, which I hope he will, then . . . actually I have no idea what he might do. But knowing him, probably something drastic.'

13

Keiran goes alone to today's hacker training session. He supposes that now his apparent cooperation has been established, they don't need Danielle around to remind him to be helpful. Laurent does not stay with him and Sophia either; only one of the bodybuilder guards.

'I need to talk to Shadbold,' Keiran says to Sophia, as she boots up her laptop.

'You can't.'

'It's something I need to tell him personally,' he lies. In fact he is hoping that Mulligan's distraction arrives while he is in Shadbold's chamber, and he will somehow be able to take the chief monster hostage. It's a slim chance, but anything that increases his minuscule odds of survival is worth trying for.

'I didn't say we won't let you, I said you can't,' Sophia says archly. 'He's not on board. He's in his private hospital in Switzerland. His condition's worsened.'

Keiran shrugs, disappointed. 'Couldn't happen to a nicer fellow. But surely you could fly me up there for a couple of hours?'

She gives him a nice-try look. He was hoping for a hint about where they are. They couldn't have been drugged for more than a day or two. But that is plenty long enough to fly them from Vegas to anywhere on the planet. There is still no land in sight, no seabirds, and the air is warm by day but cold by night, so his guess is somewhere in a northern ocean, but they could well be off Cape Town or Tasmania.

Not knowing where in the world he is, or even the date, makes Keiran feel strangely disconnected, as if in a parallel universe, or dreaming. As if whatever happens on this boat is not part of real life, cannot truly affect him. The feeling should make it easier to deal with the horrible certainty – barring some miraculous intervention – of his impending death, but Keiran makes a point of rejecting it utterly. He has devoted his life to rational thought. He won't let irrational comfort ease his death.

'Get on with it,' the guard growls. His accent is South African. 'I've been advised I need to keep your head and your fingers intact. Everything else is optional.'

Keiran looks at Sophia.

'You think I won't let him?' she asks.

'All right,' he says. 'Where were we?'

'Exxon Mobil's corporate intranet.'

'Right. Let me drive a moment. I'll show you how to own an oil tanker.'

Lost in the intricate details of Exxon Mobil's virtual private network, it takes Keiran a few moments to realize that some new sensory input is tickling his brain, somewhere on the edge of awareness. A kind of low buzzing sound, coming from the east, the direction of the bow. Sophia and the South African look at one another uncertainly. The strange noise intensifies, clarifies into a recognizable auditory signature: a helicopter, approaching.

'Are we expecting a visitor?' the South African asks.

'No,' Sophia says. She taps at her laptop, and a window called WHEELHOUSE materializes on it, above a diagnostic diagram of a ship. Keiran starts paying very close attention. She opens a new window, a radar screen with a ship in the middle and a red dot approaching from the east, and studies the ancillary data scrolling on the margins of the screen for a moment. 'It's not Coast Guard, no transponder. We're outside the two-hundred-mile limit anyhow. I'm going to raise anchor and start the engines, just in case.'

She closes the window, returns to WHEELHOUSE and types a few commands. Beneath them, the *Lazarus* begins to hum with power. Then she opens up four camera windows and tiles them across the screen. The oncoming helicopter is barely visible in the bow camera, the size of a gnat on a windscreen.

Keiran watches, partly from fascination, partly because he is memorizing the layout of the vessel as shown on screen. His guess when he first visited this vessel was correct; the *Lazarus*, like dot-com billionaire Jim Clark's yachts *Hyperion* and *Athena*, is almost entirely automated, run by this WHEELHOUSE software, via a ship-wide wireless network. This explains why he has seen so few people on board; Laurent, Sophia, the several burly thugs including the South African, and the five Filipinos Keiran saw this morning in the galley, one cooking breakfast, two dressed like chambermaids, two dressed in overalls. Cooks, servants and a couple of mechanics in case something physical goes wrong, that's all the crew the *Lazarus* needs. He is impressed.

The helicopter noise crescendos, and then holds at a level sufficiently loud that Keiran cannot hear Sophia's keystrokes as she reopens the radar screen. The red dot is circling the *Lazarus*, maintaining a constant distance. Again she opens the four camera windows and tiles them across the screen. The helicopter passes through each in turn, circling around the ship. It does not say US NAVY on it, as Keiran had hoped. It is painted plain black. It seems bigger than police or news helicopters, but doesn't look military. There are at least a half-dozen people inside. Most of them carry assault rifles.

The door to the library opens, and the helicopter noise becomes thunderous. Laurent is there. 'Gunther!' he calls. 'Secure him and get down to the weapons room!'

The door closes. Gunther, the South African, is already on his feet, pulling Keiran's arms behind his back, cuffing his wrists and lacing the handcuff chain through a metal bar at the base of the chair, unaware of the paper-clip concealed between two of Keiran's fingers.

'I'll come with you,' Sophia says, and Keiran sags, dejected.

'No,' Gunther says. 'He ordered me to come. Not you.'

'If there's a situation, you need me there.'

Gunther gives her a patronizing look. 'Girl, this is a security situation. You do what you're told. Stay where you are.'

He closes the door behind him. Keiran has already opened the handcuffs.

'Fucking *asshole*,' Sophia says furiously. She stands up and picks up her laptop, obviously about to follow him. 'Don't go anywhere.'

'Same to you,' Keiran says, standing up, holding the metal cuffs looped around his clenched right fist, ready to beat her unconscious if he has to.

It takes Sophia only a moment to internalize the suddenly changed situation.

'I'll do what you want,' she says quietly.

'Sit down. Stay quiet.'

She does. He grabs her arms, pulls them roughly behind her and handcuffs her in the same way he was just restrained. Then he takes a piece of paper, rips off a corner, chews it into a tiny wet ball and shoves that into the handcuff keyhole. It will be difficult to remove before it dries. Finally he stands and looks down at her for a long moment.

'What?' she asks, scornfully.

'I'm deciding whether to strangle you to death.'

Sophia's eyes widen.

'I should, you know,' he says. 'It's the logical thing to do.'

Then he picks up her laptop, opens the door and walks out of the library. He emerges from the galley on to the deck and starts towards the aft of the boat, towards the brig where Danielle is imprisoned.

'Come on,' Keiran commands, as he opens the door to the cabin that holds Danielle prison. 'To the stern. Hurry.' He doesn't know where exactly the weapons room is that Laurent and Gunther and the other thugs have disappeared to, it isn't marked on the WHEELHOUSE ship schematic, but he doesn't like the sound of it, and he is sure they don't have much time.

The aft superstructure is like an apartment building in the middle of the deck. A narrow walkway fenced by waist-high metal bars goes around it on either side, to an aft space about ten feet deep, across the width of the ship, which terminates at the very end of the boat. Most of this space is taken up by two touching giant metal plates, which Keiran guesses fold upwards like basement-access panels on New York streets. The two WaveRunners are parked at the back corners of the ship. There are more doors into the superstructure; one of them he remembers as the door to the scuba room.

The helicopter's ear-splitting din is returning. He sees it sweep back along the ship's port side, only a hundred feet up, approaching close enough that the yacht's mainsail billows as it passes, and Keiran and Danielle have to grab the fence to keep their footing in the rotor wash. Keiran isn't sure what Mulligan intends with the helicopter. Hopefully some kind of daring rescue. One obvious problem: the helipad above the aft superstructure is already occupied by Shadbold's private helicopter, and Keiran doubts the newcomer can land anywhere else on the deck.

Then he sees a rope ladder fall over the black helicopter's side and dangle down thirty feet, as the helicopter begins to descend towards them.

'Drop the laptop,' Danielle warns Keiran.

Keiran hesitates. He doesn't want to, Sophia's laptop might yet be insanely useful, but he can tell Danielle is right, it will be all they can manage to grab the ladder as it swoops past and hang on long enough to make it into the helicopter—

—and then sudden brightness shines from the bow of the ship. Something burning streaks across the sky, smashes into the side of the black helicopter and explodes with a loud *crump* and a burst of light so bright it clouds Keiran's eyes for a moment. Something hot tears at his left arm. He is surrounded by the maddening rattle of metal raining on metal. As he watches, dazed, the helicopter's rotor flies free of the shredded hulk that was once a vehicle, gliding away from the ship like a frisbee. The wreck of the cabin plunges unceremoniously into the sea and vanishes with an anticlimactically small splash. The rotor, still spinning, hits the ocean at a narrow angle and actually skips off the surface three times, like a thrown stone, before disappearing.

'Holy shit,' Danielle whispers.

Keiran looks down at his upper arm, and the shallow line of newly traced blood on it. The deck around them is pockmarked and furrowed with a dozen scars, some of them inches deep. If the shrapnel that grazed his arm had been six inches to the right it would have gone right through his heart. Their avenue of escape has been closed by a rocket launcher. And their would-be rescuers are dead.

'Come on,' Keiran says, recovering – they have no time to be stunned, speed is the only thing that might save them. 'We need to buy some time.'

Danielle looks at him, dazed and despairing. 'What? What for?'

'There's still a chance. Follow me.'

At the absolute back of the ship, a pair of ladders lead down the exterior hull, towards the engines, to three-foot-square platforms which jut out slightly. Doorways lead from these platforms into the interior of the ship. According to the WHEELHOUSE schematic, these doors lead to the ship's engineering rooms. One-handed, Keiran starts to climb down the nearest ladder. He keeps Sophia's laptop clamped tightly under his arm. It is now their only hope.

Danielle follows Keiran down the ladder, to the platform above the engines, where a door leads into the aft of the ship. It opens into a dimly lit tunnel that smells of grease and oil. Keiran looks up before entering – and sees Laurent's face appear over the edge of the aft deck, above Danielle's descending form. He looks amused. Keiran advances into the tunnel, hoping to soon wipe that smirk off Laurent's face.

He hears Laurent's boots on the rungs as Danielle shuts and locks the watertight door behind them. Laurent looks in through the door's porthole as Danielle and Keiran flee down the tunnel, which opens into a wider room full of gleaming machinery, lit by fluorescent light.

'Stop this nonsense now,' Laurent threatens. He is shouting, but only a dull, warped echo of his voice makes it through to them. 'Or neither of you is going home.' He lifts his hand to the porthole. Sunlight gleams from the gun he carries.

Keiran looks at Danielle.

'Is this going to do us any good?' she whispers.

'I don't know. If we can buy some time here, it might. If it works, I'll need your help.' He swallows. 'But, truth be told, it probably won't work.'

'But it might.'

'It might.'

'That's good enough for me,' Danielle decides.

Keiran nods. 'We have to block off all the other doors.'

This room appears to be some kind of mechanical workshop. Small industrial machines, lathes, bandsaws and less identifiable equipment, are spaced out around its perimeter, beneath shelves that hold racks of tools, safety and welding glasses, gloves, coveralls, rubber boots, propane tanks, lengths of wood, clamps, metal and plastic tubes, various types of wire and cable, and other assorted mechanical debris. In the middle are two large work-tables and a few chairs. There are two other doors, at the bow end, on either side of the room. Unlike the aft door, these ones open out and cannot be locked from this side. The first thing Keiran and Danielle do is tie the handles of each door to the base of a nearby machine with lengths of steel cable, so that they will open an inch or two but no farther.

'Wish we'd hit the electrical room instead,' Keiran mutters. 'But this ought to do.' He drags one of the worktables to an aft corner of the room, where it will not be visible from any partly opened door, plugs the laptop into a power outlet beneath the lathe, and sits at the table.

'What are you doing?' Danielle asks.

'Basically,' Keiran says, typing furiously, 'this is a mutiny.'

'What?'

'We're taking over the boat.'

Danielle looks at him. 'Looks to me like we've locked ourselves into a room with no hope of escape.'

'That's because you're not a hacker. This ship is fully auto-mated, and it's one big wireless hotspot. Stupid bastards brought me into a totally computer-controlled environment. And now they will pay.'

'You're not the only hacker on board,' Danielle says. She starts as one of the other doors rattles, somebody trying to open it, but the steel cable holds.

Keiran smiles. His furiously flying fingers do not cease or even slow as he speaks; he is resetting all the system passwords. 'No. But by the time they get her loose, I'll have locked her and everyone else out of the system.'

'Then what?'

'That depends on where we are. But with luck I sail us home.'

'And without luck? Those doors won't hold for ever. And they have guns.'

'Without luck I even the odds,' Keiran says.

'How?'

'Sink the ship.'

Danielle opens her mouth, then closes it again, before saying, 'And how exactly do we get out of here then?'

'Look, I never said I'd thought through all the ramifications,' Keiran snaps. 'But at least now we've got some leverage. Now please be quiet for a moment. I've never hacked my way into a ship before. It's going to take some figuring out.'

WHEELHOUSE is an elegant and powerful piece of software that gives Keiran full control over every electrical, mechanical and hydraulic system on board the *Lazarus*. But he doubts that will be enough to save them. The more he thinks about it, the less he likes their chances. Laurent could fill the room with oil and drop in a match. Their enemies are armed with rocket launchers; they must have other weapons too, grenades, explosives. He and Danielle are easy to kill. Laurent still wants them alive, and the ship undamaged, but if any real risk becomes apparent, he won't hesitate to destroy them.

Maybe they can summon more help? The small-scale radar map reports their position: the Pacific Ocean, off the Oregon coast, ten miles outside the two-hundred-mile limit that demarcates America's sovereignty. A sensible location, from Laurent's point of view – international waters, but close enough for helicopter commutes to and from the all but undefended Oregon coast.

'We're off Portland, Oregon,' Keiran says, 'but that's an eight-hour sail. At least an hour for any help to get here.'

'We'll never make it,' Danielle says.

'No.'

They look at one another.

'Can you really sink the ship?' Danielle asks.

Keiran hesitates. 'Good question. I own the system, but I'm not sure what the system can do yet.' There appears to be a seawater ballast system, big tanks all along both sides of the ship, with maintenance doors that open into them from the engine room. There will be safety constraints that prevent these doors being opened while the ship is at sea. If such constraints are hardware, there is nothing Keiran can do. But if they are software, the safety issue is sufficiently funda-mental that such constraints are likely hard-coded into the system, but it might be possible for Keiran to decompile and rebuild the software without its safety provisions. Possible but very difficult. Like programming an autopilot to crash into a mountain.

'The short answer is maybe?'

'Correct.'

'What about the fuel tanks?' Danielle asks.

'What about them?'

'Do they open up too?'

Keiran checks. 'Yes.' There's an emergency dumping system that voids the fuel tanks into the ocean in case of fire; he would have to trigger an emergency alarm, but that should be relatively trivial. 'Do you want to . . .'

'I'm not sure. But get that ready. And sink the ship.'

'Then how do we—'

'Just do it,' she says.

Keiran nods. 'I'm on the motherfucker.' He leans over the laptop, his face intent, his fingers a blur of motion but the rest of his body as still as a meditating Zen master.

*　　*　　*

'Danielle,' Laurent calls out, from the port-side door, which is open the available inch. 'This is ridiculous. I appreciate your need to try to escape, but it has failed. Open these doors or I can no longer guarantee your safety.'

'I never believed in your safety in the first place.'

'I'm serious. We'll use explosives to break in if we have to. The shock wave will probably kill you. Without counting the way shrapnel will fly around the room. Neither of you will survive. Please don't make it necessary.'

'Keep him talking,' Keiran says, his voice low. 'I think I'm close.'

Danielle says, loudly, 'You're going to kill us both anyways.'

'That's not true! Fucking *merde*. I want you to live, Danielle. I'd like you both to live. I respect you both. I'm sorry there is no way out for Keiran. But there is still an escape for you.'

'Prove it,' Danielle says.

'How?'

'I don't know. Up to you. But if you convince me that you'll really let me live, I'll open that door.'

Laurent grunts with frustration and retreats, presumably to think.

'You mean that?' Keiran asks, keeping his voice distant, as if discussing the weather.

Danielle shrugs. 'Hardly matters. I can't think of any way he can possibly prove it.'

'Enough,' Laurent says, his voice taut. 'There will be no more conversation. You will have no more chances. Open this door now or we will blow it open and kill you both.'

Danielle looks at Keiran.

'I'm there,' he says.

'So do it.'

'I already did.' At least he thinks so. He has rebuilt WHEEL-HOUSE from source, without any safety constraints whatsoever, and ordered it to open the ballast access doors; but there are no sensors attached to those doors, no indication as to whether he has succeeded or whether some subtle, tiny bug has caused his attempt to fail. 'It'll be slow if it works. Half an hour at least.'

'Then do the other thing,' she says.

'I already did.' That much he is confident of. Fuel is venting from *Lazarus*'s tanks into the open ocean at the maximum possible rate.

Danielle smiles and calls out, 'I have some bad news for you, sweetie.'

Laurent sighs. 'Do tell.'

'You set off that bomb of yours, and you kill everyone on this ship.'

'Really,' he says. 'What do we die of, broken hearts?'

'No. If Keiran doesn't type a special password into his laptop every sixty seconds, the electrical systems go haywire, sparks fly in this baby's gas tank, and everyone goes boom.'

There is a brief buzz of conversation. Then Laurent calls out, 'Nice try. Even if you could cause a spark, the oil tanks are airtight. Nothing burns without oxygen. No more talk, Danielle, it's time—'

'Oh, they've got plenty of oxygen now,' Danielle says. 'You should stop paying quite so much attention to us and take a look behind you. If you did, you might just notice that we're bobbing up and down in the middle of a big-ass oil slick.'

This time the conversation outside goes on longer and is considerably more heated. Keiran grins. It's a bluff, he can't make sparks fly inside the oil tanks, but they don't know that. 'You're brilliant,' he says.

'Thanks.'

'I've disabled all the safety systems. I don't think anything can stop the ship from sinking now. Unless they can bail eighty gallons a minute.'

'Great. Can you drop the lifeboats on to the deck?'

Keiran nods. There are four lifeboats hanging on the sides of the fore and aft superstructures; the harnesses they hang in are controlled from WHEELHOUSE's control panel.

'Do it,' Danielle says.

'I don't suppose you ever learned how to fly a helicopter?' Keiran asks, as he remotely lowers the lifeboats.

'I think I was sick that day in grade school,' Danielle says sarcastically. 'That's how they get out, not us. We paddle.'

Keiran shakes his head. 'They won't let us get to a lifeboat. They'll kill us first.'

'Not if they have to leave in a real hurry. Like, for instance, if that huge oil slick all around the ship was on fire.' Danielle looks into the corner of the room. 'Oh, look. A welding torch.'

14

Danielle has never used a welding torch before, and has only seen it done once before, long ago, in Oakland. Fortunately it isn't complicated. The torch is already connected to a propane tank. She slips the welding goggles on, squeezes the trigger, thumbs the ignition switch, and a long needle of white flame hisses from the torch's nozzle. A rubber band around the trigger ensures it will stay on as long as needed.

No one is waiting for them at the aft door. Not a surprise; the platform is awkwardly narrow. Probably there is someone on top of the ladder in case they try to escape that way. That won't be a problem. No one in their right minds will climb down that ladder, starting about thirty seconds from now. Danielle opens the door, pushes up the welding goggles and looks out. The oil slick that surrounds the ship extends out for a good hundred feet in every direction, flat as a pancake; the ocean's swells travel only about five feet into its thickness before dissipating. The oil shimmers with fantastic, kaleido-scopic rainbow swirls, unexpectedly beautiful. She wishes she had time to admire it.

Behind her she hears Laurent's voice: 'What in the name of God are you two *doing*?' She smiles. She has never heard him sound frightened before. She supposes that what she is about to do is crazy, but better that than let him win.

Danielle checks the rubber band on the welding torch, lobs it underhand off the ship, and shuts the door immediately.

She expects a massive Hollywood explosion. Instead, through the door's porthole, she sees a mound of flame erupt and spread, until the flames have climbed high and far enough to swallow all her field of vision out to the horizon. It looks as if she has set the entire Pacific Ocean on fire.

'Sweet mother of God,' someone says reverentially, in a South African accent.

Keiran enters the hallway. Like her, he wears canvas coveralls and gloves, rubber boots and a welding mask. 'I think you got their attention,' he says quietly.

'Did you do it?'

'Yes. Ten thousand SOSes. Bit redundant if you ask me. They'll see this fire from orbit.'

Behind them they hear Laurent's voice say, sharply, 'Immediate evacuation. Get to the chopper. Now.'

The whole ship shudders violently then, sending both Danielle and Keiran hard into the corridor wall; they barely get their hands up to slow the impact. The fire must have entered the still-half-full fuel tanks; in that enclosed space, the conflagration would have been much like an explosion. The ship rights itself – but not completely; it has developed a pronounced list.

'I think it's better we go sooner not later,' Danielle says.

'Yeah.'

They look at one another. Danielle reaches her gloved left hand out to Keiran's and squeezes it, tightly. Then she takes a deep breath, flings open the door and steps out into what looks like the fires of hell.

The actual flames from the burning oil don't quite reach the platform at the base of the ladder, but both the air and the metal – including platform and ladder – are already too hot to breathe or touch bare handed. She scrambles up the ladder as fast as she can, trying to ignore the brown burn-scars appearing on her gloves, the agonizing protests of her broken finger and the searing pain where her skin is exposed at wrists and neck. She wants to breathe halfway up the ladder, her upward exertion seems to have consumed all her oxygen in just a few seconds, but she holds her breath with desperate discipline. The air is thick with black, acrid smoke. The deafening sound of the flames, all around her, is like the roar of an enraged god. She throws herself over the edge, on to the aft deck, and into the door farthest to the right.

The interior air of the scuba room is cool and breathable. Keiran follows her in and she slams the door shut. It feels like closing a furnace. They peel off their coveralls and pull on wet suits. She has to help Keiran, who doesn't realize that the zipper goes on the back. He is no use at all assembling buoyancy vests, scuba tanks and the 'octopus' breathing apparatus that connects them. She tries to work as fast as she can, but it isn't easy with a broken finger and hands shaking with adrenalin, on a ship prone to sudden lurching shifts. Outside, the flames have died down a little, but the ship is listing further. By now Laurent should be gone in the helicopter. They can't hear anything over the roar of the flames.

At least the scuba tanks are filled to 5,000 psi, far more than she had hoped for; 3,000 is more usual – these tanks must be specially made. Enough to stay underwater for more than two hours if they don't go too deep. She pulls on neoprene gloves, hood and boots, and inserts the hem of the hood under her wet suit's neck. Keiran follows her example. He is trembling, and she realizes it is with fear. Danielle once spent a whole summer diving every day, but this is his first time.

'It'll be OK,' she says. 'You just have to trust me. There's no time for a lesson. Whatever happens, just stay limp and keep breathing. Don't ever hold your breath. If your ears start to hurt, pinch your nose and breathe through it, like you're on an airplane. Hold your mask and regulator on with your hand when you jump.'

'Regulator?' he asks.

'The mouthpiece. The thing you breathe from. Once I put your fins on, if you see me start swimming, you kick too, but otherwise just go limp and *do nothing*, not even if you're sinking. You have to trust me completely. Understand?'

Keiran nods and forces a smile. Danielle makes herself smile back. She knows that understanding and following instructions are two very different things, especially when you've never before been exposed to the dizzying cold and weightlessness of an undersea environment. And she knows that the instructions she has just given Keiran could easily kill him.

They help one another put their weight belts and vests on. Danielle has to guess the weight required for both of them. Too much will drown them; too little will condemn them to involuntary cremation. Fortunately the margin of error is large.

The view through the door's porthole, which earlier was like a vision of hell, is now utterly black with smoke. She can feel the warmth of the floor through her neoprene boots. Metal is a near-perfect heat conductor, and the hull and all the floors and walls must be hot enough to blister exposed skin. The air will soon be too warm to breathe. They pull on masks, the last piece of gear.

'I always wanted to be an astronaut,' Keiran says.

Danielle smiles grimly. In full wet suit, with a scuba tanks on his back, he does look straight out of *2001*. 'All right,' she says. 'We'll put the fins on underwater. I mean, I will. You won't do *anything* but breathe. And let go of the fins when I take them from you, and help kick when I start swimming.' She reaches for the flippers that will strap over their feet—

—and the interior door to the scuba room opens and Laurent walks in, followed by two khaki-clad guards, Vijay and Sophia. Half of Laurent's left cheek is blistered by a puffy red burn, the others too are burned and singed, and Sophia leans heavily on one of the guards, coughing uncontrollably.

The two sides of the unexpected stand-off goggle at one another in mutual amazement for a moment. Then the ship makes another of its unexpected lurches. This one is a shipquake, it goes on for several seconds, knocking all of them on to hands and knees, and sending scuba gear tumbling around the room. A tank hits Danielle's shoulder, hard enough to bruise, and narrowly misses crushing her hand. She looks up. Laurent is on his feet, rushing across the room towards her. Without really thinking about it she grabs the tank that just struck her, aims its nozzle towards him and twists its valve fully open.

Even with her ears shielded by neoprene the resulting scream almost deafens her. The air inside the tank is stored at four hundred times sea-level air pressure, and is correspondingly eager to escape. The tank bucks in her hand, but she has a good grip on it, and holds it steady as a jet of air erupts from it as if from a fire hose, knocking Laurent almost off his feet as the ship lurches again. He staggers away from her, somehow keeping his balance on the tilting floor, and backs out of the room. She hurls the tank towards the open doorway, and as it spins there like a top, still venting its ear-splitting shriek, she grabs Keiran's arm. 'We have to go!'

He nods.

'Hold this and don't let go!' She gives him another air tank. They may need it. Laurent is still here. The flames and superheated air must have been too much for the helicopter to take off. And Laurent may yet survive the sinking. She grabs a spear gun from the wall rack, runs her arm through the rubber loops of four fins, puts her mouthpiece in, and opens the door.

The metal door handle is so hot that, even though she opens it as fast as possible, some of her neoprene glove melts. But at least the door hasn't welded shut. Danielle steps out into the black superheated fumes of burned oil, breathing through her regulator, moving as fast as she can with a forty-pound scuba tank on her back and twenty more pounds in metal plates on her belt and in her pockets. She can feel the exposed skin around her mask and mouthpiece start to blister, as if white-hot metal is being pressed to her face. She looks back once en route to the edge. Keiran is only a few feet behind her but she can barely see him in the dark clouds of smoke. At the edge of the boat she sees the fire still raging below her, as the smoke rises and allows more oxygen to reach the burning oil. They are only ten feet above it now – the ship has sunk more than halfway into the ocean.

Without hesitation, hesitation would be lethal, Danielle uses her momentum to step up on to the middle bar of the railing around the ship, using it as a ladder, then on to the top bar, and leaps out as far as she can into the immolating sea of flame. In mid-jump she presses her hand tightly against her mask and mouthpiece. Then she is falling, falling fast, and plunging through the burning oil slick and into the dark cold Pacific.

15

Visibility is zero. Only the top layer of oil, exposed to air, can burn; the rest of it, opaque as ink, blocks the sun's light entirely. Only the telltale pinching sensation inside her ears tells her she is sinking. Danielle works her jaw furiously, opening her eustachian tubes to equalize air pressure before her eardrums burst or her sinus cavities rupture. With her free hand she pushes the inflation button on her buoyancy vest, her BCD, flooding its bladders with enough air to slow her descent. All this in only a few seconds, operating purely on instinct. She hasn't gone diving for years, but the shock of immersion has brought it all back, made that summer in Baja California seem like yesterday.

She feels a disturbance in the water to her left. A splash. Keiran made it off the ship. But he is helpless, doesn't know the first thing about diving, she can't even see him, and her fins aren't on, she can't manoeuvre. Danielle reaches her arm out, clutching desperately, and her fingers close on something. A strap. Enough to connect them in the dark water. He is not as overweighted as she – he is sinking, but much more slowly than she had. She grabs him and pulls him closer. She can tell by feel that he is curled up into a taut ball around the scuba tank he carries, breathing as furiously as an Olympic sprinter. But at least he isn't kicking and flailing.

Even so, their situation is desperate. Both of them are sinking, she thinks fairly slowly, and that is a good thing, but she can't even see her gauges to determine how deep they are. They don't dare ascend for fear of surfacing in the midst of the flames; and if they go too deep, nitrogen narcosis will set in like a powerful drug, they will lose their ability to reason, and even if they somehow manage to ascend after that, they will certainly get the dreaded bends. They need to get out from under the burning oil right now. But without fins, in full scuba gear, Danielle can't swim much faster than an infant crawls. And they may well sink to a lethal depth before she can even strap on her fins.

She takes a deep breath and tries to focus. No sense brooding about their predicament; better start trying to do something about it. She lets go of the spear gun, she can't spare a hand for it, tucks an arm through one of Keiran's straps to keep them connected, and then, working awkwardly in darkness so complete she might as well be blind, with thick gloves on, she slips off one of the fins looped around her arm, and tries to pull it on to her right boot as fast as she can. The attempt is not successful. But after its failure she realizes she can see a metallic glint in front of her. She squints and it coagulates into the rim of the spare tank Keiran carries. Vision has returned.

Of course: as they sink, they fall out of the cone of darkness beneath the oil, to where ambient sunlight can reach them at an angle from the edge of the slick. She quickly looks at her gauges. They are a hundred feet deep already. Danielle relaxes when she sees this. It's farther down than she'd like, but they can manage a good ten minutes at this depth before it gets dangerous, time enough to get themselves together.

Something drifts through the corner of her sight. The edges of her mask are clouded, they weren't able to spit and clean them out with seawater, she can see clearly only straight ahead. She turns her head, sees the discarded spear gun drifting slowly downwards, and reaches out to grab it. Maybe they can afford to keep it after all.

Keiran, thankfully, is following instructions, remains a motionless lump wrapped around the spare scuba tank. His whole body is shuddering. The water around them is extremely cold, and it takes a minute or two for body heat to warm the water between wet suit and skin, but Danielle knows Keiran's spasms are not due to the temperature. He is fighting panic, and the need to do something instead of trusting his life to Danielle, with every iota of his will. So far he is winning. She finds his BCD's controls, inflates him to neutral buoyancy so he will hover near a hundred feet deep, and then, with slow precise movements, keeping an eye on him, straps the fins on to her feet.

The difference is enormous; she is able to manoeuvre and swim again, in a way impossible without fins. She carefully puts the last two fins on Keiran's feet, then takes him by the arm and begins to swim towards the light. After a moment he catches on and starts to kick furiously as well. Moving awkwardly, encumbered by the spare tank and spear gun, it takes them several minutes to swim a few hundred metres, past the farthest edge of the oil slick. Danielle makes sure they ascend as they go, to save air, improve visibility and minimize the risk of nitrogen narcosis and decompression sickness.

About halfway there, the water around them suddenly roils violently. Then a powerful current sucks them backwards and down. Even though they are kicking as hard as they can, they drop thirty feet in a few seconds, making Danielle's ears pop painfully, before the disturbance ends as suddenly and mysteriously as it began. She keeps moving, utterly bemused. Nothing like that has ever happened to her while diving. She's never even *heard* of anything like that. Then she realizes: the eddy current from the ship, as it sank. As if the sunken vessel were trying to reach out with its last pulse of strength, drag them down to join it in Davy Jones's much-fabled locker. Had they been a little farther back they might well have been sucked down. She hopes that's what happened to Laurent.

Danielle keeps kicking. Her legs are tired, but at least the exertion helps fight the cold. By the time clear unslicked ocean is above them, they are only twenty feet below the surface. Danielle inflates Keiran's BCD and hers a little further, and slowly, finger on her BCD purge valve, ready to descend again if the air is too hot or smoky to breathe, they ascend to the surface. Keiran's breathing has slowed a little, but he has already used half of his air. Danielle has consumed less than a fifth of hers.

The transition from water to air is as always disorienting. It feels a little like being born. They are downwind from the thick black cloud that obscures the ship, a cloud fed by ten thousand tongues of flame beneath it, but smoke rises; the air here at sea level is clear. And the warmth from the flames is welcome after immersion in near-freezing water. Danielle lifts her regulator from her mouth and takes a tentative trial breath. The air is clean and cool. She inflates Keiran's BCD, and then her own, so they act as life preservers, holding their heads above the waves, and gently pulls the regulator from Keiran's mouth. He has bitten down on its rubber mouthpiece so hard that his mouth is bleeding, but his eyes are focused, he seems otherwise OK.

'You all right?' she asks.

He says in a shaking voice, 'I don't think I like scuba diving.'

'It's more fun under better circumstances.'

'I'll take your word for it. Do we have to go back down?'

'Probably not,' she says.

He releases a deep sigh of relief. 'Thank Christ for that. Now what? Wait for help?'

'Yeah. I hoped one of the lifeboats would come free and float loose when the ship sank. But I guess not.'

'You never know. We'll see when the smoke clears. Looks like it's letting up.'

The smoke does seem to be thinning out, and the edge of the flaming oil slick already seems farther away than it did when they reached the surface. The oil is finally burning itself out. She hopes Keiran is right and a lifeboat somehow survived the sinking and the inferno. It is at least possible – they are made of metal, and would have been shielded from the flames right up until the ship sank. With no lifeboat, they will have to hope that help arrives very soon. It isn't water or sharks which will kill them. It is the cold. Even these full wet suits will protect them only so long in the North Pacific water. It is only hours, not days, until they freeze to death.

'Holy Christ,' Keiran says.

Danielle follows his gaze and gasps. A lifeboat has survived. And it is occupied. She stares at the twenty-foot-long metal hull as it emerges from the cloud of black smoke, carrying two men in fire-ravaged scuba gear. Their suits have melted and run ragged on their bodies, burning the skin right off their body in places, leaving raw patches soaked with blood. The lifeboat's metal hull is marbled and warped with the heat. The men's faces are awful to look at; their lips have been burned away, and sheets of charred skin hang loose from their cheeks, reminding Danielle horribly of roast chicken. They are still alive, still moving, but not for long.

'Oh my God,' Danielle says, her voice low. They must have gambled that the ship would not sink before the fires burned out, and lost. Maybe they were inexperienced divers, and didn't dare make the jump into the sea. Maybe they didn't put on weights, bobbed up to the surface and desperately pulled themselves into the lifeboat as they burned.

But Laurent is not an inexperienced diver. He has told her tales of diving off Djibouti when he was with the Foreign Legion. And the fact that the dying men on the lifeboat had time to put on scuba gear means that he did too. And that, in turn, means that Laurent too is alive somewhere in this ocean around them, and very likely not alone. Danielle holds her spear gun tightly. It seems like an inadequate weapon now. Do they get on the lifeboat, and call attention to themselves? Or do they wait, hope to remain hidden in the waves of the North Pacific and that help somehow finds them?

The decision is taken away from her when one of the near-corpses raises a shaking arm and points somewhere in the distance, about a hundred feet away from Danielle. Somehow the charred victims on the boat muster enough strength to ship oars in its rowlocks and begin to paddle the lifeboat towards whatever they have seen. Danielle cannot see over the waves, but that has to be Laurent and any surviving companions.

The lifeboat is moving too fast to catch. She watches as two men and a woman in untouched wet suits climb the ladder on its back. One of them pulls off his scuba hood. Laurent. The other man is Vijay. The woman is Sophia. She seems weak, and Laurent has to pull her on to the lifeboat.

The first thing Laurent does, when on board the lifeboat, is to disconnect the scuba tanks from the two burned human wrecks, the two men who just spent their dying strength to get to him. And then, in an act so astonishingly callous it makes Danielle gasp, he pushes them out of the lifeboat, into the ocean. They are too weak to resist.

'What did he do that for?' Danielle asks, her voice low. 'There's help coming.'

'They don't know that,' Keiran says. 'After I sent the SOS I shut down the ship's communications. As far as they know they have to paddle to America.'

'Good. Then they'll leave us here. They'll figure we'll just die in the water. They won't waste time looking for us.'

And indeed Laurent and Vijay waste no time in turning the lifeboat to the east and beginning to paddle. Sophia doesn't help; she has collapsed weakly into the lifeboat, coughing violently.

'This is good?' Keiran asks.

'I don't know. But we've got a chance. If someone gets here in time.' Danielle looks at the lifeboat, still only a hundred feet away. She is armed, and they are not. If she could somehow sneak up on it . . . But she can't swim as fast as they paddle.

'Do you think they'll make it?' Keiran asks.

'If anyone can it's probably Laurent,' Danielle says grimly.

'Shit.'

'Yeah. Wait.' An idea races into her mind, like an electric shock.

'What?'

'We can't let him get away. This will all start over again. Even if it doesn't we'll be looking over our shoulders for the rest of our lives.'

'Too late,' Keiran says. 'He's gone.'

'No he isn't. Give me that tank.'

He looks at her for a moment, and then his eyes widen with comprehension. 'You can *not* be serious.'

'Give me that tank,' Danielle repeats, not letting herself think about what she intends to do with it. 'This is the only chance we'll ever get.'

Keiran shakes his head violently. 'No. No, let me do it. I'll do it.'

'Don't be an idiot. Who's the divemaster here? Stop wasting time. *Give me the tank.*'

Keiran passes the spare tank over wordlessly.

'Wish me luck,' she says.

'Don't do this. This is insane.'

'Close enough.' She purges her BCD and descends back into the ocean.

She levels off at about fifteen feet, close enough to the surface for good visibility, deep enough that she will not leave a visible trail. She rotates so she is facing directly away from the lifeboat, holds the extra scuba tank tightly to her chest and twists open its nozzle.

Air pressurized to 5,000 pounds per square inch, or roughly 400 atmospheres, roars out of the tank she holds. And, as Isaac Newton once observed, for every action there is an equal and opposite reaction. The tank, and the woman holding on to it, are propelled in the exact opposite direction, and at considerable speed.

It is like holding on to a small rocket; the tank shakes in her hands so violently that her teeth rattle, it is impossible to hold a steady course, and she has to look over her shoulder to see where she is going. But as she zigs and curls her way through the Pacific, holding her improvised compressed-air engine with an iron grip, spear gun under her arm, she sees a shadow appear on the otherwise unbroken surface of the water behind her. She approaches it until the convex shape of the lifeboat's hull is visible, protruding into the water. Her jury-rigged underwater rocket grows weaker and weaker as she approaches, but by the time it finally runs out of air she is a good thirty feet ahead of the lifeboat.

Laurent and Vijay are inside the boat, and her scuba gear is too heavy for her to be able to just lift herself out of the water, especially while holding the spear gun. She must rely on that which killed the cat. Danielle moves up to about ten feet below the surface, and as the prow of the lifeboat approaches her position, she lets go of the empty scuba tank. It floats up and hits the hull with a metal-on-metal *thunk* that Danielle hears even underwater.

Danielle watches, spear gun in one hand, the other on her BCD controls. She has to remind herself not to hold her breath. A moment passes. And then she sees a dark face, shimmering through the water, appear over the lifeboat's gunwale. Vijay. He doesn't see her; it is far easier to see out of water than in.

Danielle doesn't hesitate. Her finger depresses the buoyancy valve, flooding her BCD with air. She flies upwards, pops out of the ocean like a cork, and pulls the trigger. From four feet away it is impossible to miss. In Baja she saw spears go right through groupers almost a foot thick. This spear hits Vijay in his throat. He topples backwards into the lifeboat. Danielle quickly descends back to fifteen feet deep. There is another bolt strapped to the side of the spear gun. She has never armed a spear gun before, but she's seen it done, and like most things that have to be done underwater it has been made idiot-simple, nothing more than inserting the spear into a hole and turning a reel like a fishing rod's until it clicks.

She has probably just killed a man. Her only regret is that it was Vijay and not Laurent, far more dangerous. Now that the die is cast she thinks of Laurent with murderous rage. This has to end, *he* has to end, for all the awful things he has done, and all he will do if he gets the chance.

It won't end here if he doesn't want it to. All he has to do to get away is just keep paddling. He is safe inside the lifeboat, she won't be able to catch him. But Danielle is certain, dead certain, that he will not let her go like this. He will come after her.

A splash on the other side of the boat confirms it. Danielle aims the spear gun at the new body in the water, is about to pull the trigger – and just as she realizes this figure is too small to be Laurent, there is another splash, directly above her.

She looks up and sees a large form plunging towards her, another diver. Laurent. He must have seen her air bubbles on the surface. He threw Sophia in first, as a distraction. She thinks all this in a flash as she raises the spear gun and pulls the trigger, which she only barely has time to do, because then he is on her, an arm wrapping itself around her throat. He has knocked the spear gun away, she is struggling but he is behind her and they are falling dangerously fast, she can't breathe, she manages to wriggle an arm into the space between her neck and his meaty forearm but she *still* can't breathe, she tries to suck air from her tank but there is nothing there. He has turned off her air. And they are plunging deep into darkness.

16

Danielle tries to reach over her shoulder and turn her air back on, but his hand is cupped around the valve, and even with near-death desperation she isn't strong enough to pull it loose. Her lungs are aflame with the need to breathe, she can feel the strength going out of her limbs. What is left of her vision, at this dark depth, begins to blur. Then she remembers her 'ocky', her second regulator, the back-up with the long hose, in case the primary regulator fails or she needs to let somebody else buddy-breathe. Barely conscious, she sweeps her arm up in a wide backward circle, just as her dive instructor taught her so many years ago, until her arm reaches the ocky's hose. Her fingers find the mouthpiece, and she spits out the primary regulator and brings the ocky to her mouth. There is enough air contained in its hose for a single deep breath. The effect of oxygen is immediate, the world's fastest and most powerful drug – her vision clears and she can think again. For one more breath. Thirty seconds.

They are very deep, so deep Danielle can hardly see at all, but she can tell that some dark fluid clouds the water around her. Blood, Laurent's blood – she shot him with the spear gun. That explains why he is content to hold her and wait for her to pass out or start breathing water. It would be nice if the blood were to draw sharks to eat him in the next twenty seconds, she thinks crazily, but she probably can't count on that. But wait. He too has an ocky. And he is wounded. Keeping one arm wedged between her neck and Laurent's headlock, she reaches up with her free hand, locates his ocky, pulls it to her mouth and sucks air in greedily. He doesn't dare cut this air supply off; now they are both breathing from the same tank.

Laurent releases his armlock and tries to pull his secondary regulator from her mouth, but Danielle, expecting that, spins to face him, so that her face is against his belly, and wraps her arm around him tightly. Then she recoils as her hand hits something in the water near his upper thigh, something so sharp it pierces her glove and her skin before she pulls back. His whole body convulses and she hears his groan through the water. The spear. She shot him through the leg. Heedless of her own bleeding hand, Danielle reaches out, grabs the shaft of the spear and rocks it back and forth. Laurent releases her immediately, tries to get away from her, but Danielle hangs on to him like a limpet. Her face is right up against his gauges. The dials are fluorescent but she still has to squint. They are 240 feet, 70 metres, beneath the surface;

130 feet is the accepted safety limit for tanks filled with normal air.

She has never been this deep before. Few non-professional divers have. She has to ascend. She releases Laurent, twists her air back on, and inflates her BCD. He is still sinking, so fast that he must have put on both Sophia's and the South African's weight belts, so he would fall on her faster when he jumped from the boat to ambush her. But he was not quite fast enough. And with a spear through his leg he will neither make it back on to the lifeboat nor survive long enough to be rescued. She has won—

—but then there is a sudden lurch, something grabs her from behind, it feels a little like having a shirt caught on a loose nail, and she is falling back down. She inflates her BCD to full but she is still sinking. She reaches down, unhooks her weight belt and lets it fall to the ocean floor, but that only slows her rate of descent; 250 feet now. She understands. Laurent has made the same calculation she has, that he can't escape. He has grabbed her BCD, determined to take her down with him.

Only one last chance. Danielle rips open the Velcro strap around her waist, takes the deepest breath she can manage, reaches for the plastic clips on her BCD's shoulder straps, and pinches them open. The vest flies open, releasing her like a sprung trap. She opens her mouth and lets the regulator out, and floats freely up through the ocean, separated from all her scuba gear, as Laurent falls farther into darkness.

She is buoyant, but not like a cork. She wants to swim for the surface, kicking as hard as she can, but she knows the important thing to do, to give herself the best chance of avoiding the bends – and the bends will likely kill her if they hit before help arrives – is to ascend as slowly as possible, without running out of air and drowning. Her ascent to the surface must take at least two minutes. And it is impossible to hold her breath half that long.

Normally impossible. But these circumstances are anything but normal. For as she ascends, the pressure in her lungs decreases. The air in her lungs right now has been compressed to one eighth its normal volume by the pressure of seventy metres of ocean. This same air will expand like a balloon as she goes up. If it expands too slowly, she will use all the air and run out of breath; if too quickly, her lungs will rupture from the pressure; but if Danielle is careful, if she breathes out constantly but very slowly, if she ascends at exactly the same speed as the air bubbles rising around her, this single breath can last for more than a minute, replenishing itself by growing as the pressure decreases.

She makes a sound in the back of her throat, to ensure that she keeps her airway open at all times. She wants to breathe, she has never before gone two minutes without breathing, but she realizes halfway up that she doesn't really *need* to, it is habit alone which makes her desperate to inhale. She doesn't time it quite right. She runs out of oxygen forty feet beneath the surface and spends the last fifteen seconds of her ascent gagging for breath, forcing herself with iron discipline not to kick for the surface.

When she emerges from water into air, it is a rebirth. She takes what feels like her very first breath. The salt air tastes like nectar of the gods.

The lifeboat is near by. Danielle treads water, shaking her head, coming back to where she is and what she's doing, to reality, to life. She realizes that her whole desperate underwater battle with Laurent, and her epic single-breath ascent, occupied fewer than five minutes of her life. A life that looks as if it will continue for some time. Keiran is already in the lifeboat. He helps her aboard. Sophia lies on the floor, pale and weak, coughing and twitching. Vijay's body is nowhere to be seen; Keiran must have pushed it overboard.

'Smoke inhalation,' Keiran says. 'He pushed her out. I saw it. She needs a doctor.'

Danielle nods. 'I might too.' Typically the bends take up to twenty-four hours to manifest. 'Let's hope your SOS got to someone.'

Keiran paddles. Danielle spends a few minutes in the prow,

watching the waves around her with a careful eye, but their smooth patterns remain unbroken. No sign of Laurent. Of course, he could stay down there for a good hour, maybe more, with two tanks at his disposal. But wounded as he is, with a spear through his leg, in the middle of the North Pacific – he won't make it. Except it is terribly easy to believe that he might.

Then Danielle sees something break the water, something that makes her smile with relief and triumphant revenge. Not Laurent. A dorsal fin. A shark. A big one if she is any judge.

'The strong inevitably eat the weak,' she murmurs to herself. 'Isn't that right?'

'What?' Keiran asks.

'Nothing,' she says. 'Paddle us home.'

But they don't make it to the Oregon coast. It takes only an hour for the Coast Guard helicopters to show up. By that time, a steady cleansing rain has blown in, and agonizing pains have already begun to stab at Danielle's knee and shoulder joints.

17

Once on board the Coast Guard cutter, Keiran strips off his wet suit and greedily wraps himself in the blankets the sailors provide for him. He is mostly ignored at first, compared to the two critical medical cases that accompany him. Sophia is given an oxygen mask; her spasmodic coughs are so violent that they have to strap it on to her so tightly that the straps leave marks in her pale skin. Danielle lies on deck, weeping with pain, her limbs contorted as if doing yoga again. It takes Keiran and the sailors several minutes to pull off her wet suit. The bends, Keiran knows, get their name from the pretzel shapes their victims assume, because doing so slightly lessens the excruciating agony in all their joints. He knows intellectually that she will be OK, they have been rescued in time to save her, but it is almost unbearable to watch her sobbing and writhing in pain, and being unable to do anything about it. Keiran has to be pulled away from Danielle's side by two sailors before he realizes that his presence is impeding more than helping matters.

After a brief conversation between a medic and a pilot, it is decided that the Coast Guard helicopters no longer have enough fuel to reach the mainland, they will have to sail her in. Danielle is put in a cot next to Sophia and hooked up to an IV drip that seems to dull her pain. The initial frenzy of the rescue begins to dissipate. Sailors start clearing up wet suit parts from the rain-drenched deck. The cutter, a vessel maybe half the size of the now drowned *Lazarus*, with two small helicopters and a crew of about thirty, throbs as its engines drive them east towards Oregon at maximum speed. Keiran retreats inside, to a tiny room with a Formica table, plastic stools bolted to the floor, and a coffee machine. Sailors pass in and out; several of them look at him, realize they don't know what to do with him and visibly decide to ignore his presence. He is sitting on one of the stools, wrapped in blankets and sipping bad coffee, when a small blonde woman with officer insignia on her shoulders comes in. The name ELLIS is sewn on to the front of her white uniform.

'Julian O'Toole?' she asks.

It takes Keiran a moment to remember that this is the false name he adopted at Mulligan's place in Los Angeles, what feels like a century ago. He nods. The woman snaps a sharp salute.

'Sir,' she says. 'Are you sure there's no one else out there?'

Keiran, slightly confused, thinks of Laurent, somewhere in the water.

'No,' he says. 'Just us.'

She nods. 'I understand you can't say much about what happened out there.'

Keiran looks at her. Some sort of response seems to be called for, so he nods.

'My brother is in the special forces,' Lieutenant Ellis says meaningfully.

Increasingly perplexed, Keiran nods again.

'We've been in touch with your unit commander. Once we get in range we'll be helicoptering you straight to the Portland VA Medical Center. There's a hyperbaric facility there where we can recompress your soldier with the bends.'

'Unit commander?' Keiran asks faintly, wondering whether he has heard correctly.

'Colonel Mulligan.'

Keiran covers his laughter with an improvised coughing fit. Lieutenant Ellis looks at him worriedly. 'Were you exposed to smoke too, sir?' she demands.

'No,' Keiran says, smiling indulgently. 'No, that's quite all right, Lieutenant, just a little salt water down the wrong pipe.'

Mulligan, you bastard, he thinks. *You never told me you hacked the military.*

'Sir?' the nurse says.

Keiran opens his eyes and the nurse, about to shake him awake, stops with her arm in mid-prod. A slender middle-aged black woman, she speaks in a near-whisper, although there is no one else visible in the hall. 'Your soldier is awake, sir. She seems to have fully recovered.'

Keiran remembers where he is and who he is supposed to be. He swings his legs over the side of the cot and follows the nurse to Danielle's room, trying to look military. He checks the Danger hiptop, which arrived at the hospital via FedEx only an hour after he did, through which he communicates with Mulligan. There is no news, which is good news. Keiran is still half amazed that their ruse has not yet been discovered. But then how would it be revealed? He managed to tell both Sophia and Danielle to keep their mouths shut on the helicopter ride over. If they were to stay long enough in the military world, they would eventually be discovered – probably – but by the time the cracks in their story appear, they will be long gone.

There is another nurse by Danielle's bed, a tiny Filipina woman. The room smells, as all hospitals do, of medicine and cleaning supplies. Danielle's eyes are open and she manages to smile weakly at Keiran. Her broken finger has been set, and her other hand, which she impaled on the spear she shot Laurent with, is thickly bandaged. Salved burns are visible on her wrists and her face, around her mouth and forehead. Keiran knows exactly how they feel; he has similar burns. There is an IV hooked up to her arm. Outside the night is a dark hue that Keiran now recognizes as city dark, not the utter blackness of the moonless Pacific.

'I need to speak to her alone,' Keiran says.

'Sir,' the senior nurse says, 'we're supposed to monitor her condition—'

'Alone,' he repeats, and then says the magic word: 'Security.' The nurses look at one another and depart.

'Hey,' he says.

'Hey.'

'How are you?'

'I guess I'm OK.' She winces, remembering. 'The bends are really awful. Everything else, the burns and broken finger and shit, they're like a walk in the park by comparison. But they say I'm OK. No permanent damage. I can go diving again, no problem. Sometimes you can't.'

'Good. That's good.'

'They fixed your nose.'

Keiran touches a finger to his bandaged broken nose. 'Yes.'

'How long has it been?'

'I guess they picked us up about a day and a half ago. They want to keep you here for another couple of days. Under observation.'

'Where are we? What's going on? Are they going to arrest us?'

Keiran explains Mulligan's military deception. Danielle's mouth falls open.

'I'm supposed to be a Navy SEAL?' she asks incredulously.

'Actually I'm not sure *what* you are,' Keiran admits. 'But nobody around here cares. At least not yet. Mulligan sent us

Department of Defense ID cards today. Here's yours.' He puts the plastic smart card on Danielle's pillow. 'That's all you'll need to check out. There're holes in the story, but it's not like anyone's seriously investigating. The ship went down in international waters. Shadbold doesn't know that anyone survived. Mulligan thinks we've got a few days yet before anyone starts asking awkward questions.'

'This is insane. So what are we supposed to do now? Go on the run for the rest of our lives?'

'You won't need to. You remember how Laurent said you'd be safe? He wasn't lying. They've issued an official statement saying that you are no longer a person of interest to the investigation. I guess he really was planning to let you go. Shadbold must have people in the FBI.'

'So they're not after me?'

'They're not after you. How does it feel to be unwanted?'

Danielle smiles. 'Pretty damn good. But wait a minute. Why didn't you just take me and Sophia to a regular hospital?'

Keiran doesn't give her the real answer, which is, *Because Mulligan wanted to show off*; he doesn't think she'd see the appeal of using military medical facilities just because they can. Not in her current state, maybe not ever. 'They're still after me,' he says. 'Not for the bombing, for a whole bunch of other things. Sophia must have got them to connect me with LoTek's colourful history. I have to disappear now, before they start asking questions and taking fingerprints.'

'Huh.'

'Sorry. I know it's a lot to take in all at once.'

'No kidding.' Danielle thinks for a minute. Then she asks, 'What about Sophia?'

'She's next door. They said she'll mostly recover. But be effectively asthmatic for the rest of her life.'

'Shit.'

Keiran shrugs. 'She's not the queen of evil, but she made her own bed.'

'What about Jayalitha?'

'I don't know. I haven't thought about her yet.'

'Find her,' Danielle says. 'She's illegal here too. Find her and take care of her.'

He nods. 'I will. Very soon. But right now, I have to move.'

'What are you going to do?'

'I'm going to be a new man. Literally. Trurl's picking me up, he's come to get me out of here.'

'You're going to spend the rest of your life on the run?'

'It's not that bad. New identity, new life, no problem. Beats dying on that ship.'

She nods. 'Yeah.'

'So. I came to say goodbye.'

'Goodbye? But . . . where are you going exactly?'

'I don't know yet,' he says. 'But listen.' He swallows. 'Not now, you have to stay here for now, but in a little while, when you get out, do you want to come with me?'

She looks at him.

'I mean, as in . . .' He stops, words failing him, and takes her hand lightly in his. 'Hell and damnation. You know what I mean. Come and live with me. Try sharing our lives again.'

'Be the girlfriend of the romantic hacker on the run?'

'Not like that sounds. But be with me. Yes. That's what I want.'

Slowly, Danielle shakes her head.

'Shit,' Keiran says dully.

'I'm sorry,' she says. 'I can't be someone else's adjunct any more.'

'That's not . . . you wouldn't be. Christ, Danielle, no, not at all, that's not what I meant.'

'I know. I'm explaining it badly. But whatever I'm doing next, I have to figure it out on my own, OK? I don't mean I want you to just disappear. You better call me as soon as you can. You better not just vanish. Or I'll find you and kick your ass. But I can't, I don't want to, run away with you. I'm sorry. I want to run away with myself this time. I know that doesn't make any sense.'

Keiran looks at her thoughtfully. After a moment he says, 'You'd be surprised.'

'Maybe when the world starts making sense again I can come visit. I'm not promising anything beyond that. But I'd like to visit.'

He smiles. 'I'd like that too.'

'Good.'

They stare at one another.

'You should go,' she says quietly.

He nods, then lowers his head and kisses her. They share a long, slow, deep kiss. Then he stands. 'Goodbye,' he says breathlessly. 'I'm going to miss you.'

She doesn't speak. He backs out of the room and closes the door behind him, bathing her once again in darkness.

'So what are you going to do?' Danielle asks Sophia.

Danielle is dressed in street clothes. She has officially been discharged from the hospital. Her parents are flying in tonight. She isn't sure how she feels about that. But she knows that whatever she feels when they meet, no part of it will be shame or insecurity.

Sophia reaches for the oxygen mask that hangs by her bed and takes a few long, shuddering breaths before answering.

'They gave me a laptop yesterday,' she says.

Danielle blinks at the apparent subject change.

'I did some research. You were right. There were lots of parents of whizz kids who got sick or died that same summer my dad got cancer.'

'I figured.'

'I did some more research. I didn't really understand all the medical terms. But I definitely understand that Shadbold's doctors have been lying through their fucking teeth every time they talked to me. My dad's cancer isn't as extreme as Shadbold's. The existing drugs, I mean Shadbold's existing drugs, should have been much more effective on him than they have been. Than they *apparently* have been.'

'They've been keeping him sick,' Danielle says.

'They've been keeping my dad sick so I'd perform. Like I'm some kind of fucking circus animal.'

'So what are you going to do?'

'Keiran could have shut down Shazam. Taken away my access. He didn't. Any idea why?'

Danielle shrugs. 'He liked you,' she lies.

'Did he really?'

'Well. No. But he respected you.'

'Yeah. He and I are the only ones now who have both Shazam and the military attack suite. Makes both of us pretty much unstoppable. We can do whatever we want.'

'For the third time,' Danielle says, a little exasperated now, 'what are you going to do?'

'First I'm going to fix my father's treatment. Then I'm going to hack Shadbold's system. It'll be easy enough. I built its security. I'm going to hack it, and I'm going to change Mr Shadbold's prescription just a tiny bit. Not that he'll notice. Oh no. The labels on the syringes will say that the right things are in them. Just like Kishkinda's vaccination needles. The labels will be fine.'

Danielle stares at her. 'What are you going to do to him?'

'First I'm going to rewrite his will. Then he's going to take some very bad medicine. Then I'm going to publish all his results and shut down everything that's left of his operation.'

'Just you.'

'Miss Leaf,' Sophia says, baring her teeth like an animal, 'you have *no idea* what I'm capable of. Give me time and motivation and I'll bring down *governments*.'

Danielle looks at her and wonders whether the world would be a safer place if Sophia had not survived the Pacific shipwreck. But at least what she is doing is the right thing. For now. And at least Keiran is out there as a counterweight to her, if need be.

'Goodbye, Sophia,' Danielle says. 'Be good.' It is a warning.

She stands, walks out of the room, takes the elevator down to the ground floor and the waiting taxi. As it pulls away from the hospital she exhales and sinks back into the seat. She is tired. But there is much to do. She thinks of Angus, his eyes flashing with rage, and of the little children in Kishkinda, poisoned by Shadbold. Danielle wonders whether she should go back to finish law school first, whether she should join an existing organization or start a new one. Details. The important thing is that she believes in her destination. Which road she takes there hardly seems to matter.

'Where to?' the driver asks.

Danielle smiles. 'A better world.'

He gives her a perplexed look. 'I don't think I know that place.'

'No? Take me to the airport,' Danielle says. 'We'll start there.'

Epilogue

Shadbold, Jack – inventor, billionaire, philanthropist. On 15 August, after a long battle with cancer.

Born to a poor family in Durban, South Africa, in 1933, Jack Shadbold worked in the Kimberley diamond mines before emigrating to Australia in 1952, where he acquired a degree from the University of Adelaide's School of Electrical Engineering. His extraordinary technical gifts quickly became apparent, and after publishing several ground-breaking papers, in 1958 he moved to California to take up a position with Fairchild Semiconductor.

Shadbold did not stay long at Fairchild; his independent streak, called stubborn intransigence by some, led him to found his own laboratory, where he spent the next twenty years inventing and patenting numerous innovative tools and processes, mostly to do with semiconductor fabrication. The licensing of these patents by Intel and IBM soon brought Shadbold enormous wealth. He is also believed to have done a considerable amount of work over a period of several decades for the Department of Defense, and in particular its Advanced Research Projects Agency, but any such records have not yet been declassified.

Shadbold never married, had no children, and preferred to stay out of the public eye; he lived as off-the-record an existence as was possible for a man of his wealth and ability. His only recognizable hobby was sailing. He quietly bankrolled at least two America's Cup teams, and indulged in a series of increasingly grandiose yachts, culminating with the massive, entirely computer-controlled *Lazarus*. A super-luxury yacht with decorations worthy of Versailles, *Lazarus* was the world's largest single-masted sailing vessel before, in a tragic and inexplicable accident, it was consumed by flames and sank off the Oregon coast, only a week before Shadbold passed away.

Jack Shadbold was diagnosed with the throat cancer that would eventually take his life in 1995, and battled it bravely for almost a decade. It was this diagnosis which triggered Shadbold's career as a philanthropist. He privately funded hundreds of millions of dollars' worth of cancer-related research, the results of which have been posthumously published and donated patent-free to the world. While it is too early to judge the long-term repercussions, initial reaction from leading scientists indicates that Shadbold's research is likely to play a vitally important part in the war on cancer.

The bulk of Shadbold's estate was left to a foundation whose beneficiaries are the impoverished residents of areas of Third World nations where throat cancers are particularly prevalent, and in particular the Kishkinda region of southern India. The remainder will ensure all-expenses-paid treatment for all American throat cancer patients, for however long they need it. These great gifts add up to a stirring and suitable legacy for a man who will long be remembered as a modern titan, a humble genius, and one of the great humanitarians of his age.